A Soldier's Honor

by

Evelyn Timidaiski

Brandon's Brigade, Book 1

A Soldier's Honor

Cover Art by *Kristian Norris*

The Wild Rose Press, Inc.
PO Box 708
Adams Basin, NY 14410-0708
Visit us at www.thewildrosepress.com

Publishing History
First Crimson Rose Edition, 2019
Print ISBN 978-1-5092-2565-1
Digital ISBN 978-1-5092-2566-8

Brandon's Brigade, Book 1
Published in the United States of America

"Mangoes. They look positively luscious." She grabbed the fruit, took a quick bite, and chewed with hunger. An expression of pleasure flashed across her face. Juice dribbled down her chin as she took another bite and closed her eyes. "Mm, it's so sweet and tart at the same time." She opened her eyes. "Aren't you having any?"

As he watched her eat the mango, a flash of heat surged through his groin. *Damn.* Where the hell had this come from? When he got home, he'd have to take a little R & R. He shut his eyes and pictured Sister Anna Louise from his high school years. Short, squat, with a meaty face and a mean attitude. The conjured image iced his libido. He swallowed the hard knot in his throat and remembered she'd asked him a question.

Praise for Evelyn Timidaiski

Golden Palm Winner
Winter Rose Finalist
~*~

"Adventure and romance are my favorite reads during dark, Minnesota winter nights. This book hits the sweet spot for me!"

~Ana Morgan, Author

Dedication

Dedicated to James
With Love

Acknowledgments

Authors work hard to bring you the best story they can. To complete this monumental task, they require lots of support. I would like to thank the following:

The **Wild Rose Press** for seeing promise in my work and offering support through the entire process.

Editor **Kaycee John**, Crimson Rose line, The Wild Rose Press, pushed and prodded me until we made the story work. She encouraged me and challenged me to meet the mark.

Cover Artist **Kristian Norris** created a wow factor cover, capturing the essence of Brandon Falcon and the Brandon's Brigade series.

Friends and **Family** who offered encouragement, applauding each tiny bit of progress as I worked toward this day.

Ana Morgan, with me at the beginning, helping me polish this story.

Thank you.

~Evelyn Timidaiski

Chapter One

Tegucigalpa, Honduras, 1800 Hours

Brandon Falcon hefted the American ambassador over his shoulder, grabbed his rifle, and ran for the jungle. "Jackson, status," he ordered as he moved, his voice clipped and urgent.

"Just a little kiss on the arm, Cap, but Frank took one in the chest. He's bleeding bad."

Brandon shifted the heavy weight on his shoulder and ran toward the helicopter. The American ambassador was free, though unconscious and probably drugged.

Gun flashes lit the fading darkness. Bullets tore into the ground and surrounding foliage. He kept running. The men of Seal Team Omega were outnumbered and had lost the element of surprise. Two wounded—one unable to walk and one dead. The mission had been compromised.

The basket lowered from the copter hovering overhead, swaying in the downdraft of the rotors.

"Put Frank in first," Brandon ordered.

"Cap, the *package*—" Petty Officer Jackson Favre said.

Cold as steel, Brandon's voice cut off any objections. "Damn the package. Put Frank in." Protocol may say deliver the package first, but he wasn't about to let one of his men die because of protocol.

Jackson slid Petty Officer Frank Decker into the basket, then followed to keep pressure on the chest wound during the ascent.

Brandon turned to see Petty Officer Rafà Gutiérrez hauling a limp body over one shoulder. Seaman Anson Miller, dead from a compression grenade, was only twenty-three years old. Intel for this mission was crap. The rebels had known they were coming and had been prepared. And the team had paid a hefty price.

From behind him, Rafà yelled, "Grenade!"

Brandon hit the ground and rolled, covering the ambassador with his own body. Dirt and debris pelted him. The concussive force hit hard—his ears rang, then popped while Gutiérrez sprayed the area with rifle fire.

The metal stretcher dropped a second time. Brandon hefted the ambassador's limp body and secured him in the basket, then climbed onto the stretcher to shield the man for the ride up. Inside the chopper, after emptying the carrier, he dropped it back down for Rafà. As an added precaution, he slipped a grenade into the grenade launcher attached beneath his rifle and took aim at the cascade of flashes in the dark.

Below, Rafà placed Miller's corpse in the basket for the ride up. As the basket neared the open door, he stepped off onto the skid and pushed the basket inside. Brandon reached to help his friend. The helicopter tilted sideways, throwing Rafà backward. Brandon lurched forward but missed the man's outstretched hand. His heart squeezed as he saw his friend hit the ground below.

"Drop the wire," he yelled. "We still have a man down there."

Signaling a negative, the pilot turned the craft toward the ocean.

"Dammit, you can't just leave him."

"Sorry, sir. I have orders to secure the package."

Brandon took one last unbelieving look at the ground below. SEALs *never* left one of their own.

Rafà, one of the best friends in his life, was gone.

****

El Liano, Honduras, Two Months Later

Dr. Mira Phelps pressed a final layer of plaster of Paris to the cast surrounding the boy's arm and turned to rinse her hands in the small wash basin. "No more climbing across vines to steal bird eggs, young man." She tweaked young Diego's nose with her damp hands, gaining a smile for her efforts. She handed him a protein bar and sent him on his way, fearing he'd be back soon. Scavenging for food in the jungle was always dangerous.

"Rosita, is this the last one?"

Silence met her question. Where was the woman? When still no response came, annoyance sharpened her voice. "Rosita?"

A loud crash came from the kitchen at the back of the clinic. A terrified scream broke the usual quiet air. "Please don't!"

Adrenaline lent speed to Mira's dash toward the kitchen. A rebel soldier stepped in front of her, clamped a muscular arm around her waist, stopping her fast and hard. She bashed ineffectively at the man's chest. "What's going on here? Let me go!"

"Enough."

The man released her abruptly, then cuffed her on the side of her head. The blow sent her crashing against a nearby wall. She slid down the rough panels—dazed, her eyes smarting with tears. Pain burned her cheek as her ears rang. Anger flared and burned in her chest.

She shook her head and tried to clear her thoughts. The metallic taste of blood filled her mouth as she bit back an angry retort. Her first priority, calm everyone down before someone got hurt. She'd known there would be risks when she came to El Liano, Honduras, but for the last two months she'd worked in the jungle clinic with few problems.

With a quick glance, she counted eight soldiers. Her heart rate escalated. The scene before her could have come from a nightmare. Infusing calm into her voice, she said, "There's no need for violence. Tell me what you want."

"Doctor, please," Jacinta Diaz, begged. Another soldier held the nurse in a rough grip, his hand fisted in her hair, twisting her head back to expose the terror on her face.

"Please don't hurt her," Mira pleaded.

Why were the rebels behaving this way? They had brought their wounded here before but never harmed anyone. Medical needs took precedence over politics. The clinic treated every patient equally, uniformed or civilian.

She rolled onto her hands and knees, ready to push to her feet. Booted feet stepped into her view. New, spotless. Her eyes traveled up his tall form. He was solid, built like a tree. In his clean uniform, shaved and well groomed, he stood out from the others in their dirty mismatched gear. Prickles of unease tingled at the back of her neck, quickly radiated through her limbs, and settled like a chunk of ice in her stomach. His eyes were like those of a shark—cold and empty. Killer's eyes. And they looked directly at her.

"Dr. Phelps, what a pleasure."

His voice was as icy as his eyes, and heavily accented Russian. "Come. We have much to discuss." He rapped out orders to the group of soldiers, before pulling Mira up by the arm.

He jerked her down the hallway. She stumbled as they entered Father Josè's office. He shoved her into the rickety chair at the priest's desk. Anger welled up at the chaos of the room. Files spewed from the lone cabinet; papers littered the floor.

"Were you looking for something special?" Mira spoke the words through stiffened lips. She tried for bravado but failed. Her voice came out too high-pitched for bravery.

"You don't get to ask the questions, doctor, I do." His voice sounded deadly, like his eyes.

"And who might you be?" *Damn.* She should bite her tongue. She didn't really want to know. His identity wouldn't help stop this madness. And now, he'd be angered by her arrogance.

"My name is Grigore Belikov." His grin showed yellowed teeth, jarring in his otherwise impeccable appearance. "I am not someone to be messed with, I believe you Americans like to say."

Did sharks have yellow—no, she best not go there. "Why are you attacking my clinic and putting innocent lives in danger, Mr. Belikov?"

"Are all American women as unrestrained as you, doctor?"

She bit her lip hard as she watched the megalodon across the desk. "I can't answer for all my countrywomen or my sex. I assure you I am only trying to—"

"Never mind," he barked. "Are you an American spy?"

Her jaw dropped. "What the devil do you mean? I work for the El Liano clinic. Father José is my boss."

"Since we liberated our country, Americans are not allowed in Honduras. How did you get here?"

Mira frantically searched for the right response. If she wasn't careful, they could all be killed. "I was part of a mobile unit for *Médecins Sans Frontières*, Doctors Without Borders. I became ill and was sent home to recuperate."

The sound of another crash came from the kitchen. Her pulse ratcheted—almost audible in the still room. The stale dustiness of the air became acrid with the smell of her own sweat. "After I recovered, the Sisters of Mercy sent me here to help out."

"How convenient," Belikov sneered. "When did you arrive?"

She stared into the dead eyes. No matter what she said, he wouldn't believe her. "Two months ago."

"At the exact time we got rid of all Americans, you come here to help?" He motioned to the soldier standing at the door. "Strap her down and give her the drug. We'll get our answers one way or the other."

Chapter Two

El Liano, Honduras, 1100 Hours, Zulu

Brandon Falcon lay flat on his stomach in the lush greenery. While ignoring the incessant buzz of a mosquito the size of an Apache helicopter, the relentless tropical sun baked the skin of his back. Stiff from lying in wait, he forced his muscles to remain still, not betraying his presence by even the twitch of an eyelid. Sweat beaded, then dribbled down the sides of his face. Despite his discomfort, he maintained focus on the target: a narrow, rugged road three hundred yards in the distance.

After his last disastrous rescue in this very jungle, he hoped this one went a hell of a lot better. Rafà, his best friend, could still be alive somewhere out there.

First, he had to save a kidnapped doctor.

An engine, low and growling, clawed its way up the steep incline. Moments later, a truck painted military green crested the hill. He rechecked the settings on his Recon rifle, rotated his head once, and exhaled through pursed lips. He took aim with his high-powered scope and fired. Crimson bloomed across the forehead of the driver as the shattered windshield fell inward. The hapless soldier crumpled against the steering wheel, his head twisted at a grotesque angle.

After the truck left the track and crashed into a tree,

a soldier armed with an AK-47 flung open the passenger door. Brandon's shot hit him between the eyes before his feet hit the ground. Flaps at the back of the truck flipped up; three more soldiers burst from the vehicle, immediately laying down ground fire. Taking his time, Brandon picked off each with three efficient shots before he approached the truck.

His gaze darted everywhere as he ran fast and low to the vehicle. Mere seconds passed, long enough to check each of the fallen soldiers. He dropped to the ground and belly crawled beneath the vehicle.

The engine ticked. Hot oil from the ruptured pan dripped over his hand as he placed the C-4 charge on the axle, and then crept to the back of the truck. Rifle ready, he crawled out and cautiously peered into the darkened truck bed.

The package.

A ratty blanket, tied with knotted rope, hid everything except a blonde curl and patch of white forehead. His gut clenched. The truck rocked beneath his weight as he climbed in and lightly touched the wrapped body. She didn't move. Before the raw pain of another failed mission tied him into knots, he grabbed the blanket-shrouded form, threw it over his shoulder fireman style, and exited the truck.

"Please, be alive," he prayed as he sprinted for the cover of the jungle.

He was rewarded by a moan from the tightly wrapped blanket.

Good, she was alive. Now to make sure they both stayed that way. He ran toward the mountains. Without slowing his pace, he activated the remote detonator. The truck exploded, drowning out the jungle sounds around him. The explosion bought him a few minutes head start.

Thunder vibrated the air around him; the heavens opened, and torrents of rain forced him to slow his pace. He welcomed the deluge. The downpour would wash away his tracks. The soldiers would pursue, and he couldn't outrun them. He'd have to hide—couldn't risk a stray bullet hitting the doctor. Ahead, the roar of a swollen stream rose louder than the noise of the rain. He slid through a cluster of shrubs, slipped into the water, and dug in against the bank.

****

Icy waves washed over Mira's body, shocking her awake. Drums pounded in her head. The bitter taste of fear burned in her mouth. Gasping, her mind foggy, she tried to remember. The clinic—the rebels. As panic seized her, she struggled against the rough ropes binding her.

Her body yanked against something solid. No, not something, *someone*. Why was someone holding her in the water? Adrenaline surged through her veins, burning a pathway to her brain.

Drowning was her biggest fear. Dear God, how had they known? She had to fight. She expended the last of her strength, arched her body backwards, and freed a small part of her face from the blanket folds. Fresh air sucked in through her lips, ready to fuel her scream.

A large hand clamped over her mouth, stifled her scream. She bit down hard on the flesh covering her face and tasted blood for her efforts.

A muffled curse rumbled. "Jesus…"

Good, she'd hurt back.

The raspy voice whispered close to her ear. "Make

a sound, and we're both dead."

Her drugged mind fought for clarity. She didn't think she recognized the voice from the clinic. Squirming, she struggled to get out of the folds of the blanket.

Wait, her foggy brain whispered. He'd spoken in English!

"Shh. Be still. I'm trying to help you."

Even through the rough fabric of the blanket, his breath smelled clean. No whiskey or rank cigar smoke—like the others. "Who…?"

"There's no time. Stay quiet. The rebels are right behind us."

The message and its urgency penetrated the blanket and cleared some part of her brain. They were in danger, and she couldn't risk more questions. She leaned in, tired of fighting.

"Shh, I've got you."

Chapter Three

"Rápidamente..."

The hissed order to fan out and search the underbrush came from a few feet away. Had he left tracks? No, he'd been careful, and the rain would have washed away any evidence. The footsteps shuffled in his direction.

"Ma'am," he warned, "we're going under water. Take a deep breath and hold it."

"No, please, I can't."

Brandon stared intently into her eyes. "There's no other way." She looked like a frightened animal, afraid to run and more afraid to remain. He put pressure on her shoulders, willing her to comply. She was clearly scared to death but gave him a slight nod.

"Now," he whispered.

Soundlessly, he sank beneath the water.

He held his breath for a minute and then rolled to his side, placing himself between the shore and her body. Her head stayed barely above water as he half walked, half floated them downstream. If they were seen from the opposite shore, his dark form could be taken for a caiman, a crocodile-like reptile indigenous to the area.

They reached a shallow spot; he pulled her from the stream. Hiding behind a thicket, he cut the ropes holding the blanket, then her bindings. Her ankles and wrists were raw and bloody. He turned her over and sucked in an uneven breath. Short, blonde curls surrounded her bruised and swollen face—her skin deathly pale.

Damn, she wasn't breathing. He placed an ear to her chest, tilted her chin back, and blew into her mouth. Arms extended, he applied quick compressions to her chest and watched for signs of life. "Come on, lady; don't give up on me now."

She coughed, then sputtered brackish water. He turned her head, allowing the water to flow from her mouth. Her eyelids fluttered open, revealing the bluest eyes he'd ever seen. The color stood out in stark contrast to her pale skin and the purple mottling of her bruised lip and cheek. Wide-eyed with fear, she stared up at him. He could only imagine what she must feel, opening her eyes to see his face painted with camouflage, looming over her.

"Are you trying to save me?" she asked, her voice husky and raw. "Or drown me?"

Not exactly the first words he expected to hear.

Before he could answer, she grabbed her stomach, turned her head, and puked. When she turned back, a rosy flush spread across her face, and her eyes darted away from his gaze.

"Don't be embarrassed, ma'am, it's the quickest way to clear any drugs from your system. Whatever they used to knock you out is bound to make you nauseous."

He reached inside one of his cargo pockets and handed her a wet bandana.

Tentatively, she took the cloth and wiped her mouth.

He bent closer. "Are you all right?"

She jerked back, eyes widening in panic.

He tried once more. "Do you think you can walk?"

Her face brightened. "You're American."

"Yes, ma'am. Lieutenant Brandon Falcon, US Navy SEALs." He flashed a smile. "Will you be able to walk, or will I need to carry you?"

"Where…how…? Your face?"

"The camouflage paint might look frightening, but it's necessary. I've been sent to rescue you. Now, we have to go."

She stared into his eyes, looking for reassurance. Her body straightened, her chin came up, and her mouth tightened. "Help me up, and I'm sure I'll be fine."

Brandon bit back a smile at her starchy tone. He'd bet a week of leave she got what she demanded most of the time. She had spunk. Good. Anything that helped get them through the next few hours was a bonus.

"We need to hurry, Doctor—

"Mira Phelps," she whispered through swollen lips. "Can I really trust you?"

Fear and uncertainty warred on her face, understandable after the ordeal she'd suffered. Well, they could work on trust later, for the moment he needed her cooperation.

He reached to help her to a sitting position. "Mira, I'm one of the good guys. Now, can you walk?"

She flinched when he placed an arm around her back to help her sit up.

"Damn," he muttered. She'd likely already suffered the pawing hands—or worse—from her captors. Dressed as he was, he probably looked like them. "Stay close. When I tell you to do something; do it fast."

Body tense as a bow, she sat up straighter in response to his harsh words, blue eyes glaring. She took his hand and used it to pull to her feet. Her legs buckled, and he caught her before she hit the ground. She struggled against his tightly wrapped arms. "I can walk. Please, just give me a minute."

"Look, ma'am, I understand your reluctance to be touched, but we're out of time. Either you let me carry you, or I'll have to gag you and throw you over my shoulder again."

Seconds passed as they studied each other.

"All right," she muttered and stilled in his arms.

Something deep inside of him shifted, urging him to reassure her. "You're safe, Mira." He resettled her weight, and then ran toward his hiding spot.

The rain stopped, and the terrain steepened as he trudged on. When he looked down, she was fast asleep against his chest. A feeling seeped through his body which he could neither explain nor wanted to explore. He shifted her to his shoulder, so he could move faster as he continued toward the cave. What was she doing here? Why was she so important that he would be called to rescue her solo? He shrugged mentally. It didn't matter. He didn't understand or always agree with military politics, but he'd been given a job and he'd damn well see it got done.

When they reached a waterfall, he waded through the shallow pool and entered an ell-shaped cave hidden behind tall shrubs and cascading water. It wasn't large but would keep them dry and out of sight. It smelled of cat. The distinct musky odor permeated the space, though faint enough to mean the cave had been abandoned for some time. He made his way toward the rear and placed the sleeping woman on a blanket.

For the moment, they were safe.

He placed a small light strip on a ledge at the back. At this angle, it couldn't be seen through the cascading water. He checked her breathing and pulse, then tucked an emergency thermal blanket around her slender body. Satisfied, he left to secure the outside area.

Brandon liked to have at least three plans for any possible situation. This mission had been dumped on him at the last minute. He wasn't even supposed to be here, much less rescuing the young doctor inside.

Ops had found him already in flight to Honduras. And though he was on extended leave, he couldn't say no to a rescue mission. They knew that about him at least, just like they had known he'd come back for Rafà, with or without their permission. His reputation might be in tatters, but at least they still trusted him.

But could he trust them? Yeah, that was the million-dollar question.

He completed his booby trap and moved into the surrounding shrubbery.

Chapter Four

Mira floated, untethered. Images dark and dangerous flitted through her brain. Armed men. Someone screaming, begging for help. Was it her? No, not her. Smells of sweat and liquor. Pain—crying. Fear! So much fear. Who were they? Why were they holding her? Ugly, leering faces. Searing pain. Then nothing.

She jerked awake. A giant man loomed over her. Green and black paint covered his face. Short, spiky, hair topped his still, grim face. Someone from her nightmare? Weapons hung all over his body. *Danger—* her mind shrieked.

"No!" She flinched. "Don't hurt me."

God, would this nightmare ever end? Her muscles tightened, ready to flee. His fiery green gaze calmly assessed her. Wait. His eyes. Would a Honduran rebel have green eyes?

Realization hit—then recognition. The navy SEAL, Lt. Brandon Falcon. *Thank God.* She wasn't back with the rebels. She relaxed against the rough blanket.

"How do you feel, ma'am?"

His deep voice rumbled over her. She fought the urge to shrink back against the blanket in fear. "I'm fine." This man was endangering his own life to help her, and all she could do was cringe when he got near her.

Get a grip, Mira.

"Let's check your injuries and get you out of those wet clothes."

She wasn't sure she liked the implied "we" in his statement, but her body shivered from the chill seeping into her bones. Pain lanced through her ribs when she reached for her boot laces. "Ouch."

"Here, let me." He brushed her fingers aside. "Save your strength for later."

She stopped awkwardly, unsure how to say what she meant. "I'm sorry."

His eyes met and held her gaze. "No need to apologize, ma'am, you've been through a lot, and...you do realize, we're not out of danger, yet?"

"We're still in the jungle? How far did we get?" She broke off, hearing the note of panic in her voice. She sucked in a deep calming breath and lay back on the blanket, while he removed her boots.

His large hands were strong, though he took great care as he massaged feeling back in to her feet, warming her skin with his touch and bringing a small measure of mental comfort with his ministrations. "We're about five miles from El Liano. We'll be safe for the night, but tomorrow we'll have to run."

"What's the plan, Lieutenant?"

"You're probably not going to like it," he said as he ran his fingers over her feet, then raised the hems of her pants.

She surveyed the swollen areas around her ankles, raw from rope burn and her struggles. Matching marks encircled her wrists. She stifled a groan as he touched them.

When she remained silent, he searched her face as if looking for answers. "Sorry, those must hurt."

Unease crept up her spine at his hesitation. "What else am I not going to like?"

"We have to stay in the jungle and keep running for the next week."

"Why can't we just get on your boat or plane or whatever brought you here? Surely it won't take that long to get back to it? I'm banged up, but by morning I'll be able to keep up."

"The problem is...the plane dropped me off and won't return for eight days."

"Why did you expect it to take so long to find me? I'm the only American woman in El Liano." She knew she sounded waspish, but her defense mechanism reared its ugly head when she was afraid. Words had been her way of fighting back since childhood.

"You weren't difficult to find." His voice remained calm. "The hard part is how to keep you hidden."

"I don't understand, Lieutenant." It all made perfect sense to her. Maybe her brain was still fuzzy from the bump on her head and the drugs she'd been given. Was she missing something? "Why can't we just leave?"

"Drop the rank, ma'am. We don't want to advertise my military connection. Please, just call me Brandon. My mission is...unorthodox. I was here on another matter when I received orders to rescue you. Travel plans had already been determined; we'll have to wait."

"I see." She was afraid in spite of all her bravado. "And your other mission?" She chewed her sore lip as she waited for his answer.

"You're my mission now, and I won't leave you alone."

His voice lowered, and she found it reassuring. She

hadn't really expected him to leave her, but some little part of her brain needed reassurance. It wasn't like she'd had much of it lately.

"And your other mission?" she repeated insistently.

"It'll have to wait." He lowered her foot beside its mate on the blanket.

"Your feet look fine except for the ankles. We can take care of those in a jiffy. I have antibiotic cream in my supplies." He rummaged through the bag he'd set beside her. "You said your last name was Phelps?"

Oh boy. Here it comes. How much could she tell him? Could she really trust him? She wasn't all she purported to be. Did she dare tell him her secrets?

From beneath her lashes, she took a quick look at the hard angles of his face. His unusual eyes, green with gold flecks, looked so intense they could burn a hole in your soul. He would be a hard man to lie to. For now, she'd stick to her cover story and hope he'd forgive the misrepresentation later.

"My name is Sister Mira Phelps. I'm the doctor from the clinic in El Liano."

Chapter Five

"Sister?"

This was an unexpected turn of events. The locals were very religious which explained her presence at the clinic. Sure as shit she didn't look like the nuns he'd met in the past.

"Well, Sister, if you don't mind my saying, you don't look like a nun."

Her spine straightened. Eyes sparkling with fire, cheeks flushed, she protested. "I do mind. You're behind the times, Mr. Falcon. Religious sisters no longer need to wear a habit or uniform to do the work of the Lord."

Trained to recognize small visual clues indicative of lying, he knew she wasn't telling the truth. Either she took him for a fool or was used to people asking easy questions. He was nobody's fool, and the questions were going to get a hell of a lot harder.

"Where's your cross?" He may not have been to church in a while, but he hadn't forgotten. Damn, he could still hear Sister Anna Louise like it was yesterday. *Brandon Falcon, you will not act like a heathen in this school. One hour's detention after dismissal.*

Mira rubbed the raw spot on her wrist and looked everywhere but at him. "It was gold—they must have taken it."

Reasonable, but a crucifix did not make a nun. He'd let it slide for now.

"I'm sorry, Sister. It's none of my business who or what you are. You're my mission. That's what matters." With those words, he was back on track. All business.

"Good. Got any betadine?" Her question acknowledged his change of subject.

"Yes, ma'am." He handed her the plastic packet.

She stared at him, eyes intense and searching. "Could you do me a favor?"

"If it's legal and doesn't cost too much."

Her laugh brightened her bruised face.

He grinned back at her. "There, I knew you could do it."

"Thanks, it feels good to laugh. About that favor?"

"Yes, ma'am?"

"Could you wash your face so I can see you?"

"I'll clean up while you slip out of your clothes. You can use one of my T-shirts." He reached into his duffel and handed her one. "Deal?" He held out his hand.

She grasped it with hers. "Deal."

Brandon turned his back. He opened a small foil packet and removed the wet cloth treated with makeup remover. As he cleaned his face, he remembered Rafà on the first day of operations prep training. The expression on his face had been comical as he'd read the label. Rafà was a man's man and wanted nothing to do with lady stuff.

The falling water rumbled at the cave entrance, reminding him he hadn't heard much movement behind him. "Are you all right, Sister?"

"Well..." Hesitancy filled her voice.

He turned to see her struggling with her arms trapped behind her back, entangled in her wet blouse. He knelt beside her and gently took her arm.

She stiffened. Her breathing accelerated. A blush started in her cheeks and flamed over her entire face and neck.

Dropping his hands, he moved back, and lowered his voice to a soothing cadence. "Wet clothes are difficult to remove, even when you're at a hundred percent. You've been kidnapped, beaten, and drugged. Cut yourself a break. Accepting help isn't a sign of weakness."

A myriad of emotions flitted across her face as she considered his words. He could tell she was unhappy with her choices. Hell, he had to be sure she wasn't in need of medical attention. He'd made mistakes earlier, and she had nearly drowned. And there was Rafà. His lips tightened. No one else was going to die on his watch.

"I could use some help, but..." She hesitated.

"Let's just get the top layer off, so I can check your wounds," he said before she could object. "Keep the blanket to cover your legs. They're okay except for the ankles, right?"

"Yes, just the rope burns."

He gently pulled the blouse from her arms, easing her arms forward.

She immediately brought them up to shield her breasts.

He looked away. Allowing him to see her like this cost her emotionally—one more insult added to the rest.

She did her best to help, wiggling to move the wet

khaki pants down her legs.

Sitting in her plain white panties and bra, she looked so vulnerable. Brandon pulled the thermal blanket around her chest and legs and made his tone impersonal. "Turn, please so I can check your back."

With her back turned, she unsnapped her front-hook bra, then slid it down her arms.

From behind he eased one of his T-shirts over her head and helped pull her arms through. When his fingers lightly touched a large bruise on her back, she winced. Was that a shoe print on her ribs? The purplish marks marring her satiny skin tightened his gut. In his stomach, rage began a slow boil.

"You have some nasty bruises, but no cuts," he said, struggling to keep anger from his voice. "Anything else I should know about?"

"I have a rib on my left side which is probably cracked. You'll need to strap it."

His fingers tightened into fists. "Did I break it when I did CPR?"

"No," she said. "A soldier flung me against the wall; I fell to the floor."

"Show me."

She raised her shirt and touched her lower rib area on her left side.

Brandon placed his fingers beside hers and grabbed the gauze. He circled her lower chest several times with the soft fabric. "How tight?" he asked as he made the first swath with tape around her ribs.

"A little tighter." She took a deep breath. "Good, I can breathe without too much pain."

"I'll clean and disinfect your face along with your ankles and wrists after you've warmed up some. Roll over." Once more he became detached and impersonal.

"What?"

"Roll over." He repeated. "I want to get this antibiotic into you ASAP. Do you have any allergies?"

"No." She held out a hand. "Just give it to me and I'll do it myself."

"Sorry, ma'am, this one goes in the butt." He paused for comic effect. "Wait a minute. That might be interesting to watch."

She huffed, and he gave her a devilish grin.

She bit her lip and rolled onto her stomach. "You're enjoying this far too much."

He swabbed her hip and quickly jabbed the needle into the meatiest part of her buttock.

"What the—" She bit back her words.

"What, Sister?" He slapped a Band-Aid on the spot. He'd give a lot to have heard the rest of her smothered words.

"What antibiotic are you using?" she asked quickly.

He'd give her high marks for the save, but the Sister had almost cursed.

He resumed his impersonal persona. "Chloramphenicol. You have any problems with it?"

"No, it's a good choice." She rolled onto her back, covering her legs with the blanket as she did so. "At the clinic, we're constantly running out of medicine. I hate to see people suffer when the medicine to save them costs so little."

She had to be in pain, and he needed her ready to hike come morning. "I understand. Do you want something for the pain?"

"Let me see that." She grabbed the bag, rummaged

through his supplies, and took out a couple of ibuprofens. "Impressive supplies, Mr. Falcon. I think you'd make quite a good medic."

"When we go on a mission, we have to be prepared for almost anything. Expect the unexpected is my personal motto." He handed her the canteen to wash down the pills, then stood.

She lifted a brow. "Mission?"

He turned to head for his large duffel of supplies. "I'm in Special Operations. I can't divulge more."

"I understand," she said. "I just want to say thanks."

"For what?"

"For doing what you do. For saving my life."

"It's my job, ma'am." He got to his feet, uneasy with gratitude. "I'm going to rustle up some grub. Got any special requests?"

"I don't suppose you have any chocolate in your bag?"

He chuckled. "Got a sweet tooth, Sister?"

"Please. Call me Mira. I must confess, chocolate is one of my vices."

"Chocolate as a vice? I can't wait to hear about the rest. Anything else?"

"Can we have a fire? I'm so cold."

"We can't risk the smoke, but I have a portable stove for cooking. It's shielded to block out light and puts out a good bit of heat." He pulled out the stove and positioned it at the back of the cave. After checking the shielding, he struck a match against his boot, and touched it to the fuel. Picking up the duffel, he moved away and began sorting the supplies.

****

As the stove put out heat, Mira grabbed the blanket and shifted nearer the small flame. As the warmth permeated her skin, tension began to ease from her bruised body. The burning smell brought back memories of summers with her uncle Max. They'd camped out and had a real fire. Her heart ached at the memories, the pain still raw after two years. He was the real reason she came here. His research had ignited her passion for—

His question interrupted her musings. "Are you doing okay?"

"The heat and ibuprofen are working wonders, thanks."

He filled a small pot with water, placing it on the burner to heat. After refilling the canteen from the waterfall, he stuck a small light into it.

"What's that?" she asked.

"It's a SteriPEN. I don't like the chemical taste of water purification tablets." He handed it to her for a closer look. "It uses UV light to kill the protozoans and other microbes. It's one of my few indulgences."

"I've read about these things." Her hands shook as she took the pen from him. "If we could pass these out in the clinic, it would go a long way toward slowing down disease. Clean drinking water shouldn't be a luxury." She handed it back to him and put her hands beneath the blanket.

"I'm sure it would," he said, capping the canteen. "Unfortunately, cost instead of results usually guides decisions."

"Your comment is somewhat unusual for a soldier, isn't it? Don't you go where you're sent and kill who you're told to kill?"

"That's rather a cynical view of what I do, but I suppose you're right. Soldiers see the worst things humans do to each other. We're like other people, maybe with a larger dose of realism."

Her voice raised a notch. "Is that how you see the rebels?"

"No, ma'am. We were discussing soldiers, patriots for their country. These rebels slaughter innocents in the name of freedom. They see and feel differently. Where you and I see poverty and misery, they see opportunity and power."

She was surprised by the depth of his thinking and obvious feelings. She never dreamed a man who made his living so violently could think and care so deeply. "You are an interesting man." She ducked her head, fearing he'd laugh at her. "I wish things didn't have to be like they are here. Silly idea, huh?"

"Not silly, but perhaps unrealistic. We both have professions where we deal with grim realities." She sensed a kind of melancholy about him as he spoke. Then just as quickly, he was back to his brisk self again. "I'm going to get some fruit to go with our supper. Do you need to go outside?"

"Yes." The cave was claustrophobic, but she felt relatively safe inside. Out there was unknown.

"You'll be fine while I'm with you, but don't leave the cave without me." Brandon handed her the boots he'd removed earlier, waited as she slipped her feet gingerly back into them. Offering his hand, they made their way beneath the cascading water. "The front edge of the pool is booby-trapped—so stay clear," he explained in a matter-of-fact voice.

"We live in such different worlds, Mr. Falcon.

Yours is filled with guns and booby traps. I'm afraid mine is quite different." She moved closer to him, wary of the darkness surrounding them.

"We live in the same world, Sister. We just have different ways of dealing with the same problems."

He'd spoken as if he'd given the matter a lot of thought.

"How can you say such a thing?" she asked, annoyed he'd compare them in such a way.

"We both go to some of the world's most ravaged places to help people," he said.

His words left nothing for her to say. He was right, soldiers did help people. It depended on which side of the line you were standing.

She fell silent. The jungle sounds changed, taking on a different cadence as night began to fall. Without the fear of rebels, she might have enjoyed listening to the different animals. Now, she listened for danger.

He guided her to an area with a large boulder. "You'll be safe here," he said after checking the shrubs and ground.

"Thank you."

She moved behind the boulder silently praying all the creepy crawly things had moved away. She had been in jungles around the world, and still, she dreaded unexpected visitors on latrine visits. It was even worse without a light. Moments later, she returned to the clearing, and he wasn't there.

A bird called, startling her. She placed her back against the boulder and froze. Something was moving through the thicket to her left. Prickles of fear danced over her skin. Her hand flew her mouth to stifle a scream. "Brandon?"

Oh, God, where was he? Her voice pitched higher. "Mr. Falcon?"

His head poked through the brush, and air rushed from her lungs in a sigh of relief.

Chapter Six

Brandon stepped out of the bushes, carrying a couple of mangoes. "It's not safe to call out in the jungle, ma'am. I could have been a rebel, or worse, a jaguar."

When fear washed over her face, he swore softly beneath his breath. "I'm not trying to scare you, but you need to take precautions. Next time you hear something in the brush, and I'm not around, just hide and wait. Don't make yourself a target."

Far off in the jungle, an animal screamed. Not a cheerful cry of contentment—but one of violence and death. She moved closer, nearly touching him as she reacted to the sound. "I'm sorry."

"Don't be sorry, Sister, be safe. The next few days are going to be rough. Calling out like you did could get you killed."

"I'm not like you," she sputtered. "I don't expect evil behind every rock."

"Something doesn't have to be evil to be dangerous." He caught himself and stopped his lecture. He couldn't expect her to behave like a soldier, but she had to be more cautious or they'd both get killed. "Come on. Let's get some food into you." He took her arm as they walked back to the cave.

Stowing her safely beside the stove, he rummaged through the duffel and pulled out a package and a metal cup. In his best butler's voice, he announced, "Dinner is served." He sent her a cocky grin as he poured powder into boiling water.

Mira got a whiff of the boiling pot, and a grin appeared on her face. The growl in her stomach echoed off the walls of the cave. "Is that hot chocolate?"

He stopped stirring and quirked his brow.

A pink flush crept up her cheeks as she quickly pressed a hand to her stomach. "I can't remember when I ate last." She tilted her head. "What day is it?" Her voice and face became serious. "How long was I unconscious?"

"Today is Tuesday, but I'm not sure how long they had you. I arrived in country yesterday. Look, don't worry about that now. You need to eat and get your strength back."

"Don't worry?" she shrilled. "I'm missing three days from my life. What happened to the rest of the staff at the clinic?"

He refused to answer, handing her a small plastic bag filled with jerky. "After you eat." He took the pot from the stove and poured some of the hot chocolate into a metal cup.

With a flourish, he presented her with the hot chocolate and a piece of peeled fruit. "Ta-da."

Her eyes lit up at the sight and smell of the food. She eyed the piece of fruit like it was an oasis in the desert. "Mangoes. They look positively luscious." She grabbed the fruit, took a quick bite, and chewed with hunger. An expression of pleasure flashed across her face. Juice dribbled down her chin as she took another bite and closed her eyes. "Mm, it's so sweet and tart at the same time." She opened her eyes. "Aren't you having any?"

As he watched her eat the mango, a flash of heat surged through his groin. *Damn.* Where the hell had this come from? When he got home, he'd have to take a little R & R. He shut his eyes and pictured Sister Anna Louise from his high school years. Short, squat, with a meaty face and a mean attitude. The conjured image iced his libido. He swallowed the hard knot in his throat and remembered she'd asked him a question.

"There's only one cup, so I'll eat when you're finished," he explained. "The jerky will help replenish your salts, so eat plenty."

When she'd finished her meal, he walked over with the needed medical items and knelt in front of her. "I'm sorry, this is going to—"

"Sting," she said, cutting him off. "You'd think physicians would have a better way of saying it. I suppose it sounds better than—this is going to hurt like hell." She gave him a look somewhere between anger and despair. "What can I say to a child who's been sliced up by a machete? So many children have been mutilated or maimed and for what? Land? Resources? I can only patch them up. I want to do more. That's why I'm here. To find…" She sank into silence.

Brandon studied her face. She'd revealed plenty with her explosive speech. She wasn't expecting any answers. There were none. As gently as he could, he cleaned her bruised cheek and the cut along her mouth. Anger tugged at his lips as he wiped, recognizing the bruise as a fist print. He would dearly love to get hold of the guy who had done this to her.

She jerked her head back, wincing at the sting of the alcohol swab. "Ouch!"

"I did warn you." He dabbed antibiotic ointment on the cut.

She stared into space as he cleaned and disinfected her wounds. There was nothing he could do for the wounds that probably hurt the worst. The bruised spirit and humiliation. The shattered sense of personal safety and the loss of control over one's own fate. They had robbed her of those things and more.

He set the used swabs aside and looked into her eyes. "Did they rape you?"

****

The cave seemed to shrink, sharpening the smell of cat and dampness. "No!"

"Mira, look at me."

She tilted her head up but kept her eyes directed at the floor.

"I need to know. I have medication—"

Her breath came in jerky gasps. "They didn't rape me," she said through clenched teeth. "The local rebels were grateful for my help and took great care around me. When the others came—"

The waterfall pounded the rocks as she took her time, thinking before she continued. How she wished she could skip the rest, but a quick glance up into intense green orbs, prodded her on. "The man in charge kept hinting at rape but wouldn't let the other soldiers touch me. He played with me like a cat with a mouse. One minute he'd tell me in gory detail what his men would do to me. Then, he'd laugh and say he'd been kidding."

"Psychological warfare," Brandon said softly. "He was trying to wear you down."

"Well, it worked. I was on the verge of confessing

to anything." She ran her hands shakily through her matted hair. "After endless questions, beatings, and drugs, they tossed me in the truck. I'm not sure where they were taking me."

"One of their camps, most likely," he said. "Believe me, that experience wouldn't have been pleasant." He turned his head and looked away from her.

Was he repulsed by what he saw? His face was guarded, so she couldn't tell.

He got up and added another fuel can to the stove, and then returned to sit across from her. "Please, tell me what happened," he said softly.

She looked into his eyes, saw his compassion and understanding. Finally, for the first time in days, she felt safe. "I heard a crash and screams. When I ran into the kitchen, it was full of men. They hit Jacinta, my nurse, and I begged them not to hurt her. One man grabbed me and threw me against the wall." She paused and touched her cheek.

"It's okay," he soothed. "Go on."

"There was a man…" She looked up at Brandon. "He looked and felt evil. His eyes were cold, empty pits. If there is a devil, he was it. He kept questioning me about things I didn't understand. When I didn't give him the answers he was looking for, they took Jacinta away. I heard her screams coming from another room." Her voice hitched, and she took a deep breath. "I tried to help her, but a guard hit me with his fist. I guess I blacked out, because things are fuzzy."

She eyed the needle marks on her arm, and her lips tightened. "Most of the time, they kept me drugged." She halted, twisting her hands to stop their shaking.

"I'm not even sure how long they kept me. Everything has become blurred. Before the Russian mercenaries came, the rebels pretty much ignored us." She paused, breathed heavily, and trapped his gaze in the dim glow of the stove. "I have to go back. I have to help Jacinta and the others at the clinic."

****

Brandon remained silent as she talked. She needed to get it all out, and he needed as much information as possible. His knuckles tightened on his cup as he slowly drank the chocolate and ate the jerky.

As he processed the details she'd just shared, he felt his body shift into hunter mode. He could sneak into their camp, wipe them all out. The imagery incited his protective instincts. Harshly, he reined in his thoughts. Retribution would have to wait; keeping her safe was his priority for now.

"Mira, you can't go back. Make no mistake; they *would* rape you this time. They'd take turns until you bled to death." He didn't want to tell her so harshly, but it was for her own good. He needed to squelch any hopes she harbored of returning to the clinic.

"You said they were Russians?" He went back to her description of the men who kidnapped her. "Did you hear them speak it, or did someone say they were Russian?"

This could be important. If someone other than the rebels was behind the recent coup, the new government could be just a puppet of a foreign power. This could have all kinds of ramifications. His commander would need to know about this.

"I heard the leader speak it," she whispered. "I was so frightened by his eyes. They had no soul, like looking into the eyes of death. He told the others to lock me up, and then he took Jacinta." She shuddered. "I can't talk about him; it makes me cold all over." She stilled and withdrew into herself.

Brandon had looked into eyes like that before. He still did in some of his nightmares. Upon occasion, he supposed his own eyes showed the same death mask of a killer. He'd like to think he was still salvageable, unlike some of the soulless eyes he had seen. He wanted to find out more, but asking further questions tonight would be unproductive. She was exhausted. She'd shown courage thus far, and she'd need every bit of it and more on the journey to come. The rest would have to wait until morning.

"We are going to get out of this safe and sound. Lie down and get some sleep. I'll keep watch, so don't worry." He tucked the blanket around her and removed the light strip, leaving only the soft glow of light from the shrinking fuel tub. He moved over to his bag and took out more ibuprofen.

He handed her the tablets with some water. "Here."

She didn't put out her hand. "No, I'm fine."

"You'll need to be as strong as possible tomorrow. We'll be hiking at a fast pace through jungle and mountains. These will help you relax enough to sleep. Drink as much water as you can."

"Yes, doctor." She smirked at him but took the pills and drank deeply from the flask.

"During the night, I might go outside to check on things. Don't panic if you wake and don't see me."

She opened her mouth, but then she simply nodded.

"Now sleep," he said gruffly.

****

When her even breathing announced she was in deep asleep, Brandon tidied up, then took out his weapons. Leaning against the cave wall, he methodically cleaned and checked each one. He had quite an arsenal. Besides the MK12 SPR or Special Purpose Rifle, he carried a 9mm SIG at his waist, and strapped to his left ankle was a Glock. On his right boot was an MPK, Mini Pry Knife, and at his waist he had his SEAL 2000 knife. An assortment of accessories like ninja stars, a garrote, and smoke canisters lay hidden in the pockets of his tactical vest. Just your everyday surprises for the enemy. In addition to the regulation materials, he had the AK-47 he'd picked up from the rebels. And there was his good luck charm. His old man's Beretta. It had protected his father in some of the world's worst war zones.

Weapons were lethal, but even if he lost them all, he himself was a killer. He knew more ways to kill than any one man should. He was only thirty-five, but he felt old, especially when faced with an innocent like Mira Phelps. She would run from him as fast as she could if she knew some of the things he'd done.

They were opposites. She healed people. He killed people. He studied her as she slept. If he had to guess, she was probably in her late twenties. She'd have to be at least that old to be a doctor, but she didn't look it.

The way she'd described her kidnapping led him to believe she was holding something back. Her description of the men at the clinic was probably dead on. There'd been some discussion about Russian mercenaries during his last mission. When Rafà had gone MIA.

So why was she really here? She had to be keeping something from him. Granted, he hadn't been exactly forthcoming himself. She had no idea of his real mission. No one did, and he intended to keep it that way. He'd suffered enough losses in the last few months. Keeping his secret from her would ensure her safety.

Done with cleaning, he made a makeshift clothesline and hung their wet clothes. He checked the stove and placed her boots nearby to dry. Finished, he found the spot where he could monitor both the cave entrance and Mira. Picking up the AK-47, he leaned against the duffel and closed his eyes. Just a few hours, then he'd get up and check the perimeter. He regulated his breathing and fell into a light sleep.

****

Moans and thrashing woke her. At first, she thought she was back at the clinic. The smell of the stove made her remember. She was in a cave with the man who had rescued her. Those were his moans. She scrambled from the blanket and scuttled toward the other end of the cave.

Light filtered in weakly through the waterfall.

Covered in sweat, his body jerked wildly. He cried a name in his sleep. "Rafà!"

She reached out and shook him.

He grabbed her hand, pulled her close, and squeezed her throat with his large hands. The face looking at her was a cold, frightening mask. She clawed at his hands, trying to release their lethal grip on her throat so she could breathe.

Finally, she managed a scratchy gasp. "Brandon, wake up."

His eyes focused. With a curse, he jerked his hand from her throat. He tossed his gun aside and stared back at her with a tortured look of shock.

"Never touch me when I'm asleep," he rasped. "I could have killed you."

She backed away from him, holding her neck. She eyed him warily, as he became more focused and awake.

"I'm sorry, Sister; I didn't mean to hurt you. Are you okay?"

He reached out to touch her, but she shied away.

He stared at her throat. "I was dreaming."

"From your reaction, it wasn't a pleasant dream. Who is Rafà?"

He averted his eyes. "Why do you ask?"

"You called his name when I woke you. Is he a friend of yours?"

He shoved up from the floor and walked over to the waterfall, dousing his face with the cold water. Turning back to her, he said hoarsely, "He was."

"Is he dead?" she asked.

For a moment, his face blazed with anguish. "I'm not sure."

If Rafà was indeed Brandon's friend, shouldn't he know if he was dead? Before she could ask more questions, his face became a closed mask.

Abruptly, he began packing the equipment and their supplies.

"It'll be full light soon. We need to clear out of here and travel as far as we can before the rain begins. The soldiers will no doubt be out early looking for us."

"Surely, they will have given up by now. Why waste extra time on someone like me?" Who was she trying to convince, him or herself?

"You underestimate your worth, Sister. You're beautiful, American, and white." He gave her a penetrating look that had her feeling a little tingly in her stomach. Quickly, she found somewhere else to look.

"You're also a doctor. They're hard to come by in this godforsaken country." He continued packing. "Add it up, and I would say you are quite valuable to these soldiers. Of course, they could be after *me*."

"Why would they want you?" She grabbed her pants from the line and put as much distance between them as possible as she tugged them on. They were still clammy, clinging to her skin as she hurried.

Brandon stilled at her words. He walked over, snagged her arm, and swung her to face him.

"How can you be so naïve? Don't you understand? These people don't play by society's rules." He pulled her roughly up against him. "I killed five of their men when I rescued you." He emphasized each word with a slight shake of her shoulders. "Do you really think they are going to forgive and forget?"

Releasing her as abruptly as he'd grabbed her, he bent to pick up his gun and duffel. In a deathly calm voice, he said, "They'll kill us both if they find us, and killing will be the kindest part. Now let's move."

She was stunned as the full import of his words sank in. He'd killed five men to save her. Her heart felt heavy as she thought of all the death and violence. She ached for him. How did he handle the burden of so many deaths?

She dropped to the cave floor and raced to put on her boots. The air between them was electric as she helped pick up the rest of the supplies.

Brandon headed out beneath the cascading water with her right on his heels. She paused and turned back with a wistful look. The cave may have been dark and small, but for a short while she had felt protected and safe there. Quickening her pace, she followed him through the underbrush.

Chapter Seven

The morning sunlight struggled to push through the densely layered canopy, creating splotchy patterns on the forest floor. Brandon pulled a machete from his backpack and hacked through dense areas to make the trek a little easier on Mira. He hesitated to cut too much for fear of leaving an obvious path. She gamely followed him, though at a much slower pace than he'd have liked.

His mood was surly at best and dangerous at worst. The nightmare followed by his manhandling Mira left him reeling. No one under his protection should have any need to fear. The look in her eyes and the redness on her neck made him want to kick himself in the ass.

With vicious strokes he slashed the blade through the vines. The exercise proved cathartic, helping to obliterate some of his anger, though doing nothing to ease his conscience. He ignored the lush scenery but couldn't help hearing the squawks and calls of the birds. Monkeys screamed and threw fruit at them as they walked under the trees. An especially juicy piece hit him in the back, and he paused a moment to look back over his shoulder.

She had stopped and stood with a mesmerized look on her face as she gazed around. Her face looked relaxed as she watched the antics of the monkeys. He watched her enjoyment of her surroundings. Through her eyes, the deadly jungle sparkled with life and beauty, where he saw ambush and danger. "Everything's so alive." she exclaimed. "I wish they'd throw something edible. We missed breakfast."

How the hell could anyone be in such good humor this early in the morning, without coffee, and in the mess they were in?

"I'm sensing a pattern, Sister. You're always thinking of food." He took a few steps back, lessening the gap between them. "We'll stop in a half hour to rest and eat. What I wouldn't give for a good cup of Kona or Sumatra right now. I'm a bear in the mornings without my coffee."

With any luck, she'd believe it was the reason for his mood. "I might be able to help you." She flashed a grin at him and pointed to some shrubs growing beneath the larger trees. "Help me pick some of those red berries and I can promise coffee in the morning."

He gave her a look, questioning her bold statement.

"Don't look so surprised, I'm not just any doctor. I specialize in plants and their medicinal uses. Keeping a grouchy man awake is definitely a medicinal use."

"And here I was thinking you were an under achiever." He reached into one of his large pockets and pulled out a bandana. He wasn't sure what she was up to, but they could both use a little rest.

"You seem to have an amazing number of useful things in those pockets," she commented as she picked berries from the shrubs. "Are you always prepared?"

"I'm no boy scout, if that's what you're thinking." Brandon tied the edges of the bandanna forming a sack. Together they began filling it with the berries. "I wasn't exactly prepared for you. I have to admit you're the first nun I've ever rescued."

He looked up, catching an odd expression on her face. She looked like one of his sister's kids when they'd been into the cookies before dinner.

"Did I say something disagreeable? You look uncomfortable." Brandon noted the way her lips turned down and a little furrow formed in her brow.

"Well," she paused, biting her lip. "I wasn't going to say anything, but I was wondering about the number of germs that bandanna has acquired in the last few days. Assuming of course, it was clean when you put it in your pocket." She looked into his eyes and gave him an impish grin. "Fastidiousness aside, I plan to enjoy some coffee tomorrow."

Her comment startled a laugh from him as he wrapped the berries in the bandana and stowed them in his pocket.

He began hacking at the vines again. "Let's go."

As they continued, the ground steepened and the plant life thinned. Rocky slopes appeared before them and rather than climb, they turned at the base of the incline. After following the edge for an hour, they heard running water in the distance. Brandon held up a hand, signaling for her to stop. He led her behind some large rocks.

"Wait here. I'll check out the area around the water." Brandon pulled the Glock-20 from his ankle holster. "Have you ever fired a gun?"

Her look of horror was answer enough.

"It's not hard. Here's the safety—use two hands, point and shoot." He deftly demonstrated.

She shook her head and backed away.

"Look, I can't be in two places at once, and I'd feel

a hell of a lot better if you at least had it with you. Don't shoot unless someone makes a grab for you. Hide if something happens to me." He repeated his words from last night.

"I'm not shooting anyone."

He continued to hold the gun out, handle toward her. He would wait as long as it took.

She finally gave in and gingerly took the gun, holding it at arm's length.

"I'll keep it with me in case a jaguar should surprise me, but I'm not killing anyone."

He nodded his approval and handed her the water canteen. He understood her reticence at handling the gun. Few people were at ease with weapons. To SEALs, they were like another appendage.

"I won't be long so rest while I'm gone." He moved quietly away but paused to throw a remark over his shoulder. "When I come back, don't mistake me for a jaguar and shoot me. I'm rather fond of my pelt." He gave a quiet chuckle as he disappeared into the undergrowth.

****

Mira first checked the rocks for scorpions and other possible hazards, then brushed off an area, and sat. A swig of tepid canteen water made the running water ahead sound doubly blissful. She gingerly placed the gun beside her on the ground, happy to be rid of it, then leaned back to view the scenery.

This place was a botanist's paradise. Lianas, thicker than her arms twisted their way around trees, hosts for a myriad of other plants as they coexisted. Higher up, bromeliads with their brilliant red centers acted like beacons for tiny insects to bathe. She could spend her entire life studying such things.

Her lips curved upward when thoughts of Brandon's parting words flitted through her mind. His pelt was rather luxurious, almost a tawny color, like a lion. Since he'd removed the camouflage paint, he was far less intimidating—and that short spiky hair—her fingers itched to touch it. *Stop it.*

It wasn't uncommon to become attracted to your rescuer. White Knight Syndrome, her medical mind automatically filled in the correct term. She shook her head. He did have nice hair.

She sighted a spot of yellow high up on a tall tree trunk and walked over, hoping to get a better look. Maybe she could climb a little way up using one of the vines. She began her assent, ignoring the scratches from the tree. A few scratches would be worth it to get a closer view of the orchid. It wasn't the one she searched for, but still fascinating.

Half-way up the tree, hair on the back of her neck rose in warning. Noise in the jungle had stopped. She was no longer alone. Had Brandon returned? No, this felt different.

She shifted, placing the tree trunk between her and the path. A cautious look below showed movement in the foliage. Her mouth dried with fear. *The gun.* She'd left it on the rock. What if it was a jaguar? They had joked about it, but jaguars could climb trees. Her heart jumped and skipped a beat. Three men, automatic weapons across their shoulders, walked beneath the tree and past the spot where she'd sat. She eased back behind the tree trunk.

She drew in a calming breath, leaned around the edge of the tree, and looked down. She didn't recognize these men, but they were dressed in the same hodge-podge manner as the rebels at the clinic and their weapons looked like the big things they'd waved around.

Dear God, they were headed straight for Brandon.

As she watched, an arm reached out and pulled the last man into the shrubs. Accomplished quickly and quietly, the move went un-noticed by the others.

She rubbed a hand over her eyes. Had she really seen it?

The men moved out of sight; then, she heard a scuffle, followed by a shot.

Her heart leaped into her throat as she slid down the tree, ignoring the sharp tears at her skin. She had to get to the gun—had to see if he was hurt. She fell the last few feet, clamored up and ran to the rocks.

Her hand touched the gun, just as another hand covered hers. She uttered a frightened squeak as Brandon took the weapon from her shaking fingers. He replaced the weapon on his ankle. Her gaze jumped to his, asking but not really wanting to know.

His eyes were hard and cold as emeralds.

They were all dead. She forced the gorge back down her throat.

"Let's go." He grabbed the canteen and without another word walked toward the stream.

Subdued, Mira followed, careful not to allow much space to come between them. She could've been killed and Brandon had proved himself an efficient protector. He had killed, but he wasn't like those other men, was he?

She'd felt his compassion and integrity. Or was she trying to fool herself because he'd saved her? She felt safe with him. Could she trust him with her secret?

Would he understand why it was so important for her to find the orchid?

Chapter Eight

As Brandon walked, his thoughts raced over the last few minutes. He'd left Mira behind and she could've been killed. How'd she get up in the tree anyway? Had she heard the soldiers' approach and abandoned her hiding place for a better one? Doubtful. And why the hell hadn't she taken the gun with her? *Stupid question, Brandon.* She never intended to use it.

He hadn't hidden her well enough. Maybe he should've tied her to the tree. Yeah, he liked that image better. Didn't the woman understand the meaning of stay put?

He'd returned from scouting the stream and found the spot where he'd left her empty. He immediately thought the rebels had taken her. How could they have gotten away so quietly? She wouldn't have gone with them silently. He'd heard the men coming and hidden in the brush. After he'd eliminated the threat, he'd returned to find her sliding down a tree trunk. The image lightened his mood a little. He didn't know many women who could shinny up and down a tree.

She was such a surprise and couldn't be a nun. His gut told him she was using the ruse for protection. Tonight, he'd get the truth. She had to start being honest with him if they were going to get out of this alive. Mutual trust made survival easier.

He set the pack and supplies down and began

unloading things. "We can't stay here long."

"Do I have time to clean up in the water before we eat? I haven't washed in days and I'm filthy."

"Five minutes." He reached into his pack and tossed her a small plastic vial wrapped in one of his bandanas. "It might not smell like a lady, but it should help with the dirt."

"Thanks." She caught the liquid soap on the fly as she ran toward the falls.

He wasn't surprised by her request. She'd stopped to pick coffee beans, left her hiding spot to climb a tree for heaven knows what reason, and now, she was blissfully showering under a waterfall in the middle of enemy territory. Oh yeah, she's a nun and a doctor. Christ, she was a handful and his patience would be put to the test.

The look on her face when he'd taken the gun from her shaking fingers would haunt him. She'd looked like a child who'd been slapped by someone they loved and trusted. Well, damn it to hell. What did she expect?

He was a soldier.

He killed to protect and was damn good at it. If he hadn't, they'd be locked up in some rebel camp, waiting to be tortured. He'd probably be dead, because he'd kill the first one who laid a hand on her. Yeah, that would help her a lot, wouldn't it? His gaze whipped up at her screech and his heart stopped. She stood beneath the water spray, wearing only her tape for her ribs, white panties and a smile. He quickly looked away only to find her reflection mirrored in the pool. Her supple body, small taut breasts, and rounded hips were all visible in the pool.

God help him if she was a nun.

He would gladly spend his time in Hell to be able to hold her beautiful body in his arms.

His groin jolted awake and he shifted position, trying to make his body more comfortable. Who was he kidding? There was only one way to ease this pain and he wouldn't let it happen. She was his responsibility and he would protect her, even from himself.

As she approached, he finished setting out the food. Two energy bars, jerky and water. A few wild grapes from the nearby vines would round out the meal nicely.

He returned from picking grapes to find her nibbling on her energy bar and sipping water. "I'm going to take a quick wash before I eat." Brandon removed his shirt, and then placed his rifle next to her. "Keep this close while I'm occupied, Sister." He emphasized the word hoping to burn the implications on his brain. "And do me a favor, don't climb any trees."

"I only wanted to see the orchid."

"Watch something else instead." He threw the words over his shoulder, realizing their provocativeness only after he'd said them.

The cold water splashing across his head and chest did little to put out the raging heat in his lower body. He felt her watching him, almost as if she knew what she was doing to his body. She was such a mixture, both innocent and intoxicating. With a groan, he gave up trying to cool his libido.

He shook his head like a dog, throwing water droplets from his hair as he walked to the blanket. He left his shirt off to allow his skin to dry.

She made room for him on the blanket, but he sat

on the grass a little away from her. Her gaze met his and then lowered to his chest.

Christ, why had he left his shirt off? He wasn't vain, but knew his body was ripped. Each muscle hard earned in his vigorous training.

She gulped her water, nearly choked, and handed him the cup.

He grasped the cup and placed his tongue against the rim—right where her mouth had been. As he licked the water from the rim of the cup, her eyes dilated, and her pink tongue touched the corner of her lips.

"I'm hungry." He picked up a few grapes, tilted his head back and dropped them into his mouth.

****

Her throat worked dryly, and her breathing quickened. Damn him. His head was thrown back exposing his lean profile as he chewed, slowly and sensuously. Those emerald eyes sparkled. He was making love to her with his eyes. Eyes, so seductive and knowing. Damn him! He doubted her vocation, and this was a test. She had to break the spell before this went any further.

"I've already blessed the food," she said softly. "Eat. You must be ravenous. A big man like you must have a huge appetite." Two could play this game. Granted, he'd probably had a lot more practice, but she had her moments.

"I'm sorry I missed the blessing. I don't get to hear one very often." His smile was gone, and his eyes narrowed.

"You could say one yourself, unless of course, you don't believe in such things." She was sparring with a master and she wasn't sure she knew all the rules.

"Oh, I believe, Sister. I was raised Catholic, but my job keeps me from observing many of the rituals of our faith."

Now she'd done it. He sounded like he was ready to discuss church doctrine. Her lack of knowledge would open up a whole new can of worms. The hole she was digging kept getting bigger by the minute. She watched as he bit into the energy bar, eating hungrily, but her appetite was gone.

"Which way are we headed? You never said."

"To perdition."

Had she heard right? Surely, she'd misunderstood. "Where?"

"Sorry. I was thinking out loud. Our direction depends on the rebels. They move one way, and then we move. Hopefully we stay one step ahead of them."

"But how will you know where they are, so we don't run into them?"

"I won't lie to you, Sister. It'll be hard. I've been here before and know some of their camps and patrols, but things change. You saw this morning how easily they nearly caught us. It's going to take trust and cooperation on your part. I'm good at what I do, and I know this jungle. Do you trust me, Dr. Phelps?" He had used her professional name, marking the seriousness of his question.

"I have faith in your skills. I'll cooperate, but trust, is something I'll need to work on."

"I can accept that. Just remember, your safety is my job. The rest, like you said we'll work on. Deal?" Like before, he held out his hand to shake on it. This time, it was accompanied by an arched brow.

After the slightest of hesitations, she said, "Deal."

****

Brandon picked up his gun, reached for her hand and turned toward the forest. He pushed them forward relentlessly, with only five-minute breathers to sip water. Mira was exhausted but tried valiantly to keep up with the murderous pace he set.

Hours later, they were miles from where Brandon had killed the patrol.

He stopped and looked at the sky. "The afternoon rains will start soon. We'll set up camp and get some rest."

Mira dropped to the ground and sat. She hadn't said a word, but the pace had taxed her. Hell, he'd worked with trainees who had dropped at this pace. "I'm okay," she said.

He looked at her, a question on his face.

"You were giving me that—is she going to flake out look."

"Actually, I was thinking how well you've kept up under the strenuous conditions."

She took a deep breath, then looked away. "Sorry. In my line of work, I've had my share of condescending remarks."

"I'm sure you have, but I don't give compliments easily, and I give credit where credit is due." he replied. "Most men couldn't have kept up with me."

"This isn't my first trek through the jungle, though I must admit, my calf muscles are aching," she said as she rubbed her legs.

"How are the ribs holding out?"

"They hurt, but it's expected. I'll take more ibuprofen when we eat."

"Here." He reached into his pocket and tossed her a

packet. "I always carry a few in my pocket."

"Thanks." She opened the packet and washed the tablets down with a swig of water from the canteen he'd handed her.

Brandon scanned the area. "I think we'll stay in the penthouse tonight."

At her blank look, he pointed upward. "We'll use the canopy to provide protection from the rain." The trunk of the large tree he chose, hosted a spiral of lianas snaking upward and disappearing into the branches. He removed the rope from the pack and attached it at his waist.

"Wait here, and when I call down send the pack up the rope to me. I'll pull you up when things are ready."

He grasped a sturdy liana and climbed. Several large branches intertwined, providing support and invisibility from below. Perfect. He tied the rope to a thick branch, moved the leaves aside, and dropped the rope. "Send up the backpack. I'll drop the rope back down for the rest of the supplies."

****

Mira followed his instructions, then watched the backpack with the supplies disappear. He was up there, but for the life of her, she couldn't see him hidden among the foliage. Left alone with all evidence of him gone gave her a sense of unease. Several long minutes passed as he worked quietly above her.

The rope landed at her feet, giving her a start. His handsome head peeked through the leaves. She fastened the rope around her waist, threw him a 'thumbs up' signal, and held on tightly as he pulled her up. He lifted her into the canopy, took her outstretched hand and helped her the last few feet.

Astonished at his handiwork, she examined what he'd done. He had utilized his oversized rain poncho to set up a plastic camouflage tent between the higher branches. Large leaves and small branches had been woven into a small nest beneath the tent. He'd placed the blanket over the branches to make a comfortable bed with the backpack as a pillow.

"I'm impressed. It looks quite comfortable." A welcome breeze stirred the leaves, bringing the scent of flowers.

He patted the bed. "All the comforts of home."

"Where are you sleeping?" The words blurted out before she could stop them.

"Next to you." His words were matter of fact and he continued to show off the accommodations without missing a beat.

"We have a room with a view." When thunder sounded, he added, "And running water." He held his hand out in the rain, a big grin on his face.

Mira returned his grin, moved to the back of the tent and tentatively sat on the blanket. She swallowed with a suddenly dry mouth. "What now?" They'd spent the night together last night, but this was very different. They were so high, isolated, and *close*.

"For now, we eat and rest. We can't have a fire up here, but we'll be safe from all predators, both two and four legged."

She nodded. She was exhausted, sleep deprived and scared. Brandon's skills had saved them, but he wasn't invincible. They had many more days to run and hide from the rebels. Her stomach let out a long low growl. "Sorry," she mumbled as she grabbed some jerky and the canteen, no longer bothering with a cup.

They shared the water as they ate. Too tired for conversation, she stretched her legs out and curled up in the nest. Her body tensed with awareness when his weight settled next to her.

Something stirred in her chest as Brandon bent his long legs to prevent them from getting wet, then placed his gun across his chest and closed his eyes. His body heat and manly smell tickled her nose as she closed her own eyes. He was a hard man, but it felt so good to have him beside her. Feeling safe, she fell asleep.

****

A poncho clad figure moved silently through the forest. Rafà Gutiérrez slowed his progress and peered through his binoculars. He couldn't see the man and woman he'd been tracking, above him in the tree. His gut told him they were there, though. They had covered an amazing amount of territory this afternoon. The forest was difficult to traverse for even an experienced adventurer; it was treacherous for a novice. He smiled to himself at the double entendre. The next few days should prove interesting. He distanced himself from their location, trudging through the wet undergrowth, silently and stealthily like a jungle animal stalking his prey. He too had to make a nest for the night.

Chapter Nine

Abruptly, the rain stopped. Birds began to screech again, and the distant sound of monkeys woke Brandon. Cleansed by the shower, the air smelled tangy and fresh. He peered over the edge of the makeshift enclosure to check the ground below for signs of unwanted visitors. Nothing moved or appeared out of place. He tapped Mira on the shoulder. The short nap worked to revitalize *him*, but he hated waking her after such a short time.

Slapping at his hand, she remained sound asleep.

His gaze fell to her relaxed face. Maybe he could allow her a few more minutes.

With difficulty, he moved away. The short time next to her had been relaxing. Even better, when he awoke, he found her snuggled against him.

He grabbed his rifle, slung the canteen over his shoulder, and then climbed from their roost. Cautiously, he crouched and surveyed the area. No footprints or broken twigs. Raucous squawks and a flash of red brought his gaze skyward. Two Scarlet Macaws chased across the canopy. His gaze searched the surrounding trees; though he saw nothing out of the ordinary, his gut told him someone was out there.

He moved slowly, circled the area around the tree, then widened his path outward. Nothing. Over a hundred missions and years of repetitive training conditioned him to trust his gut. With no evidence of danger, he decided to do a little foraging to supplement their supper. He found a Cassava bush, pulled his utility knife and dug the roots. Survival training had provided the necessary knowledge and skills to find edible plants. The Cassava or Manioc tubers produced cyanide in the raw form. The early natives had coated darts with a cyanide derivative for hunting. The roots had to be cooked before eating to rid them of the poison.

As he continued to forage, he found plantains. He picked a few and headed toward the nearby stream where he refilled the canteen and washed the roots in the water. With his scavenged meal in hand, he made his way back to the nest. God, he hoped Mira hadn't awakened while he was gone. He couldn't handle another disappearance today. He prayed this morning's incident would keep her in the roost if she woke.

****

Her tired muscles relaxed, finally getting some of the rest they deserved. Something intruded upon her bliss. Her unconscious mind hadn't identified what was bothering her, but she was irritated regardless. What was with the tapping anyway? She sleepily slapped at her shoulder and the tapping stopped. With a sigh, she sank deeper into oblivion.

Images from the waterfall came back in vivid flashes. From beneath the shield of her lashes she watched as he stepped under the water. His skin glistened as the water washed over his highly defined muscles. He was indeed a fine specimen of manhood. If she had to have a protector, she couldn't find a better looking one.

She joined him in the spray of the water. They

touched—skin to skin. Ripples of excitement rushed through her body. She reveled in the feel of his arms around her and the soft, yet fiery feel of his lips upon hers. One look from those emerald green eyes sent waves of anticipation down her spine. Washboard tight, his abdomen rippled as it tapered toward his belt. A fine sprinkle of curly hairs rose from his chest and followed his midline down. She ran her fingers across his chest and circled the hardness of his male nipples. They tightened at her touch.

His eyes narrowed—burned with desire. Her exploration continued down past his waist. His breath caught. A surge of power zipped through her body at his reaction to her touch. Her hands glided up his chest and traced his shoulders. Slowly, her fingers glided down his muscled, sinewy arms. Her heartbeat rocketed as he took the initiative.

He slid his cold hand down her arm.

Wait!

Why was his hand cold? The tapping started again.

Annoyed, Mira groggily slapped her arm. Alarms sounded in her foggy brain. Brandon wasn't cold, and he didn't have rough, scaly skin.

Slowly, she opened her eyes, turned her head, and froze.

His voice came from beneath her. "Don't move a muscle, Mira."

Not to worry, Brandon. She couldn't move, but her body trembled. Staring back at her, only inches away from her face, was an enormous snake. Bright green scales amid an aqua blue background should make this animal beautiful. She found no beauty in its color, elliptical eyes, or the deadly pits along its face. *A Pit*

Viper. She hated snakes and had treated so many victims of their bites. Most died before they reached the clinic.

Its forked tongue slipped outward and tasted the air. Cold fire burned the oxygen in her lungs as she tried not to panic. She clamped her mouth down to prevent her teeth from chattering. She willed the rest of her body not to shake. Icy tendrils of fear threatened to immobilize her brain. Dear God, was this how she was going to die? She'd been kidnapped, beaten, and drugged. She'd survived all those atrocities, surely this couldn't be the end.

Think, Mira. She stared into the reptilian eyes and worked to slow her breathing. Her heart might fail even if the thing didn't bite her. Way to go, Mira, that's the way to think positive, she rebuked her wayward brain.

"It's okay. I'm right here," he assured her in a soothing tone. "I won't let it hurt you."

She grasped at his voice as if he were a horse whisperer. God, if only it worked on snakes. His calmness bolstered her courage. She could do this; she was in charge of her own destiny. No mere snake would control her future.

****

Brandon infused reassurance into his voice as he spoke to her. Secretly, he prayed the snake wasn't poisonous. He'd have to be fast to get it away from her without it inflicting a nasty bite. Even a non-venomous bite could be dangerous in the tropics. She had to stay calm while he figured out how to deal with it.

"Don't say anything but look at the eyes of the snake," he said softly, soothing and reassuring her. "If the lens is round, make a slight noise in your throat. If

61

the lens is elongated—don't make a sound."

God, he prayed she wouldn't panic and scream. Several, agonizing, seconds passed, as he waited and listened.

No sound.

Shit. It must be venomous.

He slid down the rope several feet and took a moment to regroup. He pulled the machete from his belt, balanced lightly with his feet against the tree, and prepared to act. "Listen carefully. I'm going to count to three. When I say three, close your eyes and slowly turn your head away. Don't move after you turn your head."

He needed her cooperation if this was going to work. "One, two, three!"

He pushed off the tree trunk and lunged over the edge of the nest. In one swipe, he struck the snake with the machete, severing its head. Blood spattered over her, as the snake's decapitated body writhed beside her in a macabre death dance. He crawled in beside her, removed the snake's body and severed head, throwing them from the roost to the ground below.

She bowed her head, facing away from him, her body trembling. Rigid except for the tiny tremors, she was like a statue frozen by fear.

"Mira? It's okay now." He tried to keep his voice steady, even though he was shaken to the core. She could have been bitten so easily and died. There was no anti-venom for many of these vipers—even if he could have gotten her to a medical facility in time.

Her shoulders began to shake violently, and he reached to offer comfort.

She jerked her head around. "Damn it to hell—what took you so long?"

His hands pulled back, stilled by her words.

"Do you know how long I stared into its eyes, wondering when it would strike? I watched as it stuck its tongue out and tasted the air around me. It—it t-t-t-touched my skin, I—I thought it was you."

She'd reached the breaking point. Brandon listened to her stuttered words—wanted to comfort her but dared not touch her when she was so panicky.

She stared down at her arms. "Get it off me! Now!" She clawed at her skin. "I can't stand the feel of it!"

He grabbed at her hands trying to stop her damaging scratches. "Stop it. The snake is gone and you're okay."

"No. It's all over me." She recoiled in horror. "Get it off. Now."

He understood. He had seen men do this in battle. It was the site of the snake's blood all over her. She couldn't stand it and was panicked. He wrapped his arms around her and pulled her tightly up against his chest, letting her flail her arms without injuring herself.

"It's over. You're fine." He felt so helpless. Fear oozed from her pores as he held her. Absently, he rubbed her back and shoulders, giving comfort. Just as absently, he dropped a small kiss on top of her hair.

Still frantic she twisted, trying to remove his arms.

Her face brushed his lips.

He didn't remember, bending his head just that little bit, but suddenly his lips covered hers in a gentle, tentative kiss. When he felt the slightest movement of her lips beneath his, he claimed hers fully.

She returned his kiss, her arms stilling, then she grabbed his shirt to pull him even closer.

Alarms rang in his head. This was so wrong. He

couldn't be doing this. No way would he take advantage of her innocence and fear. He was a soldier, sworn to protect. Now, here he was, kissing a nun. In shock or not, it took all his willpower to push her away.

"Brandon?" Her voice was unsure and quivering. "What's wrong?"

"Us." The word came out cold and hard. His body stiffened. "In your panic, Sister, you may have forgotten your vows, but I haven't. You're forbidden fruit. My soul may be on a fast track to hell, but I have no intention of dragging you along with me."

****

Fear at watching the snake—eye to eye—feeling it's body writhing beside her, the blood everywhere, it took a few moments to understand the ramifications of the kiss. While she had received comfort, Brandon was in pain. Not physical pain, he would ignore that, but his pain was real none the less.

His pain gouged much deeper—a man of honor, he'd broken his own code.

This honorable man had saved her life more than once and yet—she was still lying to him. He was attracted to her but fought his feelings. She felt the pull too, but for him it was much worse. He thought his soul was lost because he had violated her vows. She had to put a stop to this.

"I'm not a nun."

She hadn't meant the words to come out so boldly. Would he think she was encouraging him? Granted, he didn't look the sort to wait for encouragement. God, this was such a mess. "You're not going to hell, because you kissed me."

He said nothing, only stared back at her.

"Talk to me—say something." Had she ruined what little chance they might have had for something between them?

He broke the silence following her announcement. "I kind of wondered when I heard you swearing."

A stoic look masked his face and he kept away from her. "I've put myself through all kinds of hell, wanting you," he growled.

"You don't seem too surprised. You knew all along—didn't you?" she accused, worry now turned to anger and disappointment. "Did you enjoy my little act?"

"Stop it. I wasn't sure, at first. However, things didn't add up. I figured you were trying to protect yourself. Being a nun does afford some protection in certain places, but it's not a given, and sometimes nuns and priests are killed to scare the people into cooperation, El Salvador in the late '80s being a prime example. Either way, you took a terrible risk. After the awful things you'd already been through, I didn't want you to feel afraid of me." His voice softened as he touched her shoulder. "Look at me," he said as she continued to avoid his gaze.

Her body quivered at his touch. Would he hate her now—show disgust at her ruse? Afraid of what she might see on his face, she slowly turned toward him.

"Oh, hell." The words wrenched from his lips. He tugged on her shoulders, pulling her against his chest and wrapped her tightly in his arms.

"I'm sorry, Brandon. I didn't mean to make you feel sinful. It was the only way I could come into the country and work at the clinic. Things were fine, until those new men showed up with the rebels."

Slowly, he kissed the tears from her cheek.

Her eyes closed at the gentle touch of his lips on her face. His touch both excited and frightened her, arousing feelings in her she'd never felt before. Now, he knew about her, she was free to explore those feelings, but did she dare?

Instinctively, she knew he wouldn't physically harm her, but what about her heart? He was a soldier. When his mission was complete, he would leave her. If she had more experience, she could indulge her cravings for him and walk away unscathed.

One little problem, she wasn't experienced; she was a virgin. He would run if he knew or laugh. She wouldn't survive either scenario.

Chapter Ten

Tasting her salty, wet cheeks, Brandon ached. He drank in her sweet softness, allowed it to soothe his tortured soul. Her curves fit against his body as if she'd been designed to match his contours. It took all his willpower, not to lay her down on the blanket and make a feast of her.

Her softness met his hardness and his erection strained against her belly.

She sucked in a swift breath and his sanity returned. The inner soldier raked the man over the coals. He couldn't put them in danger for his own gratification.

"I'm sorry." He pulled back abruptly and placed her away from him. She had the look of a young fawn separated from its mother. Lost and bewildered. He shouldn't have tasted one so innocent. It had been the tears of course. He could face the worst torture in the world without flinching, but the tears on her face had been his undoing.

"Let's get you cleaned up and start supper." He reached into the duffel, pulled out another of his shirts, and tried his best to forget the last time he'd given her one of his tees.

As soon as his feet touched the ground, he made sure the snake's body was totally out of sight. She had experienced enough traumas without seeing it again.

"You can come down," he called up to her. She clasped the rope and began her descent. He reached up and grabbed her before she touched the ground. As she slid down the front of his body, his breath hitched. He steadied her on her feet and abruptly moved away.

To calm himself, he set up the stove. The image of her face to face with the snake was burned in his mind. Admiration for her grew in his chest. She'd been a trooper since he'd found her tied and unconscious in the truck. All right, his brain reminded him, she'd been a pain in the ass, too. But she was a fighter. Maybe admiration wasn't all he felt for her. Jesus, things were getting complicated.

****

Mira refused to look at her reflection in the water, dipping her hands in to break up the image. She wasn't proud of what she'd seen there. A liar and a coward. Stripped of the bloody shirt, she rinsed it, and then used it to wipe the remaining blood from her body. As she pulled the clean shirt over her head, his masculine scent surrounded her. She looked back, eyed his strong back, and wished things were different. Why couldn't she be like other women? No wonder he'd turned from her.

He looked up from the fire and watched her approach. "Are you okay?"

"I'm so sorry," she whispered. "I guess everything finally caught up with me. I can't stand snakes. They give me the willies. Thanks again, for saving my life."

"You have no reason to be sorry and there's no need to thank me. After what you've been through, you deserve a good breakdown. I don't think any less of you for it. Besides, snakes give me the willies, too." He smiled at her chuckle.

"What? A big, strong soldier like you, afraid of a snake? I don't believe it."

"Just ask my buddy, Jackson, when he picks us up. He'll tell you all about my aversion to snakes."

Mira walked to the stove, her mood lightened by its cheerful glow. She picked up the cassava roots. "These will be great for supper. I wish we had some oil to fry the plantains." She fondly remembered the meals she'd shared with the nurses at the clinic. "The cook at the clinic had more ways to serve plantains than you could shake a stick at. She even cooked them with whiskey one night."

Her hands stilled as her thoughts turned inward. What had happened to them since she'd been kidnapped? Were they alive? She had to get back there. Her moment of introspection was interrupted when Brandon touched her shoulder.

"I can make a stew with the cassava and what's left of the jerky."

"Good, tomorrow I'll go hunting. Unless—" the words hung in the air between them, "—we eat the snake."

At his words, she threw the cassava roots at his chest.

He grinned. "I take it, that's a no?"

She turned her back to hide her grin at his joke. God—she hoped he was joking. "I'll start supper."

"Okay, I'll take care of the mess." He grabbed the rope and disappeared into the leaves.

She tried not to think about what he was doing. All the blood. Cooking pot in hand, she went to the stream. A deep sigh escaped her lips. She didn't want to think, period. Right now, she wanted to sit by the stove, eat a hot meal, and pretend they were camping.

He slid down the rope, blanket in hand. Mysteriously, a large portion of the blanket was missing.

He threw it on the ground and sat beside her. "I hope what's left of this will fit the two of us."

"Coffee." Mira blurted.

He stared at her, a blank look on his face.

"Where did you put the beans we picked?"

"They're still in my pocket. I'm afraid they're a little squashed." He gave her a sheepish look and pulled out the nasty looking bandanna.

"They're perfect." She grabbed the slimy bundle. "We only use the seeds anyway." She began to sort the seeds from the mashed fruits. When she had a handful, she dried them as best she could and placed them on a large leaf.

"We'll let them dry out some, and then roast them in the pot when we finish dinner," she said as she stirred the stew. "Was it only this morning we talked about coffee?"

"You must really want a cup bad."

"The coffee is for you remember? I'm not the grouchy one in the morning. Besides, it's only the best for my hero." She dramatically placed her hands on her chest and batted her eyelashes like one of the sappy heroines in old-time Southern romances.

Brandon laughed and quipped, "Damned right. I'll have my eggs over easy with wheat toast and a double rasher of bacon to go with the coffee."

They both laughed and settled closer together on the blanket. They watched the flames for a few moments and a companionable silence fell between them.

"It was the last straw," she mumbled.

"I know. You don't need to explain."

"How do you do it?"

"Do what? Kill?"

She nodded.

His face hardened and the easy atmosphere chilled.

"Are you sure you want to know? After all, I'll be sleeping beside you in the nest tonight."

His voice and words were meant to curb her questions and curiosity, but she dug in her heels. "That's exactly why I want to know. You are a soldier, a SEAL. I've heard they're trained killers. How do you kill and keep your soul intact? How do you separate what you do, from who you are?"

He stared into the flame, his face still, as if searching for the words to answer.

She removed the pot from the fire and placed it on a rock beside him. He ate the hot stew slowly. Neither spoke. When he finished his share, he passed the pot to her. "Each time you kill, a little part of your humanity dies." His voice came from deep within and sounded hollow. "If you're lucky, you don't see the light fade from their eyes. *That* image, you carry forever, and it lives in your nightmares."

Mira felt the pain he carried but wouldn't show. He was a warrior, a protector, not a killer. The man at the clinic was a killer. "I'm sorry you have to see and do the things you do. But if there were no people like you, the rest of us wouldn't stand a chance."

"Don't make me out to be some kind of hero. Hell, I'm far from that. I'm just a man with the same flaws as any other man."

"Well, for what it's worth, I'm proud to have you at my back." Her words hung in the air, as she grabbed the pot and went to the stream to wash it.

When she returned, Brandon sat lost in thought. She used the last of the stove light to clean and check her wounds. "You go on up while I make it look like we weren't here."

She took the rope in her hands and began her climb. " Okay."

Chapter Eleven

Mira greeted him as he entered the nest. "It's so dark up here. I miss the fire."

He pulled mosquito netting from the pack and hung it over the opening. "I'm sure you've had all your shots, but we won't have smoke to keep the insects away."

"How thoughtful."

"It's not a matter of thoughtfulness—it's survival. The jungle will kill you given the slightest opportunity. I don't give an inch, especially when it comes to safety."

Did he realize how much those last words revealed about his nature? Probably not. He was like a rock, hard and unforgiving. After settling in beside her, he broached the subject they had both avoided. "I know it's hard for you to talk about it, but we need to discuss your abduction."

He reached over and stopped her from plucking at her shirt. "Take your time, but I need to hear everything, no matter how upsetting or embarrassing."

"I've already told you everything. You rescued me. Isn't that the important thing?" She pulled her hand back and continued to pluck the edges of her shirt.

"I need to know why *you* were the one kidnapped." His voice was soft but determined. "What makes you different?"

"You mean why kidnap a Caucasian, American

nun who happens to be working in a clinic in this quagmire of a country?" Her words were angry. "I don't really know. I don't have any money, so they couldn't have wanted me for ransom."

"But you're not a nun. Maybe someone figured it out. They might have suspected you were spying for the Americans."

Her breath sucked in at his words. "The leader, Grigore Belikov, asked me if I was a spy. I told him he was crazy to even think such a thing."

He sounded amused. "How did he take that?"

"He told his men to strap me down and give me truth serum."

Her hand found his face in the dark. His stubbly beard rasped as she ran her fingers across his chin. "I'd make a lousy spy with my schedule. Doctors don't get much time off. Besides, I never left the clinic, so how could I learn information and pass it on?"

"You'd be surprised what kind of information you can gather from sick or hurt people. As for passing it on to someone, there are numerous ways," he continued, "I'm not suggesting you *are* a spy. I'm explaining how it might appear to someone with the right agenda."

She shifted her body, saying nothing as she stalled for time.

"What aren't you telling me? I need complete honesty and all the facts. Full disclosure is the only way I can plan for all possible dangers "

She stalled for a few more moments. What would he think of her after she told him her secret? Would he think she was driven by shallow motives? Would he still look at her with admiration in his eyes or would he condemn her for endangering others for her selfish goals? In the dark it would be easier to tell her story. She wouldn't have to look into his face and see his disappointment and condemnation.

"I came here under false pretenses."

Beside her, his body tensed.

"Remember, I told you I studied plants for their medicinal uses? There's one plant in particular which interests me. It's a flower, the *Blue Spider Orchid*. It's supposed to be extinct. Legends about this orchid say it has regenerative healing powers. My Uncle Max traveled all over the world, researching any information about the plant. The Mayans mentioned it in some of their writings. Vague references have also been found in writings from parts of Asia."

She sensed his impatience to hear more about the kidnapping and not her botany liturgy. "This is important. I have to tell all of it for you to understand."

"Okay, but if there's a science test when you're finished, I probably won't pass."

She smiled at his attempt to ease the tension between them. With a sigh, she continued. "Two years ago, my uncle disappeared. As his only relative, I inherited his possessions. There wasn't much but in his personal things, I found his journals. They contained documentation and evidence he'd collected concerning the orchid." She reached out in the dark to touch him. "This is the exciting part. He had information gathered from natives, which led him to believe the plant is not extinct. He gave descriptions of this very rainforest as the last known sighting of the orchid." She sighed and shifted in the tight confines of the shelter. "This plant could provide miracles for injured people and save so many lives." She reached out and touched his shoulder, trying to make him understand her zeal.

Brandon stiffened, then sat up. "You risked your life for a flower?"

How could she have been stupid enough to think he would listen and not think her an idiot? "I knew you wouldn't understand."

"Make me understand." His voice softened, as he shifted toward her. He took her hands in his, gentle despite their size.

He really wants to understand. She relaxed and squeezed his hands. "My parents were killed in Somalia when I was sixteen. Both were doctors, trying to save lives in a country being destroyed by genocide."

He interrupted. "Were you there?"

"Yes."

"How did you get out?"

"My parents saw how bad it was getting and arranged to smuggle me out of the country with a man they trusted. By the time I arrived in the US, they were already dead."

"You've seen your share of tragedy."

"I'm determined to follow in their footsteps." She continued. "Uncle Max raised me and fostered his love of plants and medicine in me. I was devastated when he disappeared. When the journals showed up in his personal effects, I vowed to come here and finish his work." She felt as if he still didn't understand. She moved so mere inches separated them. "Haven't you ever felt duty bound to accomplish a mission at all costs?"

****

Brandon sucked in his breath. She had him there. Hadn't he come to Honduras for the same reason?

When the last mission ended in disaster, he'd been lucky he hadn't been sent to some desk in Siberia. But he'd pleaded, and then argued with the brass, to allow him this one last mission. At thirty-five, he was already pushing the age limit to stay in the field. They'd turned him down and given him thirty days LWOP while an investigation into the last mission could be undertaken.

It was a bunch of crap—the team wasn't at fault— someone had warned the rebels about the planned attack. At least the thirty days allowed him time to take a vacation and come on the mission anyway. He'd risked everything he had to come here and search for Rafà. Death was a very real possibility, court martial almost a given, except—the last-minute call had given him sanction, but little else.

"Yes, I understand believing in something that much. I also know what that type of determination can cost personally. I bet you've sacrificed a lot to get to this point as quickly as you have."

"I don't think of it as a sacrifice. It was a choice, requiring a great deal of determination and one to which I was happy to dedicate my life."

"How old are you?"

"I'm twenty-eight. Why?"

"How much time have you lived for yourself?" He waited for her to come back with a scathing remark. Instead she switched topics on him.

"I've had to trust you with my life, and now my secrets, yet I know nothing about you. Since we're baring our souls here, don't I deserve a little return trust? Why are you here?" She bravely pushed the conversation onward. "Am I just a side trip? What are you really supposed to be doing?"

He allowed a few moments to pass, deep in thought. He weighed his words carefully before answering. "You're very perceptive, Mira, but I'm not at liberty to discuss why I'm here. Let's just say I'm going to look up an old friend and leave it."

Brandon was hesitant to discuss anything further. He couldn't let her get too close to the truth. His mission was Black Ops and totally off the books. If he were captured or killed, no one would ever hear about it. Officially, he did not exist and neither did his original mission. She was the mission now, along with a few other things. He stalled any more questions by ending the conversation. "We should get some sleep."

She lay down on the blanket with her back to him.

He heard the deep sigh escape her lips. She wasn't satisfied, and he knew she'd keep digging. She was smart, and he didn't like lying to her, but it was all he could do for now.

He relaxed as he heard the even breathing of her sleep. He lay down on his side and pulled her soft body up next to his. In the darkness he could allow himself this small indulgence. Maybe, he rationalized, his touch would help keep her dreams peaceful for a few hours.

In her sleep she snuggled closer. Somewhere in the vicinity of his heart, he felt a jolt. She meant something to him. He'd been with many women before, but this was the first time he'd felt this way—he cared, dammit. Wrapping a protective arm around her, he brushed a gentle kiss over her curls. Lord help him, he was lost.

Chapter Twelve

A hand covered her mouth. Her eyes flew open and she tried to get up. Brandon's warning sounded harsh and urgent in her ear. "Men. Coming down the trail toward us."

Their eyes met and held. Instantly awake, she understood. At her nod, he released her and leaned close to say, "Lie on your stomach facing the tent flap."

Mira complied with quiet haste, watching as he reached inside the backpack and pulled out several weapons. She'd only been around him two days and already she recognized several of them. His sniper rifle, the AK-47, a handgun, and several clips of ammo for each, all formed a line near the edge of the tent. When he reached back once more, he pulled out what looked to be pieces of metal fruit.

Dear lord—he held grenades. She shouldn't be surprised; after all he was a SEAL. The knowledge didn't stop her mouth from drying in fear or stop her heart from crawling into her throat. This was serious shit. She cringed at her thought but smiled as she realized he was probably thinking something ten times worse.

"How many are there? You look like you're expecting an entire army."

One look at his face made her want to be anywhere but up in this tree. She'd never seen him look so serious. The face that had smiled last night was now an implacable mask. His green eyes were cold, his body taut, all his movements practiced and precise.

He held up his field glasses and looked for what seemed like endless minutes.

"It looks to be about fifteen to twenty soldiers," he said with undeniable calm. "I'm sure they have scouts out of sight and possibly a sniper somewhere in the canopy. I'm afraid things could get a little nasty. Stay as still as possible. They might not find us up here. If we're lucky, they'll pass right by and never know we're here. I don't want to shoot unless it's unavoidable; the return fire could take both of us out. If need be, I'll go down the back of the tree and draw them away. Here, take my handgun. If I need to leave, shoot anything that comes near this tree."

She stared at him, mouth agape, speechless. She'd never heard him say so much at one time. Unfortunately, his words made her stomach feel like she *had* eaten the stupid snake.

She shook her head and whispered, "I won't let you leave and take all the risks to save me. Besides, I'd never find my way out without getting caught." She reached out and placed her hand lightly on his chest. "What can I do to help?"

For a moment, the cold mask slipped from his face, replaced by a lopsided grin. "Pray for a miracle, Sister." His mask slipped back into place as he laid belly down, the AK-47 in hand.

He was probably arrogant enough to think God would accommodate his schedule. "It doesn't work that way. God helps those who help themselves."

His large palm curved around her face, as he stared

into her eyes. Then, he kissed her.

Mira breathed him in. He smelled of man, danger and raw lust. She'd never shared a kiss like this. How could a simple touch make her forget everything but his palm touching her face and the tip of his tongue, sliding softly along the line of her mouth? Her body ached with need as his lips slid across her own. Her nerve endings jolted with excitement.

She reached out to touch him, to pull him closer. She wanted more—but he broke the kiss and turned to look out the tent flap. Brandon, the soldier, was back.

Surely, he couldn't be so unaffected. Her world had just tilted, and he calmly stared into the field glasses. Miffed, at his casual attitude toward the life-changing kiss—she had to say something. "What was that for?"

Without removing the glasses, he quipped, "I was helping myself."

She wanted to hug him for saying just the right thing. With those few words, he had put her at ease again. Right now, he needed to focus. Their lives depended on his skills. Thank God, one of them could concentrate on the situation at hand.

She had been given her assignment and like a good soldier, she would obey—*this* time. Ignoring the gun, she settled down on her belly, closed her eyes, and prayed.

****

He kissed her because he couldn't stop himself. If he had to die—a distinct possibility, this was the perfect moment. He was already halfway to heaven when he tasted her sweet lips. The urgency of the situation only intensified the moment. Though a simple kiss, she had branded him. Her taste would forever fill his senses. He should have kissed her like this much earlier. As it was, he could only sip her sweetness quickly before turning to face the danger below them.

As he watched, three rebels dressed in ragged, camouflage uniforms tramped into the small opening where he and Mira had camped last night. The way they trampled the shrubs and leaves, Brandon felt certain they would find no evidence of their occupancy.

His shoulders stiffened as the next four men came into view. They were definitely foreign to this area. They stood much taller and wore new, matching camouflage uniforms, their weapons the best money could buy. Each man walked carefully, eyes constantly scanning the area around them. These were well trained soldiers and must be the mercenaries she had mentioned. They were the true danger. One of the mercenaries spoke to his two nearest companions, in Russian.

Here was the confirmation he needed; a foreign power was behind the coup, which had recently overthrown the local government. He needed to find out as much as he could about them, then live long enough to get the information back to headquarters.

The first thing, however, was Mira's safety. He didn't care if the entire Russian army moved into this place as long as he could get her as far from here as possible. Telling himself he would feel the same about anyone he'd just rescued, would be a lie. He'd completed scores of rescue missions, and not once had he felt like this.

The kiss they'd just shared still had his senses swimming. To clear his thoughts, he quietly shook his head. Their lives depended on his ability to clearly read the situation and respond accordingly.

As the Russians continued to talk, ten more rebels moved out of the brush and stood behind them. Their conversation completed, the tallest of the three mercs walked away and continued into the surrounding shrubs. There, he was the sniper. Now he had a slight advantage. He concentrated on the others, now he knew the sniper's location. Thirteen rebels in all, with the three mercenaries, the total was sixteen. It could have been worse, but it could be a hell of a lot better.

He was glad Mira's eyes were shut, as several of the men relieved themselves near the bushes. They kept up a continuous conversation in Spanish. Some of the soldiers lit up cigarettes and pulled out canteens for a drink. The distinct smell of marijuana wafted upward as one of the men enjoyed a joint. As there wasn't much discipline in this army, the odds shifted in their favor.

On a bad day a SEAL could easily take out five or six men without breaking a sweat. Of course, there was the luck factor. Even on a bad day, the *worst soldier* could make a lucky shot.

Tension radiated from her body as she lay flattened against the floor of the nest. He reached over and squeezed her arm in reassurance. He could only imagine her fear at what was about to happen. This was his chosen life—he was prepared for it, she on the other hand, had been thrown into this.

The loud crack of a rifle blast pierced the jungle. Brandon stilled. Mira shrank even further into the twisted vines and limbs. Chaos broke out. The men below scrambled to their feet, threw their lit cigarettes away, and quickly grabbed their guns.

Where had the shot come from?

"Get the hell under cover," the merc barked at the rebels. The motley group stopped swarming in circles and found cover. Moments later, the sniper ran back to the clearing. He spoke quickly to the obvious leader. "Fall in and follow Niko." Another order spurred the group. The men scrambled to their feet and ran back down the trail.

Brandon couldn't believe it. The shot had drawn the entire group away from him and Mira. *Could it be Rafa?*

"Pack up. We're getting out of here." Brandon urged her to her feet. "We'll stay out of sight by using the back side of the tree."

She asked no questions and quickly helped him pack everything. She climbed down the tree and once on the ground, dropped to a crouch.

He watched her descent and sent the rope and backpack down as soon as she touched ground. He used the lianas to swiftly climb down. Sliding the pack onto his back, he grabbed the machine gun in his right hand and pulled Mira to her feet with his left.

Neither spoke as they raced through the jungle. The tangled vegetation made running difficult without a path, and he had no time to hack it with the machete. They had to get as far away from the area as fast as they could. He hoped the gunfire was from his friend, but he couldn't be sure. If fighting broke out, he couldn't risk being caught between two different forces.

An explosion sounded behind them and he threw Mira down, covering her with his body. A hail of bullets and shouts followed the explosion. Seconds later, they continued their escape into the forest.

Brandon didn't believe in coincidence. Someone had deliberately diverted the troops away from them. The explosion and the rifle shot were timed exactly right. If it was Rafà, why hadn't he contacted him?

They ran as fast as the tangled mass of vegetation allowed. He needed to get Mira to a safer location. He looked over his shoulder and saw her holding her side.

He walked back to check on her. "Are you hurt?"

"Just my ribs reminding me they're still there. I'll be okay. I won't slow you down," she murmured breathlessly. "I know we have to keep moving to stay ahead of them."

"We'll be in the mountains in a few minutes. If you can make it a little longer, we can stop for a short rest when we move into the clouds."

She nodded.

The vegetation thinned as the ground steepened. Moss covered boulders jutted out of the ground before them. Ferns and epiphytes clung to the damp branches or hung from aerial roots. Higher, a mist obscured the height of the mountain. Brandon reached for her hand and they began a slow ascent into the rocks. At times the eerie mist surrounded them like a blanket. Though only mid-morning, it appeared much later.

"We have to be careful as we walk through here. Rocks slide from under your feet, and people have been known to simply step into nothingness because of the mist," he warned.

"At least it's cool and refreshing after our run."

"Here, let's stop and rest." He removed the pack and put it on the ground next to a large boulder.

She took his proffered hand and sat with her back against the rock. "Thanks." He handed her the canteen and she drank thirstily.

"Do you think we've lost them?" She took a long drink and waited for him to speak.

"For a little while," he replied. "We'll move up higher on the mountain and make camp."

Chapter Thirteen

Mira's muscles burned from the constant running. Her tight legs cramped and shook. All were signs of muscle fatigue and dehydration. She forced herself to drink more water, then handed the canteen to Brandon. He was much larger than she and would need the extra water. The cool mist would help regulate their body temperature, but they had to continue hydrating themselves or risk serious injury.

"*Baaaa.*" The sound came from ahead and was followed by a gentle tinkling sound. They tilted their heads and tried to locate the sound. The bell tinkled again. In unison, they jumped to their feet and moved toward it.

"There must be a farm nearby. If we can catch up with our four-legged friend over there, we might get a real meal for a change," he said.

"You're not going to kill it, are you?" She was hungry too but didn't like the thought of killing an innocent lamb or goat.

"I say we follow it as closely as possible and find the farm. There's bound to be someone there who can help us." He picked up the pack and walked toward the sound.

"How do you know we can trust them? Won't we be taking a big risk exposing ourselves?" she asked. Seeing some sort of civilization after her trek through the jungle was tempting, but could they chance it?

The mist swirled as they moved through it. Brandon held her hand tightly as they tread over some loose rocks. "Sure, it's possible they're connected to the rebels, but most small farmers are very solitary. Usually, they only associate with groups of people when they need to get supplies or medical attention." He paused and listened once more before moving ahead. "We might be able to strike a bargain with them for some food—if we play our cards right. I can offer to help do some work for them in repayment or I have money. We'll need to be very careful when we approach them. If we look menacing; we might get shot instead of fed."

She paused long enough for him to look back. "And just whom might you be referring to?"

He laughed. "Why—me of course, you couldn't look menacing if you tried."

The bell tinkled again.

"There." She pointed. "It's moving down the slope. I'm glad you aren't going to eat it." She hastened to keep up with his pace.

"I didn't say we wouldn't eat it." He grinned at her indrawn breath. "I said we'd follow it first."

She laughed, happy to be teased again. For a little while, she had wondered if they would make it. They followed the small goat down the slope until a clearing appeared ahead.

"Do you speak Spanish?"

Her question stopped him in his tracks. "Only the basics. Where are you going with this?"

"Spanish is my second language." She preempted his next question with a burst of explanation. "I should approach the house first and ask for help. If they're friendly, I'll explain you're in the forest and didn't want to frighten them. You stay here and cover me from the woods."

His expression told her what he thought of the idea. It went against all his protective instincts. But it was the best way to prevent them getting shot. Surely, he had to see. "I won't look like a threat—unlike you, covered in weapons and looking very much like a soldier."

His expression hardened. "It goes against all my training and I don't like it, but you're right. I'll have my rifle trained on you the entire time. Stay clear enough to give me a clear shot."

"You won't miss, will you?" Her question begged for reassurance.

He rubbed her cheek with the back of his hand as if he needed reassurance also. "Mira—I never miss."

She didn't relish the idea of going alone but walked out of the woods toward the ramshackle farm house. The place was small, built with scraps of different wood, some adobe and rusted tin. Chickens pecked in the weeds near the fenced pasture, which held a cow and a few goats. Up on the rocky hill a small donkey and a few sheep grazed on the sparse grass.

Near the house a young girl, about four years old played in the dirt near the door. Barefoot but dressed in clean clothes and her hair in a long plait down her back, she played with a doll, singing a song to it.

Her song stopped abruptly as she looked up and noticed Mira. She didn't appear to be frightened, which encouraged Mira to kneel in the dirt beside her. "I would like to speak to your parents, please."

"Papa's gone," the little one replied and pointed

toward the house. "Mama's sick."

Mira sat back on her heels and tried to think of the best way to continue. The screen door creaked open and a middle-aged man came out. The girl ran to him babbling in her native tongue. The man motioned for the child to go inside as he approached Mira.

From the corner of her eye, she caught sight of Brandon approaching from the woods. The man turned toward Brandon and she jumped up. She had to act quickly. "Please, señor, we mean no harm. My friend and I would like some food. We can pay if you wish or work in repayment." She spoke in rapid Spanish, hoping she'd said things clearly enough, so he would not misunderstand.

"Is your man with the rebel forces?" the man asked in perfect English.

Brandon quickened his step and approached with both hands open and visible. Though he'd left the pack in the woods, Mira guessed he still had enough weaponry hidden on his body to feel secure. "Sir, my name is Brandon Falcon, and I am an American," he said, looking directly into the man's eyes. "I am not a rebel, but I am a soldier. This is my friend, Dr. Phelps. We mean you no harm and just wish to obtain a meal. If you would rather, we will leave."

Mira watched what could only be described as a manly display—a standoff—something you would see in an old Western movie. Sweat trickled down her back as the man scrutinized Brandon closely, raking his gaze over him from head to toe and settling on his face. He studied the green eyes and unwavering look staring back at him. He must have found what he needed to know.

He offered a nod. "My name is Rico Velázquez. You and your woman are welcome to eat at our table. Several months ago, my son was taken by the rebels and we have not heard from him. My wife, Lucia, and I pray daily he is safe and will return to us. We must be vigilant with visitors."

Brandon lowered his hands but kept his eyes trained in front of him. "I understand your protectiveness of your family and I'm sorry to hear about your son. Things must be difficult on the farm without him. We don't wish to cause you any hardship," he reassured the man. "We'll gladly pay for the food or work for our meal."

Rico straightened, standing as tall as his willowy frame allowed. His voice carried a ring of pride when he spoke. "One does not pay for hospitality, Mr. Falcon. There is plenty of food in my home, though it is simple. Please come in and be at ease."

Brandon dropped his head in an almost courtly bow, then took Mira's arm. Following Rico inside, he ducked to pass through the low door, which opened into a very hot kitchen.

Mira sniffed as she passed a bubbling pot. The steam wafted across her, bringing with it a hint of garlic and onion. "Those beans smell wonderful."

An older woman entered from the back. "This is my wife, Lucia. She will attend to your needs." Rico indicated she should go with his wife while Brandon was shown to the pump and sink in the kitchen.

She followed the woman through a curtained door into a small room with a simple bed. A beautiful pitcher and basin painted in vibrant colors rested on a small table beside the bed. Lucia indicated she should bathe.

"Thank you." She picked up the cloth and small soap and began to wash some of the grime from her skin. Out of the corner of her eye, she saw the other woman place an embroidered white blouse and tiered blue skirt on the bed near her.

She didn't want to offend her, but suspected Lucia didn't have many clothes. "Please, I can't take your clothes—they are far too nice."

"They are yours," Lucia said. "With a scarf to cover your hair and these clothes you will be safer in your travels."

She was overwhelmed by the generosity of these people. She unabashedly hugged the other woman, who looked taken aback by the emotional American. "Please allow us to repay your kindness in some way."

Lucia's face suddenly lost all vitality. "Are you truly a doctor?"

Mira held on to her hands, giving the woman a quick professional look. "Yes. Are you ill?"

The woman became agitated. "My son's wife is very ill. Could you help *her*?"

"Of course, I'll look at her. Where is she?"

"No, first you must refresh yourself and eat—then I will take you to see Ana. Please, take your time and come to the kitchen when you are done." Lucia pulled the curtain closed behind her as she left.

For the first time in days, Mira was alone in a place where she felt safe. She would have hot food, a bath, and clean clothes. Months ago, she'd taken all these things for granted. Now she relished the opportunity to enjoy them.

Stripped of her clothing, she sponged off her body, enjoying the feel of the soapy water on her skin. The loose skirt and blouse would feel cool after wearing the shirt and pants. There was a comb beside the basin, and she worked to remove the tangles from her curls. A quick look in the small mirror above the basin brought a smile to her reflection. The cuts and bruises were still there but starting to heal. What would Brandon think of her in her new clothes? She couldn't wait to see his reaction.

Chapter Fourteen

Bare chested, Brandon leaned against the sink drying his hands. A movement caught his eye. Mira stood in the doorway. He had known she was pretty, but cleaned up and wearing the local clothing, she was breathtaking. He straightened and dropped the towel in front of him, hoping she wouldn't notice his body's reaction.

He had trouble making his voice work and cleared his throat. "You look lovely."

"Thank you." Her voice sounded husky—sexy. "You clean up nice, too,"

He yanked his shirt from the back of the chair and covered himself. Her eyes followed his movements. Awkwardly, they stood gazing at one another.

The moment of intimacy shattered with Rico's words. "Please, Ms. Phelps, Mr. Falcon, be seated so we can enjoy our meal. I'm sure you must be hungry after your journey."

He held the chair for Mira, then sat across from her at the small kitchen table. "We'd like to thank you again for your generous hospitality, Señor Velázquez."

"It is nothing, and please call me Rico."

Lucia came in from outside and filled the plates at the counter. She smiled shyly as she served the filled plates. Rico waited while she completed her task, then joined them at the table. He murmured a simple blessing over the food.

Brandon bowed his head but kept his eyes open—not letting his guard down for a moment. He felt an undercurrent of unease but remained silent and dug into the meal of beans and tortillas filled with meat and vegetables.

"The fajitas are wonderful," Mira said between mouthfuls.

"I agree, ma'am," he added. "You are a superb cook."

Lucia responded with a shy smile. After everyone had eaten their fill, she filled a large pot of coffee and set it to perk on the hot wood stove. After pulling small glass cups from a lattice front cupboard, she set them on the table.

The smell of fresh ground coffee teased Brandon's nose; he did his best not to drool. He took a sip, savoring the robust, full bodied coffee and sighed. Café solo; he remembered having it once in Spain.

He shot a look at Mira and she smiled. Was she thinking of the smashed beans, which had gone unused?

"Tell me, Mr. Falcon," Rico asked. "Why is an American soldier hiding in our forest? And Ms. Phelps, if you are indeed a doctor, you must have come from the clinic in El Liano, yes? If my memory serves me correctly, the clinic doctor was a woman of the cloister. Are you indeed a doctor and a nun?" Rico's questions were hard-edged.

Brandon looked into the intelligent eyes of the man beside him. This man was no poor farmer. He came off as self-assured and well educated. Why was a man like this here on a run-down farm, living such a poor life?

Mira spoke up. "Sir, I am indeed a doctor, but I am

not a nun. The Sisters of Mercy encouraged me to pose as one for my safety. The rebels learned this, and they questioned me. As their prisoner, I was beaten and drugged. They would have killed me if Mr. Falcon had not rescued me." She touched her fingers to the raw wound on her wrist. Her gaze dropped along with her voice.

He reached across the table and squeezed her hand. He turned and met Rico's gaze. His jaw muscles tightened as he controlled his anger. Was this man going to turn against them? "I assure you, señor, we are not a threat to you or your family. Dr. Phelps has suffered greatly these last few days. I won't let *anyone* harm her with words or deeds." His words had started out softly but ended on a very harsh note.

"Mr. Falcon, the way you defend her, one would think you have feelings for this woman. I am merely trying to ascertain who has come into my house and how they will affect my family."

He took a sip of the black coffee before speaking. When he spoke, no one was left in doubt of his meaning. "*My feelings* are not your business, señor. As to your family, we are not a threat. What *I* would like to know is, why an educated man like you is farming up here in the wilds away from civilization? Are you hiding from someone also?" He watched as Rico's eyes became pained and Lucia left her untouched plate and walked quickly from the room.

His words hung in the charged atmosphere between them for several silent moments. A fly buzzed around the single light bulb suspended by a wire.

With great care, Rico folded his napkin before placing it beside his plate. "I brought my family here, to my parent's old home, to keep them alive. The government position which I previously held became dangerous when the rebels took over. Many were killed for doing their jobs. Here, away from everyone we live simply, but safely. Except now...the rebels have taken my son. We are no longer safe anywhere."

Brandon had seen firsthand the terror inflicted on the citizens and foreigners alike during his earlier visit. He could well imagine how dangerous Rico's position had become. As the men talked, Lucia came back in and nervously waited in the corner.

"Is everything all right?" Mira asked the agitated woman.

Lucia's face flooded with tears as she spoke to Rico in rapid Spanish.

Rico turned to Mira, "My son's wife, Ana, is worse. Could you help her, please?"

"I don't have my medical supplies, but I would be happy to look at her." Mira was up and ready in seconds. "Brandon, could you fetch your bag and first aid materials?" She threw the words over her shoulder as she quickly followed Lucia from the room.

"Mira, wait!" He grabbed her arm to stop her from leaving.

She tried to pull free of his hold. "Ana could be dying. I don't have time to stop."

"We are not going to separate." He was torn between the desire to help the sick woman and his need to protect Mira. "Anything could happen while I'm gone. What if the sick woman is a ruse to separate us?"

"Now you're being paranoid. Please, go get the supplies. Rico will make sure I'm safe. Ana can't wait any longer." She turned and followed Rico and Lucia.

Frustrated, he let her go. He sped from the house and into the forest, wanting to get the supplies as quickly as possible. Could he trust Rico completely? No, not when it came to Mira's safety. He had given up trying to explain away his feelings for her. She was the most important thing in his life right now. The rest would fall into place later. He grabbed the duffel and ran back to the house at breakneck speed.

****

Mira followed the couple past the small room where she'd bathed. They came to a set of steps, leading to a small loft. As soon as she entered the space, she became all professional. She could almost smell death in the room. The small woman, a girl really, lay curled in a ball atop a quilt on the floor, moaning in pain. Her skin, once brown, was now ashen. Sweat covered her body and her eye sockets and cheeks were sunken.

"How long has she been like this?"

"Two days. We thought it was the flu at first, then she complained of stomach pain. She's been feverish and can't sleep at all." Lucia sank down beside Ana and wiped the young woman's face with a cloth.

"Did she eat anything different or come into contact with anyone sick? I need as much information as possible if I am going to help her."

She checked Ana's eyes. The pupils were fine, but the sclera showed a slight yellowing. Jaundice. Her hands pressed against the girl's throat but found no swelling or stiffness. She tapped the girl's chest and then moved to the upper quadrant of her abdomen. With a gentle pressing motion, she circled her abdomen until she reached the right lower quadrant. Taking a deep breath, she pressed hard on the spot where the appendix would be, releasing hands quickly. An anguished cry erupted from her patient. N*ot good.* If only she had some equipment for needed blood tests and scans to help make the correct diagnosis. *Lord help her,* even that would be useless if there was no operating room. Especially if it was appendicitis as she suspected.

"She was in the village two days ago, but I don't think she was near anyone sick." Lucia continued to wipe the girl's face. "Please, doctor, what is wrong?"

Mira took a deep breath and reached for the calm professionalism these people needed. She couldn't allow her fears to show, only her strength.

Brandon's strong steps sounded on the stairs. She readied a smile for him as his head appeared in the loft. He set the duffel down and reached in to collect the supplies, shielding the contents from Rico and Lucia. Good—seeing all those weapons would just infuse more fear in them.

He handed her several sealed containers. "How is she?"

"Not good. She has a fever with abdominal pain. She's slightly jaundiced which could indicate some form of hepatitis, but without blood work it's impossible to tell." She stared directly into his eyes. He would know the danger without having to be told.

"I think she has appendicitis." She gazed at the worried looking couple. "Your daughter-in-law will most likely die if she does not have surgery."

She never sugar-coated bad news but wished she could when she saw the crestfallen faces. These people had taken them in, fed and clothed them. The couple had placed themselves at great risk. She only hoped she could repay their kindness by saving Ana.

"Lucia, get fresh water and continue to wipe her down. It will help with the fever and bring me some boiled water with a spoon. Rico, could I please have a moment alone with Brandon?"

"Certainly, doctor—but what can I do to help?"

"Figure out the fastest way to get Ana to the clinic."

After Rico left, she approached Brandon. "We have to get Ana to the clinic in El Liano as fast as possible. She still might not make it, but it's her only chance. If her appendix bursts, the infection will spread through her already weakened body and kill her."

"I understand your concern but if we go to the clinic, we all could be killed—or taken hostage. We can't take the chance. Can't you operate here?"

"Should I put her on the kitchen table and cut her open with a butcher knife and no anesthesia? That would be a death sentence."

His face took on a stubborn look. "It's a better choice than risking all our lives."

She knew he was only trying to keep her safe. He cared what happened to Ana. The dilemma darkened his eyes. He didn't want to compromise *her* safety. It would be hard to convince him. Gathering her courage, she walked over, placed one hand against his cheek, the other flat against his heart.

"You are a good man, one with a strong sense of honor and duty. You've risked your life to protect me because of it. Now, I may have to put mine on the line. I swore an oath as a physician to heal the sick and I truly care about these people and what happens to them. I can't do this alone, and I won't just let her die. Please, help me to help them."

"That's not fair." He grabbed the hand against his chest and wrapped it tightly in his. "You played the honor and duty card—not to mention staring at me with those innocent blue eyes." He ran a frustrated hand through his spiky hair. "It's not like I don't want to help, but *your* safety is my priority. There are too many unknowns. For all we know, the clinic could still be crawling with rebels."

Ana's shallow breathing was the only sound in the small space—the smell of sweat and illness all too familiar. She waited quietly—gazing at him with pleading in her eyes.

"Are you sure this is the only way?"

She nodded, relief brought a smile to her face.

"Damn, I don't like it."

A hollow moan came from the sad figure lying on the blanket.

"We're running out of time. She's going to die a horrible death."

"Okay. We'll do it. However," he stared intently at her, "we do it by *my* rules. You concentrate on the doctoring and I'll take care of the rest."

He took both her hands between his. "But if it comes right down to it—I'll protect you first. At the first sign of trouble, I'll get you out of there, regardless of what happens to anyone else."

Her chest tightened. This man had woven himself around her heart—a heart that would probably come out of this broken. But what did such things matter when life was so precarious these days?

He leaned down and brushed his lips across hers. She closed her eyes and savored the feel and taste of his lips. A whirlwind of sensation engulfed her, giving her a single moment in time untouched by the chaos surrounding them. Reluctantly, she opened her eyes and stepped back. "You help Rico with transportation, and I'll prep Ana for travel. Take the duffel with you downstairs and I'll bring the rest of the supplies when I come." She turned back to her patient as Brandon left to help Rico.

Lucia returned with the warm water and spoon. Mira took them and rummaged through the medical supplies. Once again, she was surprised at the variety and completeness of the kits. She pushed aside the scalpels and stitching materials, found syringes and morphine, then grabbed the acetaminophen.

She placed two tablets in the spoon, crushed them, then filled the spoon with boiled water. She'd work on the fever first and prayed by the time they arrived, her patient would stand a better chance.

Lucia dribbled the medicated water down Ana's throat while Mira administered an antibiotic and morphine in a shot to the girl's arm.

"I need sheets to wrap her in and some pillows to cushion her," she instructed as she gathered the supplies and waited for the men to return.

Lucia placed the requested items into her hands. "Go with God, doctor. Please take care of Ana. I must stay with my granddaughter."

"Gracias." She understood how difficult it had to be for the woman to send her loved one off into the unknown with strangers. She squeezed Lucia's hands reassuringly as the men arrived.

Brandon and Rico entered the loft and between them moved the girl gently to the lower floor. They continued outside, placing her in the back of an old truck.

Lucia handed Mira a black scarf. "Please, remember to keep your head down and covered, hopefully you will have no trouble." She kissed Ana on the forehead and stood back as Rico started the truck.

Brandon jumped in, his duffel tucked beside him. They did their best to cushion the girl from the worst of the jostling. The road to the river was rough, but mercifully short. Minutes later they arrived at a small dock on the edge of the forest.

The dock was in bad shape, with missing or broken planks. She prayed the boat was in better shape.

The two men examined the small boat. "It'll do." Brandon said.

As she boarded, the boat rocked precariously. Using her arms, she balanced and sat facing the rear where Brandon would steer.

He stepped into the back with practiced ease and reached up to take Ana from Rico's arms. Gently, he placed her in the middle of the boat. With an outstretched arm, he took a firm grip on Rico's hand.

"Thank you, my friend. We are grateful for your help."

"No, it is I, Mr. Falcon, who is thankful you and the good doctor came to our home." Rico looked at her. "She and my granddaughter are all we have left. Please do your best to save her."

"I will, Rico. I'll do my very best."

The boat motor sputtered and caught. Rico threw Brandon the line and the small boat maneuvered out of the dock area. As soon as the dock was out of sight, Brandon sped up and reached into the duffel beside him. He grabbed the A-K-47 and placed it on the seat within easy reach.

"I'm not taking any chances. Beneath the bench seat, there's a tarp, extra petrol and food. If we need to, we can bypass the clinic and go aground somewhere safer."

She gave him an anxious look. "We can't bypass the clinic. There isn't time. Ana won't last long."

"I told you to take care of the doctoring and I'd handle the rest. That's one promise, I intend to keep. You've got to trust me on this. I won't come ashore without checking out the clinic first. It won't do Ana any good if the rebels have the place."

"I have faith in your skills, Brandon, but don't forget, I'm still working on trust."

Mira wished she knew what they would face when they arrived at the clinic. Surely the rebels had all left by now. She couldn't remember much about her trip in the truck. Had all the rebels left with her?

"How long before we get there?"

"According to Rico and the map, the trip should take about three hours. I'll try to be as quick as I can. Now try to relax a little."

****

Rafà watched as the two men loaded the woman into the boat. What the hell was Brandon thinking? How many women did he plan to rescue before he got caught by the rebels and killed? He was like that, always the hero, always fighting for the underdog. Where had Brandon been when he'd needed him? Why had it taken him so long to comeback for him?

He could've confronted Brandon as soon as he'd arrived. But he had his own reasons for wanting to *stay dead*. No matter what, he still owed Brandon for the many times he *had* been there. Well, he'd just have to follow them and intervene if necessary. Brandon seemed uncharacteristically oblivious to his own danger right now. The episode back in the jungle had been close. If he hadn't intervened…Rafà stopped thinking and began the cross-country hike to intercept them at the village.

Chapter Fifteen

Brandon searched continuously as they passed heavily wooded areas and rocky outcrops along the shoreline. Each time the nose of the boat rounded another curve in the small river, his muscles tensed.

He studied the strain etched on Mira's face and the drooping of her head. Each time she began to nod, she'd start, then reach out to check Ana. Her constant attention told him things weren't looking good for the young woman. Still—watching and waiting were all they could do for the time being.

"There's nothing you can do for her now," he murmured. "Why don't you lie down and catch an hour of sleep while you can? I'll keep an eye on her. I promise to wake you if I notice any change."

"I hate feeling so helpless. I've been trained to help people, not sit around and watch them die. It's so frustrating." She shifted on the seat, seeking a comfortable spot. "You're right. Ana deserves my best efforts. The only way I can help her now is to rest and be at my best when we arrive."

"Could I have that in writing?"

"What?"

He gave her a grin. "You know, the part about me being right."

"Fat chance." She returned his grin. "Sleep couldn't hurt."

"Good girl." He encouraged her as she slipped off the bench and lay beside Ana on the floor of the boat.

She sent him a half-hearted wave and closed her eyes.

Brandon studied her rosy cheeks and riot of curls before turning his gaze to the shoreline. The surgery would be physically demanding for her. Not to mention the emotional ramifications of returning to the clinic, the place where she'd been beaten and abused. She'd suffered so much in a short amount of time. If she shattered at this point no one could fault her, but he'd seen tremendous strength in her from the beginning. She'd managed to survive a kidnapping, a beating and the sheer mental torture of capture and evasion. Grit. She had lots of it. He admired the trait in *anyone* but hadn't expected to find it in such a small, delicate package.

He chuckled to himself. *Delicate like dynamite.*

Yeah, Mira was something all right. She'd thrown his mind and body into a nosedive. His steely nerves and unshakable concentration had suffered massive neuroses since he'd pulled her from the back of the rebel's truck. How could one small, adorable woman wreck such havoc on a man? He had years of military training, which always kept him in command of his emotions. He was a finely tuned weapon, lethal against opponents. Yet, one look from her soft blue eyes could send this warrior into a tailspin. Could she ever love someone like him? *Damn.* He sounded like one of those sappy novels. Next, he would be spouting poetry.

With an effort, he gathered those thoughts, and pushed them far back into the deep, nether regions of his mind. He had a mission to complete. Mira's safety depended on his clear head. It would take quick thinking and fearless determination to stay ahead of the rebels. No way would he let her down. He straightened in his seat, double checked his weapon and renewed his vigil of the riverbanks.

He planned their approach and arrival at the clinic. The rebels *shouldn't* be there when they arrived. However, he'd learned from experience, people always showed up where they weren't supposed to be. No plan covered everything, but he needed a contingency in case things hit the fan.

A quick look at his watch and the map, and he eased up on the throttle, slowing the boat. They were almost there.

Gently, he nudged Mira with the toe of his boot.

She stretched and rubbed her eyes, looking tired and groggy "How much longer?"

"About ten minutes. When you leave the boat, get inside the clinic as fast as possible. We can't trust anyone, so we can't be seen." Brandon relayed all this in his calm matter-of-fact tone. Though he made it all sound simple, they could be killed if anyone saw them.

Five minutes later, he cut the motor and steered the boat to the riverbank. He paddled the boat under the overhang of some trees. He tied the boat, pulled out the tarp and covered the women. For one moment, his eyes met and held hers. He ran a finger down her cheek.

Soundless, he slipped into the water beside the boat. "I'll be back soon."

"Be safe," she whispered as he waited quietly for her to cover her head with the tarp.

He swam ashore and found his way to the edge of the woods near the clinic. It was dusk, and few people moved around the small compound. Lights were on in the building and he moved in for a closer look. Blending with the shadows, he rose to peer through a window.

The same woman he'd encountered before moved from bed to bed, smoothing and tucking covers. She looked recovered from the scare he'd given her, and she was alone. As he watched, a man in black priest robes walked into the room. Through the open window, he heard the priest ask about a patient. *Damn*, he'd hoped the clinic would be empty, but at least there were no armed guards or rebels. He made his way back to the boat for Ana and Mira.

The dock was empty when he pulled the boat up and tied it. He lifted Ana from the boat and moved quickly to the clinic. They entered through a back door into the employee section of the building. Doors hung off hinges, scuff marks decorated the walls, all evidence of the rebel's raid.

Mira shook her head at the disarray, but as he watched, she stiffened her back and moved on. She pushed open a door to the simple treatment room, which doubled as an operating room. No high-tech equipment here, but enough to suffice for the emergencies a small village might need.

"Brandon, I can't do this alone. I have to have someone to help."

"There's a priest and a woman in another part of the building.

"It's probably Rosita and Father José. We can trust them."

He placed Ana on the table. "I'll get them."

Mira had already stripped Ana and placed a sterile

blanket over her body. She only nodded as he left the room.

He followed the sound of voices to the end of the corridor. He opened a door and found the two people he'd seen earlier, calmly sipping coffee from mugs at a small table.

At the sight of him, the woman dropped her cup and jumped back from the hot liquid, an exclamation of horror on her lips.

"What do you want?" the priest asked calmly. "We have no drugs or money if that is why you're here."

Brandon took stock of the man. Dark hair and eyes, a mustache and olive skin, probably South American, he surmised. He wasn't large, but something about his demeanor seemed out of place for a priest. Most men facing him, wearing all his weaponry as usual, at least showed *some* fear. The priest didn't. Interesting.

"Well, Padre, I guess a cup of coffee will just have to do." He smiled as he replaced his gun in its holster. "But first, I need you and your friend to help Dr. Phelps. She has a patient who needs surgery immediately."

The priest jumped to his feet. "Sister Mira is here? Is she all right?"

"No time for explanations. She said to hurry." The words barely left his mouth before the two hurried past him and down the hall.

He eyed the coffee hungrily, then turned to follow them. When this mission was over, he promised himself he was going to drink a gallon of the best coffee money could buy.

"Rosita," Mira called out happily as she deftly arranged her surgical supplies on a tray near the table.

"I'm so glad you are safe. Please—finish prepping her for me while I scrub up. Father, if you don't mind, I need someone to help with anesthesia. Brandon, don't go anywhere. I may need you, too, before this is over."

Blood didn't scare him—it poured copiously in his line of work. Most of it, however, was a result of battle and the adrenaline rush allowed him to work without thinking. This was a different story. The antiseptic smell reminded him of all the hospital stays he had endured as a result of his wounds.

"Don't flake out on me."

The authority in her voice brought him out of his reverie. He quickly moved to the sink to wash up. She was so different here. This was her world, and she was its mistress.

He gloved up and helped her and the others into surgical gowns. Stripping his outer shirt, he donned one himself. The weaponry beneath the sterile coverings brought him a scowl from Mira and her staff. He shrugged and pulled on his mask. He wouldn't let down his guard, regardless of the need for a sterile environment.

The patient was prepped with coverings, IV's inserted, and oxygen in place when the team approached the table.

Chapter Sixteen

Mira closed her eyes and swallowed the ball of fear lodged in her throat. A silent prayer passed her lips beneath the mask. Her attitude set the tone for the others. She couldn't show the gut-wrenching terror gnawing at her insides. This was the first time she had done an appendectomy—alone, without other doctors for backup.

"Swab," She held out her hand not looking up from her patient, intent on cleansing the exposed flesh of Ana's abdomen.

"Scalpel." She willed her hand to steady and made a clean cut on the lower abdomen. "Suction. Brandon?" Blood continued to pour from the wound. Rosita's deft hand removed it with the tube.

Mira had no time to wonder where he had gone. He was supposed to be helping. "Retractor." She deftly moved the bowel aside. There it was, all red and inflamed, the appendix.

"Clamp." She isolated the appendix, cut it, and caught it in the pan, keeping the poisonous material from spilling into Ana's body. "Rinse—suction." Her hands worked quickly as she sutured the clamped area. "How does she look, Father?"

Father José chuckled. "I think she is doing much better than your friend."

Mira couldn't help a quick glance behind her. Her

brave soldier was sitting on the floor with his head between his knees. He lifted his head, a look of embarrassment, covering his ashen face.

****

Two hours later, Ana rested in one of the two small wards. Father José sat with her, silently tolling worn wooden Rosary beads while Rosita scrubbed the operating room. Mira pulled off her bloodied scrubs and mask, tiredly rubbing her hand along the back of her neck. "What happened to my extra help in there?"

Brandon shed his medical garb and gently massaged her neck and shoulders. "Sorry, that's never happened. It was the smell—not the blood."

"Don't be ashamed. Some of the best doctors I know fainted during their first surgery."

"I guess I'm better at shooting them than fixing them. *You* were fantastic."

She laughed, and some of the tension eased. "I suppose we make a great pair. You break 'em. I'll fix 'em. We could put it on a business card."

He spoke softly as he continued to knead her shoulders. "Even though I got queasy, I feel like I'm on a high."

Her aching muscles relaxed under his ministrations. "What you're experiencing is an adrenaline rush, sort of like when a woman gives birth. I felt the same way the first time I did it."

"The first time you did what?" he asked with a devilish tone in his voice. "A lot of *first times* can give you a high," he whispered into her ear.

"You're incorrigible." She elbowed him in the stomach and twisted from beneath his hands. "I know where they keep the coffee," she purred and got exactly the response she expected.

"Lead on, woman."

Father José entered the small kitchen area as they sat sipping coffee and relaxing at the table. "May I join you for a moment?" He hesitated before sitting at the table with them. At their nods he sat and heaved a heavy sigh.

"Thank God for your talent, Sister," he said without looking at her.

"It was a team effort, Father," she murmured evenly. "Everyone played a vital part, including God." The air became charged with undercurrents. They had serious matters to discuss.

"Mira, is there somewhere I can shower?" I'd like to clean up before we move on." Brandon stood, and they exchanged a look—hers thankful for his tact and his one of understanding. His words gave her a moment to collect her thoughts.

"There's a shower down the hall near my room. Use anything you need."

"Padre," he continued when the priest looked up, "I need to discuss some things with you after my shower." His words were said lightly enough but could only be taken as a demand. He touched Mira on the shoulder reassuringly and sauntered from the room.

Alone with the priest, Mira felt her heart drop to her toes. The next few minutes would be difficult. She'd lied to this man and all those at the clinic. Yes, she'd had her reasons, but guilt for her deception weighed heavy upon her.

"Father, I have a confession to make," she spoke without looking up.

"That is my line of work, if you will forgive an old

man for making light of a serious subject."

She raised her bowed head.

"Speak your mind, child. When we bury things in our hearts and cover them with guilt, everything looks dark and unmanageable."

She looked into his eyes. "I'm not a nun, as I'm sure you've guessed by now. I'm sorry for lying to everyone, but the Sisters back home thought it would protect me. Not that it did much good in hind sight. Father, how did they know about me? I didn't present a threat. Why target me and not someone else?"

"First, I am sure God has already forgiven your deception. No one was harmed, and many have been helped by your medical talents."

"What about Jacinta? She was harmed, wasn't she?" Mira was afraid to hear his reply. She'd almost forgotten the young woman while racing through the jungle.

"She left with the rebels. I know this only second hand from people in the village who saw them leave. They claim she went willingly, though one never can tell with these things. She may have been cooperating to spare herself more abuse."

Her heart lurched at his words. Had her deception caused the rebels to do this? Was she responsible for Jacinta's pain?

"I doubt your subterfuge would have changed her outcome one way or the other," he chided. "Don't add this to your burden, Dr. Phelps."

"Please, call me Mira. I think dispensing with all my titles might be best."

"All right, Mira. At this point, I think you need to ask yourself, what's next? You can't change what has happened. Now, you must concentrate on getting to safety. If you stay here, they will come back. I can't say why you were chosen out of the others. I only know you have to leave."

"I agree completely, Padre," Brandon drawled behind him. "Now Ana is safe, we need to get as far away from this place as possible."

A startlingly handsome Brandon stood in the doorway. He'd taken his shower in record time and was gorgeous. Well, manly gorgeous anyway. No man should have such a lethal combination of good looks and heavenly physique. His clean smell wafted across the space between them. Water droplets clung to his hair, like they'd done at the waterfall. She wanted to wrap her arms around him and breathe him in. His words jarred her from her sensual perusal.

"I can't go anywhere right now."

He opened his mouth to argue and she held up her hand to prevent his comment.

"The first twelve hours after surgery are the most critical. Ana may need me in the night, so I'm staying right here. Besides, I want to sleep in a bed for a change." She hadn't meant the last words to sound so petulant and hoped he wouldn't comment on them.

"Your safety is my primary concern. It may sound callus, but that's the way it is. The longer we stay in one place, the more likely the soldiers will find us."

"Please, don't argue," Father José interjected "You both have valid points and I may have a solution." Two sets of eyes turned his way.

****

"What do you have in mind, Padre?" Brandon pulled out a chair, turned it around, and sat astride it.

He deliberately projected the appearance of someone relaxed and at ease. His senses, however, were alert as he attentively examined the priest's face. "I'll hear you out, but when it comes to Mira, I reserve the right to do what I think is best."

Her body snapped to attention. "*You* reserve the right? I am perfectly capable of making my own decisions—thank you very much." Her eyes flashed like darts at him, as she got up and flounced over to the refrigerator.

She reminded him of a kitten he'd once rescued from a ditch. He'd ruined his favorite loafers crawling down into the culvert—only to have the half-drowned kitten scratch and spit at him the entire time. She probably wouldn't appreciate the comparison. He'd let her spit and claw and then, he'd do what he thought best anyway.

"As I said, I have a solution," Father José continued. "I can get Diego, one of the orphans, to take your boat upstream and hide it. Rosita's husband, Carlos, can stand watch down where the road splits. You and Dr. Phelps can sleep while Rosita and I care for our patient."

Brandon watched each nuance in the priest's face. He was more than a little suspicious. Everything sounded too well planned. Was the priest trying to get them to fall asleep and then turn them over to the rebels?

****

Mira's world had been turned upside down and everything had gotten out of control. Brandon was only doing his job, but did he have to be so macho-superior while he did it? Food. She needed to eat; it might help her attitude. She opened the fridge.

He watched her as he listened to Father José. What would it take to wipe the superior look off his face?

No chocolate. *Damn.* Disappointed, she rummaged around and found the makings for a sandwich. She made a small one for herself and a gigantic one for him. Mumbling beneath her breath about egotistical tyrants, she poured two glasses of cold milk. Was that a smirk at the corners of his mouth?

She sat down at the table as the two men talked.

"Thanks." Brandon took a huge bite of the sandwich and washed it down with half the milk.

She eyed him curiously; he'd never eaten like this in the jungle. Had he hidden his appetite because he had rationed the food to include her? Guilt flooded through her. She ate her sandwich hungrily as she listened to Father José's plan.

"Sounds great. I think I'll follow Brandon's example and get a shower. I can't wait to sleep in a bed." She smiled at the men, then jumped up and started down the hall. The decision was made, and she was happy to have some small measure of control returned to her. The look of annoyance on Brandon's face gave a little boost to her mood. This time, she'd gotten the last word. She stifled a chuckle as she made for her bedroom.

She pushed open the door to her room. *What on Earth?* Her mouth clenched, and anger welled in her chest. She hadn't been inside her room since the kidnapping and wasn't prepared for this.

Her mattress lay askew on the floor along with all her books from the shelf. Her toiletries were overturned, and her clothes were scattered throughout the room. How dare they go through her things? She felt her little bit of regained control slip away. They weren't even here and still they were jerking her around. She knelt on the floor beside her photos. The heat of tears welled in her eyes. The framed picture of her parents and herself lay shattered, the photograph wadded in a ball.

"Damn them. Damn them to hell."

Having voiced her thoughts, she felt a little calmer. Gently, she gathered the pictures, and moved to place them on the nightstand. That's when she noticed her uncle's journals were gone.

Frantically, she picked things up as she searched the entire room. They weren't here. Her money was still in the bedside drawer, but her passport was gone. Why would they take the journals and her passport? This wasn't random. It was personal. Tendrils of fear raced down her spine. They had chosen to kidnap *her*—no one else. What did they want?

She looked up to see Brandon standing silently in the doorway. How had he known she needed him? He opened his arms and she wrapped herself around him. She felt the reassuring beat of his heart as he pulled her up against his body, his strength seeping into her watery bones.

"Why does someone hate me?" she hiccuped and sniffed between the words. "What have I ever done to cause them to hurt me this way?"

"I don't know their motives. Some people don't need a reason. Don't imagine you have done anything to deserve this." His hands gently massaged her back as his mouth dropped tiny kisses over her hair and temple. He stepped back and placed her away from him.

"You get your shower, and I'll pick up this mess. You'll miss out on a soft bed if you stay up much longer."

His words were meant to draw a smile from her, and she didn't disappoint him. It was a bit wobbly, however.

****

He watched her disappear down the hall before bending to pick up her things. He examined each item carefully before putting it away, learning more about Mira through her things. From her reaction to the smashed photo, he could tell how much she missed her family. It didn't seem right. Someone so talented and beautiful shouldn't be alone. He'd lost his parents a while back, but he hadn't had the close relationship with his folks like she'd had. Of course, she'd also been a lot younger. She seemed so vulnerable, so...*hell,* he didn't have time for psychoanalysis.

He cleared the rest of the room, and then searched the room with safety in mind. Only one small window high above the floor and one door. Good. They should be safe if the padre could be trusted. If you couldn't trust a priest...nope, he wouldn't go there.

He removed a mattress from one of the cots in the room next to hers and placed it on the floor.

Her screech jerked him to attention, and he bolted from the room.

Chapter Seventeen

Brandon raced down the hall with his gun cocked and ready. The scream had come from the bathroom and it was locked. A swift kick and the flimsy door gave way immediately. His breath sucked in with a loud hiss.

She stood in the shower surrounded by debris from the ceiling. Someone had crashed her shower, evidenced by the tumbled rod and shower curtain at her feet. She held a sorry excuse for a towel, trying to cover her curves. Her face held a look of irritation.

He quickly scanned the tiny room for intruders but saw no one.

"Don't just stand there—do something."

"Exactly what am I supposed to do?" he asked, raising one brow.

"Get him out of here."

"What? I don't see any bad guys—so why'd you scream?"

She pointed to the crumpled shower curtain at her feet. "There."

He followed her direction as the curtain moved. As he watched, one of the biggest iguanas he'd ever seen nonchalantly crawled from beneath the wet plastic and blinked at him. A relieved chuckle escaped his throat. "Damn, Mira, if I had known he was this big I'd have brought my other gun."

"Funny-ha-ha, now get rid of it. He totally ruined my lovely shower."

Brandon was far more interested in the picture she made as she stood in the tub, pulling at the towel. The cloth wasn't much bigger than a hand towel, and thin enough to show intriguing hints of pink. The damp terry clung to her breasts.

Noticing his preoccupation with her predicament, she nearly dropped the towel in her effort to conceal her nakedness.

"Ogling my half-naked body isn't helping," she chided but had a little wisp of a grin forming.

"Well—now, that's what they call perspective— and from my perspective…" He laughed and dodged the soap thrown at his head.

She tugged at the damp towel. "Don't stand there, help me."

He casually placed the gun in the band of his pants and walked toward her.

She managed to twirl around, keeping her curves partially hidden. "Be careful. He might snalt you. You might not mind, but I don't want salty snot on my clean skin."

"This big guy won't hurt anyone." He picked up the iguana and got sprayed as it sneezed salt and water from its nose.

"Maybe he won't, but *I* will if you don't hurry and get rid of it. And keep your eyes to yourself, while you're here."

"Now is that any way to treat your hero? After all, I saved you from Iggy." He held the iguana out toward her. "I think maybe I deserve a little reward for my bravery, don't you? How about, oh, let's say, one little kiss. Surely it's the least you can do for my efforts in saving you."

"Did your mother ever use the word incorrigible when speaking about you?"

"Can't say I remember that one—she used things like, adorable and cherubic—you know the everyday kind of words for boys."

When she looked at him, he noticed her look of irritation had been replaced by an impish one. "Well," she dragged the word out slowly, "I suppose I could spare one tiny one, but don't bring that thing anywhere near me. I don't want to get salt on me after my shower."

Brandon smiled rakishly as he held the iguana far away from her and leaned in. She bent just the slightest bit and placed a peck on his cheek—immediately moving back from him.

"Thank you. Could you please close the door on your way out?"

His anticipation was quickly erased by disappointment. The kiss still caused intense heat in his body. The bathroom began to feel like a sauna. A hasty retreat seemed in order, if he wanted to keep his hands off her beautiful body.

"You're a hard woman, Mira. You could have at least kissed my lips." He turned and walked out the door.

****

"Everything's okay, Padre." She heard his voice in the hallway. "Dr. Phelps doesn't want company while she showers."

The priest's voice held a note of shock. "I should hope not, my son."

She quickly dried off, grimacing when she looked at her robe. Debris from the ceiling and water from the shower had covered it. Brandon would probably laugh at her dilemma. She had only this wisp of a towel for cover.

The back door slammed, and she ran, hoping she could make the cover of her room before he returned. As she rushed down the hall, she silently prayed Father José had left the area. Encountering him dressed like this was a scenario she didn't want to picture.

She rushed through her bedroom door and turned to shut out would-be oglers. She twisted around and tripped on a mattress by the door. Her arms flung outward to break her fall and her towel fell by the wayside at the precise moment Brandon walked through the door.

She looked for a hole to crawl into, found none, so laid her head on the floor.

He knelt beside her. "Are you okay? I forgot about the mattress when you screamed."

She didn't answer. Face down, totally naked. What could she say? Heat blossomed in her cheeks and she felt the blush spread over her face and body. How would she ever be able to look at him?

His voice filled with concern when she didn't reply. "Mira?"

Her shoulders began to shake. Laughter bubbled up and spilled out. She couldn't help it. After all the angst and pain of the past few days, she had to have some release—and she refused to cry. She wouldn't allow them that much control over her. But laughter—she could use it. He snatched a blanket, covered her, and let her laugh.

He moved to lie beside her on the outside of the blanket. "Do you know how wonderful your laughter sounds?"

Embarrassment, humor, and relief flooded through her. He understood.

She rolled beneath the blanket, so she was face up. "I feel safe, for the first time in days. I hadn't realized how freeing it can be. I'm alive and they didn't win."

Chapter Eighteen

Brandon leaned on one elbow and watched the emotions flit over her face. He wrapped his arms around her, pulled her close to his body, and inhaled the heady scent of soap, shampoo and woman. Arousal stiffened his body and quickly he moved his hips back from her.

She had come to mean so much to him. It was more than just wanting. He'd wanted lots of women. None had made him feel this intense *protectiveness* or tightness in his chest. She was attracted to him, but did she have feelings for him? He didn't want feelings of gratitude for rescuing her from a group of depraved rebels. He wanted her to…

"Brandon?"

Her voice sounded breathy and he hardened more. "Hmm?" He wound his fingers around a wet tendril of her hair, preventing it from sliding down and touching her damp skin. One wrong move and he might do something unthinkable.

"Is there someone special in your life?"

"My job hasn't allowed me the time—so no. Why?" His heart-rate accelerated as he anxiously waited for her answer.

"Because, I'd like you to make love to me."

Dear lord, did she know how sexy she sounded? He doubted it. His hand stilled. "Mira, you—"

"No, don't put me off. I know you're attracted to me, and well…you make me feel things I've never felt before."

"You are worth so much more than just sex. You need to be loved."

Her face flashed, a look of longing blended with equal parts curiosity and just a little bit of uncertainty. He'd bet his last dime, she was a virgin. College—medical school—research—when had she had time to explore a relationship? Then again, college could be a sexual playground these days, but Mira? He didn't think so.

"A thousand different things could happen before tomorrow." She rushed to fill the silence after his words. "We could die or get captured by the rebels. I don't want them to touch me like that. I want to know what it's like to feel loved."

She had no idea how much she'd betrayed with those last words. Mira had never known love. The realization smashed him hard in the solar plexus. How could he push her away—but was it right? *Hell no*, but what if he refused? He wasn't the first-time—I want to experiment, kind of guy. Nor was he about to shatter her fragile feelings.

"Remember, I told you I wouldn't let anyone harm you?" At her nod, he continued. "I include myself in that statement."

Emotions ran high in a dangerous situation like theirs. He didn't want her to regret her decision later. She was right though; they could die or get captured. No. He would breathe his last breath before they took her from him and hurt her.

"Have you ever been with a man?" His voice came

out low, guttural and God—his hands were shaking.

"No, but I'm a doctor remember." Her grin was cocky. "I think I can figure it out."

With a gentle hand he touched her chin and turned her to face him. "It can't be undone, and I don't make a habit of having sex with women I rescue."

"I didn't ask for sex. I asked you to make love to me. I know the difference and so do you. There are probably a hundred rules against it and just as many sane arguments, but right now I don't give a damn about rules and sanity."

"I don't want you to regret this. Are you sure?" *Hell*, was he really contemplating doing this?

She leaned in, found his lips, and kissed him tentatively. "I'm sure. I've never been more sure of anything in my life."

Damn right he was. His lips crushed her mouth. Passion rose hot and quick between them, like a flash fire burning everything in its path. His breathing sounded like he'd run a mile on the beach. He pulled back, taking in her rosy cheeks and bemused expression. And then he looked into her eyes, seeking the answer he needed before committing to this. It was there for him to see—desire and yearning.

She wanted him, as much as he wanted her. No more asking questions. He was tired of always doing what was right. He'd spent his life fighting other people's fights and righting wrongs in places all over the world. Never had he taken time for himself or reached out for something *he* wanted with both hands and grabbed onto it. He needed her and damn his soul to hell if he was wrong—he was going to have her.

Mira might be innocent, but she wasn't shy. Her

hands roamed his shoulders, tentatively at first, and then with more sureness as her deft fingers explored his tensed muscles. Lips soft as rose petals touched the pulse in his throat, eased upward to tease the underside of his chin.

"You have on way too many clothes," she whispered as she nuzzled his ear and then licked it with her tongue.

His mind soared at the touch of her tongue. She was killing him with her needy exploration. Did she understand what her touch did to his control? Achy desire filled him, emboldened him. With unsteady control he allowed his fingers to brush gently across the top of her breast. Her hitched breath brought a groan to his lips. "I totally agree." He started to sit up.

****

"No—Let me." She rolled to her knees, deliberately allowing the blanket to fall.

Astonishment—followed by blatant desire flashed across his face. His eyes filled with fiery passion. *She'd done that to him*, the heady thought made her pulse race.

"I want to see all of you, this time. I want to see what you've carefully tried to keep hidden from me these past few days."

His brow rose at her pronouncement.

"Yes, I noticed all the times you pulled back from me. I might be inexperienced; but I felt you against me in my sleep. I wanted you then, and I want you now."

His face took on a pleased look and a Cheshire smile curved his lips.

"You have become rather daring since your return to the clinic. Have pity on an old soldier's heart."

"It's a command thing. You should know all about it. Here, *I'm* in charge. Didn't you know most doctors are brash and daring?" she sassed. She intended to show just how 'in charge' she was.

"I've never heard it, but feel free to enlighten me." He wiggled his brows.

A giggle slipped out before she could stop it. Her hands moved to his waist, sliding the edge of his shirt up, allowing her fingertips to skim over his flat belly and ribs as she did so. His muscles tightened at her touch and she smiled directly into his eyes. She felt intoxicated, wanton and powerful. This beautiful, sexy man was hers for the taking, and she intended to do just that. Blue eyes sparkled at green.

"Are we doing this with or without the loaded gun?" Her voice lowered.

Brandon chuckled and reached down to move her hand away from the Sig Sauer tucked inside his waistband.

"I think we'd better...unload it...don't you?" she asked coyly and watched as he removed the gun and placed it beneath the mattress near his head. It would be his only concession to disarming himself. The gun must stay within his reach. She respected his caution and her breath hitched at the thought of how dangerous this man really was.

"Yeah, I do. Loaded guns can be dangerous, you know." His eyes held hers as she pushed the shirt over his chest, teasing his skin with her nails as she went.

"You're enjoying this aren't you?" he asked when she tugged the shirt over his head and threw it behind them. "You like being in control?" He laughed as she straddled his hips and eased her butt down and sat directly over the front of his pants. His groan supplanted the chuckle when she rubbed her naked hips across his straining pants.

"You're killing me." His voice burned with need.

"Aren't you glad I'm a doctor? I can resuscitate you." She giggled, enjoying what her body did to him, but her own breath became labored when his erection grew even larger. And when it touched the spot at the apex of her thighs, she clenched her knees and rocked. She leaned forward, allowed her breasts to hang over him, tempted and teased, to the delight of both.

"Don't tell me you learned this in med school, if so, I might be tempted to go back to school." His hands cupped the weight of each dangling breast. He lifted upward and took a nipple into his mouth.

A moan of pure pleasure erupted from her throat. "Ooh, Brandon," she crooned as his hot tongue licked tiny circles around her nipple. Lightning flashes of pleasure pulsed through her breast down to her womb where it set fire to her center. Her breath rasped, and heat pooled between her thighs. Any moment she would melt around him.

As he continued to feast on her breast, she rocked against his groin following the rhythm of his tongue on her nipple. His hardness was exquisite. The feel of his rigid sex rubbing against her mound through the fabric intensified her growing need. Eyes closed, head thrown back, she ground her body against his length, straining for something just out of reach.

"You're so beautiful and sexy." He eased a finger between their bodies and touched her bud.

Her body jerked in response, suffused in intense pleasure. "Too much." She pushed at his hand.

In response, he grabbed her hand, interlaced his fingers with hers, and continued to tease her with his other hand. Wetness poured from her as he used his finger to brush her nub, and then move away. He was well tutored in the art of making a woman feel fantastic and she was a willing pupil. Her body picked up the rhythm and moved against his hand. Then, slowly he eased a finger inside her warmth. She felt tightness followed by pure pleasure. He sucked on her nipple harder, teasingly caressed her nub...and his finger pushed deeper.

Everything around her disappeared. Her world narrowed to just this moment of feeling—just Brandon—just her. As he pushed into her hot flesh and suckled her breast, her world began to spin—she was headed to a place she'd never been.

"Brandon?" she spoke his name uncertainly.

"Go with it, Mira; let it take you. I'll catch you."

Lost in a euphoric haze, his words came from a distance. She climbed ever higher and then stepped off into the clouds, shattering. Her muscles clenched around his finger as tingling pleasure rocked her to her core. Aftershocks pulsed, bringing wave after rippling wave of rapture. She sagged against his chest, unerringly reaching for his mouth. Their lips met in a tender kiss. Surely, she'd died, and this was heaven.

Brandon held her as she floated down from the dizzying heights of her orgasm. He turned and placed her on her side facing him.

She opened her eyes, and smiled the biggest, goofiest grin ever. "That was so amazing," She kissed his hand and placed his palm against her cheek.

"That was just the appetizer and I'm still hungry."

A note of shock tinged her voice. "You still have your pants on."

He rolled onto his back. "I think someone got distracted and failed to do her job."

She grabbed his belt and unbuckled it before his hands had the chance. She felt playful as she unsnapped the pants and slowly inched the zipper down. Reaching beneath him, she grabbed the waistband and tugged. He lifted his hips to help her pull off the offending clothing. Her hand stopped, surprised.

"You're wearing swimming trunks," she voiced with puzzlement. "Right, you're a SEAL. You never said much about your work."

"I couldn't. My mission is secret, and I have to kill anyone who finds out," he said with poker straight face.

Her head jerked upward; her eyes met the twinkle in his. "Soldier, I don't intend to die a virgin, so you have some work to do before you kill me."

"A man's work is—Oomph." Breath rushed from his lungs as she hit him hard with the pillow.

Mira dispensed with his pants, and then sat back on her heels admiring the view. "Have you been wounded many times?" Her voice softened as she saw the scars on his shoulders and abdomen.

"A few. How about I show you all the places and you kiss them better?"

"*Now* who's being daring?" She watched him study her, as she reached for his swim trunks. They were tight, and he had to help pull them down. When they were off, she sat quietly and stared at his proud erection. She had seen naked men in her line of work, but this was the first aroused one she'd seen intent on her.

"Don't be afraid, touch me."

"I'm not afraid, Brandon, I'm speechless—you're so big."

He chuckled softly. "Haven't you heard size doesn't matter? Besides—a woman's body is very accommodating."

"Accommodating, huh? I bet you've done a lot of research."

"Now, Mira, I'm not one to kiss and tell."

She swallowed hard, then looked into those jade green eyes. Her curiosity took precedence over her nerves, strengthening her resolve. It would hurt, but this was Brandon. She wanted to be one body with him.

She reached out and ran her index finger down the length of his hard shaft, smiling when he jerked in response. Oh yeah, she liked that she could make him feel this way. He felt like satin over steel. Emboldened by his response, she ran her fingertip around the silky tip, watching as he strained toward her. His reaction filled her with excitement.

"Are you enjoying my body?" His voice was husky with feeling.

"Oh yes. Your body is perfection."

"Well it's starting to feel a little neglected."

She wanted to explore him, learn every detail, touch every sinew and kiss every pulse. His stomach muscles tightened when she ran her fingers lightly across and then upward to feel the hairs on his chest. There she found his nipple and felt it harden at her touch. Just like hers. She pushed him back and used her tongue to traverse a path from his navel upward. Her journey ended at his tightly budded nipple.

"Damn, that feels good. Are you sure you haven't

done this before?"

"Shh. I'm concentrating." She giggled. She nuzzled his nipple with her mouth and was as turned on as he at the feel of her tongue brushing him. She suckled him as he had with her. A growl rumbled from his throat and she was pulled up into a steamy kiss.

She pulled back and grasped him, her entire hand wrapping around his shaft. He was thick—and very hard. Slowly, she moved her hand up and down as she'd done with her body earlier. He became even harder.

****

Brandon was suffering a sweet death. But if a man had to die—his breath held as her fingers worked him—this was one hell of a way to go. Her expression was so intense, a tiny smile curving her lips. Her inexperienced exploration was sexy. She was playing with him and enjoying his reaction. Patience, he chided himself. He desperately wanted to slake his desire but held back, letting her enjoy her playful exploration of his body. Later would be his turn—right now belonged to her.

She bent down and flicked her tongue over the head of his sex.

He nearly blew a fuse and grabbed her hair, jerked her upward, crushing her breasts against his chest. "Enough," he panted. "You're a fast learner. A few more minutes and you'll still be a virgin tomorrow." He caressed her cheek with the back of his hand then trapped her mouth with his own. Need for her body, burned in him like jet fuel. She was so soft—so right for him. He kissed her eyes, tongued her ear, and then slid his mouth down to feast on her breasts.

135

She arched toward him as he suckled her. Her fingers dug into his hair and he was pulled tightly against her breast. She held him there. *Sweet Jesus*, she was the most sensuous woman he'd ever known. Her body was made for loving and responded to his slightest touch.

He couldn't wait much longer. Her gleeful exploration was about to break his control. He rolled her onto her back, his knees gently spreading her legs. Bending his head, he took her lips softly, reassuringly. *Honey—so sweet.* Her tongue met his in a sensuous dance as he deepened the kiss. Downward, across her silky skin and rounded hips, his fingers traced a path to her mound of blonde curls. Her body arched against his hand when he teased her with a finger and then slid inside her wet velvety folds.

"Brandon…" Her breathy voice breathed his name as her body twisted in pleasure.

"Mira, look at me."

Her passion glazed eyes gazed up at him and with one strong thrust, he joined them. His mouth covered hers, swallowing her cry. He paused, allowing her body time to grow accustomed to him. When her muscles relaxed, he moved again. Such sweet agony. Her body was like a slick vise around him. He had to hold on; he wanted her with him when he came.

She began to move with him—tentatively at first, then more frenzied. Soft moans accompanied the movement of her hands up and down his back, caressing one moment, leaving claw marks the next, as tension built between them.

"Come with me," he whispered encouragement.

Her body tensed, clamped around him as a moan of

pleasure escaped her lips along with his name.

"Oh, Brandon..."

He thrust deeply one last time, cried out her name, and emptied himself into her moist depths. "Mira." His body shuddered in ecstasy.

Braced on his arms, he leaned down and kissed her with more tenderness than he'd ever shown anyone. With their bodies still connected, he smiled down into her eyes. "Thank you, for such a beautiful gift."

"No. *Thank you,* the pleasure was all mine."

"It's debatable, but the hour isn't. We need to sleep. Dawn will come soon."

"Did you have to remind me? Where's the blanket?" They shifted on the small mattress until she was spooned against his chest, his arms wrapped tightly around her.

"Are you okay? Did I hurt you?"

"If only all pain was as sweet, life would be blissful," she murmured softly.

He savored the touch of her skin against his own.

"Brandon?"

"Hmm?" he answered tiredly.

"I love you," she whispered and turned over to go to sleep.

"You love me?"

He lay against her back not ready to face her after those words. "Mira, *I* don't need pretty words or promises, *do you?*" A trickle of fear slid down his back. He'd made love to her with all his emotions flying free. His feelings for her were so different from anything he'd ever felt, and quite frankly it scared him to death.

"No, I don't need a declaration of undying love from you just because we made love. I'm simply telling you what I feel. If it bothers you, I'm sorry, but I've never been one to back down from the truth." She ran her hand along his arm wrapped around her middle. "I know we've only known each other a short time, and under very dangerous circumstances. You were doing your duty when you rescued me, but tonight—you didn't have to do that. You didn't have to show me how beautiful it can be between two people."

He ran his thumb down her cheek, pausing to softly rub the outline of her lips. She was so beautiful—not just physically. She had a beautiful soul.

"What happened between us wasn't typical. Very few men ever get a chance to make love to a woman as responsive and delightful as you. You were born for loving. I've made love to many women before, but I've never *been* in love. What I feel for you is special and tonight only allowed me to show you how I feel. I'm not very good with words—"

"Don't—leave it," she interrupted him. "I only wanted you to know how I feel." She pulled away from him, got up, and pulled on clothes from the pile on the floor. "I'm going to check on Ana before I go to sleep. Don't trip me when I come back in."

"Wait, I'll go with you and check out the place before we settle down." He pulled his pants and shirt on and caught up to her. He grabbed her, held her with arms like a vise.

The kiss wasn't gentle. His lips ground against hers, his tongue forced her lips apart in an invasion, rather than conciliation. A touch of pique made him a little rough. "No woman leaves my bed without a kiss." He wrapped his arm around her waist and walked with her down the hall.

Chapter Nineteen

On the steps outside the kitchen, Father José scraped a match on the door frame, momentarily spotlighting his face in the dark night. He touched the flame to his cigarette before snuffing the match beneath his shoe. He did not often partake of the bad habit, but occasionally felt the need. He inhaled deeply and blew smoke out through his nose in a long exhale. The taste and smell of the American cigarette was something he savored, as many would a fine wine.

He took another long drag and turned at the sound of a footstep in the darkest part of the compound. "You may come out from the shadows, my friend. I know you are there."

The masculine voice came from the darkness. "You're developing good ears, Father. Not many would've known I was there."

"It wasn't sound, amigo, but your smell. I fear you have been too long without a bath. Come, Rafàel, join me for a quiet smoke."

"Where are the others?" The younger man moved cautiously into the small circle of light by the door.

"They have all gone to sleep. We are quite alone."

Rafà moved to sit on the steps beside him.

Indeed—he did look in need of a bath. Dirt covered his face, and his hair fell in a scraggly mess nearly to his shoulders. He looked like any other soldier about the area, conspicuously armed and disreputable enough to discourage even the most curious citizens.

He held out the pack, raising an eyebrow when Rafà shook his head. "Don't tell me you quit. Where will I get my American cigarettes if not from you?"

"Don't worry, I won't make you suffer. I just don't want one right now."

A few moments of silence passed between them as both sat lost in thought.

"How are they?" Rafà asked quietly, hesitantly. "Is…is everyone all right?"

"You mean, is *he* all right, do you not, my friend?" He stabbed his scruffy companion with a penetrating look.

"Well, is he?"

"Señor Brandon is alive and well. He brought Dr. Phelps here and helped to save Señora Ana's life. I find him to be a most agreeable chap."

A smothered guffaw spewed from Rafà. "If he's *agreeable*, then you better watch out. That's when he's liable to sneak up behind you and cut your throat."

"I thought he was your friend. Surely, you must have high esteem for him to risk so much?"

"Sorry, Father. What I'm trying to say is, Brandon can be very dangerous. He is my friend, but I still don't know if I can trust him."

Father José turned a serious eye on his friend. "Should you not speak to him and clear this matter up?"

"I will, when the time is right. How 'bout I stand guard and you scout out some coffee and pie?"

"Rafàel, it is always best to speak while there is time. Who knows what will happen tomorrow?" He tossed his cigarette butt to the ground and moved toward the door. "Think on it, amigo." He went inside, closing the door quietly behind him.

****

Rafà *had* thought about it. In his heart, he knew Brandon hadn't pushed him from the helicopter. They'd had to leave him behind to save the ambassador. The knowledge didn't make him feel any better. Why hadn't Brandon come back sooner? He'd survived two long months stranded in the jungle. He'd dodged bullets and rebels, hid in the worst kinds of places and scrounged for morsels of food. He wasn't complaining. He'd been trained to do those things. He just wanted the truth about what had gone wrong.

Luckily, his parentage allowed him to blend with the locals. As long as he was careful, he could come and go in the small towns without much risk. That had been how he'd met Father José. The first time he'd shown up in the village, he had been scrawny. The priest had befriended him and made sure he had food to eat though he turned down the offer of a place to stay. His trust of anyone only went so far. So, he came and went as he pleased, always staying in touch with Father José. Through him he'd learned of the doctor's abduction.

He smiled as he thought of the doctor. If they were together, Brandon had met his match. The good doctor was outspoken and independent—just the type to stir his friend's dander. He'd met her once when she'd cleaned an infected wound for him. She hadn't known who or what he was, but she'd patched him up and treated him kindly. They'd spoken only in Spanish, so she couldn't possibly guess his identity. He was glad Brandon had saved her, but why come back here?

Surely, they knew it wasn't safe.

"Damn it to hell, Brandon, why are you taking so many risks?" He muttered under his breath as Father José opened the door and handed him a mug of coffee along with a huge wedge of pie.

"So, what do you plan to do? Are you going to speak to him?"

"Right now, I'm going to enjoy this pie and coffee. Afterward, I'm going to search the area and make sure things are safe, then—I'll think about it."

"How have things been with you? It has been some time since you visited."

"I've had to do a lot of running lately." He paused for a bite of pie and a slurp of coffee. "The area is crawling with rebels."

"I should have been here," Father José muttered. "I might not have been able to stop them, but—"

"They'd have killed you. The men who took Dr. Phelps aren't your local rebels. They're mercs, paid killers on a mission. I haven't figured out their mission yet so be careful, they might return."

Father José placed his empty cup on the step and released a heavy sigh. "If they discover the doctor is back, you can count on it. They've probably put a price on your friend's head."

He laughed. "It's not the first bounty on his head, and it probably won't be the last."

"Rafàel—I hope you will make the right choice. You are both good men and true friendships are hard to come by.

"I know." He fell silent.

"I think Señor Brandon has met his equal in our Dr. Phelps—sparks fly when they talk."

Both men laughed.

Rafà finished his last bite of pie and placed the empty plate and cup on the step. "I'm sure he finds it a welcome change from dodging bullets."

"Well, my friend, I must go and relieve Rosita. Promise me you will think about what I said."

"I promise."

The priest picked up the empty cups and plates, turned to him and nodded. "Good night, my friend. Stay safe."

Rafà pushed off the steps and disappeared into the shadows.

****

Mira entered the ward where Ana slept. She ran a critical eye over her patient, quickly felt her pulse and forehead, then lifted the sheet to check the incision. Good, everything looked great. Her hand gently smoothed the hair back away from the woman's forehead.

"You've had a pretty rough time. I can't promise miracles, but I think you'll be up and around in a couple of days. Your daughter looks just like you." Her soft words were meant to sooth both her patient and herself.

Rosita kept vigil in a straight-backed chair near the bed. Her nimble fingers busily crocheted a colorful scarf. "You have already given her a miracle. If not for you, her beautiful child would have only her grandparents. It's so sad she has lost her man. Too many of our women have lost their husbands, sons and dignity."

Mira had never fully understood the politics of the region. "Why did they take her husband?"

Rosita's fingers stilled, and she took a moment

before answering. "Many are taken to fight. Others are taken as hostages to control people in the government. Some are used as slaves to work the mines." She crossed herself and bent back to her scarf.

"Take a break," Mira offered. "I'll sit with her for a few minutes. She should be waking soon. When I leave, give her only ice chips and keep her on the IV for the next twenty-four hours."

Rosita wrung her hands as she stood. "What will happen to you? Where will you go?"

"I don't know. Regardless, you can't let anyone know I came back. They'll torture you for information. You were lucky to get away from the clinic the first time. I couldn't bear it if something happened to you because of me."

"I understand. Please be careful." As Rosita headed toward the kitchen, she turned back. "These people get joy from killing."

Mira sat beside the bed and leaned her head back against the wall. Where *would* she go—and how could she get the journals back? The people who had them wanted her dead. How would she stay alive while she did it? It all came back to one person. Brandon. She needed to convince him to help get the journals back.

Chapter Twenty

Nerves on high alert, Brandon moved silently through the halls, checking doors and windows. In the jungle he had an advantage, run or hide—his choice. Stealth was his friend when securing a rescued hostage. Yet, here they were in the very building where the kidnapping occurred. They might as well paint a target on their backs and stand in an open field. No matter what arguments Mira presented, they were out of here at first light. She was a dedicated doctor and would fight to stay near Ana the next few days.

He entered the kitchen just as Father José placed several cups and plates into the sink.

"Midnight snack, Padre?" he asked absently, barely paying attention to the man as he double-checked the back door.

"Just making sure I stay awake." Father José ran water in the sink and rinsed the dishes. "Couldn't you sleep? Don't tell me a soft mattress instead of the hard ground is troubling you."

"Many things bother me, but the sleeping accommodations aren't high on the list. We both know there are things to discuss. Don't take me for a fool and I will return the favor." He heard the hard edge in his own voice and tried to relax the tight coiling of his muscles.

"I doubt anyone would ever take you for a fool,

Senor Falcon. If they did, they are most likely dead and not around to tell about it."

"I'm shocked. Your opinion of me is so low."

"On the contrary, my opinion of you is very high. Predators have their place in nature, and you are at the top of the food chain."

Brandon looked at the priest, *really looked* at his demeanor, his eyes, and recognized a fellow soldier.

"I think, Padre, you are a man with secrets, not necessarily all good."

"We all have secrets. Things we would like to forget; things we must do for the higher good."

"I'm not concerned with the higher good at the moment. I need to know more about the rebels and why they took Dr. Phelps. How did they know she wasn't a nun, and why did they care? She's not exactly a public menace, and she certainly couldn't harm any of them." His gaze remained focused on the man's face as he spouted questions.

"Please, sit down." Father José invited as he crossed to the table and sat. "You must understand my awkward position. I am accepted here because of my position as a priest. The clinic is my responsibility and the employees are local. We have a visiting doctor who comes once a month, while the nurses and I do what we can the rest of the time."

"I'm listening," Brandon said when the priest paused. "Cut to the chase."

"When I received a letter from Dr. Phelps, offering to help out, I was delighted. After the *coup*, I was afraid she would not come. Imagine my surprise when she showed up and had a letter from the sisters saying she was one of them."

Brandon jerked out a chair, plopped it down with anger as he faced the priest. "Did you know she wasn't a nun? Did you rat her out?" Anger burned his stomach. How could this man, who was supposed to help people, turn on someone like Mira?

"No...It is not like you think. I had my suspicions but kept them to myself."

Relentless, he continued the interrogation. "Then how did they know?"

A look of resignation passed over Father José's face. He looked uncomfortable, obviously distressed. He sighed, reached into his pocket, and pulled out an envelope.

"I received this letter two weeks ago from the Sisters of Mercy in Chapel Hill."

Brandon grabbed the letter and read.

Dear Father José,

I fear I have a confession to make. Please understand, I meant only to help.

The sisters and I felt Dr. Phelps would have more protection if she was one of us. So—we gave her the proper credentials and sent her to help you. She is most anxious to be there and is an excellent doctor.

Please forgive our deception and please watch out for Sister Mira.

Yours in Christ,
Mother Angelica

"So, you did know."

"Only these last two weeks. The problem is—the letter arrived opened. Someone read it before I got it."

"Who?" Brandon demanded, putting an edge of cold steel in his voice.

"I can't say for sure. You must understand, Señor

147

Falcon, I don't want to accuse anyone unjustly."

"We'll decide on justice later, just spit it out. You have a good idea so level with me. My life and Mira's could depend on it."

Tension, thick as the steamy air, hung between the two men. Several moments passed as he kept the priest pinned with a flinty gaze.

"Once a week I have someone go into the city to run errands and pick up the mail. She had access to the letter before I received it."

"Who?" A nerve in his cheek twitched, and his mouth tightened.

The priest looked down at his folded hands and spoke softly, "Jacinta."

"Damn it." Brandon speared him with a look that would have had his men cringing. They'd have found a hiding place or made themselves invisible, if possible. His entire body tensed as he clenched his fists. "Mira has berated herself with remorse and guilt—and the entire time *her nurse* is the one who helped her kidnappers?"

He saw red. He had killed men over less. In his eyes, the woman who had sold out Mira deserved the same. For a moment he allowed his face to show his feelings—a rare occurrence. Rage, raw anger, and murderous intent passed through his mind as he thought of the nurse's betrayal. He felt like an animal defending his mate, a man ready to kill.

"Señor Falcon, I cannot be certain she did anything wrong. Please think before you act. Do not do something you might regret."

"Regret? I regret few things, Father. Killing a traitor would not be one of them. Believe me—if Mira comes to more harm, that *traitorous bitch* will welcome death."

He stood abruptly and paced the room like a caged lion. Suddenly—as if a veil had lifted, comprehension hit. He swung around and slammed his palm on the table. "*You're* the one who contacted Washington." Brandon wasn't asking, he knew. "You informed them Mira had been kidnapped, but why? She isn't the first American medic to go missing. Washington isn't in the habit of rescuing fools who go willingly into hostile situations like this. Why is she so important the Department of Defense took a call from a lowly priest in the middle of nowhere and sent me to rescue her?" Brandon caught himself. He hadn't intended to do his thinking out loud.

The priest looked down at his hands. "I cannot answer your questions."

His voice dropped to a dangerous level. "Can't or won't?"

He knew when someone was hiding the truth. The man wasn't lying to him—exactly, but he was dancing a fancy two-step around the truth. Whether some church rule or for his own self-preservation, the padre wasn't telling him everything.

He didn't push. In a pinch, he figured the priest could be counted on to help. He didn't want to delve too deeply into the why or how. A tiny bit of information to file away until the right time. Another thought popped into his head. Just for the hell of it, he cocked his head and asked, "Do you know a man named Max Sanderson?"

Father José blanched and looked away.

"I understand a whole lot more now." Brandon's

mind spun with possibilities. If Mira was indeed related to Max Sanderson, one of the CIA's best European operatives, all kinds of shit would likely hit the fan.

He paused in the doorway and watched as she slept in the chair. Her head lolled to the side and her torso slumped down, making her look young and even smaller. His gaze roamed over the mass of curls which defied taming—just like her. She was wild and alluring, like those spiky strands. He ached to make love to her again. Once had not been enough, and a thousand times wouldn't quench his lust for her. Need clawed at him as he walked over and lifted her into his arms.

She startled, then nestled against him, as if her body recognized his touch. As he brushed a kiss across her forehead, he entered her room, and placed her in her own bed. He longed to sleep beside her—to hold her soft body for the last few hours of the night, but no, if he held her, he would take her—and they both needed to sleep.

He pulled his mattress in front of the door, curled on his side and tried to sleep. Her scent rose from the blanket, the same blanket which had covered those beautiful curves and witnessed their blissful joining. A sigh escaped him, as he pushed his gun under the pillow and inhaled her essence. Thoughts of her naughty innuendos about his weapon teased a small curl to his lips as he closed his eyes.

Chapter Twenty-One

The mouthwatering smell of frying bacon and fresh perked coffee, teased Brandon's senses awake. He'd slept soundly. His body had needed the rest and his mind—well his mind never totally rested. A quick look toward the bed assured him Mira slept soundly. Quietly, he gathered his things and followed the aromas down the hall.

A young girl of about thirteen, stood at the stove, turning the bacon and stirring a pot of something that looked like oatmeal. As he entered, she flashed him a shy smile, then lowered her eyes. She poured a steaming mug of coffee and placed it on the table. "Sit, Señor." She indicated the chair and turned to her cooking.

"Something sure smells good." He pulled out a chair and savored the first sip of a really great cup of coffee. "What's your name?"

"I am called Concepción. I cook for Father José and the patients at the clinic. He wishes you to come see him at the church after breakfast." She shot another quick glance at him before turning to the stove. She filled a bowl and plate then placed each before him.

After swirling what Concepción told him was local honey over the oatmeal, he chowed down. The bacon crunched as he savored the most heavenly taste he'd had in quite a long time.

No, he'd tasted Mira. The essence of her sweetness lingered on his taste buds like a fine Kona blend brewed with spring water. Smooth and aromatic with a strong jolt. Erotic images of her clinging to him, calling his name, drifted through his mind, and his groin tightened. He stifled an impulse to rush back to her bed and devour her instead of breakfast.

Just then, she sashayed into the kitchen, a gentle sway to her hips as she approached him, looking good enough to eat.

****

Mira's breath tightened at the dark, hungry look in his eyes. Her gaze flitted to his throat as he visibly forced down the last bite. Her eyes riveted on a tiny crumb at the side of his lip. Unconsciously, she flicked the edge of her tongue to the side of her own lips, wanting to bend down and take the crumb with her mouth and savor the taste of coffee and bacon on his.

Her nipples budded tightly beneath her cotton shirt, and she felt heat flood her cheeks when his eyes darted to the level of her breasts. He'd noticed her reaction. Electricity filled the air, and she was surprised the table didn't ignite from the supercharged heat flowing between them.

Plunk! Startled, she was drawn back to reality as Concepción set a second cup of coffee on the table. "Thank you," she said absently and sat across from Brandon. She ran the tips of her fingers around the rim of her cup. Aware of the alert ears of their adolescent audience, she ate and drank quietly. She dared not speak of the important things which begged to be discussed.

Brandon stood and downed the rest of his coffee.

"I'll walk around the village while you check on Ana. Why don't I meet you back here in an hour?"

"Sounds good." Though his words had been innocuous, she'd gotten the message. He was scouting the area and they would be leaving in an hour. She grabbed a few pieces of bacon and wrapped them in a tortilla. When the kitchen door slammed behind him, she was already half way down the hall.

She desperately needed to talk with him to discuss their plans. They'd enjoyed a few brief hours of feeling safe, but they were at risk here at the clinic. If they stayed, others like Ana were in danger, and that was intolerable. Still crunching bacon, she walked into her patient's room.

"Good morning," she greeted her patient who sat up supported by pillows. "You gave us quite a scare." Methodically, she checked Ana's vitals and wrote on her chart.

"Thank you, doctor. I don't remember much about your visit, but Father José told me how you and your friend brought me here for the surgery. When can I leave? I can't wait to get home to see my little one."

"You'll need to stay here a few more days. You have hepatitis in addition to the bad appendix we removed. Take your medications and get stronger before you go home. Father José has sent a message to your family and they know you are well."

She wanted to sit with her patient and put her more at ease but was conscious of the time. She had to gather her personal things and leave. "Your family was very kind to us when we needed help. Helping you was the least we could do to repay them. I'm sure they will be glad to have you back safe and sound."

Ana's fingers plucked at the sheet covering her frail body. Nervously, she said, "My husband, Miguel, was taken a few months ago. Things have been very hard for us without him. I wish..." She broke off, clearly overcome by emotion.

Mira rubbed her shoulder gently, trying to give some small measure of comfort. She couldn't offer any reassurances. The rebels were ruthless, and her husband had probably been tortured and most likely killed. "I don't know what has happened to your husband, but you've got to stay strong. Your daughter is going to need you."

When Rosita walked in, Mira stepped back from the bed. In hushed tones, she explained how to take care of the sick woman. She felt guilty for leaving her patient but was confident in Rosita's skills. She sent a smile of encouragement, then left to pack.

There wasn't much time and she'd have to carry everything on her back. She reached under the bed, elated when her hand grasped the old worn out medical bag. It had belonged to her father and was her most prized possession. Somehow, the rebels had missed it in their search of her belongings. If only she'd kept the journals there. Never mind, she'd just have to retrieve them somehow. She tossed a clean set of clothes into her backpack, topped by her photos. In the storage room, she filled her father's bag with medical supplies. The way Brandon went around shooting people, someone was bound to need medical attention. Of course, most people he shot didn't live long enough to need help. Why such a morbid thought should bring a smile to her lips was just a small sign of how her life had changed in the past few days.

****

Brandon viewed the clinic's perimeter with the eye of a warrior. His guard had been down too long. It was time to prepare for their escape to the Mosquito Coast. Caution guided his steps to the church for his meeting with the padre. No doubt the coming conversation would prove interesting, whether he would learn anything useful remained to be seen.

He wasn't about to disclose his plans. He trusted few people, and then only with certain information. Their escape route was not up for discussion. The church was a small adobe structure at the edge of the village and looked like an afterthought. It backed up to the forest, making it vulnerable from the rear, or—an excellent escape route if trapped. His mind registered this without conscious thought. It was a part of him, this constant surveillance of his surroundings. A SEAL always planned for escape.

Few people were about this early. Those he saw were purposeful in their activities, as they began the day's work. A couple passed him, leading a scrawny burro, sticks perched precariously on the animal's back. The woman lowered her eyes as she passed him, while the man nodded his head in acknowledgment. Neither, projected vibes of secrecy or danger.

He passed a small store with broken windows and crumbling walls. Times were hard for these people and most couldn't afford to buy from a store. Instead, they eked out a living as best they could from the land or bartered for supplies.

He pulled his Glock from his waistband and eased soundlessly through the side door of the church. In deference to his surroundings he kept it close to his tactical vest instead of out front leading the way. He'd been raised Catholic but hadn't kept to his religious roots as he bounded around the world. He'd like to think God was still on his side though and crossed himself and bowed slightly before the dimly lit altar. The scrape of a shoe on stone caused him to wheel, positioning his gun in a practiced move.

"Ah, Señor Falcon, you are prompt." Father José stared at the gun, quirking one brow as he rose from a wooden kneeler positioned in a small alcove in the wall. "Do you fear me, or your surroundings?"

"Neither, I'm just a cautious man. Now, why did you call me here?"

"Straight to the point, eh? One misses the pleasantries of times past in today's brash world. I brought you here to help you, of course."

At Brandon's raised brow, the priest smiled and motioned toward an open door leading into a small office. "Please, what I say is best said outside the sanctuary."

Brandon scanned the room with a sharp look and then sat on a chair, his back to the wall. "What do you have in mind?"

"I know a place where you might take Dr. Phelps to keep her safe, while you make your way to—eh, wherever you plan to go."

"Why are you suddenly interested in helping us?" he asked skeptically. "I thought you had to remain out of the politics of the area. Helping us would certainly put you right in the middle of a hornet's nest. Unless," he leaned forward, "you're working for someone other than God."

Father José stared directly into his questioning

gaze. "Sometimes God's work must be done by those not chosen for my path. Often, he uses those at hand to accomplish his miracles."

"Look, I'm not above helping those I can, but don't look to me to be some avenging angel or some such shit. Mira's safety is my first concern."

"Ah, but you have a second mission, do you not?"

He rose to full height, using his powerful stance to intimidate. "What the hell do you know about any of my missions?"

Far from intimidated, the other man smiled. "Let's just say…what you are looking for is near at hand."

Both men looked unflinchingly into the other's eyes, searching. Each took the measure of the other. When the silence became almost unbearable, Brandon broke it. "Who are you? You sure as hell don't act like any priest I've encountered."

"I am whomever I need to be to get God's work done. I have, let us say, unusual contacts. With my help you can keep Dr. Phelps safe and find what, or should I say whom you wish to find."

He had Brandon's full attention now. Who was this man who offered his help? Could he be trusted? Who was he working for and what did he know about Rafà? He quickly sifted through all the possibilities and made his decision. "Is he okay?" He had to know.

"Yes, but he is angry about being left behind."

"We didn't leave him by choice. I've been working the system for the last two months trying to come back and look for him. When the system didn't work—I changed the rules. Coming here could cost me my career and my freedom."

"So, why did you risk everything to come back if it

was so costly?" Father José probed.

"I suppose," Brandon paused, "I valued my soul and his friendship more than my freedom and career."

"Ah, I believe you to be an honorable man, Señor Falcon. I pray all will work out for you."

Brandon didn't like spilling his guts to anyone— least of all some priest who didn't act like a priest. He'd exposed himself to this stranger enough, time to get back to the purpose of his visit. "All right, Padre. What's this going to cost me?"

"I need you to do a little job for me."

He studied the other man, looking for clues to the truth. "Go on."

"Tonight, men from the rebel camp will come into town for tomorrow's celebration, a local festival. Few guards will remain at the camp. I need you to see if Ana's husband, Miguel, is there. If he is, help him escape. In return, I will provide a safe place for you and Dr. Phelps, all your supplies and put you in contact with the one you seek."

"That's all? I thought it was going to be something difficult." Sarcasm dripped from his words. "Are you sure you don't want me to wipe out the entire camp while I'm at it?"

Father José waited while he said his piece, then, quietly asked, "Well, are you in or not?"

Thoughts spiraled through his head as he assessed the information he'd just been given. Rafà was alive and this man knew how to contact him. Thank, God. He hadn't realized until now, he'd more than accepted the idea that his friend was dead.

Now, his job was ten times easier. He had a safe place to keep Mira while waiting for the rendezvous at the Mosquito Coast. He'd take her to the safe place, meet Rafà, and then get the hell out of here. "Remind me never to play poker with you, Padre. Yeah, I'm in, but this place better be secure, because I'm not leaving her alone with anyone but me."

"Good," the priest said with a brief nod. "Let's get down to the details before Dr. Phelps comes looking for you, shall we?"

Brandon nodded, wondering why the back of his neck still tingled.

Chapter Twenty-Two

Brandon entered the back door, the edginess hard to shake as he placed his pack on the floor. All softness he'd shown last night had been buried beneath his cold warrior persona—steel edged and cold eyed. He had changed from passionate lover to deadly protector, like a chameleon.

Mira raised her head and met his eyes.

He stood before her unashamedly—all soldier, covered in weapons and ready to take on the most dangerous enemy. Her gaze touched each deadly weapon and then moved back to his face. This woman had seen him naked with all his scars, physical and mental—at his most vulnerable. She accepted him for what he was, and still she loved him. Love glowed in her eyes as she silently approached. What had he ever done to deserve this angel before him? Granted she had a sharp tongue—but her tongue had been oh-so-soft and gentle as it played across his body last night. His heart rate galloped when she leaned into him and placed her lips against his.

"I've waited all morning for this." She pulled his arm and tried to get him to sit at the table. "While I have your full attention, I need to talk to you about a few things."

His lips softened—his only concession to her sensual kiss. Those same lips hardened as he swung her around to stand before him. "I would like nothing more than to sit and talk. Hell, I'd like to drag you back to bed—but we must leave immediately. Tomorrow is a festival; the rebels will come into the village to start celebrating today."

She tucked the last of the protein bars in her backpack and closed the top. "Damn, I'd forgotten about the festival. This place will be crawling with people."

"Is this all your stuff?" He picked up the medical bag. "Let's get going. We'll have plenty of time to talk after we get out of here."

Mira shrugged the small pack onto her back and then relieved him of the medical bag. "I'll carry my things. You need to keep your hands free."

He gave her a quick peck on the cheek and headed for the door. "You're starting to sound like a SEAL." He chuckled but allowed her to take the bag.

Moments later, he looked up at the sun, then flipped open the cover on his watch. He pressed a button and instantly a GPS reading appeared on the screen. He rechecked the sun's position and slipped into the forest behind the clinic. By his calculations, they had a three hour walk before reaching the coordinates the priest gave him.

He hoped they weren't walking into a trap, but short of hiking circles through the jungle, he had no safe place to hide Mira until the pickup time. Besides, if Rafà had trusted the priest enough to discuss the mission, he figured he could trust him, too. Then again, he'd feel better once he knew more about Mira's connection to Max Sanderson. He had to broach the subject, soon.

****

Without questions, Mira followed him through the jungle. After the tension at the clinic, the forest sounds were reassuring. Brandon needed to be alert, so she turned her thoughts inward. Everyone near her was in danger as long as the rebels were looking for her. But why did they still want her? She wasn't into politics or in possession of state secrets.

The only things she considered valuable were the journals and they already had those. Why would they want them anyway? Uncle Max had left them to her because of her interest in medicinal botany. Surely, the rebels had no need for such knowledge. Perhaps they thought she would come after them. Was that it? Were they baiting her in hopes of capturing her?

"Can we stop for a moment and drink some water? I've gotten lazy without my daily jungle stroll."

He turned, giving her a searching look. "You're keeping pace with a Navy SEAL, carrying two bags and dodging vines and limbs as you go. Don't sell yourself short." He looked around, then pointed to the right. "Let's move under that large tree for more cover."

She found a relatively clear rock, eased the pack to the ground and sat. "Thanks." She took the canteen and sipped at the tepid water. "Where are we going?"

"Father José told me about an abandoned mine a few miles from here. There's an open area in the side where we should be able to stay out of the rain and out of sight."

"Yes, I've heard of it, such a tragedy." She took another sip and handed him the canteen.

"The villagers believe it's haunted by the men killed there when the mine collapsed."

He took a sip of water from the canteen and cast a look of concern her way. "You're not afraid of ghosts, are you?"

"I certainly believe in spirits, but it's not dead men I fear. They can't hurt me. It's those who are alive who inflict pain."

He reached out and smoothed the skin on her wrist. "No man will ever hurt you again. I give you my word."

The silence between them was shattered by a howler monkey's resounding call. He put the canteen away and helped her stand. "Time to go." He repositioned his bag and started out.

"Aye, aye sir." She gave him a mock salute before following his lead.

The jungle gave way to stubby brush and the occasional tree. They had reached the mine site. Much of the area had been cleared with bull dozers, and piles of rubble littered the landscape. Once abandoned, the area had grown over with weeds and vines. Small forest trees had sprouted from the rubble and quickly grown straight upward to beat others, competing for light.

Rusted mining equipment lay overturned amid the debris. Broken support timbers and rotting lumber lay piled near the caved-in opening. The perfect home for spiders, snakes, and all kinds of vermin. Water trickled from a spring above the mine, providing the only softening touch to the harsh visage before them. Brandon motioned for her to stay, raised his rifle and checked behind machinery. He continued through the area, disappearing through an opening in the side of the mine.

She sank to her knees and waited. She hated it

when he left her behind. She felt so alone, exposed and vulnerable without him. What would happen if someone came while he was inside? Her gaze darted around as her body tensed. Thunder rumbled announcing the impending rain. The first fat drops landed on her skin as his head emerged from the opening, followed by his motion for her to come.

"Welcome to our temporary home." He took her hand and guided her over several obstacles in their path. "I'd like to leave everything untouched out here, including the spider webs, so it looks like no one has been here."

Once, this had been the mine's office. Broken in several places, the floor beckoned careless feet. What furniture survived was covered in dust and rocks. An old metal file cabinet listed toward the wall, its papers strewn across the floor. The mine workers abandoned everything after the cave-in.

He clicked on his flashlight and led the way to what might have served as a large storage room. Behind the solid door, everything was intact. The modest room had been cleared and a single cot sat in the corner. Two overturned crates served as chairs and were positioned next to a sloping table.

A lantern, complete with fuel, rested on the table. Brandon lit it and held it up to view the room. The flickering light cast eerie shadows on the wall but showed the room's tidiness. Even the cot looked fresh. A small cupboard, upon inspection, contained a gas hot plate, a cylinder of gas, and several bottles of water. Tinned food, metal plates, cookware and utensils filled the other shelf.

He whistled through his teeth. "I think Father José

has used this place before. I wonder who else he's hidden here."

Fatigue weighed her steps as she removed her pack. Neither of them had gotten much sleep. The cot looked inviting.

"Could you make us a snack while I secure the perimeter?" he asked. "After we eat, we can have our little talk."

"You and your booby traps." She made a face but was happy for his protective instincts. Rummaging through the cabinet for materials, she set about making a meal. There was no natural light and the solitary lamp cast dark shadows about the tiny room. She felt caged. Thunderous rain pounded the outer room changing her thoughts about their shelter. Now, instead of trapped she felt cozy.

Brandon returned, water dripping from his spikey hair. As he turned to slam the sliding lock, he paused, a strange look on his face.

"What's wrong?"

"The lock is on the inside of the room."

"So, what's the problem?"

"This room was used to store dynamite and other valuable supplies. The lock would need to be on the outside. Who'd want to lock themselves inside a store room with no means of escape? I know I wouldn't." He moved to the table. "I'll have to check on escape routes after we eat."

"Dinner is served."

They pulled out the crates and sat to enjoy their meal. For the moment the matter of the lock was forgotten as they ate hungrily.

Chapter Twenty-Three

Silence reigned during the meal. Images of last night's lovemaking danced through her mind as she savored the simple lunch of tinned chicken and peaches. She shot a quick look at him from beneath her lashes. What was going on behind those green eyes? He looked the same, yet different. No, maybe she was different.

She was hopelessly in love with him.

It sounded so simple when she thought of it that way, but nothing was ever simple. He didn't love her in return. He cared—and lord knows he wanted—but love? She had very little experience with love or men, having lived a very solitary life. Few of her friends had experienced it. At least not the happy ever after kind of love she wanted. They were more apt to 'hook up' than fall in love.

"About last night," he spoke the same words just as she did.

She broke into a nervous giggle as his face blossomed into a huge grin.

"I suppose we know where our minds have been." He reached across and effectively stopped her nervous fingers from shredding her nails. "Stop." He enveloped her hand with his big paw. "Last night was one of the most beautiful experiences I've had in my life."

Her startled gaze flew to his face.

"What? Don't you believe men are capable of having sensitive feelings?"

"I don't know much about men or love. I know how I feel, but I don't want you to feel obligated to express similar declarations."

"Feelings scare most men. Give us something to blow up or shoot and we'll be just fine, but love? Emotions? We usually run the other way." He leaned forward, his expression serious. "I'm not running. I can't explain how I feel in the pretty words women want to hear, but I *can* say right now, you are my life. You matter more than living."

"See—you *can* say the words. I don't want to disappoint you with my inexperience. I want to…"

"Practice?" Laughter laced his question. "Believe me, you're already good, but—I'm willing to put in some extra practice time—just to help out."

"Such a sacrifice. I'd hate to be a burden." She turned away from him, intent on escape.

Strong arms swung her up into a tight embrace. His mouth crushed hers in a kiss which should have hurt, but only made her body want more. She turned and straddled him, returning kiss for kiss. Her breath hitched when she felt his taut muscles flex beneath her exploring touch.

His lips left hers, finding her earlobe. His hot tongue laved her outer ear, then delved inward. Reality slipped away at the warm, moist invasion. "Please," she begged.

"Hold on, we have a long way to go." His whisper sent a warm breath across the wetness of her ear, shooting another shaft of delight to her core.

He took his time, kissing and nipping his way

down her neck, paying special attention to the throbbing pulse at the base of her throat. In a swift move he stood and laid her across the table. Her arms flung outward and her legs spread invitingly. Her brain felt a moment's trepidation at her total vulnerability. Her body, on the other hand, ached to show him more.

"God, you're beautiful," he rasped. Reaching for the buttons of her blouse, he unbuttoned each one slowly—teasingly. His gaze never left hers.

A spark of wanton pride flared as she watched the flame ignite in those green orbs.

He tugged off her shirt and threw it carelessly to the floor. His breath sucked in.

She reveled in the sound. Her nipples pushed against the lace fabric of her bra, desperate to feel his mouth. Her body became molten as she gazed up at him. "Brandon, love me please…"

"Believe me, I will." He growled the words and then pulled her body toward him, pushing her center tightly against his hardness.

His body grew harder against hers and when he lowered his hot mouth over her lace covered nipple, she moaned her pleasure.

He blew on the wet cloth covering her hardened nipple. "Do you like that, sweetheart?"

"Oh yes. Again."

He slid his tongue along the edge of the lace, teasing one hard nipple before moving to the next. Deftly he unhooked the front clasp of her bra, exposing her breasts. Her chest strained upward, seeking. He licked circles around her engorged nipples. The feel of his warm tongue against her bare skin was magical. He stood and removed the rest of her clothes, tossing them to join her blouse on the floor.

"Look at me." His voice both commanded and teased. "It's time for a new lesson."

Her startled gaze flew to his when he lifted her feet and placed them on the table.

"Brandon?" Her voice held a small note of fear.

"Shh," he whispered. "Trust me, we're both going to enjoy this."

She gazed up through heavy, passion filled eyes into a fiery storm. The way he looked at her, she felt *beautiful*. She reached for him—had to touch him.

His hands caught hers, pushed them above her head and held them. Moving back to her breast, he suckled. Unable to move, she surrendered herself to his passion. A moan ripped from her throat. She thrust her hips, her body on fire, searching for release.

Ripples of pleasure moved across her stomach as his warm breath teased her skin in a feathery touch. Kissing a path downward, he nipped tiny bites on the insides of her thighs. Her muscles tensed in anticipation of his next move. He fingered her curls, parted her inner lips and touched her bud. Her body arched off the table. When his mouth settled on her soft inner flesh, she cried out in surprised pleasure.

Threading her fingers tightly in his hair, she tried to stop his sensuous assault. "I can't stand it. Take me," she begged in a husky whimper. "I can't stand much more."

He tongued her sensitive bud, suckled her as he'd done with her breast.

She writhed, her mind in another world—so attuned to his touches, she forgot all else. Her world became one of sensation—pure, sensual, pleasure.

Could one die of pleasure? The thought was fleeting, blotted out by more sensation. Her muscles tensed, tightening her body like a bow. Hot all over, her world momentarily stilled, then her dam burst. Waves of sensation centered in her bud, flowed like hot—molten—lava over her body. Tears of happiness trickled down her cheeks as pleasure rippled through her womb.

****

Brandon ripped his pants down and entered her in one quick thrust. Ripples of her orgasm surrounded him. He pumped her hard against the table, feeling the exact moment she became aware of his pounding into her flesh. Rather than fear, her face lit with excitement. She met his thrusts, pushing back. The table bounced on the uneven floor. She reached down between them, encircling him with her fingers, adding pressure.

He cupped her buttocks, pulled her tighter against him and continued to thrust within her. He uttered a harsh growl and plummeted over the edge. She tensed and cried out as her muscles gripped him, milking him of his seed. *Mine. My woman.*

He lay heavily against her body, reveling in the feel of her nakedness against him. He wished he'd taken the time to rid himself of his own shirt, to better feel her sweet wet skin against his own. He rose up on his elbows to look at her, and the earth moved—no—the table...*Kablam!*

He grabbed Mira protectively in his arms and clung to her as the table crashed beneath them. Hell, he should've known the sorry excuse for a table wouldn't hold them. If he'd hurt her with his stupidity—Squeals, followed by a chorus of giggles, echoed off his chest as he lay covering her face.

The absurdity of the situation hit him, and he let loose a deep belly laugh. "You okay?" He shifted to check her body for damage.

"I would be if I didn't have a GI Joe Gorilla squashing me." She pushed at his chest to move him.

He wrapped her with his legs and arms and executed a perfect roll, landing clear of the table, with her lying on top. He grinned up at her. "How's that?"

Chapter Twenty-Four

She whistled between her teeth. The big-headed devil had managed the entire move while keeping their bodies joined. "That's a smooth move, sailor. Do the SEALs teach this to all their trainees, or is it something you invented on your own?"

"I must admit we teach it to all, but for use in quite different circumstances."

"I should hope so. Was my lesson about gravity?"

"Something like that. What are we going to tell Father José about his table?" He rolled to his side and turned to fasten his pants. "We better come up with a good cover story."

As his body separated from hers, insecurity sprang into her heart. In moments of intimacy with him her confidence soared. When he moved away, doubts crept in. She picked up her clothes and began to dress.

He gathered the remains of their meal and pieces of table from the floor. "The rain has stopped. Do you want to make a quick trip outside?"

She grasped the opportunity for a bit of fresh air. The room wasn't hot, because of the surrounding cave, but it was closing in on her. She followed him to the side entrance and paused when he turned back to her. "Stay to the edges where there is grass and rocks and try not to leave any foot prints. You should be fine by those old trucks." He pointed to rusted-out hulks that looked like giant toys left outside after baby dinosaurs played.

She was grateful for his understanding her need for privacy. Following his directions, she jumped from grass to rocks, then ducked behind the dump truck. After a quick check for all manner of vermin, she did her business quickly, then looked around.

The thought of returning to the tiny room wasn't a welcome one, so she dawdled, putting the moment off as long as possible. There was no sight or sound from Brandon, though it didn't surprise her, he moved like a ghost. *That* thought made her pause. The mine had ghosts, according to the locals. Her skin prickled as a shiver passed over her. Hopefully they were friendly. Attracted by the sound of running water, she moved to the rocky embankment. After the rain, steam rose from the metal of the old mining equipment. She pulled a handkerchief from her pocket, wet it in the running water, and wiped her face and neck. The hair on the back of her neck stood up in silent alarm.

Someone was watching her.

She felt eyes boring into her from the jungle. Acting naturally, she turned and searched the bushes and trees. Nothing. Fear stabbed along her spine. Brandon was near and would keep her safe. She opened her mouth to call and remembered another such time in the jungle. Loath to make the same mistake twice, she backed up against the embankment, feeling somewhat safer with her back protected. She pushed into the dirt, trying to become part of the hill. Small pebbles from several feet above her head loosened and fell onto her shoulders.

****

Unease crawling up his back, Brandon stilled. Instinct told him the someone out there watching, wasn't a threat, only a presence. This place was getting to him, or maybe the legend of ghosts was true. He moved to where she had gone behind the truck and saw her hunkered against the embankment, apprehension in her stance. Instinctively he crouched and drew his gun, his gaze darting everywhere, looking for the enemy. Had she felt it, too?

Her eyes met his, and then she disappeared.

"What the hell?" He took off at a run. "Mira? Where the hell are you?" He pounded the embankment, searching for her. In the mud he found clear imprints of her boots and what looked like drag marks. Sweat rolled down his back and fear gripped his belly. Dammit, what had happened? One minute she'd been looking at him, the next she was gone. He stilled at the sound of scuffling and a muffled call.

"Brandon. Help me. Get me out. It's dark in here and I'm covered with spider webs."

The sound of her voice reassured him. If she could still yell at him—she had to be okay.

"I'm trying. You must have fallen into some kind of tunnel." His mind raced as he pushed on the embankment. Without warning, an earthen door pushed inward. He held it ajar and pulled her toward him.

"Thank God," she said. "I was so scared. It felt like someone was watching me, so I backed up against the hill. Then I fell in. I kept pushing, but it wouldn't open. I heard—"

"Are you hurt?" He interrupted her nervous babble, running his hands down her body, feeling for broken bones.

"I'm just a little shaken. Let's get out of here; this place gives me the creeps."

He pulled her into the sun and wrapped her in a tight embrace. His first reaction was to sweep her up into his arms and run, the second was to shake her. She attracted trouble like perfume attracted mosquitoes. He compromised and placed a kiss on top of her head and growled. "I'm never letting you out of my sight again. You scared years off my life." With her arm firmly clasped in his, he started for the storeroom. "Let's get the lantern and check this place out, it might be a back door." Now, with sanity returned, he had work to do.

"A back door?" She quickened her step to keep up with him. "Do you mean another way into the mine?"

"No. I'm talking about an escape route from the locked room. I wondered earlier why someone would lock themselves in with no way out. I think this is the way out. The priest has all his bases covered."

"So, we're going to get a light and follow the tunnel to see where it leads? That sounds a little dangerous. The mine is unstable."

"Actually, *I'm* going to check out the tunnel and you're going to stay in the storeroom with the door locked." At her mutinous expression, he hastened to add, "I need back up in case the door is one way and I don't find the opening to the room."

"You just said you weren't letting me out of your sight. Now you plan to lock me up and take off on some adventure, leaving me to cover your butt if you get into trouble?"

"That sounds about right." He sauntered across the room and picked up the lantern.

Her gaze followed his movements and fixated on

his derriere. "You're lucky it's a nice butt. Otherwise, I might be tempted to take a nap and let you get yourself out of trouble."

"Thanks, I knew you were a good sport." He dug through the drawer and found several candles. "I'll light these, so you won't be left in the dark. If I'm not back in an hour, come out and push the door open for me."

"Please, be careful." Her smile faded, and her voice thickened. "The tunnel could be a dead end and the supports could be compromised. I don't want to spend the rest of my life locked in this dark room."

Brandon heard the underlying fear in her voice. She wasn't afraid of the dark, she was afraid for him. It felt good to have someone worry about him. He could definitely get used to it.

"Don't forget, the lock is on your side of the door. No need to panic."

"Come on. Let a girl have a bit of drama."

"No way. A little drama today, tomorrow you'll expect an entire performance." He stepped out of the storage room, pulled the door closed behind him and spoke against the wooden door between them. "I need to hear the lock click."

Once the lock slammed home he went outside, heading for the embankment and the hidden door. A touch to the correct spot and he pushed the door open. He entered the tunnel, closing the door behind him. The feeling of being watched earlier made him extra cautious as he lit the lamp and moved forward.

The tunnel was tall enough for him to stand, and he turned, checking the heavy beams. These supports were relatively new. Someone had kept this place in order, which added validity to his escape route theory.

Counting steps, he moved along the narrow corridor. Thirty-seven, thirty-eight. A draft caught at the flame. A few more steps and another tunnel branched off to the left. Picturing the location of the storeroom in his mind, he reasoned a left turn would take him away from it. He noted the position of the other tunnel, planning to check it out later. He continued forward. Fifty-five, fifty-six—a dead end, but he was positive he was beneath the store room.

He held the lantern up, checked the walls and ceiling, looking for a lever, but found none. To his right, carefully camouflaged by root-like vines, he spotted an alcove with a ladder.

Pay dirt.

Chapter Twenty-Five

Mira slammed the lock home with more force than necessary. She heard his muffled chuckle as he walked away. Darn him. He'd guessed she planned to follow him, well, not right away, but after he'd entered the tunnel.

The only reason she hesitated was the logic in what he'd said about the tunnel door. It wouldn't do for both of them to get locked in. Why was he always one step ahead of her? It wasn't like she was stupid. She had a good mind, but when it came to this type situation, he was an expert. Deflated, she flopped onto the cot. It would serve him right if she fell asleep and left his sorry butt in the tunnel. The thought made her smile as she curled up for a rest.

She studied the low ceiling, concentrating hard to keep claustrophobia at bay. The door was locked on her side, and she could get out if she wanted. The candles burned brightly. Her mind shied away from the dark corners of the room and wandered to happier thoughts.

Making love with Brandon earlier had exceeded anything she'd ever imagined. She'd always thought it would be a gentle, loving act. There'd been *nothing* gentle about it but loving—oh yes. She'd allowed her love for him free reign and it had bloomed under his tutoring hands. Had she really been that wanton woman crying out, wriggling her body against his swollen sex?

Heat burned her cheeks as moisture pooled between her thighs. His method of teaching about gravity had been fun, but a little unorthodox. The lesson she decided, was only fun because of the teacher. *Hmm, wonder how good he'd be at anatomy?* She covered her face with her hands. Was it possible to embarrass oneself with thoughts alone?

Thump.

She rose up on the cot and listened. She'd definitely heard something, coming from the floor just beneath her. Jumping up, she grabbed the closest candle and peered under the cot.

Thump-Thump. The sound came from over by the cupboard. She cradled the wavering candle and moved to the wall by the cupboard. The candle flickered as she came close to the wall. "Brandon? Is that you?" A muffled response filtered through the wall. She tapped, searching for a door or some evidence of an opening. She put her shoulder against the wall ready to push when—it opened.

"A secret passage. It feels like I'm in a mystery novel." She reached to brush cobwebs from his spikey hair. "Did you find anything exciting down there?"

"I found evidence this place is well tended. The walls are secure, and someone left a ladder in an alcove leading to this door. I believe the padre is running some kind of safe haven for escapees. At least, I hope his purpose is noble. The man says a lot but reveals little." He closed the secret door and instantly it blended into the wall.

"If you didn't know where to look, you'd never see it. Someone put a lot of careful work into this place. These doors had to be crafted meticulously for them to move so easily and stay concealed.

She took the lantern and placed it on the makeshift chair. "Surely you don't think he's involved with the rebels?"

"No, but I'm not too sure about some of his associates. He could be working with any number of people. I think he can be trusted, but I'm holding out total acceptance."

She set the candle down and pulled a crate over for a chair. "Do you think he's really a priest? It would be weird if I pretended to be a nun and he was a pretend priest."

"I can't say for sure, but in a pinch, I suppose I'd let him give me last rites." His lips crooked up into a wry smile.

"Don't say that. Are you trying to tempt the fates?" She gained insight into the man she loved in those flippant words. He had a religious background even if he made light of it. His central core of honor probably came from those roots. She had so much more to learn about him. Would they ever have time to get to know each other?

As if reading her thoughts, he took her hand and eased her gently down on the overturned crate. He moved the lantern to the floor and sat on the other, facing her. "We need to talk about some very important things. No, let me finish." he said as she tried to interrupt. "I need to know about your Uncle Max."

"Why on earth do you need to know about my uncle? My family history can't have anything to do with our situation. I need to talk to you about the journals. They are extremely important. They contain vital data which will be lost forever. All his research, my coming here, will all be for nothing without them. I must get them back."

"I believe both topics are connected and are critical to our situation."

"I don't understand. He's dead. How could he possibly have anything to do with our current situation? Unless—Are you talking about his journals? I just explained how important they are to me, but they'd be worthless to anyone else."

"Humor me, will you? Did you and your uncle share the same last name?"

"No, he was my mother's brother. His last name was Sanderson, not Phelps. Why is his name so important? Most people have uncles with different last names."

"I'll be damned," Brandon cursed softly, a look of disbelief sliding over his face. "Tell me what you remember about Max Sanderson."

"It's really important, isn't it?"

She still didn't understand, but one look at his face had her convinced. She took a deep breath and closed her eyes. It was hard to picture Uncle Max these days. She dug deep and dredged up memories of him, blinking back tears, threatening to fill her eyes. "I've told you about how my parents were killed in Somalia. Uncle Max was my only next of kin. When they died, he came home from his travels and took care of things. When I was younger, he would show up without warning. I'd wake up, and he'd be there with presents from faraway places. We'd sit around a campfire in the backyard and talk for hours. He always spoke to me as an equal, never as a child. He told me stories about the places he'd explored and showed me drawings of the plants he'd studied. I used to copy his drawings and color them. We had this silly kind of code we used when we wrote to each other. It was great fun. I always looked forward to his letters, though they were infrequent. God, I miss him."

Brandon's face alerted at her mention of the code. "What did your uncle do for a living?"

"I told you, he was a scientist, researching plants all over the world. Weren't you listening?"

"This might come as a shock to you, but the Max Sanderson the rest of the world knows is a very different person."

"What do you mean? I know...knew, my uncle."

"Calm down." He took her hands in a gentle but persistent grip. "What I'm about to tell you might hurt and I'm sorry, but we have to get this sorted out."

She tried to stand, and he stopped her. "Be patient. This is very important. Your uncle may have studied plants, but his real job was with the CIA. Uncle Max worked for Uncle Sam."

Her body stiffened, and her hands shook. She tried to pull away, but his grip tightened. "I don't believe you. My uncle was a gentle man of science. You're saying he was some kind of secret agent? You have to be mistaken."

He didn't back down but continued to look directly into her eyes, his face serious.

She turned her head and closed her eyes. What was happening? Her whole world had turned upside down. If she believed him, all those childhood memories were false. The loving uncle who had spent hours teaching her about plants couldn't be a spy. Could he?

Wait a minute, didn't spies kill people? No, not the

gentle man she knew. Did he understand what he was doing to her? With a few spoken words, he'd shattered the last thing she had to cling to, her memories. Hot tears squeezed through her lids and slid down her cheeks. Why did life have to be so unfair?

Chapter Twenty-Six

His gut twisted at the look of anguished dejection on her once happy face. How much did she really know about her uncle? Could Max have hidden his secret life from her completely? Sure, she was a kid who'd lost her parents. It would make sense for her to idolize the man who had swooped in and rescued her. She'd believed her uncle a saint. Now she had doubts about all her memories. Her tears fell like drops of acid on his soul, a painful yet helpful reminder he still had one. God, he wanted to pull her into his arms and smooth away all the pain and confusion, but he couldn't do it. He could only be here for her when reality set in.

His soldier's instinct told him this whole mess revolved around her and those journals, and thus Max Sanderson. He couldn't tell her all he knew. He had crossed paths with her uncle in several black ops missions. Her uncle was good at what he did, *deadly good*. Then again—so was he.

She snuffled one last time and swallowed with a hitching breath. She made a swipe at her wet eyes, and then looked at him. Understanding dawned in her tear-streaked face. She believed him. The pain in her eyes as she grappled with the knowledge made his chest ache. He watched as her childhood beliefs crumpled like a sandcastle in the tide. Her spine stiffened, and she leaned back to look at him. "Tell me everything."

He struggled to find a painless way to explain about her beloved uncle. There wasn't one, so he began telling her what he knew. "Max Sanderson was recruited right after college. With his brilliant mind and science background, the CIA felt he'd be able to move freely around the world. His academic credentials would allow him to mix with the upper echelon of society where he'd be privy to a vast amount of information. He was one of the best and his reputation as an operative is almost legendary."

"Please tell me he wasn't a killer." She looked up into his face. "He only gathered information, right?"

"I can't. He was an excellent CIA operative, and I'm positive he had to kill to maintain his cover. It doesn't make him evil." He squeezed both her hands. "Am I a bad person because I'm good at my job? I've killed too many men to think about. Where would you be right now if I hadn't killed?" The hidden plea in his questions had his nerves stretched expectantly as he waited for her answers.

"That's difficult." She pulled her hand free and took a moment before she answered. "The doctor in me hates the idea of killing. I've seen so many atrocities, most involving women and children. You're not responsible for those things. The woman in me is glad you and others like you help keep the world safe. You're protectors. The rebels and people like them shouldn't have such an easy time, taking what they want, ignoring the consequences to others." She shifted closer to him, nearly touching his face. "No, I don't think you're evil, and I know you have a job to do. You keep the rest of us safe, but you pay a heavy price. It eats away at your soul, doesn't it?"

"I'm not some superhero." He turned away from her penetrating gaze. "I've killed people and thought nothing of it. They needed to be killed, and it was my job. Sometimes, I can't do anything to help people and they die. I'll admit *that* erodes my insides. Someone is always ready to step in and take the place of those I killed, so there'll always be a need for people like me. It's endless, and you get trapped."

He stopped talking suddenly, realizing how much he'd revealed about himself. He'd never opened up to anyone. He turned back and searched her face, looking for the revulsion she had to feel at his self-deriding speech. Astonished, he saw only love. She saw who and what he was and accepted him. It was a gift beyond belief.

"It's all right. I understand. I suppose what hurts the most, is having to question all those childhood memories of Uncle Max."

"There's no need to question those memories." He stood and paced the cramped space. How could he make her understand? He dropped to his knees beside her. "Mira, Max loved you. The experiences you shared together are still just as meaningful. In a way, by not telling you, he showed his love. He wanted you protected from the darker things in life. Losing your parents, at such an early age in such a tragic manner, was enough to scar you without adding subterfuge into the mix."

"So why does it matter if he was a...*spy*?" She stumbled over the word. "He's been dead over two years and his journals are all about the Blue Spider Orchid, not some weapon of mass destruction."

His face stilled, once again the emotionless soldier.

Her eyes widened with surprise. "You think he hid something secret in the journals?"

"I do. Think about it. He traveled the world, collecting information and keeping the CIA informed. Yet, before he disappeared, he made sure you received the journals. I find that interesting, don't you?

"I suppose…"

He watched her struggle to assimilate all he'd told her, then reconcile it with what she knew of her uncle. It wasn't easy to rock someone's world, and then expect them to take it even further and speculate on something as serious as espionage.

"You talk like he's hiding somewhere and not dead," she said.

"That's just it. Nobody knows exactly what happened to him. He could very well be alive and hiding somewhere."

"How do you know these things?" She clenched the front of his shirt in both fists. "If he's alive, I have to know."

"I can't tell you more. I've broken all the rules by telling you this much. I can speculate, though. If someone thought Max was still alive and had important information, which they didn't want compromised, they'd do anything to draw him out, including kidnapping his niece and using her as a pawn. They might have the journals, but I think you are the key to deciphering them."

"It's all too fantastic to comprehend. If my uncle is still alive, wonderful, but if the rebels think I can help with the journals, they're wrong. The only information is about the plant."

"But *they* don't know that. Of all the people at the

clinic, *you* were the only one kidnapped. Don't you find it strange? Why not the priest? Surely, he would make a more important pawn in some political game? Why didn't they just kill you if they wanted to send a message to America? I think they kept you alive for a reason. We have to get those journals back and study them."

****

"Finally, you're making sense." She raised her arms in an exasperated display. "When do we go?"

His features hardened. "Go?"

"Yes, when do we go to the rebel camp and steal back the journals?" It made perfect sense to her. Why was he giving her a *have- you- lost- your- mind* look?

"*I* will be going to the camp this afternoon to look around. Later tonight when most of the people are at the festival, I'll sneak in, find the journals, and meet you here where we'll hide out until tomorrow. We'll make our way to the Mosquito Coast and Jackson will pick us up day after tomorrow. If everything works out, you'll be home resting in a few days."

"You are not leaving me behind. You're going to need my help finding the journals."

"There's *no way in hell* I'm letting you anywhere near the camp. Are you out of your mind, or plain crazy? It would be like Jonah crawling back into the whale."

"I'm perfectly sane and able to make my own decisions. I won't let you do this alone. I want to help."

"It's too risky. If you go with me, my attention will be divided, which puts everyone in danger. This is what I am trained to do. Please accept it and let me do my job." He stood silent, waiting for her capitulation.

"Well, are you going to cooperate?"

Her face tightened as defiance surged through her body. She was tired of being left behind while he took all the risks. Yes, he was the expert, but the journals were her responsibility, not his. She should help retrieve them. The thought of him sneaking into the camp alone, without backup, made her shudder. He could be captured or killed. No, she couldn't let him do it alone. Smart enough to know he'd insist on her staying behind, all she could do was agree with him, then see how things went.

"Mira, I need to know you are safe. If you insist on coming, we'll forget the entire thing. Maybe we'll be able to retrieve the journals another time. We can safely stay here another day and then head for the coast."

"No. If Uncle Max hid something in those journals, we've got to get them and keep them safe. He could have died for the information hidden in them. I couldn't live with myself, knowing the information could have caused his death, and I allowed someone else to take it. Who knows, maybe it *is* information about a weapon of mass destruction? We have to get them."

"Agreed. I'll get them, but you stay here. I know you don't like it, but it's the way it has to be. Promise me, you'll let me do this alone."

Long moments of silence passed as Mira thought through her options. She knew her face was like a screen broadcasting all her emotions to him, the anxiety, the indecision—the fear.

"I don't like it, but okay. I promise. I need you to do one thing for me though."

He would have a hard time with her request, but it was non-negotiable as far as she was concerned. "What is it?" he asked hesitantly.

Her chin lifted, daring him to say no. "Leave me an automatic weapon and show me how to use it."

He searched her face, then nodded. "It's a deal." He took her chin in his fingers and lowered his lips to hers. "Sealed with a kiss," he murmured and pulled her tightly against his chest.

Chapter Twenty-Seven

She learned fast. Her strength and willingness to do something so against her convictions made him proud. He'd chosen his M240 machine gun for her. The gun was lightweight, packed a powerful punch, and didn't rely on close quarters for accuracy. She could literally point and pull the trigger. The gun would do the rest. Leaving her alone strained his nerves, but at least she would be armed and trained in the rudiments.

It took little time to teach her how to load it, sweep an area with bullets and reload. He'd have been happier if she could've felt the gun fire, but they had to keep their location safe, so no bullets.

"When you pick up the gun, make sure it's turned away from you. Here's the safety." He touched the mechanism with his thumb. "Click it off when you're ready to shoot. God, I hope you never have to use this." He pulled her up against his body and straightened her shoulders. "I chose this weapon for you because you don't actually have to aim; just make sure you have it pointed in the general direction of the enemy before you fire."

Her body tensed when he used the word enemy. As a doctor, human life was sacred.

"Mira, you can't think of them as people or you'll never be able to kill anyone. You must always shoot to kill; otherwise, they'll have the opportunity to shoot you. They won't hesitate, so you can't either."

"I understand. I don't want to kill anyone, but if it comes to my life or yours, I'll do what's necessary." Her muscles relaxed, and he felt her calm.

In that moment she sounded more like her Uncle Max than she knew. She had determination and resolve, both would help her more than accuracy at shooting. She was tough, compassionate, and loving; all wrapped up in a killer body. *Damn,* she was one in a million.

"Besides, if I don't kill them, I'd probably stop and try to fix them up." She looked over her shoulder then leaned back into him.

"You probably would." He sighed then broke into a laugh. Her bottom moved against him intimately. "Stop your shenanigans, or you'll get a lesson in something besides firing weapons."

He did his best to keep things light, not wanting to think about his mission tonight. She was worried about him but there was nothing he could do to make it easier.

As if reading his thoughts her smile vanished. She turned into his embrace and hugged him tightly to her soft body. "Brandon, I'm so scared for you. I know you're trained for this type of thing, but you're not super human. You can die as easily as anyone else. Promise me you'll be extra careful and come back to me in one piece, so I won't have to worry about using this gun."

He leaned back to look into her pleading eyes, and his heart turned to butter. "I can only promise to do my best. Unexpected things can happen regardless how well you prepare for a mission. By staying here, you're helping me. The knowledge you're safe allows me to concentrate completely on the mission." He took the gun from her and picked up the clips. "Let's go outside for a while before I leave. I know how much you hate being cooped up in here."

He scanned the area around the mine entrance, listening to the birds calling as they flitted from tree to tree. Satisfied all was as it should be, he strode toward the undergrowth away from the clearing and sat on the ground with his back against a tree. "Come here, sweetheart." He softened the command by smiling and tapping his hand against his leg.

"Aye aye, sir." She made a sassy salute and flopped into his lap with a laugh.

"You need to learn discipline and respect. Your blatant disregard for my authority is appalling. What would my men think of me if I allowed them the liberties you take?"

"I hope you wouldn't command any of them to sit on your lap." She grinned, as she rested her head against his chest.

Brandon chuckled. "You can be dammed sure." He wrapped his arms around her and bent down for a light kiss. "I don't think Jackson, or Rafà swing that way. Besides, it would break too many female hearts among their leagues of female admirers."

"And what about you, do you have leagues of women chasing you?" Her voice was casual as if his answer meant nothing.

"Would you mind if I did?" he asked, laughing at the flare of jealousy in her eyes.

"I'd scratch their eyes out."

"You don't have to worry. There's no harem or competition. I don't really have anyone, except my sister out in California. The SEALs are my family.

Though some men manage, it's hard to have a successful relationship with the kind of life we lead. Successful is the only kind I will accept, so I'm alone." He felt an ache in his chest and realized he'd never felt alone before now. He hadn't known what he was missing before.

"You've got me now, and I don't care what kind of life you lead."

Her sincerity squeezed his heart like a fist. "I love you, Brandon. Don't *ever* forget it."

Before he could contain it, passion flared, razing like a fire through a dried forest. The rainforest disappeared, along with the danger surrounding them—everything but the moment and their desperate need to touch, to feel. Clothes disappeared to suddenly be used as a blanket. His head filled with the scents of arousal, the damp earth and the surrounding forest.

His breath came in short, quick gasps. With every ounce of discipline, he had, he reigned in his passion and slowed down. He wanted to worship her body, wanted to show her all the things he couldn't say with words. She was the most responsive woman he'd ever touched, her body arching toward his, demanding a completion to their erotic foreplay. His erection strained against her soft belly, pleading for entry into her blissful sheath.

When he could no longer stand the strain, he pulled back. "Look into my eyes, Mira. See my words." He commanded in a guttural voice, as his muscles tautened with passion. Slowly he pushed inside her.

Passion drooped eyes widened as he entered her. He might not be able to say it, but by *God,* he'd show her. Together their bodies moved in a slow rhythm, as the wave began to build. There was no frenzied grasping or hurried climb, just a silky rising of ecstasy, which claimed them. He bent and gently kissed her. Looking into her eyes, he slipped over the edge. *I love you.*

He held her quietly in his arms and allowed his breathing to slow to normal. Above them the sunlight filtered through the leaves, painting their sated bodies with mottled shadows. He sensed the lateness of the hour. He'd have to leave soon. If all went according to plan, he'd take a quick look around the camp and be back here before the moon was fully up in the sky. Later, he'd go back, at a time when even the most ardent sentry relaxed his guard, as evening became morning.

"It's time, isn't it?" she whispered against his chest.

"Yes." he answered reluctantly, not wanting this moment to end. For a few moments he'd tasted heaven and wanted to savor the feeling. Years of training and self-deprivation brought the soldier back to earth. He stood, and took one more look at her beauty, lying there naked and well loved. Her white skin glowed with moisture and the heat of passion had brought a rosy hue to her cheeks and breasts. Her hair, as usual, was a riot of golden curls. Resigned, he took her hand and pulled her upright. Quickly, they gathered their clothes and dressed.

"Please don't be sad." He tried to reassure her. "It's going to be okay."

As she fastened the last button on her shirt she looked up and smiled. "I know. I'll be okay."

Hands clasped together, they returned to the mine.

****

Through the lens of his scope, Rafà found Brandon and the Doc in a most compromising situation. Shock followed by envy filled him. Damn if Cap hadn't fallen hook, line and medical bag. He thought of the SEAL nickname Brandon had acquired over the years. It had a double meaning only someone with sniper experience would understand. He was their captain, no matter what his rank, and he could cap any target at a thousand yards. He had known him since becoming a SEAL. He respected him and loved him like a brother. How could he have been so stupid as to believe he had intentionally left him?

He was happy for the two of them. Now all he had to do was make sure the couple didn't get themselves killed. He might even get to be 'Uncle Rafà' someday. He grinned at the thought.

He turned his scope away from them, allowing them this fleeting moment. Since they had sensed his presence earlier, he was keeping his distance. They hadn't heard him. No pride—just fact. Rafà knew he was that good. People had been known to nearly step on him and never see him. He was a master at blending in and becoming almost invisible.

Some people were just good at sensing things. Those people were the survivors. He slowly moved off through the underbrush, putting more space between himself and the lovers. They didn't have much time before Brandon would leave for the camp. He found a liana covered tree, climbed silently upward, and lay down to sleep before this evening's activity.

Chapter Twenty-Eight

Brandon checked the placement of each weapon and its location on his body.

He double checked the M240 which he'd attached to a belt. He held it out to her, wishing there was some other way. No healer should have to face the act of killing. Her hands shook as he placed the weapon on her open palms. "The belt might be a little large, but it'll help support the weapon, and ensure you don't drop it while running. Remember, hide first and use the gun as a last resort. If anyone manages to get inside, leave through the tunnel. Don't shoot inside the tunnel unless you have to—the entire thing could collapse on your head."

He paused to grab her around the waist. "Mira, there's a side tunnel down there, take it. I think it leads back to town and possibly the church. The padre will help you."

She pulled back and busied herself with tidying the small room. "I understand."

He knew she kept busy, so she wouldn't have to think but her gaze tracked his every movement. His gut hurt as he looked at her. She was putting on a brave front—no tantrums, no tears. He was proud to call her his woman.

She smiled up at him. "I'll be fine."

The smile didn't fool him, and if he heard her say

"I'll be fine" one more time, he might cancel the whole mission. Before he could change his mind, he leaned down and branded her lips with a searing kiss—a kiss of goodbye. He turned quickly and left through the door. He waited to hear the lock click and then made his way out and into the jungle.

He walked quickly but silently toward the rebel camp. For the first time on a mission, he had trouble shoving thoughts to the back of his brain, putting everything aside and keeping his full attention on what was at hand. God, her face—the look of anguish she couldn't quite hide. *Put it out of your mind. Concentrate on the mission.* Too many lives are at stake if you slip up. You can't save Mira if you're dead.

He jerked to a stop, took a deep breath, and reviewed what he had to do. Father José had asked him to bring Miguel out; Mira wanted the journals and he needed to gather more intel on the Russians. The job wasn't an easy one, but most SEAL assignments were difficult—if not impossible. That was why they existed—what they lived for—what they died for.

He took a circuitous route to dodge any straggling rebels heading into town. The festivities would certainly cut back on the number of people at the camp. There'd be a few guards, but their number and specialization would be low. Officers and soldiers in good standing would leave the minions to guard while they played in town. He hoped they played long and drank freely. It was going to be a long night, but first— he had to check out a hunch.

****

"Goodbye, my love," Mira whispered against the rough boards. As she slammed the metal latch into the lock, her heart shattered into tiny pieces. Her mind screamed—he won't come back. She couldn't explain the nagging premonition but felt it all the same. Tears she'd held in check slipped beneath her lids and streamed down her cheeks.

Her body continued to shudder when she could no longer produce tears. Eventually, she calmed, got up from the floor, and drank some water. She was terrified he wouldn't return. How on earth had women through the ages survived their men leaving them to go off and fight?

Had they felt this quivering emptiness in their bellies? Had they, like she, wished they could grab hold of them and keep them by their sides, safe? In her heart she knew, if something happened to Brandon, she wouldn't want to go on. Did it really matter if she knew how to shoot? Would she care?

Unless…some part of her subconscious whispered, *there is a child*. Oh God. She could be carrying his baby. They had taken no precautions. Hope rose in her heart. Until she knew for sure, she'd keep on hoping, and she would live.

She straightened, moved to the sink, and splashed her face with water. Her fingertips touched her lips where his had seared hers with a kiss of goodbye. To stay here while he was in danger was intolerable, but should she follow him? She had made a promise— could she break his trust? Her inner argument was short-lived; of course, she was going to do it.

Hadn't she planned to do this all along? He needed her, and *she* needed to be there for him. Having settled the issue in her mind, she entered the storage room, picked up the extra ammo and crammed it into her back pack. Making sure she had water and the gun on safety she stepped out into the hot afternoon. Okay, which way did she go?

Trusting her instincts, she took off in the direction she thought Brandon had taken. She hoped it was the right way. The jungle looked more daunting without him to clear the path as she walked. Her self-confidence ebbed as she plowed through the tangled undergrowth and her progress slowed. The animal calls sounded closer, louder—or maybe her senses were over-stimulated. Frustrated, she stopped to slow her breathing. Brandon was faster, but it hadn't been too long since he'd left—surely, she'd catch up to him soon.

The oppressive heat closed in as she struggled against vines and damp, rotting vegetation. *Think positive thoughts.* She pushed the idea of him in danger, hurt, or dying completely to the back of her mind. Engrossed with her thoughts and determined struggle with the vegetation, she was caught by surprise when the arm reached out of the bushes and clamped across her mouth.

Panic prodded her to kick out, struggling to get away. Sound rushed to her ears. She jerked back and met a solid wall of flesh. Enough—she was tired of being manhandled. With all her strength she bit down on the hand covering her mouth and prayed for release.

"Ouch! Damn it, Mira. Leave me a little skin."

She sagged against him in relief. "What are you doing here?"

"I thought it was obvious. I was waiting for you to follow me."

Adrenaline subsided as anger took over. "Did you

have to scare me to death?" She pushed against Brandon's sinewy arms. "What do you mean you were waiting for me? How did you know I would follow?"

"I had a hunch," he said curtly. "You acquiesced way too easily to my suggestion to stay in the tunnel."

"Suggestion?" She spat the word at him. "Is that what you call it? I got the distinct impression it was an *order*."

Arguing with him was the last thing she wanted. She *wanted* to take him in her arms and hold him close, but his look of utter arrogance and supreme superiority had her ire up. How could he stand there looking for all the world like this was a normal conversation they might have on the street?

"It doesn't matter. You're here now, and I don't have time to take you back before dark. You'll come with me—and you'll follow my *orders,* or I will find a convenient tree and tie you up." The look on his face was one of total frustration. "Dammit, I'm a military man—a commander—people jump to obey my orders. In one week, you've done more to upset my training than some of the world's worst terrorists. I do believe you could make *Rambo* forget his training."

They stood eye to eye, both stubborn—both breathing rapidly with exertion and emotion.

She looked away first, staring down at her feet. Her anger died as she touched his chest.

"I'm so sorry. I know I promised to stay but I couldn't. Please, I'll listen and…"

He pulled her to him and fiercely took her mouth in a punishing kiss.

"Why'd you kiss me?" An echo of confusion sounded in her voice. She'd expected a thrashing at least. He'd looked so terrifying when he'd grabbed her.

"Sweetheart, don't you understand?" His breath feathered across her cheek. "I had a choice of kissing you or shaking you. I find kissing far more satisfying."

"I'll listen—but I won't jump." She felt better when she'd added the last bit.

"Okay, no jumping but stay close and follow my hand signals. Few people should be left at the camp, but we can't take chances."

They walked for about fifteen minutes, before Brandon motioned to her to crouch. She didn't need him to tell her how close they were to the camp. In the jungle heat, the smell of human waste, rotting food and unclean bodies assaulted her nose. She wasn't sure what she'd expected; but this wasn't it. Suddenly, she was aware of the reality of soldiers and prisoners living in primitive conditions.

She followed his lead as they crawled through the edges of the greenery. In nearby pens, pigs grunted contentedly as they wallowed in the fetid mud and scrawny chickens pecked among the debris littering the compound. A row of cages lined the middle of the camp. She bit her lip and a heavy ache filled her chest. Men sat hunched against the wooden sticks with no room to move. They were half-starved and many needed immediate medical attention. Open sores and raw slashes covered their bodies. Flies and insects crawled undisturbed over them.

Gorge rose in her throat and tears burned her eyes. Dear God, how could anyone mistreat human beings this way?

Chapter Twenty-Nine

Horror flashed across her face. God—he wished she hadn't witnessed this. His fingers squeezed hers as his throat worked. Swallowing his own pain, he shifted his gaze away from the occupants and to the layout of the camp.

Anger flowed like acid through his brain, etching the horrific image into his mind. Men in unbelievable pain and despair, caged like animals. He felt it, he knew—he'd been there. Vivid flashes of his own capture and torture—and the loss of so many fellow SEALs, threatened to overwhelm him. Almost changed his resolve and turn this into a rescue mission instead of recon.

Instead, he closed his eyes and took a steadying breath. Anger was dangerous. Soldiers had to use their brains. Emotions gave the enemy an advantage. When he opened his eyes, cold steel burned in his veins and icy calm took over. Once more, he was all soldier.

Mira hunkered down at his signal.

"I'm going closer and look around," he whispered directly into her ear. "Stay hidden and quiet."

He dropped to his belly and crawled through the shrubs. He took his time, inching around the perimeter, creating a mental map of the camp. No fence. Who would expect anyone to walk in or visit? At the back of the camp, a large tent sat on a platform, a foot off the ground. A sloppily dressed sentry slouched in a chair in front of the tent flap. His presence differentiated this tent from the rest. The leaders would bunk here, and the journals would probably be there as well.

A truck approached on the rutted track, bringing the lazy guard to his feet. He straightened his shirt, trying to appear alert as two men exited the tent to meet the arrivals.

His gut told him the truck was bad news, and he never ignored his gut.

Who was important enough to bring the guard to attention? He didn't have long to wait. The vehicle screeched to a halt and a tall, blond, European man swung down from the driver's side and swayed toward the tent. He continued to celebrate, taking long swigs from a half empty bottle.

A woman lay half in, half out the open passenger window, her long dark hair covering her face. The smell of vomit drifted on the breeze. Spanish curses fouled the air as she banged her fist on the side of the truck. The sentry jumped forward to open the door. She slapped impatiently at the man as he tried to help her. She wobbled toward the blonde man, grabbed the bottle, and downed his whiskey. Tossing the empty bottle, she grabbed him, running her hands roughly over his body. Unperturbed, he returned her groping in a wanton display of debauchery

Brandon crawled frantically toward Mira. Instinct screamed at him to get to her.

"Jacinta." Mira gasped aloud.

What the hell? His blood turned to ice. All his fears had come to fruition. As soon as the startled outburst left her lips, he sprang to his feet, launched his body forward to cover hers, and prayed the soldiers' aim wasn't good.

Damn his luck.

Pain tore down his right leg as he tackled her and slammed them both to the ground. *Get out of here.* His mind commanded, but his leg wouldn't move. *"Dammit!"* He struggled, but it was useless.

"Brandon?"

She spoke from beneath him, as her hands tried to push him off. "Let me have a look."

His vision grayed, and her voice shrank in volume.

"Brandon?" A sharp slap accompanied the voice.

Someone pounded on his chest. He fought hard to stay alert. *Get Mira out of here—no time to lose.*

"Let me up. I need to check your wound."

Gunfire flew overhead, cutting the tall grass close by. He pressed her deeper into the dirt, and then rolled off her, firing three quick shots at the soldier running in their direction. A barrage of bullets fired back.

"Fools, don't *shoot* her," Jacinta shouted above the din. "We need her."

Brandon took advantage of her shouted reprimand and grabbed Mira's arm. "Run as fast as you can, and don't look back. You know where to go."

"I can't leave you—you'll bleed to death." She tugged and released his belt, pulling it from his waist. Quickly, she fashioned a tourniquet around his upper thigh to slow the pulsing blood. "You'll die if I can't slow the bleeding."

He had to make her understand. She was in full doctor mode—oblivious to the fact she was now in the middle of a war zone. He grabbed her by the shoulders and shook her. "Dammit to hell, listen to me. You have to run, *now*. I'll be fine, I'm trained for this, remember? We do this all the time." He stared intently into her eyes, giving her a half smile for encouragement. "Please, if you love me, leave now. That's a request," his voice went close to a whisper. "Trust me, I'll find you, no matter what. Go, before they catch you."

What he asked would tear her to shreds when she had time to think about it. Right now, there was no time to think—just take action. Tears streamed from her eyes as she stared back at him.

Footsteps pushed through the tall grass, ending her hesitation and spurring her into action. She kissed him, a mere brushing of her lips against his, handed him her rifle and ran.

Brandon grabbed the gun, rolled, and fired. Two men fell, and another dropped behind cover. He couldn't get them all and he couldn't run. Die or get captured? Neither choice was enticing, but he opted for the last. He'd wanted to see the inside of the camp. What better way than as a prisoner?

He had one last ace to play before this game was over, an ace which could save Mira and himself. He dropped flat on his back in the grass and yelled at the top of his lungs. "Rafà? GEESE!"

The code word barely escaped his lips when pain exploded like hot phosphorus in his left shoulder—another hit. Shadows moved inward shrinking the sky and then...dark.

****

Mira ran as if the entire rebel army chased her.
Traitor.
Jumbled images flashed through her mind as she ran. Jacinta wasn't a prisoner as she'd thought, and her

disgusting companion was the soldier who'd slapped her. God, she'd been so stupid to startle and gasp the woman's name. Hadn't she learned anything from Brandon's tutoring? She'd done all he'd expected and worse. Her stomach twisted in knots.

Now, the most precious person in her life lay bleeding and alone. She'd abandoned the man she loved to be tortured or killed by those maniacs. If she'd stayed, they would both be lost. She was free; she'd find some way to get help for him or die trying.

"Trust me," he'd said. For the first time in her life, she did trust someone. She trusted his good judgment, his experience as a soldier, and by God, his bravery. Earlier, he'd said he wasn't a hero, but she knew better. He was the kind of man countless others tried to emulate. He didn't try to be a hero, he just was.

The jungle reached out, tearing at her body as she fled, mixing her blood with Brandon's which stained her arms. Heedless of her tearing flesh, she pushed on. Why hadn't she been the one? That bullet had been hers. She had to get away, had to find help. Blinded by tears, all sense of direction lost, she ran until—her body was stopped mid stride, by something long and muscular encircling her from above.

Hideous images filled her mind—of a powerful python, sliding its coils down from the trees to slowly squeeze the life from her. Powerful muscles clamped around her mouth and she was quickly pulled up into the shadowy foliage.

"Shh, I'm trying to help you," an unknown voice whispered against her ear.

Mira experienced a moment of *déjà vu*. Hadn't she heard similar words at the beginning of this nightmare?

Her throat constricted at the thought of who'd said those words. Did it really matter who had pulled her up into this tree? She ceased her struggles. Without him in her life, there was little meaning.

"Don't worry, Doc, we'll get him back. Now, stay still so I don't drop you. We've got to go upstairs for a while. Things are getting a little hot down below."

Shock pulsed through her veins. Who was this smooth-talking man, giving her hope with his promises? Hanging upside down, suspended from a rope in the tree, made it difficult to see him. Her impression was of tanned skin and black hair—and strength. His steely muscles rippled with the extra weight of her body. They began to move upward in a smooth, sliding motion, like a lift. She startled, afraid of falling. His arms wrapped around her in a protective, almost comforting gesture.

She wasn't sure what to expect next, certainly not a well-built platform in the upper reaches of the canopy. He lowered them to the platform and Mira got her first good look at her rescuer. Before she could speak, he motioned her to silence and pointed below. She stretched out on the platform and looked down. What was she supposed to see? He handed her a foot-long scope and indicated she should look again. Astonished, she saw orange-looking figures below.

My God—she'd been there, mere seconds before. They would have her now, if not for her rescuer. He took the scope from her, observed the figures below, and sat up to face her.

She openly studied the ruggedly handsome face framed by dark black hair, which brushed his shoulders. A shaggy mustache and beard added to his dangerous look. He wore ragged clothes, like those worn by the locals, but she could tell he wasn't one of them. His dark-brown eyes held far too much worldliness to be a local. His assessing gaze was keenly intelligent.

He might blend in, but he certainly wouldn't *fit* in. *A wolf in sheep's clothing.* Though he had helped her, his dangerous persona made her nervous. He emanated an air of restrained violence—like a snake coiled and ready to strike.

They waited several long minutes. He slid the scope together and turned to her with his hand outstretched. "Good to finally meet you, Doc. I'm Brandon's friend, Rafà."

Relief swept through her like a strong wind. Weak with emotion, she gave him a bleak smile and took his hand. "I've gotten him killed, haven't I?" Her voice was low and filled with hurt. "I only wanted to help, but he got shot, protecting me."

Her body shook in reaction to the violence—the run—the loss. Tears streamed freely down her cheeks. "He had to stop looking for you to rescue me—and now—I've gotten him shot—or worse." Words stuttered from her mouth as she tried to explain.

Rafà sat across from her, silent, and looking very uncomfortable.

She snuffled. "You must hate me."

"You can't hate, Doc. It gets in the way. *Damn.*" He shook his head as if to clear his thoughts.

His quiet epithet made her look at him. "What's wrong?"

"Nothing to worry about. I just realized I should have been practicing what I preach. If I had trusted Brandon and put my own hate and anger aside, we might be out of here by now."

She went back to his earlier comment. "In the way of what?"

"It gets in the way of thinking and taking action," he replied. "Cap gave me an order before he fell, and I intend to follow it."

"What order, and why are you calling him that?"

"*GEESE.*" He chuckled at her puzzled expression. "Cap is his SEAL moniker."

She ran her gaze over him in a quick clinical appraisal. "Are you sure you haven't been wandering around in the jungle too long?"

He offered a cheeky grin. "Get Everyone Else Safely Evacuated—or GEESE. He was telling me to get you safely out of here and not to worry about him. Geese fly in a Vee formation, with the lead goose taking most of the headwind. When he tires, he moves back, and the next strongest flock member takes lead. I'm now lead goose—in a manner of speaking."

"More like LOON, as in *crazy as a loon*, if you think we're leaving him behind and getting out of here."

"I see he's going to have his hands full with you. Of course, we're not leaving him behind, but first we must plan. It must to be tonight. There are only a few men left in the camp, but the Ruskie has a bad look about him. Cap's hurt already. If they discover he's a Navy SEAL, he'll be killed—slowly."

"We can't let that happen." She squared her shoulders and continued. "I don't know much about rescues, but you have a willing partner, Rafà. Let's get to it."

"Atta a girl. Ready to ride?"

She gave him a disbelieving look. "Don't tell me you have a vehicle hidden up here."

He chuckled and pointed upward. "Jump on my back and hold on tight." He touched her arms in reassurance, then they were being pulled up even higher into the canopy, stopping as they reached yet another platform. As soon as they stopped, he grabbed a harness and strapped her into it. He gave her no time to speak as he attached the harness to a cable above their heads, snapped on a safety belt, and attached it to the cable. Without a word he wrapped his arms around her and jumped off the platform.

Mira bit her lip to keep from screaming. She jammed her head into his solid chest and held on for dear life. They were flying across the canopy at a dizzying speed. She'd always enjoyed amusement park rides, but this was even more exciting. Under different circumstances, she would have enjoyed the experience tremendously.

He reached above them, activated some sort of break, and they slowed down to land on a lower platform. They continued the process until they reached an area which looked vaguely familiar.

They were near the mine. She unbuckled the harness, climbed down from the tree and paused at his all too familiar gesture. She waited for him to check the area, and then followed him through the secret door in the hill. The total darkness inside the tunnel was daunting, and she grabbed the back of her guide's shirt. Silence reined as they made their way through the tunnel and to the ladder. Moments later, they were back in the room where she had been a few hours earlier.

"Hey Doc, you forgot to leave the lights on."

Reaction was setting in. "By the door, on the floor."

"Not to worry." He fumbled in one of his pockets and pulled out a slim flashlight.

He grinned as he shut the hidden door. "Home sweet home." Her knees threatened to buckle as memories of Brandon and all that had happened in this same room, overwhelmed her. She staggered to the cot, grabbed the blanket, and curled into a ball. The room brightened as Rafà found and resurrected the lamp.

"I should have stayed, like he asked. He'd probably still be safe." She turned away and faced the wall. What had she done? Her mind grappled with her loss and then switched to self-loathing. Her stupid arrogance had cost her the best thing ever to come into her life.

"You don't know for sure. Second guessing is useless." His words came from just behind her and were meant to sooth, but somehow, they fell flat.

She kept her back to him, not acknowledging his attempt to console her. "They'll kill him, won't they?" Her voice was low and filled with hurt. "I wanted to help, but it all went wrong." Her body shivered—reaction to the violence—the run—the loss. Tears streamed freely down her cheeks. "He had to stop looking for you to rescue me—and now…"

Words stuttered from her mouth as she tried to explain. "He'll be tortured, won't he?" Her fingers dug into the rough blanket on the cot. "It should be me laying in the grass with a gaping bullet hole in my chest—not him."

Rafà leaned closer but didn't touch her. "Hey—you okay?"

She grabbed the pillow, swung around, and threw it

at his head. "Of course, I'm okay. Brandon's the one who's hurt. I'm just sitting on my *ass*, wallowing in self-pity."

Dodging the missile, Rafà threw up his hands. "Women," he exclaimed, his voice full of frustration. "How did Cap ever get you to cooperate?" he asked in mock horror.

At the mention of Brandon, she turned to face him. She gave him a look which said, *you asked*, and cleared her throat. "He kissed me," she said in a sultry, sweet as sugar voice.

The look of horror on his face was comical. "We need to come up with a better solution. I value my head."

"There is nothing better," she muttered the words and then laughed outright when his jaw dropped. "It's okay, Rafà. Thanks for making me feel better." She patted the cot beside her, indicating he should sit.

"If you don't mind, I'll just sit on the floor, ma'am." He handed her the thrown pillow and sat on the floor. "Now, to the plan, we'll need more than one, because something always goes wrong." He started ticking off the supplies they would need

"First, I'll get the truck up and running while you plunder through Brandon's things for some dark clothes."

"I don't mean to put a damper on things, but how do you intend to get one of those dinosaurs outside to run?"

"Not those trucks—and it's my job. You take care of getting camouflaged."

"Brandon told me to go to Father José if something should go wrong. Shouldn't we get him to help?"

"There's not enough time, besides he knows already, and he'll do his part." He paused and turned even more serious. "This isn't going to be a picnic. We could get hurt or killed. Are you sure you don't want to stay here while I get him out?"

"I realize I shouldn't have followed him to the camp, but you're going to need my help. If he's still alive—if he's still alive, he's going to need immediate medical attention. Before I left him, I had to put a tourniquet on his leg. It's the only thing keeping him from bleeding to death. If they haven't killed him in the meantime, we have to get to him soon or it'll be too late." Fearful her voice would break, she said the last part quickly.

"Then let's get to it," Rafà said. "SEALs are used to things going wrong, we just deal with it and go to plan B. Are you going to be okay with shooting people or blowing things up? People are going to die, and we'll be the ones doing the killing." He was blunt—letting her know the worst and giving her an out.

"At this point, I'd shoot all of them including, Jacinta, and then gladly blow up the entire stinking place, sending them all to hell."

"Good girl. I don't mind blowing things up, now to plan B."

Chapter Thirty

The shock of cold water splashing across his head jerked Brandon from the black pit of unconsciousness. For the span of two seconds, the coolness felt great, soothing even. Then pain seared through his leg and shoulder, and he began to crave oblivion. The metallic smell of blood—his own, brought reality into focus. He had to concentrate; he had to survive, to find Mira.

"Welcome back, Mr. Brandon. You must forgive the familiarity. I did not catch your last name." The woman stared at him inquisitively.

He raised his head and examined the harsh face of the woman from the truck—Jacinta. Her wiry, tangled hair reminded him of Medusa, writhing with her every move. Makeup, heavily applied, smeared across her face. It looked cheap and emphasized her ugliness rather than enhanced her features.

This woman had worked with Mira as a nurse? How had she hidden her duplicity? He looked into her eyes and saw pure evil. He'd seen the look before—on some of the faces in his worst nightmares. Oddly, he'd never seen it in the eyes of a woman. Well, so much for being the gentler sex.

"Nothing to say? We'll see how things go."

The guards grabbed him and laid him spread-eagled on the floor. The taller one took out a knife. His muscles tensed—ready to fend off any attempt to kill

215

him. The man bent and slit the leg of his pants to the edge of the belt Mira had wrapped tightly above his wound. He hadn't expected this. Were they really going to help him?

"I'm afraid this might be a little painful, but necessary. We can't let you bleed to death before we question you."

Her voice held a harsh almost anticipatory sound, and suddenly he had a clear vision of what was to come. He clenched his teeth and worked to slow his rapid heart-rate as the woman pulled a glowing red knife from a brazier of fiery coals.

She held the hot knife close to his face, watching intently, almost with excitement, as the metal glowed red just above his cheek. "Where is Dr. Phelps? Tell me and I will have the guard knock you out, and this will hurt less."

He wasn't a fool. They would kill him regardless of what he told them, but he intended to stay alive as long as possible and look for an opportunity to escape.

"You are needlessly stubborn, Mr. Brandon. One way or another, I'll get my answers."

He sucked in his breath but remained still as she slid the very tip of the knife down his jaw. His skin sizzled audibly and the stench of burning flesh filled his nostrils. Nerves in his body jerked at the intense pain, his jaw clenched tighter and his cheek jerked uncontrollably. His stomach roiled in revulsion, but he remained strong. He would not scream for this bitch. His stoicism seemed to anger her. Good, anger caused people to make mistakes.

"I see you are a strong man. We're going to have lots of fun." She bent down and ripped the belt from his leg, allowing blood to pour from his wound. "This will stop the bleeding." She placed the flat edge of the knife blade against his leg, dragging it across the torn flesh.

He bit down hard on his teeth, clenching all his muscles. Blood and spittle spurted from his mouth. Searing pain tore through his body. Each nerve burned as if lit by white phosphorus. *He would not scream.* He refused to let her have the satisfaction.

His mind turned inward, blocked out all sound, escaping to a place where the non-soldier part of him could hide. It was a familiar place, shielded from pain and sorrow, a place where his humanity could survive, hidden from those who would try to steal it. As darkness enveloped him, he entered his sanctuary and slammed the door.

****

Brandon woke to pain and stifling heat. Tied against the rough wood of a tent support pole, his body slumped forward. Blood covered his shirt, but he'd seen worse. Ignoring the pain, he struggled to look around. A desk, a folding chair and a small cot. Not the Hilton— but at least he was off the ground and not in a cage.

The lamp on the desk was lit, so it must be dark. He'd been out for hours. How much time did he have before the *real* fun began? Heavy footsteps warned him a split second before the tent flap opened and a slight breeze poured in. Needing to gather strength, he inhaled the fresh air, but feigned unconsciousness.

A booted foot kicked him in his wounded leg. He couldn't suppress the pained cry escaping his lips.

"Ah, I see you are awake." The soldier spoke with a discernible Russian accent. "It's time for you and me to have a little chat."

The smell of cheap whiskey wafted toward him from the soldier's breath. It might not be top shelf—but he'd give anything for a shot of it to deaden the pain

The merc stared at him with eyes devoid of feeling. "What is your name and why are you here?"

"Smith," he lied as he looked the other man in the eye. "My name is Brandon Smith." His lips quirked into a mocking smile at the look of disbelief on the man's face.

"Well, Mr. *Smith,* I suggest you be a little more candid when my 'lady friend' returns. She has a fondness for—how do you say, painful pleasures?"

Brandon gave the soldier an accessing look. They were merely dancing with words. "That *woman* may be many things, but *lady* isn't one of them."

A chuckle escaped the soldier's throat. "I cede you the point."

"Rutgar?"

The high-pitched nasal call announced the arrival of Jacinta. She looked cleaner, as if she'd taken the time to wipe off some of the smeared makeup. Her hair still writhed, and the smell of her perfume nearly choked him when she swept into the tent. She wound herself around the soldier and kissed him open mouthed on the lips. "There you are, darling."

Brandon watched the by-play between the two. They certainly had lust in common—and something else. He looked closer and it dawned on him; both were manipulators and deadly. The soldier was probably the less dangerous of the two and more predictable. He'd been trained in a similar fashion as himself. In a fight, he'd give them even odds. Well, maybe a little less with his wounds.

Now Jacinta, she was a snake—and you couldn't trust a snake. They were vicious and unpredictable. He'd have to be very careful with that one. God, he hoped he got the chance to eliminate her. Normally, he wasn't one to wantonly kill, but he figured offing her would be a service to more than just his country.

After biting her companion's lip, she rubbed against his body and giggled. "All this excitement makes me hungry." She turned to him and suggestively fingered her breasts. "Maybe, it will take two men to satisfy me. What do you say, darling? Mr. Brandon may be a little damaged, but I imagine he is still strong enough to perform."

"Well, ma'am," he drawled in his best imitation of a Southern accent, "you just untie me, and I'll show you what I can do." He banked down his disgust and played to her ego.

She laughed, coarse and crude. "Mr. Brandon, you have *mucho machismo*, but first, we have a little matter to discuss." She went to the desk, opened a drawer and pulled out two leather bound books.

His eyes sharpened, but he said nothing. She was holding Max's journals. He pretended ignorance as she slapped them against her palm.

"I'm afraid I am a little old for bed time stories, but I'll indulge you if you like."

Her brittle face hardened; she dropped all appearance of civility. Her talons scraped his face leaving a blood trail. "Tell me about these books."

He stifled the urge to bite her as she bent close. Nope—he might get blood poisoning. "What's the title? Maybe I read it in school." He was playing with fire now. She was dangerous, but anger messed with your good judgment. If he could rile her enough, she might make a mistake. He'd strike at any opening.

"I'll leave you to your *fun,* darling," Rutgar said from the front of the tent. "You enjoy this much more than I. Let me know if you have any luck." He chuckled and walked down the steps.

Mentally, Brandon slapped himself. He had forgotten the other man. The merc had watched the woman dealing with him and said nothing. He shouldn't have taken his eyes or mind off such a dangerous enemy.

"Do you think me a fool?" Jacinta's shriek broke the stillness of the night. "That little blonde-haired American doctor is the fool. She thought she could sneak into our country and carry secrets out with her. Tell me what I want to know, or things are going to get painful."

"I'm not sure I should answer the first question, ma'am. As to the second, I don't know anything about secrets. I merely rescued a *beautiful* woman in distress."

Her face clouded with anger and jealousy. He'd pushed the right buttons. She was jealous of Mira's beauty. Agitated, she paced, her movements' jerky, all signs he was rattling her. If she didn't kill him first, he might shake her enough, to make a mistake. He only needed the right moment to make a move. Oh, and his hands free. Blood trickled on his wrists as he worked the rope and taunted her with words.

A sharp painful jab from the crack between the boards made his knee jerk. Damn. Had he been bitten by a scorpion or something worse, on top of all his other troubles? He looked down in search of the culprit, surprised to see the tip of a sharp knife barely showing through the crack beside his leg. His heart raced, and hope flared. Adrenaline pumped through his veins and he quickly drew Jacinta's attention to his face.

"How did you meet Rutgar?" He hoped she would grasp at the conversation change, and not be interested in coming too close to him—at least not yet.

"He came to the club in the city where I worked. Instantly, we were attracted to each other."

His stomach roiled as she preened. "He told me about his work, and I offered to help him. He is going to take me away from here and show me all kinds of beautiful places."

Brandon kept his attention on her, doing his best not to grimace when the knife cut the rope and nipped his skin. Immediately, he felt the tension ease on his legs as the bindings were sliced. All he had to do was move his legs to break the last tiny strand holding it together.

Through the tent wall behind him, he felt the blade of another knife as it sliced through his bonds. Startled, he stiffened when he recognized the feel of Mira's slim fingers.

Damn Rafà. How dare he put her at risk like this? He fought against his anger. The knife sliced the ropes completely, and then a small hand squeezed his palm. She might as well be squeezing his heart. Warmth rushed through him as he returned the pressure and palmed the knife.

"Come now, Mr. Brandon—let us contin—"

An explosion ripped through the camp, cutting off her grating voice. She whipped around toward the flap. Sounds of chaos floated through the opening.

It was time. He jerked his good leg, snapping the rope, and hurled the knife as she turned back to him. The blade found its mark. Jacinta collapsed to the floor without another sound.

As he looked at the lifeless body, her vacant eyes staring, he felt nothing.

Spurred by the commotion outside, he dragged himself over to the body and removed the knife. Rolling her body over, he grabbed the journals and tucked them into his shirt. At the sound of a step, he drew back to throw the knife but stilled when he recognized the face peering in at him.

"You disobeyed orders. Now help me up so I can slam my fist into your sorry face." He swore as he pushed up on his good leg. He was angry at Rafà—for so many things—but *damn* it was good to see him.

"I love you too, *Cap*, but can we save the hugs and kisses for later? I'm going to be a little busy in the next few minutes." Rafà armed him with a Sig Sauer, then grabbed him fireman style. Two books fell to the floor.

Brandon struggled against his friend's shoulder, muttering about the books.

"I got 'em, Cap." Rafà shifted him on his shoulder, scooped up the books sliding them into his vest, then carried him from the tent.

****

Mira ached to reach in and wrap her arms around Brandon after releasing his hands from the ropes. She pushed feelings and needs aside for now. She had to stick to the plan and make this escape work. Leaving the knife with him, she ran in a low crouch to the tall grasses. Dressed like a man with her hair tucked under her cap, she blended with the shadows. Rafà had enjoyed rubbing mud over her face and hands to complete her disguise. Another preset explosion went off, briefly silhouetting the two men making their way toward the jungle.

She fell in behind them, sweeping the area to the rear with her rifle as they'd practiced. Anyone crazy enough to come out to check on the explosions was kept at bay by the rapid gunfire. They made their way into the jungle unscathed and went quickly to the zip-line.

Rafà had anticipated Brandon's injuries and rigged a special sling to support him. She went up first and turned to help direct Brandon up the rigging. She lowered him to the platform, suppressing an exclamation of horror at his wounds. He was in bad shape. No way would he last the entire route on the zip-line. The jarring motion would break open his wounds and cause serious blood loss.

Her face must have shown her concern because Rafà picked up on it immediately. "Cap, looks like we're switching to plan B. How do you feel about female drivers?"

After the jarring race to the trip line, Brandon was barely conscious, but he raised his battered face and stared at Rafà.

She bent and kissed him softly on the forehead, the only visible spot on his body not covered in blood. As she did so, she noted he was fading in and out of consciousness. "Quick, Rafà, he could go into shock."

He rigged Brandon for the zip-line. "You run the zip-line first and start the truck. I'll be right behind you. We don't have much time before the soldiers get back from town to check out the explosions."

She patted Brandon's arm, and then hoisted herself to the next level. She took only a moment to reattach her safety harness before she jumped off and flew though the darkness. God, she hoped there were no vines or creatures in the way. Her feet had barely touched the platform before she unharnessed and shimmied down the tree. She ran another fifty feet to the spot where they'd left the old mining truck hidden in the underbrush.

The truck was huge, having been used at the mine for loading ore. Rafà had somehow worked a miracle and made it run. It was as good as a bulldozer in the underbrush. She climbed into the cab and started the diesel engine. Smoke sputtered out of the snorkel exhaust and the body of the truck shook all over.

Moments later, she felt the weight of Brandon's form as Rafà placed him in the back, followed by a sharp rap on the roof. Her signal. She took off, running without lights, and wearing Rafà's night vision goggles. Identifying objects was difficult—so she dodged anything that looked big or very solid. When they had planned this, it had sounded easy. Reality check. Driving through the jungle at night, without lights was a nightmare.

She reached the old road leading to the mine. It wasn't one of the main roads, but a track the locals used for their carts. Ahead was a waterfall which fed a small river. Following Rafà's instructions she slowed, grinding the gears as she struggled to downshift to a lower gear. With the lower gear engaged, she eased the heavy truck into the water. Back and forth, the truck pitched precariously over the river bottom as she drove straight into the waterfall.

God, she hoped Brandon was okay with all this movement.

The truck slowed and sputtered as water cascaded down over them. She experienced a moment's panic. Heart in her throat, she stomped the clutch, shifted gears, and pressed the gas pedal to the floor. The engine gave a shudder as the truck whined momentarily, then with a surge of energy it pitched forward into a dark cave. She slammed on brakes, stopping a foot from the rock wall. The old truck stalled and shut off. The sound of rushing water was muted in the truck cab, allowing her to hear the loud pounding of her own heart. Her hands and knees shook, and her mouth was bone dry. Jerking off the goggles, she dropped her head on the steering wheel, trying to ease the shakes, spreading through her body.

Muffled bumps from the rear of the truck brought her swiftly back to the moment and she swallowed hard, trying to get her voice to obey her. "Is he all right?

She held her breath, waiting for his reply.

****

"Depends on what you mean by *all right.*" Rafà had excellent night vision but even he couldn't see anything in this darkness. He struggled with the slippery truck bottom, and then managed to sit upright.

"He's…damn it Cap, why'd you have to go and do that?" He reached down to remove the fist clawing into his calf. "What am I going to tell all the pretty senoritas when they see claw marks on my sexy legs?"

"You won't be able to tell them a damn thing, if I cut your tongue out first," Brandon rasped, his breathing labored. "Whose hair-brained plan, was this?

You know how I feel about women drivers, and you go and let Mira drive at an ungodly speed through the jungle, with no headlights. Now get me up from here so I can beat your sorry—" He fell back to the truck bed, his strength gone.

Rafà suppressed his laughter. "I'd have to say he's alive and clawing." Secretly he was glad to see Brandon had some fight left in him. He was going to need it because even though they were out of 'the woods' so to speak—they weren't out of trouble. They still had to take care of his wounds, and then get out of here.

Chapter Thirty-One

Mira struggled with the door on the heavy truck, managed to shove it open, then fell out. With no light, she clung to the side of the truck and made her way to the back. She froze when the sound of an approaching vehicle cut the night air. It slowed as it reached the stream they had just driven through. She held her breath as a whirling spotlight created sparkles on the falling water. God, would the light penetrate the water and come into the cave? Another explosion sounded in the distance and the truck motor gunned, crossing to the other side of the stream. A collective sigh of relief sounded and Rafà switched on a small lantern.

Her gaze riveted on Brandon's bloody and bruised face. Unspoken words and emotions electrified the air. Rafà shuffled awkwardly showing his awareness of the charged atmosphere. "You two want me to leave?" he interjected into the quiet.

Mira became all business. "Let's get him upstairs."

She scrambled into the back of the truck and helped him drag Brandon to the tailgate. Lantern in hand she led while Rafà hoisted his friend across his shoulder. A few yards into the cave they entered a metal cage. She closed the mesh door and pushed the button. Slowly, the elevator moved them upward.

The lift stopped abruptly, jolting Brandon's body against the metal grating. He groaned.

Rafà shifted Brandon's weight. "Sorry, Cap."

Moments later they entered the secret door. Rafà released Brandon, sliding him onto the cot. Her lips quirked as she knelt beside the cot. Even half dead, Brandon still held the sig tightly in his hand, jerking when she tried to pry it from his fingers. "You can let it go now. You're safe."

His eyes popped open, fixing her with his hard gaze then released his death grip on the weapon. She eased the gun from his now relaxed grip—placing it under the cot out of the way, but not out of reach. "Help me get him out of these clothes and boots."

Rafà reacted to the urgency in her voice, pulled his knife from its sheath and cut what was left of Brandon's clothing. She made short work of his boots then had him down to swim trunks and layers of blood. Her heart rate quickened at the sight, and she ached to pull him into her arms and hold him. She shoved her feelings aside; for now, he was her patient, one she'd lose if she didn't hurry.

As soon as his flesh was exposed to the air, he began to shake all over. With the combination of blood loss and adrenaline burn, he was going into shock.

"Turn the water back on to heat and then help me wipe him down," she ordered in a brisk professional manner.

She'd known Brandon would need extensive care and had prepared as much as she could before going to the camp. The equipment was set up beside the bed on the table, which Rafà had rebuilt and reinforced. She grabbed the small plastic wrapped emergency blanket and covered his shaking form.

Her parents' medical bag, restocked before leaving

the clinic, could make all the difference. She'd anticipated using it to patch up people *he* shot, not the other way around. The IV solution she'd placed inside at the last minute could very well save his life.

With the water already heating on the stove, Rafà grabbed a cloth and poured liquid antimicrobial soap on Brandon's arm and started cleaning.

She continued the process with alcohol swabs, and then quickly found a vein inserting the IV. Rafà brought the pot of water over; she placed the IV bag in it. Within a few minutes, the warmed fluid began to calm the shaking and brought needed warmth to his ravaged body. His eyes fluttered open.

"Hey *Cap*, the doc and I are going to get you all fixed up." His eyes followed her movements as she gently slid her hands over his body wiping away blood with the warm cloth, while keeping most of his body covered with the silver space blanket.

"It's good to see you, Rafà. I was beginning to think I'd never find you. No!" The abrupt exclamation halted her from placing the syringe of pain killers in the IV tubing. "I don't want any narcotics—I have to be able to think clearly."

Mira held the needle aside. His raised voice hurt, but she needed to get to work on him immediately.

"Sorry I snapped," he mumbled. "I've got a few things to take care of—before I get all fuzzy. Would you leave Rafà and me alone for a few minutes? We have issues to discuss in private."

"Are you crazy?" Her voice was incredulous. "You have major injuries and pain puts more stress on your body. You might think you're superman—but *damn it*, Brandon, you're only human."

He tried to chuckle, but it came out as a rumbling cough. "Isn't she something? She must be really riled if she's damning me."

Rafà gently lifted his head and shoulders and placed a pillow beneath him.

Brandon continued to look at her with that same beseeching stare until she relented. Whatever the two needed to discuss must be important. He wouldn't needlessly take the risk for anything less.

"All right," she said grudgingly. "I'll give you five minutes while I go out and remove some of the mud your friend had so much fun applying. When I return, you're getting the meds and *anything* else I deem necessary." She picked up a clean, wet cloth and left through the door into the tunnel.

The air was much cooler in the tunnel, refreshing after the harrowing escape. She stayed near the closed door, giving the two men privacy, yet available if needed. She used the respite to collect her ragged nerves and still her thoughts.

"Please God, help me to save him." She'd been raised without a formal religion but had seen enough miracles in her work to believe. What if she wasn't good enough? Operating on Ana had been frightening enough, but this was Brandon—the man she loved. Too many things remained unsaid and undone. They had to have more time together.

Nervous, she walked to the opening, drawing in fresh air with deep calming breaths.

"Get a grip, Mira," she told herself. She had to prepare herself to be strong for him. She listened to the sounds of the forest and inhaled the sweet scents of the blooms. Off to the right, she could just make out the glitter of twin stars. The scientist in her knew all about binary planetary systems. Tonight—she decided the scientist needed all the help she could get.

She smiled up at the stars, "Mom, Dad, if guardian angels exist, please watch over me while I try to save the man I love. I can't afford to make any mistakes." Her voice faltered for a moment before she continued. "I miss you and I love you." Her voice broke and she caught herself up. She took one last cleansing breath and used the cloth to wipe the tears and mud from her face and hands. Her shoulders pushed back, stiffening her spine, then she turned to go back inside.

****

Father José stood in the dark archway beside the church and watched intently as the sky lit with fireworks. The festival was in full swing and the participants reveled with boisterous outbursts as the evening progressed.

He paid close attention to the soldiers—noting their position as he made his presence visible. He liked to think the presence of a priest on the street kept violence and debauchery to a minimum. The rebels, for the most part, were hungry disillusioned peasants who were sold a story of a better life. The foreigners leading them were the ones to fear. The soldiers drank freely, he happily noted, and most were soon unable to stand. *Good.* Tonight's success depended on their ineptitude.

A loud explosion brought squeals of excitement from the crowd, as they looked skyward, expecting a large light display. A giant fireball rose—not over the crowd—but over the jungle. Surprise quickly changed to confusion and children screamed in fear. Another explosion sounded. Lacking leadership, the soldiers ran in several directions at once. Gunshots rang out, followed by loud yelling. The drunken soldiers raced to their trucks and drove wildly out of the village.

He watched the mass exodus, a smile on his lips and spring in his step. *It seems the Lord is busy tonight.* His gaze swept the village once more, watching as the locals calmed and continued to celebrate. He hung around a few more minutes and then moved inside. *The Lord might need a little help.* Whistling a hymn, he made his way to the alcove and down to the basement. He grabbed the bag of supplies, the light, and then moved swiftly into the hidden tunnel.

Chapter Thirty-Two

His gaze followed Mira as she left reluctantly. He turned to Rafà and stared up into his eyes. Rafà stooped down by the bed, making it easier to talk. "I need you to do something for me."

"Now, don't go asking me to do stuff for you after you're gone. Doc and I are going to fix you up, if I have to drain the blood from my own body and pour it through a tube into your ornery hide."

His eyes misted at the outburst, knowing Rafà meant every word. Most people went their entire lives, without having someone care that much. The SEALs had bonded his men into a group of lifelong friends, brothers, willing to die for each other. Now, he had only two of his brothers left. "I want you to fetch the padre," he interjected when his friend paused for breath.

"Weren't you listening? You're not going to die."

"If you don't mind, shut up and listen for a minute." His voice radiated irritation. "I want Father José to marry Mira and me."

Rafà's face contorted comically, but quickly morphed into a wide grin. "Now you're talking. But I think you need to wait until after we patch you up. You look a little, *worse for wear*, if you know what I mean?"

"No. I want Mira to have my name and all I own before…well let's just say I don't want to put it off.

I've used up a lot of my nine lives on this mission. You know me. I always have a backup plan."

"That's the way we operate." Rafà looked around as if searching for Mira. "This mission was crap before we got started. We've been playing catch up instead of getting things done."

"There's one more thing." Brandon paused and looked away—then decisively turned to his friend "There might be a baby."

Rafà's jaw dropped. His face serious, he quickly lectured his friend. "How many times have you cautioned us before a mission? You had plenty of protection in the—"

"It was a choice," He interrupted. "She's the one, Rafà. The one I've waited for all my life. I've seen so much death and destruction in my lifetime—if we created a baby when we made love—well, I figure it's a good thing. What I need from you is a promise. If something happens to me—I can't think of anyone I would rather have watching over them."

Rafà's throat bobbled and he swallowed hard. For once he said nothing. Wordlessly, he reached over and squeezed Brandon's good arm. It was as good as an oath.

A look passed between the two men. Nothing spoken: Everything said in one shared look.

"Now, you have so much to live for, you better be nice when the Doc gets back and be a good patient. She's quite a lady—and she's got spunk. I think you've met your match, Cap. So, have you asked her yet?"

Brandon froze. "I plan to tell her when she comes back."

"Hold on. I wouldn't *tell* her anything if I were

you. You might…better ask her. She's kind of stubborn."

"I know all about her stubborn streak—but, how do you? You've only known her a few hours."

Rafà gave him a sheepish look. "I sort of, had to *negotiate,* to get her to follow my plan, and I couldn't get her to cooperate any other way. There was no way I was going to kiss her, like she said you did to make her agreeable. I'm not stupid and I value my head too much."

He laughed a full-throated chuckle. Pain shot through his shoulder and blood oozed from his wound. Hearing Mira's return, he quickly masked his exclamation of pain and covered the bloody wound with the blanket.

Both men turned as she walked through the door. Tension thickened to an uncomfortable level. Rafà flashed his friend a look of pity and fled through the secret door into the tunnel.

She knelt beside the cot and pulled the blanket back. "Where's Rafà running to? I'm going to need his help to tend this wound."

"Claustrophobic. When things close in, he goes outside. He'll be back soon."

He winced as she started a careful examination of his shoulder, continuing down his leg.

"Okay," she said in a tone that sounded true doctor. "I'm giving you some pain meds so I can dig more thoroughly into these wounds. I'll be honest with you—they're bad. I can probably fix your shoulder, but the leg may already be infected. In a tropical climate like this, that means you could lose it."

The harsh reality of her words had no effect. He

was a soldier and prepared to hear news like this. Talking to her about his feelings was the harder thing. "I don't want any medication. Rafà has gone to get the padre for me." He grabbed her hands and pulled her onto the side of the cot, working up the courage to explain.

"I know you're religious," she barked, "but we don't have time to wait for a priest to say some words over you. I don't intend to let you die."

"Are you challenging God now, Mira? I thought he was the one who controlled life and death. Besides, the priest isn't coming to give me last rites—though I would like to receive them. He's coming to marry us."

Damn, now he'd done it. She was going to get all mad and he'd probably have to kiss her to calm her down. The thought made him smile. Her silence puzzled him. Why was she sitting quietly and just looking at him? "Say something. You're scaring me."

"Why?"

He felt a little panicky at her stillness. "What do you mean—why?"

"Why do you want to marry me?"

Raw fear filled his gut; sweat beaded his brow.

"Damn it, you took a bullet for me without flinching. You faced the enemy without fear, yet you're scared to death of feelings and words. Will I die an old woman before you ever work up the courage to say it?"

He saw real anger—and hurt—in her eyes.

"Sometimes—a woman needs to hear the words, to know for sure. If you really care, show me some of that courage now, Brandon."

He turned her face with his palm, drank in the sight of her lashes against her skin—the blueness of her eyes—those eyes that saw way too much. If he died and never told her how he felt, then God would rightly send him to hell. Still—he didn't feel like he deserved her. Maybe if he lived long enough, he would get the chance to earn her love. She gave it so freely to him. Well he'd just have to bite the bullet and '*soldier up.*'

"Mira, I don't deserve someone as innocent as you—but I want you, and," he swallowed painfully, "and I love you." He held his breath waiting for her reaction. This was harder than waiting for an enemy attack.

"Thank you, Brandon. I know how hard it was for you. I love you. I promise, if God cooperates, I'll be around at least fifty more years, so you can practice saying those three little words you find so difficult. Now I need to give you a shot."

She started to rise.

Brandon grabbed her arm and held her there. His muscles tightened with frustration.

"Well? What's your answer?"

She stared at him, unsmiling. "Maybe, I'm being obtuse, but did you ask me something?"

"Come on Mira, don't do this to me. Will you marry me?" He held his breath and waited for her reply. Damn, how did men do this all the time? He'd rather jump into a crocodile infested river than talk about feelings.

A beautiful smile bloomed across her face and her eyes sparkled with feeling. "Yes, Brandon, I would be happy to marry you." She took his face in her hands and gently placed her lips on his.

A noise at the secret door startled them apart. Rafà's head popped through the door. "Is it safe to come in?"

"This is a safe house you moron, of course it's safe."

Rafà reached behind him and pulled Father José though the entrance. The priest carried a large pack. "Look who I found. Father must be psychic. He was already on his way for a visit." Rafà moved to the cot.

Brandon flashed a happy look at his friend, but he couldn't hide the spasm of pain shaking his body down to the bone.

Mira sent an urgent look to Father José.

Brandon read the look and interpreted it accordingly. "Let's get this show on the road, before Mira changes her mind."

She fiddled with the IV, and then picked up the syringe. He started to protest, but she gently placed a finger over his lips to prevent his words. "I understand your need but try to understand mine. I'm only going to give you a little something to relax you. When I kiss my husband for the first time, I don't want him wincing."

"I'd hate to disappoint a lady." He nodded, and she injected a small dose of morphine into his IV line.

The pain eased immediately. His muscles relaxed, and his breathing became less ragged. He looked up at her with his best grin. "I should have taken the shot before I asked you to marry me. It might have been less difficult."

"Don't get sassy with me, soldier." She slipped his arm back under the blanket and pulled the cover up to his chin.

Father José wore a satisfied smile as he moved to the cot. "There's going to be a wedding? I'm glad I stopped by. Here I was thinking Rafà and I would have a little game of checkers and now it looks like I'm going to be busy." The priest sat on the box Rafà had pulled over.

He quietly studied the priest.

Father José returned his candid, searching look.

Brandon recognized the signs of past wars, the pain of loss. He didn't know the priest's story, but he understood him. Soldier to soldier, they reached an understanding.

He hadn't talked to a priest in a very long time, now he said what he needed to say with his eyes. "Padre, Mira and I would be honored if you would marry us. I know we haven't met all the criteria, and we don't have a license but, we're a little pressed for time."

"In light of the present circumstances, I'm sure the Church will overlook our lack of procedure—As for the license, I always keep one in my bible. I have it on good authority," he nodded at Rafà, "you're a man of good character."

He flashed Rafà a sharp look, causing the priest to chuckle.

"I would be happy to join you in Holy Matrimony." He motioned for Mira to come closer. "I take it you are both doing this willingly, and are of sound mind?" He looked at each as they nodded.

Brandon lifted his eyes to his friend. "Would you be my best man?"

"I'll always be your best man, Brandon." His use of his real name spoke of the seriousness of his promise.

Mira moved to sit beside him, taking his hand in hers. The two of them silently listened as Father José spoke the words joining them as husband and wife.

When it came to the part for exchanging rings, everyone frantically looked around.

Noticing the dilemma, Father José reached into his pocket and pulled out a ring rosary. "I'm afraid this isn't supposed to be used as jewelry but will do." He handed the rosary to Brandon.

"Somehow, this seems appropriate. Thanks, Father." He reverently made the sign of the cross, kissed the rosary and slid it onto Mira's slim finger. "With this ring, I thee wed." His words resounded with promise—and love.

Mira cleared her throat before responding. She removed the rosary from her finger, repeated his movements and placed it on his finger.

His heart swelled with emotion at the simple words and the rest of the brief ceremony passed in a blur.

"You may kiss the bride." Father José intoned.

Using the last of his strength Brandon pulled her down to him and gave her a long, passionate kiss.

"Cap, it's not time for the honeymoon yet," Rafà said. "Suppose you let your best man have a kiss."

Never one to miss an opportunity, he took advantage of the poorly worded request. "Sorry, Rafà, I'm saving all my kisses for my wife."

"Smart ass," Rafà quipped and bent to give Mira a kiss on the cheek.

Father Jose handed the bible to Brandon with a pen and the license.

Brandon, then Mira and Rafà scrawled their names and handed the book back.

"I hate to pour water on the party, but I think we should start on those wounds," Father José said, as he rolled up his sleeves.

Mira kissed him on the cheek and became all professional again. "We can't risk moving him yet, Father, but I'm going to have to cut into his leg. I think it's infected and the bullet is still lodged in there somewhere. I would appreciate your help with the surgery. It's going to be primitive—but I'd like to try and save his leg along with his life."

Those were the last words Brandon heard. His vision blurred and then all was black.

Chapter Thirty-Three

"Thanks," she said as Rafà removed the syringe from the IV. "I was beginning to think we'd need a hammer to get him under." She wrapped surgical tape around the ring rosary, securing it to Brandon's hand. They needed all the help they could get. She moved to the sink, where she scrubbed her hands and arms.

"No problem," Rafà said. "He'll probably slug me when he wakes up, but he was being a little difficult."

Following her example, the two men washed up and sterilized as best they could.

Using a wet cloth, she cleaned the blood on his thigh. "I'm sure the cauterization was horrible—but at least it kept him alive." The horror of what they'd done to him rattled her inner calm. Reaching way down, she pulled on professionalism to center herself.

After another deep breath, she began to assess her patient. "I can ignore the shoulder for now," she mused as she slipped on gloves, "and concentrate on the leg. I'm going to try and get the bullet and see if the artery is completely sealed. Rafà, I need you to hold his leg down in case he moves. I pray he won't wake up during the procedure. Father, I hope you managed to bring some antibiotics in your bag of goodies." She busily prepped the leg, placing sterile gauze pads around the ragged entry wound. "If you had an X-ray machine and some anesthesia, I'd really be impressed."

"No x-ray machine, I'm afraid, but I do have chloroform. I can administer it, if you'd like." He placed several items on the table.

"Bless you." She breathed easier, knowing Brandon would remain unconscious during the procedure. "Rafà, open the door and push the secret door back. We need some cross ventilation. I'd hate for any of us to fall asleep from the fumes."

"I managed to bring several medications, including IV antibiotics." Father José said. "Don't ask where they came from; my sources are sketchy. I heard the explosions and knew things were happening at the camp. As soon as we finish here, I need to go to the clinic to see if any casualties show up. I wish I could bring you back with me."

The priest covered Brandon's nose with a gauze pad and dropped small amounts of chloroform on it. The sickly-sweet smell quickly permeated the room, reminding all of them of the primitive conditions.

As Mira made her incision, fresh blood seeped from the wound along with a few small clots. After a visual and by touch exam, she breathed easier. "At least there are no leaks coming from an artery. I sure as hell wish I could see well enough to sew things up."

Her words met with silence. "Sorry gentlemen, I tend to get a little 'adjective challenged' when I'm upset."

Rafà laughed at her explanation. "That's what it's called? I'm going to have to remember your definition. I'm afraid my genteel ears have never heard such fierce adjectives. Must be Brandon's influence."

Mira laughed at his antics, the tension between her shoulders easing just a little.

"Bring me the night vision goggles and take his scope off his rifle. If he asks later, tell him it fell off, the man's positively *anal* about the gun." She didn't bother to look at her assistants, just continued working on the wound.

Rafà returned with several parts along with those she'd requested. "Okay, Doc, what do you need me to do? Where are we going with this?"

"Can you rig something to hold the scope at an angle and steady?"

"Sure thing." Within minutes he had managed to scavenge parts from rifles to make a primitive microscope attached to a sniper gun prop. At her nod he slid it into place over Brandon's leg. Pressing his upper body over Brandon, he held him down while using his hands to hold the scope steady.

Mira found several oozing vessels. "I'm not going to be able to stitch them all—they're too ratty." She looked at Rafà over her mask. "I'm going to have to re-cauterize."

"I've got an acetylene torch; we can use it to heat something," Rafà added helpfully.

"You never cease to amaze me," she murmured. "Take this probe and heat it out in the tunnel away from the fumes. I've seen enough fireworks for tonight. How's he doing, Father?" The priest looked up from the head of the cot. "He's okay for now. How's the leg?"

"I'm withholding judgment until I get this bleeding stopped."

"Ready, Doc," Rafà called before entering with the glowing probe.

She took the probe while Rafà held the night scope over the wound. Looking through the eye piece, she gently touched the seeping areas of the ragged vessels. Instantly, the oozing stopped.

"Put the night goggles on me," she said. "And turn the light down."

Rafà grabbed the goggles and gently placed them on her face. "I don't follow you, Doc. You won't be able to see any detail."

"I'm hoping the bullet will show up colder than the tissue surrounding it. It'll keep me from digging too much and tearing other vessels."

"Pretty smart. Are you sure you're not a SEAL?"

She chuckled. "I'm afraid I wouldn't make a very good one. I can't swim."

"What?" Shocked disbelief flashed across his face. "We'll have to take care of that as soon as we get home."

The two of them kept up a conversation, while Father José quietly passed instruments and monitored the chloroform. His lips moved in silent prayer as she continued to search the ravaged flesh for the bullet. Comfortable with his silence, she was glad for his help and the prayers. For an untrained layman, he was remarkably adept in surgery.

After a moment, Mira stilled. "The bullet shattered the femur—the thigh bone—and is mixed in with the splinters. I can see it as a black spot where the surrounding area is red." She pushed the goggles off her eyes with her forearms. "Turn up the light and hold him tight." She cut deeper into the muscle, removing pieces of bone, followed by a mangled slug. Blood poured from the spot as she cleaned and swabbed the area.

"Hang on to him, this is going to hurt like…" She didn't finish her sentence as she poured peroxide into the wound—let it sit, bubbling as it cleansed and slowed the blood flow. As she swabbed it out, Brandon began to stir. "Father, I don't want to give him anymore chloroform, it might compromise his lungs. How are we on morphine?"

"We have more. How much do you want to give him?" the priest calmly asked.

"Start with four milligrams. If it doesn't hold him, give him one milligram at a time till you reach a max of eight. I've still got a lot to do."

Not bothering to look up for a response from Father José, she began the tedious task of stitching muscles, one layer at a time. Afterward, she left the outer layer of skin open. It looked awful but would lower the risk of infection forming in the deep wound. With Rafà's help, she carefully wrapped his thigh with a thick bandage. With no x-ray equipment and no special tools, there was little she could do for the bone and the knowledge pained her. Brandon would need more surgery, most likely a pin. A wound like this was a career ender for a soldier. Hopefully it wouldn't be a life ender.

No—she wouldn't let herself think of what *might* happen—she had to stay focused on the here and now.

She looked up from her work. "Father, I need something for splints."

The priest looked around, grabbed the crates and swiftly broke them apart. For a man of the cloth, he demonstrated tremendous strength. He handed her the slats and helped her to tie them in place.

After finishing the leg, she immediately went to work on his shoulder. Shifting Brandon with Rafà's help, she determined it was a clean through and through shot. She cleaned and applied a dressing with antiseptic cream, then wrapped the entire shoulder.

She chose a broad-spectrum antibiotic from Father José's pack and administered it through the IV. Having done all she could do, she pulled off her gloves and ran from the room into the tunnel.

Her gorge rose as she dashed to get to fresh air, barely managing to make it to the opening before retching. Tears poured freely as she remained doubled over, emptying the contents of her stomach. Her body shook from reaction. She covered her face with her hands, and finally allowed all the fears and emotions to release.

After a moment, gentle hands took hers and lowered them.

****

Rafà wiped her face with a damp cloth and then pulled her close and held her. Brandon was one lucky man. This woman had fought for him, doctored him, and loved him. Something cold deep inside of him thawed just a little. Would there ever be another woman like Mira who would do the same for him? He doubted he was so lucky.

She shuddered a little, hugged him tightly and stepped back. "Thank you."

"No problem," he said lightly. "We all have to let off steam sometimes. You ready to go back in? Father José needs to leave, and we could all use some 'spirits' to settle us down. I just happen to have a wee flask I keep for just such occasions."

"Why doesn't that surprise me?"

"Now, Doc, don't go getting any ideas. It's strictly medicinal." He made his words light—though he felt a little squeeze in his chest when she smiled.

They both entered the room—only to realize there was nowhere to sit. They fell to the floor, laughing. Brandon now wore the only chairs as splints.

Rafà pulled out the flask and offered some to Father José who refused. He handed it to Mira and grinned. "Ladies first."

She grasped the flask and took a large slug, choked and sputtered.

He pounded her back. Brandon would enjoy a description of her face as she took the slug of pure brandy. He'd make sure to tell him about it. It felt good knowing he'd be able to talk to his friend again.

He raised the flask and made a toast. "To Brandon and Mira, may you live long, love hard, and tell your grandchildren about their uncle Rafà." He tipped the flask and drank deeply.

"Keep your celebrations to a minimum, my friend. Dr. Phelps, eh, Dr. Falcon is going to need a lot of help with the patient. I'm afraid it's going to be a long night for everyone."

After admonishing Rafà, the priest moved to the cot, and laid his hand on Brandon's forehead. Murmuring a few words in Latin, he bade the two of them good night. Before entering the secret passage, he turned to Rafà. "Have you figured out how you're getting out of the country? I'm sure there must be some sort plan in place for your return."

Rafà slipped the capped flask into his vest and looked up at the priest. "I'll be in touch as soon as Brandon wakes and we get all the details. Be extra careful at the clinic. Those rebels are going to be really pi—" He caught Mira's eye and quickly changed his word choice, "*upset.* I sort of blew the sh—" Another look. "—*heck,* out of the whole place." Having a lady around could be quite an inconvenience. How did Brandon manage it?

Father José laughed at his dilemma. "Take it easy, Rafà. Good luck, Mira. God go with you."

"Thank you for everything." She jumped up and gave him a big hug. "Please keep praying for Brandon, he's going to need it," she whispered as he returned her hug.

"Don't worry, child, I think God has more plans for Mr. Falcon." With those words he disappeared through the hidden door.

Chapter Thirty-Four

Silence filled the small room after the priest left. What was left to say? It was a waiting game now. She checked on Brandon, wishing she had the means to do more to help him.

"I feel so helpless. With all the modern medicines and technologies, we've been cast back to the Stone Age. There's an entire jungle out there with thousands of potential medicines and cures. What we don't cut down and burn, we make inaccessible because of revolutions and politics. Mankind is far too violent to survive."

"Don't give up on the world, just yet. I think we've fu—screwed up some things, but we still have hope. That's why soldiers keep fighting. We're trying to keep the good safe and rid the world of those trying to destroy it."

"I'm sorry," she murmured. "Normally, I'm not so pessimistic. Must be the brandy."

"Cap and I have to be in places like this, but why are you here? You could do clinic work in thousands of similar villages without the risk of hostiles. Believe me there's no shortage of poverty and medical need. How'd you end up here?"

Brandon made a groaning sound, then moved his arms. Mira jumped to his side, noting his glazed eyes were slightly open. Using a wet cloth, she wiped his face with a gentle touch and saw recognition dawn in his eyes. He was coming around.

"Mira?" His was voice dry and husky. "I had a dream—we got married." Then he smiled and faded back to sleep.

She brushed the hair back from his forehead before pressing her lips to his skin. He was hot—too hot. His body was at war with the myriad of microbes attacking him. The bullets, knife, dirt and the filthy truck ride, all of which carried microscopic armies of invaders into his wounded flesh. Poor Brandon, even now he was at war.

She plopped back down on the floor beside the bed. "How will I get him to remember our anniversary? He doesn't even remember the wedding."

"Don't you worry, he has a memory like an elephant. Besides—men usually remember more about the honeymoon than the wedding."

"Great. I hope our honeymoon is somewhere a little less exotic."

"What I meant to say was—"

"It's all right. I understand. I'll just be happy for him to wake up, regardless of his memory."

"It's that bad?"

"I wish I'd been able to find the orchid I came searching for. It's has miraculous healing powers, and we could use a miracle right about now."

"You came all this way looking for a flower? It must be pretty special."

"Information from my uncle's journals led me here. He'd studied all the known records of the plant. Some of the stories he heard made him believe it still exists, in some of the remote jungles here. I suppose it doesn't matter now. He's gone, and Brandon could be dying." Her voice broke. "I've waited all my life for a man like Brandon Falcon. I refuse to lose him after such a short time."

****

Rafà wasn't much of a talker, especially when it came to consoling weepy women, but he had to do something to take her mind off her worries. She had shouldered a heavy burden the past few weeks. Lesser women, *hell* most men, couldn't face what she'd faced and still manage to fight. *Damn.* She was one tough woman.

"Tell me more about this miracle plant. I've had plenty of time over the past two months to study the plants here, not much else to do when you're hiding."

He congratulated himself as her eyes lit up and she started a botany lecture.

"It's called the *Blue Spider Orchid,* because it's blue and the petals are shaped like a spider. The Mayan, Egyptian and even the Chinese people all make vague references to it in their histories. I wish Brandon had been able to rescue the journals before you blew everything up. You're very destructive you know."

"Now, Doc, I only blew up bad things, besides, the whole area should smell a lot better. About those journals, they wouldn't happen to be about the size of a diary and bound in leather, would they?"

With a gasp, she jerked around to face him. "Do you mean to tell me, you've *seen* them?" Her excitement grew at his words, her face becoming animated. "Where?" She was on her knees leaning toward him—waiting.

"Are these journals important?" he asked, as if he

had no idea of their significance.

"Important enough for Brandon and me to risk our lives to get them back."

"Oh, I wondered why he was carrying diaries around the jungle stuffed in his shirt. I was hoping for some juicy reading, but I suppose they're filled with all kinds of scientific jargon and the like." Enjoying each minute of her mounting excitement, he dragged out handing down information.

She grabbed his shirt with both fists, getting right in his face. "Thirty seconds. Where are they? Tell me right this minute before I find something to throw at you. This time it won't be something soft."

He gave her his best smile—the one he saved for grandmothers and small children—then spoke the words she'd been waiting to hear. "They fell from Brandon's clothes when I picked him up; and I put them in the cupboard."

Mira was off the floor and in the kitchen before the words were completely out of his mouth. Her squeal of excitement woke her patient. She stopped long enough to soothe him. Sitting near the cot, she cradled the journals to her chest as if they were golden. "Thank you, Rafà. You can't know how much this means to me."

"It was Brandon, not me. I just happened to notice them. Do you have any pictures of this flower in the book?"

"There are no *real* pictures, but there are sketches of it from descriptions. Uncle Max let me help with the drawings. We enjoyed working on them together." Her voice became momentarily wistful. "Come here and I'll show you," she patted the spot beside her.

Together they flipped through the pictures and descriptions. Before long he noticed her eyes droop. She had to get some rest, or she would be no good to Brandon if he needed her. "Hey, you look all done in."

Closing the journals, she yawned, "I need to get some sleep."

"You curl up here beside the cot, while I make a security check, then I'll probably crash outside somewhere. If you need me just give a call."

"No. Brandon said not to call out in the jungle. You might not be the one to answer."

"Smart man, our Brandon. Can you whistle?"

"Not very well, but I'll make do. I won't call unless I need help with him, we both need to rest." She scrunched in beside her new husband. At Rafà's questioning look she lifted her chin. "I have to be near him and not just as his doctor. I need to hear him breathe—feel his heart beating. I need to help him have the will to live," she lowered her head. "Sorry, I guess I want him to know I'm here for him."

"Don't ever apologize for loving someone. Get some rest." He watched as she closed her eyes, drifting off to sleep with her palm over Brandon's heart.

By the time her breathing was even and relaxed, he was gone. He was a man on a mission, not doing a security check—he was going flower picking. There were some exotic looking, blue flowers up the mountain. Climbing in the dark was risky, but worth it, if it would save his friend. He would risk anything to put hope back into the eyes of the lovely woman he had just left.

Chapter Thirty-Five

Brandon woke to faint light provided by a single candle guttering in a tin plate on the table. He was hot, especially his left side. A weight pinned his chest and legs. He suffered a moment of panic. Was he paralyzed? Where?

Everything flooded back like a nightmare on steroids. He'd been shot, tortured, rescued, married and...his heartbeat accelerated. He and Mira had been married. Talk about reality checks. The heater beside him had short blond curls and her head lay across his chest. He was a little fuzzy about details, but recognized her delicate features, remembered how soft her lips were, how silky her skin felt against him.

He ignored the overwhelming heat and pain bombarding his body, fascinated by her head moving up and down with each breath he took. He had made it through the surgery. They were together but still not safe.

Where was Rafà? Surely, he hadn't taken off again. He'd strangle his friend with bare hands if he'd left her unprotected. No. He'd given his word and that was an oath to Rafà. He was around here somewhere, hopefully near enough to help him out of this bed. Nature was making an urgent call and he didn't want Mira to have to haul his bulk out of bed.

She must have sensed his watching eyes and jerked

awake. He tightened his arm around her and pulled her close. "Brandon, don't put so much pressure on your arm. I don't want to lose the IV." She gently shoved against his arm and sat up beside him. "How do you feel? You've had a rough couple of days."

"I'm burning up, my bladder is about to explode, and for some reason…I have this overwhelming urge to kiss you."

He covered her mouth with his, drinking in her sweetness. "Mm—best medicine in the world," he murmured against her lips.

She pulled back and eyed him with a professional look. "You've lost a lot of blood and you can't put any weight on your leg. The bone is shattered. There's nothing I can do for it."

"Straight to the point, no frills or sugar coating. I like that in my woman." He moved his hand to take hers. "I'm alive, Mira, and I have you. To quote an old friend, 'the rest is lagniappe.' "

"What?"

"It's Cajun for *something extra*. It seems to fit don't you think? We're alive and together, more than that is a bonus."

"Lagniappe." Mira tried the strange word on her tongue. "I like it, but if it's okay with you, I'd like lots of lagniappe." Her face became serious again. "You're going to need extensive procedures when we get out of here." She lowered her head. "All I could do was patch you up and try to control any infections."

Her chin in his hand, he tilted her head up and looked at her tormented face. "Baby, don't torture yourself. You did your best and gave me a chance. It's what a person does with a second chance, which makes

256

a difference. I intend to dance at our children's weddings."

A smile blossomed across her face. "I suggest you wait until you get better before you start thinking about children in the *plural*. They can be quite a handful."

"Help me up out of this bed. I'm burning up and I need to…"

"You weren't listening. I meant it when I said you can't get up. I'll find you a bucket." Mira wandered off to the cabinets pulling things out until she found a plastic bucket. "As for burning up," she continued, "you have a fever. I'll give you a cool sponge bath when you finish."

He frowned at the bucket. Did she really expect him to do this lying flat on his back? He tried to sit up but dropped back down as pain pierced through his leg. "Damn it, Mira," he spat the words out. "I can't do this lying down."

She bit her lip. A delightful laugh burst from her throat as she watched his dilemma. Even gritting his teeth, *he* had to smile.

****

She gently removed the blanket and helped him roll to his good side. "I'll prepare your bath now, sir," she said in her brisk professional voice and walked over to the stove. She banged two pots together at the sink, making noise to give him as much privacy as possible.

"I need your help."

She knew how much those words cost him. She took the bucket and helped him roll onto his back.

"Where's Rafà?" he asked as she bathed him with the cool water.

"He left to make a security check and then sleep

outside. Is he claustrophobic? He doesn't seem to like enclosed places."

"How long ago? Shouldn't he be back by now?" His voice held a note of uneasiness. "Rafà has spent most of his life outdoors—but he shouldn't have left you inside alone."

"I lost track of time when I fell asleep, but by the looks of your IV, I'd say he's been gone about three hours." She straightened the covers and tucked them around his washed body. "I'm supposed to whistle for him if I need him. He needs to discuss your arrangements for leaving the country. It's supposed to be tomorrow, right?"

"It *has* to be tomorrow." He stayed her arm as she reached to check the IV. Her eyes met his in question. "This entire area will be a hornet's nest after what happened at the camp." He paused to look directly into her eyes. "If we don't get out tomorrow, we might not make it out at all."

"You're not well enough to be moved. The bone fragments I didn't get could move and puncture another artery." She abruptly stopped at the adamant look on his face. There was no use arguing further. Brandon—the soldier was back.

"Our rendezvous on the Mosquito Coast is tomorrow evening. Jackson will be waiting there to pick us up, but he can't hang around long without being spotted." He smoothed the worried crinkle in her forehead. "I promise, somehow, I'll get us there."

Rafà walked through the door and set down a large sack. "That's mighty big talk from someone lying flat on his back, don't you think?"

"Where the hell have you been?" Brandon

growled. "You left Mira alone."

"You should give her some credit, Cap. She is quite a capable woman, with or without help. If we could teach her to swim, she could fill in on our team anytime."

Mira wasn't sure what was going on between the two, but she didn't like it. Tension bristled between them. Brandon acted as if…she looked at his face and saw it. He was jealous because his friend had complimented her. She reached over, picked up his hand and kissed it. "I'm already on a team, Rafà."

His face softened at her words. Rafà's face, on the other hand, had a distinctively devilish look.

"You jackass—quit trying to bait me. I should've known you'd try to stir things up." Brandon threw a disgruntled look at his best man, who laughed and sat on the floor beside the bed. "What happened while I was in la-la land, and where have you been?"

Rafà pulled the sack toward him. "Well—Doc has been so sweet and all, so I went out and picked her some flowers."

Brandon's face tightened into a scowl. "The hell you did. Rafà, I'll…"

"You found it!" With a stunned look on her face, Mira bent to touch the flower. "Do you realize what this means?"

"I could only get the one. There might be others higher up, but it was dark, and I didn't want to be gone too long." He gave Brandon a meaningful look. "I wasn't sure what you needed so I pulled the entire plant."

She was too busy examining the plant to listen. This was a miracle. Thousands of people could benefit from the research she would conduct. There was no limit to the possibilities. She would need to set up some sort of equipment to extract the essence of the plant. Even with her specialized training, it would be difficult and a gamble. Rafà's words penetrated her fanciful musings. This was the only specimen and she would have to destroy it to save Brandon. The scientist in her screamed NO. She looked into her husband's eyes and knew what she would do.

"Mira?" His voice was subdued. "Is this the plant you told me about—the *Blue Spider Orchid*?"

"Yes." She gently lay the flower back down. "Thank you, Rafà." She jumped up and became all business. "First we have to update the journal and do another sketch. Even if we must destroy it, we can get as much information as possible. Rafà, while I'm doing that could you take the dry bouillon from the cabinet and make some broth. We have to get Brandon's strength up if we're going to take a trip tomorrow."

"Yes, ma'am." He cast a helpless look at Brandon.

A chuckle escaped Brandon's throat followed by a cough.

Mira's pulse leaped at the sound. Please, God, don't let him have pneumonia on top of everything else. The faster she got the plant extracts into him the better. He was strong—but even he couldn't survive this without help.

His head sank back down on the pillow, weakness evident in his slack muscles. She exchanged an uneasy look with Rafà, before the two of them commenced their jobs with added haste.

Chapter Thirty-Six

Early in the predawn hours, Father José walked with tired steps from the clinic. Either the explosions had wiped out all the soldiers or they had left for safer territory. The only people who came to the clinic were some of the escaped prisoners. He and Rosita patched them up, fed them and then sent them off with a reliable associate. They would have to lie low until things cooled down in the area, and then they and their families would be relocated to remote villages.

At times, it seemed the world was constantly destroying itself. Everyone wanted what wasn't theirs and no one took time to talk and work things out. He caught himself in his musings. "Forgive me, Lord," he murmured as he hastened his steps. He hoped it wasn't too early to make a call. Inside the small church, he waited as his eyes adjusted to the darkness, then moved to the front of the church and knelt before the altar.

"You've had a busy night, Father." The man's voice came from an alcove near the side wall.

He finished his prayer, crossed himself and moved into the main part of the chapel. "God's work is not an hourly job, I'm afraid. Things often happen in the middle of the night and can't wait until morning. I believe you of all people should understand this, Agent Morel."

"After all these years, you still won't call me by

my given name?"

"Our association is one of necessity, not friendship. I prefer formality."

"Fine. I stopped in to see how you and our friends are doing. I'll be leaving the country for a while. All vehicles are being checked and I would hate for anyone to be subjected to an arrest or worse. Of course, as a priest, your position does allow a certain freedom of movement, even in a war-torn country. Thank you for the inspiration."

"Are you ready to move on, Joseph?"

"Not yet. I still have work here."

"Then I would advise you to be very careful. It's hard to know who to trust these days." The door to the alcove opened and then closed.

The appearance of the American agent hadn't been a surprise. He'd been in the area for a year and popped in at the oddest times. He often thought the man was burning too many fires at the same time, but as long as God's work was done, he'd still keep piling on the wood.

He entered the alcove and pushed the button for the tunnel door. Once there he climbed down a ladder to a small room, removed a key from his pocket and opened another door. He flipped the light switch as he entered the room. An array of computers and high-tech communication devices lined the walls of the room. Lights blinked, and machines hummed as he moved to the Hip-Link Encoder and sat. He had a message to send, another mission to complete. Soon he would need to destroy this room; it wouldn't do for the rebels to find it beneath his small church.

After coding the message and sending it on its way,

he waited in silence. Moments later the reply flashed onto the screen.

"GET PACKAGE OUT AT ALL COSTS."

****

Mira worked furiously, keeping accurate records, while trying to extract the healing chemicals from the orchid. If this plant had been used in ages past, their equipment couldn't have been very sophisticated. At least she had years of medical training and was an expert in botanical pharmacology. Even so, this was a first—there had never been a living specimen to work with in modern time. She had no idea what part of the plant held the regenerative compound. She would use the entire plant in different ways.

First, she removed the stamen with its pollen, and then the pistil. As the reproductive parts of the flower, the most important part of the plant, she hoped the chemical was concentrated there. She ground the parts in a makeshift mortar and poured some of Rafà's whiskey over it. The alcohol should extract the chemicals, similar to how perfume was extracted. The method was crude, and it wouldn't have enough time to steep, but it was the best she could do. Brandon needed help now.

If her theory was correct, the extract needed to bypass the digestive system and be placed directly into the bloodstream. She was so thankful for the IV already in his arm. The roots, leaves, and stems, she chopped and boiled. God, she hoped she was doing the right thing. Brandon thrashed on the cot and she paused to wipe his face and soothe him with whispered words.

"I'm here. Fight, my darling." He was burning up and delirious. "Rafà, find me some sort of strainer for this, I'm going to try every way I can to get this plant into him."

He removed the cleanest shirt from the duffel, tore it, and handed her the pieces. Together they strained the two mixtures and left them to cool.

Normally confident in her work, she was now a bundle of doubts. When the life of the one you loved was at stake, things were so different. "What if I'm doing the wrong thing? I could kill him. I have no way of knowing the strengths of these chemicals—or if the plant has some kind of poison to protect it. There are too many unknowns."

"Cap always tells me you can't go into enemy territory knowing everything about it. You just have to work with what you *do* know and hope for the best." He paused beside the cot and ran a hand gently over Brandon's brow. He turned back to face her. "Tell me. What do you know?"

"I *know* if something isn't done, he will die." Her voice broke at her last word. She took a deep breath and continued. "I *know* from what I've read—this plant is his best chance for survival."

"*I know* he would tell you to follow your instincts." Rafà's voice was soft but filled with conviction. "He'd tell you he trusts you to do what's right. Now we've got that straight, how do you want go about this?"

She closed her eyes a moment—then grabbed the medical kit and knelt on the floor by the bed. "I'm going to inject the alcohol mixture into the IV. That will get it into his system the fastest." She drew the liquid into a syringe and slowly injected it into the IV.

"I hope he appreciates the sacrifice. You just injected a fine brandy into him."

She spared him a look before turning back to her patient. "Take the strained plant material and pack it directly into the leg wound. We'll use the boiled leaves on his shoulder and try to pour the juice down his throat a little at a time."

****

Rafà uncovered the wound, then used the tips of his fingers to pack the warm plant material onto the ravaged skin. A tingling sensation moved up his arm, then his groin tightened. *Damn*—what the hell was the matter with him? He cast a sideways glance at Mira, before moving to work on the shoulder wound.

She laughed unexpectedly. "I'd forgotten that part of the legend."

"What part?"

"It's a good thing we cut those swim trunks off." she said, turning her pink face away as she covered Brandon's aroused body. "One of the reasons this plant was thought to be extinct was because it was an aphrodisiac. It was over-collected and used for, shall we say, non-medicinal purposes. It does give one a little boost, doesn't it?" She turned, running a finger down her husband's chest. "If the plant works this quickly, Brandon may just walk out of here."

Rafà began to feel a little bit uncomfortable. The look on her face combined with the tingle running down his body brought him to his feet. "If you have things under control, Doc, I think I'll do another security check."

She laughed and laid her head beside Brandon. "Go ahead."

He waved and walked stiffly from the room, sucking in fresh air as he moved outside. The effects of the plant were indeed potent. A few more minutes and he might have embarrassed the Doc. He checked the area then ventured into another section of the old mine.

No one knew of his discovery, not even Father José. He'd found the hidden tunnel only a few weeks ago and hadn't explored much of it yet. The tunnel led into the bottom of what was certainly a pyramid, though it couldn't be seen from the outside. The entire structure was covered by jungle and looked like any other small hill in a series of similar landforms. If the rebels found this place it would be pillaged for what artifacts, precious metals, and gems they could find.

He'd come here for something he'd seen earlier. The beam from his light moved around the edges of the room. He spotted the altar, and removed a vase, small enough to fit into his palm. He admired the beautiful artwork hand painted on the pottery. Some ancient writing, most likely Mayan, was below the etched blue orchid. Yep, this was the perfect wedding gift for the Doc. Like him, she'd know what would happen if the rebels found the pyramid. She'd keep his secret. He wrapped the fragile vase in his kerchief and made his way back outside.

Chapter Thirty-Seven

Mira woke with a start when Brandon jerked restlessly. She rose and checked the almost empty IV. If only she had another. She injected the last of the antibiotic into the IV while it still ran. The fiery heat of his skin burned the damp cloth she used to wipe his skin. His body was waging war against an army of invaders. Wearily, she sat beside the cot with her head on his chest.

She jerked her head up. How long had she dozed? Guilt bit at her. She had to keep fluids in him. Mixing the last of the plant juices with broth, she would try to get some of the mixture down him. She pulled her backpack over and propped his head up. She tried to dribble some of the mixture into his mouth. Most of it ran down the sides of his face.

Before she could wipe it away his eyes popped open. "I'm not a baby. Help me sit up some and I'll drink your goop like a good boy."

She gave him the grin she knew he expected. "I'm so glad you're awake." Her spirits soared as she ran her fingers over his damp but cool skin. "Your fever has broken." She supported him with her body, replacing the pillow and backpack behind him.

True to his word, he drank the liquid from the bowl, contorting his face into a horrible grimace before falling back against the pillow. "Look in my bag and find me some clothes, will you please? I can't traipse around the jungle in my birthday suit. The mosquitoes would have a field day."

"You're not ready to move anywhere. I'll get your clothes, but I'll have to do some cutting before you can get them on."

"What day is it? Where is Rafà?" Lines of strain etched the skin around his beautiful eyes. He might be talking the big talk, but he was still weak as a kitten.

"Can I do one thing at a time please? First, how do you feel and how bad is the pain?"

His face tightened in irritation at her impertinence. She wasn't jumping to follow his orders and he couldn't do much about it. Yep, he was on the mend. She moved quickly to the notebook on the table. *Patient is awake and responsive after only six hours. His fever is broken, and he shows amazing stamina. He is alert, clear minded and his color is back to normal. In view of my administering the essence of the Blue Spider Orchid, this could prove significant...*

"What are you doing?" he demanded,

Irritated at being interrupted, she snapped, "I'm recording data. Answer my questions."

"All right." Sarcasm dripped from his words. "I feel like a tank ran over me and I hurt like hell. No, I do not want any pain medicine and yes, I will take a kiss to help it feel better."

"You have such a charming way with words. It's a wonder I didn't fall at your feet the moment I heard you speak." She kissed him lightly on the lips.

His hand gripped the back of her head as he ground his mouth against hers. Her tongue met his in a tangle of need. She wasn't sure which one of them groaned.

Passion flared between them, only curtailed when she pulled back, remembering his wounds.

"You're killing me woman."

Heat rushed to her face when her arm accidentally brushed against his swollen sex.

He rubbed her cheeks with the back of his hand. "You blush so beautifully."

"The orchid lived up to its reputation. Your virile response is proof of its powers as an aphrodisiac. I hope it's regenerative powers are equally impressive."

"I suggest you find those clothes or you're going to be stitching me up again."

With a laugh, she reluctantly left his side. She'd like to freeze this moment in time, protected from the insanity of the real world. This room felt safe, but she'd risk the danger to have a life with Brandon.

"Rafà—um—he excused himself a couple of hours ago. It was getting kind of stuffy in here for him." She rummaged through his bag, finding a shirt and pants.

Brandon chuckled at her bashfulness. "I take it the flower affected him, too? Forget it, love. Men are men, best friend or not. I'm sure he didn't want to embarrass you. Besides, I manage to do it without anyone's help."

"We're leaving today." Her voice sobered. "Rafà and Father José want to talk to you about your plans. I'm sure the two of them will show up in a little while." She prattled while straightening the contents of the duffel.

"Come here," he commanded—his voice seductive.

She moved to the cot, the clothes in her hands.

He patted the bed beside him, and she sat. "I know you're scared. I can feel it vibrating off you. We have to leave here, and it will be risky. I won't be much help physically, but I swear to you, no one will harm you. Rafà and I will see to it."

"I'm not worried about me. I don't want anything to happen to you. You could have died—could still die from your wounds. I feel so helpless."

Laughter burst from him and he pulled her close. The secret door opened. "Do you hear that, Rafà? Our Mira thinks she's helpless."

"Hey, you're looking better. I'd hate to be someone threatening you with your *helpless* woman around. Did I tell you she can shoot, Cap? With a little practice she could be downright dangerous."

Rafà moved closer to the cot. "I don't know if now's the right time, but I have a wedding present for you two. I didn't figure you guys could drag pots and pans around the jungle, but you might find a little spot for this." He reached into his pocket, removed the wrapped vase, and placed it carefully in Mira's hands.

She gasped in disbelief as she unwrapped the delicate artifact. The beautiful vase had to be at least a thousand years old. "It's painted with the Blue Spider Orchid, and there's writing below it. This is fantastic. Where did you find it?"

"I found it in a pyramid in the forest. No one can know about it. With the revolution, the site would be pillaged, and the treasures sold. When I saw it, I knew the vase belonged to you."

"Thank you." She rose up and kissed his cheek. "Maybe one day we can come back and explore the pyramid."

Brandon growled his displeasure.

She turned swiftly to kiss his lips. "I had no idea you were so possessive. I'll just shake his hand the next time he brings me a gift."

"There better not be a next time. Now where are my clothes? As long as this big oaf is here, he can at least help me get dressed."

Both men ignored her as she placed the clothes on the bed. They began discussing coordinates and plans for the trip. Once again Brandon was in soldier mode.

She escaped into the tunnel and followed the fresh air outside. She had thinking of her own to do, like how would they find a way to transport Brandon. Rafà couldn't carry him the entire distance to the coast which was miles away. The terrain was mountainous and covered with jungle. Somehow, they would need to traverse those miles, carrying an injured man.

Dear Lord—they needed another miracle.

****

Brandon punched the pillow and said nothing while Mira was still within earshot. "So, what's the plan?"

Rafà sank to the floor next to the cot. "You can't walk, and I can't carry you and defend us at the same time. I'm assuming Jackson will be the one picking us up?"

"Get my maps and GPS from the bag and clear off that miserable excuse for a table." Brandon smiled at the memory of what had happened there. Now, bandages, syringes and tubes of medicine cluttered the top. "Never mind. Just throw the map on the floor and let's get started."

He tried not to grimace as he dealt with the pain of moving his leg off the bed.

Rafà didn't say a word.

"Find me a pointer." *Damn*, it felt good to give his friend orders again. He took the wooden spoon Rafà grabbed from the counter and pointed to a spot on the map. "We're here." He drew an incredibly long line to a spot on the coast. "It's roughly forty miles. Right?" He looked at Rafà for confirmation.

"Sure, as the crow flies, but the area is mountainous with ups, downs and switchbacks. It might be closer to sixty miles if you consider the obstacles. What time are we supposed to meet Jackson?"

"Any time after dark tonight. He'll land in the small lagoon just before sunset. We need to be there early and make sure it's safe. It'd be easy for someone to pick him off as he's setting down." He felt the familiar rush of adrenaline flash through his body. Finally, he was doing something proactive.

Mira walked through the door and moved to the cot. "Join us," he said and patted the bed invitingly.

****

"Gentlemen," she said as she looked down at the map and then at the two men "The way I see it, we'll need transport and some way to move out in the open without drawing attention to ourselves."

The two men looked at each other and laughed.

She looked from one man to the other. "What's so funny?"

Brandon grabbed her hand and pulled her closer. She glanced pointedly at his arm which was missing the IV and received an unwavering stare in return.

"We were just discussing the same thing," Rafà said. "You summed up our entire conversation in a single sentence."

"Have you figured out what kind of transport we can use?" she asked.

A noise below them in the tunnel caused a startled

silence to fall upon the group. Brandon and Rafà pulled their guns and shoved Mira beneath the cot. The secret door creaked open and Father José peeked in.

Mira crawled from beneath the cot. "Father, I hadn't realized we'd see you again."

"God has his plans and it seems I am to be a part of yours." He walked into the room armed as usual with a smile and a bag of provisions. "Mr. Falcon, you seemed to have improved greatly in the last few hours. The orchid must have helped you."

"I'm not up to a hundred percent, but the medicine and the orchid seem to have greatly increased my odds. How has God placed you in our plans, Padre?"

"I'm sorry to hear that you died, Mr. Falcon. I think my sorry *ass* will be transporting your body to the next town for burial."

Identical looks of puzzlement appeared on the trio of faces.

It was Rafà's face that was the first to change and he let out a loud cackle. "I think the good father, is offering you a ride in his donkey cart, Cap. He often transports bodies in his cart. It'll be the perfect ruse."

"Exactly," the priest commented. "There's a special place beneath the seat where Mira can hide safely. You my friend"—he pointed to Rafà—"will follow out of sight in the woods."

Brandon listened to the two men outlining their plan. He didn't like it. They'd be out in the open, exposed for far too long. There was only one alternative. "We'll never make the entire distance by nightfall." He looked at Rafà.

"There's no way we're leaving you behind, Cap, so don't even suggest it. We all go, or none. You married this woman; I doubt she wants to become a widow before her honeymoon."

"Excuse me you—you—cavemen." She stuttered. "I'm as much a part of this, as the rest of you, and I won't agree to anyone staying behind. We're the remaining members of SEAL team OMEGA and I'll be dammed if anyone is going to split us up."

Damn, she could be such a little fireball. He loved watching her when her eyes flashed hot darts at him. She was his wife. The fact still amazed him. "Excuse me—*Mrs.* Falcon. Since you can't swim, you can only be an honorary member of the team." His teasing brought a flush to her cheeks, letting him know she enjoyed the use of her new title.

"We are indeed honored to have you, Doc," Rafà interjected.

"Might I suggest we finalize the plan and get started?" Father José interrupted.

All eyes turned on him as he continued. "We will only take the cart part of the way. Another mode of transport waits, once we reach the next village. For the ruse to work, Mr. Falcon, you must appear to be a corpse. The rebels have set up checkpoints and we will be stopped. Can you do it?"

"Padre, I won't need to do much acting. I'm sure I can handle it."

"I'll give you a muscle relaxant to help with the pain," Mira said.

He was about to protest the injection but changed his words at the inflexible look on her face. "I need ready access to my weapon in case something goes wrong. Promise the med won't interfere with my ability to think and I'll take it."

At her nod, he looked at Father José. "What do we need to do for this trip, Father?" It was the first time he had called the priest by his correct title. It was a sign of the trust he was placing in the man before him.

"Pack up and let's get started. If we hurry, we will blend in with the other foot traffic going to market." He turned toward the door.

Chapter Thirty-Eight

Mira grabbed her backpack and her parents' medical bag and started packing. The journals went in first, followed by the vase wrapped for protection in her clothing. She rechecked the medical supplies and withdrew a syringe.

"Gentlemen, give us a few moments?" Brandon asked.

"Sure thing, Cap. We'll get the cart ready." Rafà and Father José left the couple alone.

He pulled her beside him and gently ran his fingers down her cheek. "We could run into trouble as soon as we leave this place. We'll be moving fast and after last night, the rebels will be everywhere."

"I know, Brandon—"

"Wait. This is important. I'm not worried how you'll handle things. I guess—I'm trying to say I'm so proud of you. You're the only woman I know who could have handled the danger and grueling situations of the last week." He wiped a stray tear as it crept from beneath her lids. "I love you, Mira, and I'm so glad you're my wife." His lips claimed hers in searing kiss.

She pulled back a little. "I'm glad I finally found you. I've been looking for you all my life. No matter what happens today—or tomorrow, I'll always love you."

"Ahem." A throat clearing separated the couple.

Rafà stood in the door with an awkward look on his face. "It's time to get started." He grabbed the blanket and pillow and handed them to her.

The two men carried Brandon to the cart, and she helped settle him on the rough floorboards. She returned to the room for her backpack and medical bag. A feeling of loss filled her as the door closed behind her. Shaking it off, she straightened her shoulders and exited the mine. She critically eyed the way Brandon lay in the cart. Cushioning his leg was out of the question. Dead men didn't need protection. She hopped into the cart and quickly gave him the injection. His hand found hers and squeezed. Her heart ached at the grueling pain he would face.

"Doc, crawl under the seat and use the pillow and blanket to cushion against the bumps," Rafà said as he organized the cart and its contents. "Brandon, keep the rifle flat beside you"

Crouched beneath the bench seat, she curled with her head against her knees and watched the rest of the preparations. Brandon placed his Glock under his body, close at hand as Rafà and Father José wrapped him in an old tarp.

"I'm sorry about this, but we are trying to be as realistic as possible," Father José apologized. He opened a container of rotting meat, teaming with wiggling maggots and splashed the contents across the tarp.

"Jesus! Are you trying to kill me?" Brandon grumbled beneath the tarp

The stench engulfed her as the squirming mass of insects crawled over the wet plastic. She covered her nose, barely managing to keep the gorge from climbing up her throat.

Rafà laughed. "I think we might have to fight the buzzards off you. That *eau de stench* will keep everything but them away from the cart." He walked over to the front of the cart. With a wicked wink, he slipped the board in place, blocking Mira's view.

****

The cart dipped beneath a heavy weight, causing the boards of the old cart to creak. Leather slapped against flesh, eliciting an indignant bray and the cart jerked forward. Brandon lay beneath the tarp, listening. His mind raced, trying to anticipate all that could possibly go wrong. He felt exposed in the open cart but gained some comfort from the knowledge Rafà would disappear into the foliage and guard them.

"Come on, Adam, we have God's work to do. I promise you a tasty carrot if you make good time." Father José chatted as the donkey clopped along its journey. He knew the man driving the cart might look like an eccentric priest with an old animal, but he'd seen the automatic weapon hidden by the padre's feet. Its presence spoke of something quite different. Father José was a complicated man.

Hoping the trip would be uncomplicated was a waste of time. After the destruction of the camp last night, the roads would be crammed with soldiers. The soldiers and citizens knew Father José, which was to their advantage. Unfortunately, the priest, the wagon, and corpses were far too common a sight.

"Brandon? Are you okay?"

The loud whisper reached his ears beneath the tarp "I'm dead, Mira—of course I'm okay." His curt reply was interrupted by a stifled groan as the cart hit an especially deep rut.

"Don't talk—we can't take any chances," he whispered curtly.

The sun's heat intensified the suffocating smell and his stomach roiled. His head pounded. He shouldn't have been so curt with her—she wasn't used to these conditions. He stopped himself mid thought. She *was* prepared for this. She might not be military trained, but she had experienced death and destruction in all the *Doctors without Borders* camps.

Sweat poured over his skin. He felt like he was being baked in an oven. His senses were in over-drive and with each bump, each creak, he not only felt it, he anticipated it. Expectations of a confrontation kept his mind sharp and his muscles tense. *So much for the muscle relaxant*, he grimaced. Even if he was caught, Mira might not be found. Rafà would take care of her if something happened to him, but—by all that was holy—he prayed they'd *all* get out of this safely.

Time dragged, as minutes slowly became hours, before the cart slowed, then lurched to a stop. His fingers moved and touched his gun. His breath stilled when shouts bellowed from near the cart. It had to be soldiers at one of the checkpoints Father had spoken about. His body stilled as he awaited the outcome.

****

"*Alto!*" Two soldiers stepped from the side of the road in front of the cart.

With their tattered clothing and unkempt appearance, they could be mistaken for inept, but a closer look at their eyes showed the hungry edge of danger. Joseph recognized the look and had come prepared for just this contingency.

"Who are you and what is your business?" The soldiers scrutinized the cart as they aimed their rifles at his head.

"I am Father José from El Liano, and I'm taking this poor man's body to the next village for burial. He died last night and is already starting to decay. I need to get him there quickly."

The taller of the two soldiers kept aim while his companion walked to the back of the cart. He turned slowly, watching as the man walked. The red dot painted on the soldier's back, gave him a feeling of relief. Rafà had the man targeted and would take him out if necessary. Rafà was a man who erred on the side of safety and would feel no qualms about killing the soldiers.

Spanish curses filled the air as the man got a whiff of rotting stench emanating from the tarp.

"*Dios*, the maggots already have him, Father. Is the body all you are carrying?" The soldier stood back from the cart, using his forearm to cover his mouth and nose.

"I have only the body and this small bottle of spirits to help with the smell."

As he'd expected, the soldiers showed a heightened interest in the bottle. "Here my friends—enjoy some of this," he said, indicating the bottle, "It will help rid your nostrils of the smell." He handed the bottle to the nearest soldier and took up the reigns again. "May I continue?" He indicated the road with the reins.

"*Si*, but you must leave the spirits to clear the air." The two soldiers guffawed rowdily. Swinging their guns in the air, they motioned the cart onward.

"My thoughts exactly. Bless you my friends." He slapped the reins, speaking to the donkey, "Come,

Adam. Just a little further and you will get a treat. One down," he mumbled to himself.

They bumped along the road for another hour, and then pulled off to the side of the road. He hid the cart behind a group of tall shrubs.

"I think you need a drink and a short rest, Adam, you are pulling a heavy load." He unhitched the donkey, then spoke to the two in the cart as he passed. "Perhaps now would be a good time for a breath of air, my friends and maybe some water. Here, we are hidden and safe."

****

Brandon pushed the tarp from his head and gulped in a breath of fresh air. Rafà materialized from the greenery and uncovered him carefully, folding the tarp to keep its contents. He reached in and removed the board from in front of Mira.

She immediately moved to him. As she held the canteen to his mouth her eyes filled with questions. "Take it slow." She wet a rag and wiped his face. "Do you need anything?"

"I'm fine. Get down and stretch your legs and cool off a bit. Rafà will take care of me." He smiled for her benefit and watched her walk down to the stream near the donkey.

"How are you really doing, Cap?"

"I hurt like hell and I need to sit up. Give me a hand." He grunted in pain as Rafà hoisted him off the floor of the cart. He sat still until the dizziness passed. "We got lucky back there. If those soldiers had been more experienced—they'd have poked my body or at least removed the tarp. I think the padre was a genius with the bottle." He slid to the edge of the cart. "Want to give me a little lift here, buddy? I want to check out those bushes over there."

"Sure thing, Cap. We might want to hurry before the boss comes back." Both men chuckled. "The little woman with a big personality." Rafà grinned at him. "She sure has a way of twisting you round her finger."

"Yeah, right—like you're not putty in her hands too." He looked at his friend. "If I didn't know better, I'd say you were smitten."

"Well, it wouldn't hurt my feelings if she was a twin." Rafà helped him back into the cart.

Brandon turned his gaze toward Mira down by the water, petting the old donkey. "Don't worry, you'll find yours—probably when you least expect it. I certainly didn't expect to find my life partner in this hell-hole." His demeanor grew serious and he looked up at his friend. "We're still not out of the woods. Remember your promise—I'm holding you to it."

"You know I'd never let anything happen to her," Rafà grinned, "but I'm going to do my best to make sure she's your handful and not mine. Besides, you might be ready to stay home and warm the hearth, but me? I have a few more hearts to break." He flashed a cocky grin and stepped away from the cart.

"Are we ready for stage two?" Father José quizzed as he led the donkey to the front of the cart and re-hitched him in the harness.

"How long before we reach the village?" He eased back in the cart as Mira walked up, her scowl, letting him know she'd seen him leave the cart.

"Another half hour or so. I'll let you know when we get close." Father José said. "The transfer will be the most dangerous part, so be careful." He cautioned before climbing back onto the cart.

"Will we make it in time?" Mira asked as she crawled into her hiding spot. "Jackson won't leave without us, will he?"

"He has his orders. But believe me, he's creative. He'll find some way to pick us up if he has to fly a balloon." With those final words he laid back down and Rafà covered him with the tarp.

"Don't worry, Doc, we've got it covered." Brandon heard Rafà reassure her followed by the slap of a board sliding home.

Chapter Thirty-Nine

Under the guise of conversing with the donkey, Father Jose kept his passengers informed of their progress. "Adam, we're almost there. Not long and you can rest and eat your treat. The town doesn't look too busy, so our business shouldn't take long. Here we are, now. There's a nice spot near that shade tree. I dare say our friend won't mind being planted in the shade."

The cart stopped and creaked beneath the weight of his footsteps. He gazed around the area, tipping his hat to an old woman who passed by. They were in a small, walled-in cemetery at the side of the village where only a few graves lined the plot and the headstones were hand-carved and very old. The graveyard backed up to a lush forest where birds kept up a steady racket. Stone benches lined one wall for sitting during the *Day of the Dead* celebrations. He entered an old storage shed and grabbed a shovel before moving to the shade splotched ground beneath the tree and began to dig.

****

Beneath the sweaty tarp, Brandon jerked awake. He tightened his grip on the rifle, breathed in deeply, then let it out slowly to steady his grip. The pain in his leg, the sweltering heat, and the God-awful smell made him anxious about his ability to shoot.

The unmistakable sound of a shovel scraped and thudded as it pierced the soil. A dull plop sounded as dirt was thrown against dirt. Listening to someone dig your grave, tested one's fortitude. A cold chill ran up his spine. God, he sure hoped this wasn't an omen of what was to come.

The digging stopped.

He bit his lip as the cart backed up. Pain sliced through his skull as frazzled moments passed. His body tensed when hands grabbed the tarp and flung it open. Relief filled him as he saw the face of Rico Velásquez holding the tarp. No one spoke. The transfer took place like a choreographed dance.

Rafà released the board for Mira and together the three of them managed to roll Brandon onto a litter. They replaced the 'body' with stuffed clothes, making it look suspiciously like a scarecrow. The trio filled the blanket with rocks for weight and the pillow added bulk. The entire structure was wrapped and tied in the tarp and the task completed in less than five minutes.

Father José moved the cart forward and gently rolled the makeshift body into the grave. He removed his sweat soaked hat, made the sign of the cross and spoke some words in Latin.

"*Deus meus amicus*. God speed, my friend." His words rang out loudly so the retreating trio in the forest could hear. Silently he bowed his head and remained quiet a few moments before he took the shovel and began to cover the corpse.

****

In minutes, they slipped into the forest behind the cemetery. Mira kept a tight hold on the rifle as she followed the three men along some unknown path. Encouraged by Father José's parting words, she concentrated on her surroundings as they sped through the undergrowth.

She'd been terrified for Brandon's safety when the soldiers had stopped the cart. The hours she'd spent hidden in the space were nothing, compared to the agony he must have suffered at each bump. It was over now and here in the jungle she felt some measure of freedom. Strange, the jungle had frightened her at first. Now it provided a safe haven.

In front of her, propped up on the stretcher, Brandon remained alert. Like the two men transporting him, he carried an abundance of weapons. He was responsible for their safety. Despite his wounds, he was team leader and command settled naturally on his shoulders.

"Dammit, I want her where I can see her," Brandon barked as the group moved through the dense foliage.

The two men quickly placed the makeshift litter on the ground. Mira touched his shoulder and his muscles tensed. She bit her tongue on the soothing words, hovering on her lips. He wasn't happy and short of him walking in front, he wasn't likely to settle.

"Would you be happy if she took point?" Rafà asked sharply.

Brandon let loose a string of expletives.

"Enough." Mira's voice caused the men to stop. "We don't have time for squabbles. I'm bringing up the rear—end of discussion."

Three pairs of eyes swiveled in her direction. The angriest face twisted her heartstrings. She knew why he'd behaved like a bastard, but she couldn't let him continue. She returned his stare with a lifted chin.

Several awkward moments passed before he relented. "I'm sorry," he murmured for her ears only.

"I'm worried and frustrated at my weakness. What if I can't protect you?"

"We'll protect each other." She touched her palm to his cheek. "Now apologize to the others. Even husbands need good manners."

"Sorry."

Rafà bent to pick up his end of the litter. "It's all good, Cap. We're a team and everyone plays a part. I'm counting on you to watch my back."

Brandon straightened. "Good, let's get going."

The air cooled as they neared the river. Blinding light assaulted them as they emerged from the shadows and stood on the edge of the rushing water. The men set Brandon down, pulled off their backpacks, and sat for a much-needed rest. Rafà passed the canteen to her first.

She settled onto the grass covered bank. "Thanks."

As they drank in silence, Rico pulled a wrapped cloth from his pack. A delicious aroma wafted to her nose.

"My Lucia sends her thanks and some of her fajitas," he said as he passed the food around. "Each of you has earned a warm place in her heart. Our Ana is getting better as is our son. We cannot thank you enough." His voice broke and he looked away. "Miguel was at the rebel camp and managed to escape when things blew up. He is ill—but we have him in hiding and hopefully he will be well soon."

Brandon placed his hand on Rico's arm. "We are the ones who are grateful. You have risked so much to help us."

She scooted next to Brandon and wrapped her arm through his. "We have some good news. Brandon and I are married."

Rico laughed. "Now why does that not surprise me? My Lucia said there was fire between you two. I wish you both well." He looked around. "It's time to get started."

Rafà followed his lead and the two men moved into a thicket near the river. They pulled back camouflage netting to reveal a small boat. Within minutes they were loaded up. Rafà pushed the boat away from the bank and jumped aboard.

Brandon sat upright in the middle, ignoring the stern looks she sent him. Rico took the helm and Rafà sat at the bow. Mira was squeezed in between the duffel and her bag. It was no accident she was the only one covered completely from the head down.

The engine sputtered, blew out a puff of smoke and started. As the boat moved through the water, Rico steered it close to the bank—in the shadows. A welcome breeze cooled her face as they moved forward. No one spoke—everyone searched their surroundings expecting danger at every turn. They steered through endless curves and passed numerous streams pouring into the larger river. Once they frightened a large tapir, interrupting its rooting among the water plants and mud flats. For the most part the journey was quiet.

"Thpat! Thpat! Thpat!"

Gunfire from an automatic weapon strafed the water and the side of the boat. Brandon sprawled across her, then brought his weapon up and fired into the jungle. As the boat sped up, Rafà tossed a grenade toward the shore.

"Get us out of here, Rico!" Brandon yelled. His heart pounded as his chest pressed against her head.

"More of them upstream—" Rafà flung the words over his shoulder as he continued to pepper the shoreline with bullets. "We're heading right into them,"

"We'll have to take another route," Rico yelled and spun the boat in a dangerous maneuver, heading into one of the smaller side branches of the river. Moments later, silence filled the boat, and the jungle. The gunmen were far behind them.

Brandon sat up, removing his heavy bulk from her body. "You okay?" He pulled her up from the floor of the boat.

She was covered in water and—*blood.*

Making frantic motions with both hands, he examined her front and back. "Where are you hit?"

She stared down at her shirt, feeling distant from her surroundings. Her arm was stained red, but she felt no pain. What was he fussing about? She was fine. Then she saw the bottom of the boat. "Brandon—there are holes in the boat!"

He tugged at her suddenly frozen appendage. "Let me see your arm."

She jerked away and pointed. "We're taking on water and I can't swim." Her breath hitched.

"It's okay; we won't need to swim. Besides you have two SEALs in the boat, remember?" He grabbed her arm, cut her sleeve, and tied the fabric around the wound. "It's not deep, just a graze,"

His words penetrated her fear-hazed mind, easing the tightness in her chest. "Thank you, Dr. Falcon." She rewarded him with a quick kiss.

Rafà called from the bow. "Hey, Cap? We got a problem."

Her hands clenched as she whirled to face forward.

Terror burned her insides, paralyzing her ability to move.

Brandon—forever the calm one, said what everyone had to be feeling.

"Shit. We're going over the waterfall."

****

"Hold on tight; it's going to get rough." Brandon's voiced strengthened in command. "Rico—steer her toward shore and give her some gas." He turned as Rafà pulled equipment from the duffel. "We'll only get one shot. You want to take it?"

Rafà's gaze met his. "No sir, you're the best man for the job."

Something dark and jittery uncoiled in his gut. He was a trained sniper and their lives depended upon his ability to shoot. He straightened. Renewed confidence directed each of his movements. Rafà would never jeopardize the lives of innocents just for friendship. His trust in him was real—he truly believed Brandon was the only one who could make the shot.

"It's getting rocky," Rico warned as he continued toward the shore.

With invisible threads the water pulled them toward the cliff edge as it rushed over the falls. The small boat bashed a jutting rock, and everyone grabbed for a secure hold as the tiny boat nearly capsized.

Rico managed to swing the boat into the current and keep it upright.

Brandon quickly glanced at Mira. Crouched in the bottom of the boat, holding tightly to the underside of the bench seat—her face showed fear, but not panic.

"Mira, I need your help. Straddle the seat. I'll lean on you to steady my arm." He pulled her up in front of him, positioning her back against his chest. "This is our one chance without swimming."

Terrified, she straddled the bench and pushed tightly against his chest.

"Good girl." He motioned Rafà over, and the two set up a tripod apparatus with a spear grappling hook. "Close your eyes—there'll be a flash when I fire. You'll feel a kick, so brace your feet on the floor." He leaned against her body and took aim. "Rico—find me a sweet spot."

Rico steered the boat between two large rocks. For a split second, the boat stilled. Brandon breathed out. Mira's lower body tensed, but her shoulders remained steady as he squeezed the trigger. He held his breath as the hook flew across the water, pulling the rope behind it. He had never doubted his shooting skills before. Now he watched the rocket propelled hook as it headed for a large tree on the shore. *God please let it be good.*

"Bulls eye—Cap." Rafà yelled as the boat jerked, halting its path toward the falls. Seconds later, he jumped into the water and swam to shore.

"Why is he abandoning ship?" she asked.

"He's going to reel the boat in so we can keep our supplies. We're going to need them without the boat."

Rafà pulled them in with the winch. With Rico's help, he pulled the boat out of the water, removed the supplies, and covered it with the camouflage netting.

Mira looked down at the bullet ridden boat. "I'm afraid we owe Rico a new boat."

Brandon laughed, Rafà whistled, and Rico stared at his feet.

"What is so funny?" she huffed.

He smiled and pulled her close. "Let's see, we've

been shot at, nearly fell over a water fall, and yanked across a raging river—and you're worried about a little hole in the boat? Don't worry about Rico's boat. Uncle Sam will help out." With renewed energy he turned to the others. "Let's get out of here."

Chapter Forty

Worried about the abuse his leg and shoulder had suffered in the boat, Mira helped Brandon settle on the stretcher. They shoved their way through spray covered vegetation and down to the cliff edge. The roar from the falls was deafening, but the vista which lay before them was breathtaking. Churning water plunged eighty feet, splashed over outcrops, forming smaller falls below. Spray caught in the breeze, forming vapor clouds over the water. Suspended in the sun's rays, the vapor formed a rainbow over the large pool below.

"It's beautiful," she said in awe. "How can something so lovely exist in a place like this?"

"The place is not the problem," Brandon replied. "It's people. Someone will always come along and spoil it for the rest." He turned to face Rico. "I hope your country will see peace soon. You and yours are always welcome in our home."

She walked beside him and saw his amusement. "Where is our home? I don't know where you live."

"Now is not the time to discuss housekeeping— let's wait until we climb down the cliff."

He spoke so tongue-in-cheek, she felt inclined to give him a good swat, but he looked beat. Her hero showed signs of wear. Love bubbled up inside her, crowding out the pain and suffering and all the danger. For just one moment, she looked at him—and felt her toes curl in her boots. Warmth pooled between her legs and her breath caught. He turned and caught her look. His eyes blazed with passion. Gone was the fatigued look. He was all man, and all hers.

He whispered a single word, "Soon."

The men placed the stretcher beside a sturdy tree, near the edge of the cliff. Rafà rigged the climbing apparatus for the descent. Within moments he harnessed himself, hoisted the duffel onto his back and dropped off the side.

Mira's mouth dried as he repelled against the cliff, jumping outward while sliding down. He made it look easy, but how would she manage it. What about Brandon? No way could he climb with his leg and arm damaged.

Rafà's feet touched ground and she released the life grip she had on her bag.

He made a quick check and motioned Rico to send the equipment. After stowing the equipment, he climbed back up the cliff. The harness he wore was similar to the ones he had used on the trip wires. His muscles bulged as he leveraged his weight up the vertical cliff.

These men had such amazing strength, not just physical but mental as well. They literally had to think on the fly. Situations changed so quickly. They had to be one step ahead to stay alive. Rafà hauled himself over the edge and stood before them. Brandon handed him the canteen and turned his gaze on her. He held a harness.

His voice took on a wheedling note. "My love?"

Her breath hitched. "Brandon?" She knew what was coming but dared not think about it.

"Rafà will take you down the cliff using the harness. When you get down there you need to watch his back while he helps me down." He explained the procedure and she listened and nodded appropriately.

"I don't suppose this is the time to tell you I have a fear of heights?" His gaze swept her face. "I'm kidding. Hasn't Rafà told you about our night swinging through the jungle for fun?"

"I sort of forgot to tell him, Doc. Are you all set?"

She nodded, stepped into the harness and knelt in front of Brandon. "You be careful coming down the cliff. I still haven't had a honeymoon, remember?"

Rafà howled with laughter. "I'd say she's got your number, Cap. Don't worry, we'll try not to bang up the important parts." He ducked the rock Brandon threw in his direction.

"*You* just remember you're carrying precious cargo, and s*he* better not have any bruises when I get down there."

"Yes, sir." He straightened and gave Brandon a salute. "Come on, Doc, he's starting to get grouchy." With those words, he clipped the two harnesses together in the front and stood at the edge of the cliff. "Hold on tight now; it's going to get a little bouncy."

She wrapped her arms and legs around his middle, burying her head against his chest. He stepped back, and the world dropped away. Her heart fell to the bottom of her stomach. Just as she was getting used to free fall, he bounced into the cliff jarring her bones. She swallowed the scream but dug her nails into his back. They continued to fall and stop until they reached the bottom.

She swayed, disoriented and dizzy when her feet

touched the ground. Rafà unclipped the harness, steadied her, and sat her down beside the equipment. "You did great. Now I suppose I have to get your grumpy husband."

"Thanks, Rafà. Please take good care of him."

"No problem. Take the rifle and keep watch. We're going to be pretty busy up there." He set off for another ascent up the cliff.

She scanned the area nervously. Admiring the beauty, she remained cognizant of the danger. The jungle hid all kinds of natural dangers. Cliffs, poisons, and killer animals. Those caused her only a little fear. Those she understood. Her true fear came from a different kind of predator, men who preyed on innocents.

Her life was one of healing and helping others. It was hard to fathom souls so evil they would take innocent lives without qualm. People like Brandon and Rafà existed to fight that evil, using the same ruthlessness to defend those innocents. Her heart swelled in pride as she thought of the job her husband and friend accomplished. But it was a job which took a toll and left bitter scars.

A rock fell near her. Startled, she blinked her eyes to refocus. She was supposed to be watching Rafà's back. She pulled the rifle from the bag and scanned her surroundings again. This time she looked with a different set of eyes. Now, she viewed the world through the eyes of a protector. Things looked far more dangerous this way.

****

"How'd she do?" Brandon asked before Rafà was completely over the edge.

These last ten minutes had been a private hell to him. He'd listened to every falling rock with his heart in his throat—fearing the worst and hoping for the best. He trusted Rafà with *his* life, but somehow placing the life of the one you loved into someone else's control was more difficult.

"Between the two of you, I've managed to acquire nail scratches on my legs and now my back. I'll have to be creative to keep the ladies from getting jealous." Rafà smiled at him. "Relax, she did just fine."

His gaze searched his friend's face. Damn, it was hellish when he was jealous of a pal.

"For the record," Rafà's tone dropped, serious now, "that's one hell of a woman you've got there."

The tension in his muscles relaxed but he continued to frown at his friend. "For the record, I know she's one of a kind. I'm one lucky devil to have found her. Now let's hurry, I don't like her being separated from us." He sulkily tossed the words at his friend and lay back on the litter. God, it was hard being so dependent on others. *He* should have been the one to take her down the cliff. *He* shouldn't have to go down tied to a stretcher.

"Thanks, Rafà." A look of understanding passed between the two soldiers.

Rico helped strap him to the stretcher, taking care to knot the ropes tightly. His weight with the added stress of wind would bounce him off rocks. "Tighter, Rico. I'd hate for that pretty woman to see me fall out of this wrap."

Rico patted his good shoulder. "It's going to be a rough trip, my friend. I'll be leaving you here. I must return to my family. I will pray for your safety and one day we will meet when times are good."

"You can count on it. Thanks for all your help."

He watched helplessly as the two men lifted the stretcher and gently placed him near the edge of the cliff. He gave them a mocking salute with the fingers of his one free hand. He'd insisted he have one part of his body under his own control.

"Don't attempt to push off the rocks with your free hand," Rafà reminded him.

He'd be lucky to make it down the cliff without adding a broken hand to his list of injuries. Mira would have something to say about that. He held his breath as the litter was attached to the winch and then gently pushed off the cliff.

Chapter Forty-One

Mira bit her lip as the stretcher teetered on the edge of the precipice, and then dropped from safety into the emptiness. The bindings were probably cutting into his flesh as the litter swayed back and forth in the breeze coming off the water.

Please, God don't let him fall. She squeezed the hard metal in her hands. "Oh hell," she muttered and eased her grip on the rifle. Nervous, she checked the safety as Brandon had taught her. Prickles of awareness crawled across her skin.

Suddenly, it was quiet.

Where were the birds? Earlier they had filled the air with their calls. No more screams of monkeys who had created such a racket. All she heard was the water pouring over the falls, hitting the rocks below. The mist blew through the air and she smelled the freshness of the surrounding trees. Something wasn't right.

Unsettled, she looked up at the cliff, Brandon continued to sway in the wind. The two men strained against his weight as they eased him down the escarpment. All seemed right there. Where was the danger? She ran her eyes over the surrounding pool area. Nothing. Then as her hands began to trickle with sweat, she slowly moved her gaze over and behind her.

Twenty feet above her and to her right was a small ledge. A beautiful spotted jaguar stared at her with eyes the color of topaz. The animal was massive—its rosette covered musculature a graceful feline sculpture against the outcrop of rock.

Awed by its beauty, but paralyzed by fear, she and Brandon had joked about his tawny skin earlier, comparing it to the jaguar's pelt. The animal in the flesh was more stunning than anything she'd ever seen.

As she watched the cat, she came to a better understanding of how she'd changed since coming to this country. She slowly lifted the rifle and pointed it up at the outcrop. She had defied Brandon once and not picked up the gun. She couldn't let the same reticence now put her or the others at risk. She squeezed the trigger.

****

The bindings pulled taut against his body as the stretcher swayed in the wind. He felt like a hotdog sandwiched between the two parts of a bun. The only thing under his control was the one hand left untied. The knuckles of his free hand whitened as he clutched the strap surrounding his chest. His gaze focused on the rope, avoiding the swaying skyline. He felt secure in Rafà's hands but was anxious about Mira. She was alone down below, and he'd be useless if something should happen.

"How's it going, Cap?" Rafà called down to him.

He heard the hard edge of frustration in his voice. "I'm fine, hurry this thing up."

"As you wish, sir." The two men eased their grips on the rope.

His breath caught as the stretcher quickly increased speed. It was like being in an elevator coming down from the top floor with no stops. As his speed increased so did the sway in the wind. He banged into the side of the cliff and bounced off.

A gun shot echoed off the cliff face from below.

"Rafà!" he yelled. "Get me down from here."

The stretcher dropped, bouncing against rocks and snagging on the roots of an old shrub. It flipped over on its side, leaving him swaying over the cliff, the ropes the only thing between him and the bottom of the cliff. He grabbed his Sig Sauer with his free hand and scanned the ground below. Where was she? She should be just below where Rafà had left her. A memory of her looking at an orchid while rebels walked below her flashed into his mind. His breath quickened, and his chest squeezed.

Rafà, attached to a second rope, flew by almost in free fall. As soon as his feet touched the ground, he took off into the underbrush.

Brandon swayed helplessly in the wind as agonizing moments ticked by. He stowed his gun and reached for his knife to cut the ropes. Mira and Rafà, emerged from the undergrowth.

"I'm okay," she called up to him. "I'm sorry about the shot, but I had to scare a jaguar away. He was on a ledge above me. He was so beautiful—I couldn't bring myself to shoot him, so I shot at the rocks below him, and he ran away."

Brandon relaxed and listened to her voice as she told him about the jaguar. She was nervous; words spewed, barely taking time for a breath. There was something else in her voice, excitement. Suddenly, she stopped talking, and looked up.

"Why are you hanging upside down? Rafà, you promised you'd take good care of him."

The two men chuckled at her fussing. Things were almost back to normal.

"I was but then I heard the shot. I figured you might need a little help so, I sort of left him hanging and came down to check on you."

"I'm sorry. I didn't think about what effect the sound of gunfire would have on you."

"Ahem." He loudly cleared his throat. "You two think you could stop your jabbering and get me down from here? These ropes are cutting off circulation in my legs."

His words spurred the two into action. Rafà quickly climbed up and released him and Rico eased him the rest of the way down.

"Good luck, my friends," Rico called to the group below then dropped the rope and winch over the side. "Take care and God speed." He waved.

"Thank you, my friend. We'll be in touch." Brandon tried to wave and was stopped by the bindings. "Do you think you can untie me now? This is getting a little old."

"Sure thing." Rafà grinned wickedly at his friend and quickly cut the ropes.

Instantly, Mira was at his side, checking his wounds. He grabbed her, enveloped her in a tight hug, and kissed her hard on the lips. She squealed in surprise.

He touched her cheek and gently pushed the riot of curls behind her ear. "I aged ten years when I heard that shot."

"I'm sorry I scared you," she said with mock contrition, but her eyes sparkled.

He felt her excitement. "You enjoyed your little

adventure, didn't you? I'll never be able to trust you out of my sight." He pulled her down for another quick kiss then pushed her away and sat up. "Rafà, let's get the hell out of here."

****

Jackson Favre banked his plane and flew over the sparkling aquamarine water. The pickup site would be difficult to see in the tangled mass of mangroves edging the jungle on the Mosquito Coast. The area was a maze of brackish swamps, making any kind of travel extremely dangerous. It also made the Caratasca Lagoon the largest and most uninhabited area to land a seaplane.

The Grumman Widgeon was one of only thirty-six left flying since their debut in the nineteen forties. Many had been used in World War II by the military for search and rescue missions. Jackson had bought the old plane when the grandson of a WWII Vet was clearing out his grandfather's collection of favorite aviation relics. He'd fallen 'in love' as his friends teasingly chided him, spending years and loads of money, lovingly refinishing and refurbishing the old *Darlin* as he fondly called her. She was on her first unofficial mission, helping to rescue his friends.

"Okay, *Darlin*, let's go see what Brandon's gotten himself into. I get the feeling it's bad and you'll probably get your new paint job chipped."

He eased the plane down and gently landed on the lagoon's surface, taxied toward the western shore, and then pulled into an area where tall grasses met the water. He was quite a distance from the shore but felt safer this way. He tethered the plane, pulled the raft from the supplies in the back, inflated it, and began loading the essential weaponry aboard. He motored into the only spot clear enough for a boat. Brandon was supposed to come this way according to the plan. He only hoped the plan was still intact.

Chapter Forty-Two

"Rafà, cut the bamboo while I lace the stems together." Brandon directed from his stretcher. "Mira, drag the bamboo over to me."

"Yes sir." The two irreverently saluted and made for the thicket of bamboo growing at the edge of the water. He was back in command mode and everyone, especially Brandon, was happy.

Soon, the three had assembled a long skinny raft. Mira eyed it dubiously as Rafà dragged it to the edge of the water. The raft looked barely large enough to support one of them much less all three. She inspected their handiwork. "If I didn't know how strong bamboo is, I'd have serious doubts about this raft."

"Bamboo is extremely strong and can even support bridges, but it's also very buoyant," he said. "Sorry, I forgot I was talking to a plant specialist."

"Don't apologize. I enjoy hearing you talk about things."

"All right then," he said, and continued. "It'll hold us and the equipment, but it's all about balance. Notice how we made it long and skinny. We'll need to sit, spaced out to balance the raft. I'll take point—you get the center with the equipment and Rafà will stand at the back. He'll use one of the poles to push the boat."

Rafà pushed the raft from shore and climbed aboard. Soon they were drifting down the river which quickly divided into smaller and smaller branches. The entire habitat changed abruptly. The tall trees with lianas and exotic blooming shrubs gave way to stubby trees with vast root systems growing from branches.

"Mangroves," she exclaimed.

"We're almost to the Mosquito Coast." Brandon's voice held renewed energy. "Can you smell the salt in the air? It won't be long now."

Her heart quickened at his words. Soon this nightmare would be over, and she and Brandon could begin their life together. No more running from rebels and hiding in fear. She would be back at her job researching plants. Somehow her former life didn't seem real anymore. Circumstances had changed her forever. She had seen death in its most violent forms, used a gun to shoot at other human beings and faced true evil. She had tasted just a small bit of the bitter poison of war. Her gaze rested on her husband. Again, she wondered how any man could see and do so much and remain whole.

The river ended in a vast expanse of tangled trees and roots. It was a navigation nightmare. How would they ever find their way through this mess? Everything was so close—the vines and roots brushing the raft. What kinds of creatures lurked in the murky depths of the almost black water? She didn't want to think of what dangers hid in the trees above them.

"Cap, this is as far as I can take the raft using the pole. I need to scout up ahead and see if we can get through." He placed the pole on the edge of the raft and slipped into the water.

"Are we lost?" Mira asked.

"No, but this is a different route from the one I

came. When we had to leave the main river and crossed the falls our route changed. We'll relax until Rafà gets back. He'll find the best way through this mess."

"Relax? You're kidding right? How can anyone relax here? There's murky water all around us with vines and roots brushing against us—not to mention the things…" She stopped in mid whine. "Sorry, I'm just a little overwhelmed at the moment."

"Don't apologize. The situation is a bit daunting. Rafà and I have trained for this, but you're handling things great for a first timer." A loud splash sounded in the water ahead, followed by thrashing, then silence.

"Rafà," Brandon's voice rose slightly. "Are you okay?"

Several seconds passed as they waited for an answer.

"I'm okay. I just had to explain to an oversized mangrove crab that I wasn't taking any hitch-hikers." He sloshed his way back to the raft. "I'm afraid we'll have to go to plan B. I can't see any other way out except walking and using a machete."

The two men studied each other for a moment, then Brandon nodded. "Can you get us out in the open?"

"I'll see what I can do." Rafà turned the raft and headed around some large roots.

"What's plan B?" Mira asked as Rafà pushed them around the tangled mass of roots.

"We're going to fire a flare. If Jackson is anywhere near—he'll see it," Brandon explained. "He expected me to return by the same route. Now, we'll wait for him to find us."

She studied the worried faces on the raft. "What aren't you telling me?"

"If Jackson can see our signal—anyone else looking for us will see it too. It's like marking a map with an 'X' and saying, 'look here.'"

"I see," she said the words calmly, yet felt the rush of fear enter her stomach.

"Don't worry, if he's is out there—he'll find us. We'll take up defensive positions and wait."

"You keep saying *if* Jackson is out there or *if* he sees it. Aren't you sure? What if he hasn't arrived yet? What do we do then?"

Brandon turned around carefully and faced her. He looked her directly in the eye. "We wait." Though several feet away, she read the unyielding strength in his eyes. "I know it's hard but it's all we can do."

She nodded her understanding, trusting in the two men's abilities. Everyone remained silent as Rafà pushed the raft out into an open space. She could see the sky once they cleared the cover of the mangroves. Her spirits rose. The air moved, a welcome change from the oppressive stillness from within the trees. It would be dark soon.

God please help us get out of here before nightfall.

Brandon pulled the flare from the pack and fired it with a muffled *poof.* Smoke and light pulsed upward as a bright red ball shot into the sky. The red ball continued to rise and then suddenly burst into a bright yellow and red explosion.

Three sets of eyes followed the path of the flare in total silence.

He checked his watch. "If we haven't heard anything in an hour, I'll fire another." No one answered. There was nothing to say. Rafà grabbed his pack and scrambled up into a mangrove. Brandon handed her the rifle and they settled in to wait.

****

Jackson saw the bright flash of the flare and cut the engine. *Damn*—they were coming from another direction. This was the only section of waterway navigable by boat, which meant they were stuck in the Mangrove Swamp. *Damn*. It would be dark soon, so he'd have to hurry.

Swinging the boat around, he pushed the throttle. No time for quiet now. He had to find them before anyone else did. If they had risked firing a flare—things were serious. He hoped no one was hurt. A hundred scenarios passed through his mind as he broke through the underbrush and into the open lagoon. There was *Darlin*, just where he'd left her. He pulled alongside the plane and stood up under the wing.

No one had touched her. His booby trap was still intact. He quickly removed the device wired to the door, flung the supplies into the plane, and climbed in after them. Strapped in, he pushed the correct sequence of switches and the engines roared as he taxied out into the center of the lagoon and gave it full throttle. The plane jumped forward and took to the air.

"*Darlin*, Brandon needs a little help. Let's go see what we can do."

Chapter Forty-Three

Eerie silence shrouded the swamp. Only the occasional splash of a fish or the faraway call of a bird pierced the quiet. He and Mira lay on the raft, head to head, drifting. Rafà kept watch while they used this time to rest. The sun hovered just above the horizon, casting a pink glow to the murky depths. The droning sound could have been mistaken for an insect. He sat up causing the raft to sway and tilt. He steadied the raft and grabbed binoculars from the bag.

"Do you see anything, Rafà?"

"Not yet, but it sounds like a sea plane."

"There's no way he can land here—we'll need to signal our position."

"Got it covered, Cap. You two keep to the shadows just in case it's not him."

Brandon and Mira used their hands to paddle and push the raft into the shadows.

"Damn, that's the brightest plane I've ever seen." Rafà laughed. "Jackson needs to work on the *covert* part of the mission. You can see it for miles."

"It looks pretty darn good from here." His tone was much lighter now. Having seen the plane—he knew they would get out. Jackson might not be able to land, but he'd find some way to rescue them.

"I'm using the mirror. There's no way he can miss it in this light."

The plane tipped its wings, signaling the group below. Elation spread through the trio as it altered course and flew directly at them.

The plane dropped its altitude to fly just above the trees.

"Be prepared for anything," Brandon warned. "He'll probably make a drop first."

A tarp sealed package connected to a rubber float dropped in front of them with a loud splash. He snagged the package and used his knife to cut it open. A radio, small chain saw, and a bag of chocolate filled the tarp. His team had always favored chocolate for quick energy, though it wasn't regulation.

Mira laughed as she greedily grabbed the chocolate. "I don't know Jackson yet, but I already like him. Any man who brings chocolate is okay in my book."

"Cap, did you happen to have chocolate on you when the two of you met?"

He looked at Mira and laughed. "Now you mention it, Rafà, I do seem to remember some hot chocolate." He touched her face, wiping chocolate from her mouth. He flipped the radio on and turned the dial to their team frequency.

"This is *Darlin*, calling Cap," a voice crackled from the radio. "Come in, Cap."

"Hello, *Darlin*." Brandon said in a deep sexy tone.

Laughter crackled over the radio. "Cap, I didn't know you cared so much. How many ducks are on the pond?" He used the code for passengers.

Brandon looked at Mira to check her response as he spoke into the radio. "There are two drakes and one hen." He watched her prickles rise. God, he loved the way she looked when her dander was up. He could have worded the message differently but had chosen those words deliberately to get a rise out of her.

"One lame duck, Darlin" he said and heard silence on the other end.

Jackson's voice crackled back, "Message clear. I'll make another pass in a few minutes. Look for bread crumbs."

"Make the bread crumbs extra spicy, Cajun," he teased Jackson, who came from the deep bayous of Louisiana and never let anyone forget it. "Thanks for coming back."

"I'll see what's in the oven. *Darlin* out." The plane disappeared over the mangroves.

"If I hadn't just had some chocolate, you'd be in deep trouble, mister. Calling me a hen, indeed." She swatted his good arm and passed the chocolate.

Brandon took a piece and popped it into his mouth. "Rafà, you better power up on some of this. It looks like we're going to saw our way out of here."

Rafà swam over and stuck out his hand for a share. "I figure Jackson will work on his end and we'll meet somewhere in the middle." He downed a handful of chocolate. "We're going to make a hell of a lot of noise. I hope those men from the river didn't move down after seeing us detour."

"Enough chocolate for you my man—you're talking way too much. Let's crank this little gem up and test her out." Brandon diverted the conversation away from possible adversaries. Mira had seen and heard enough depressing information. Right now, he wanted her to concentrate on their rescue and forget the other horrors.

"You got it, Cap." Rafà primed the saw and pulled the string. A satisfying *brurrrriiing* erupted from the machine. He revved the engine and then turned it off. "She's a beaut. We'll be out of here in no time."

The droning of the plane's return caught their attention. The plane flew low over their position and then headed southeast. It banked, then turned to make another pass. As they watched the plane fly over again, something trickled from the body of the plane. The breadcrumbs he had spoken of turned out to be a yellow, oil-based dye, floating on the water leaving a clear trail for them to follow.

"This is *Darlin*." The radio crackled again. "I estimate one hundred yards to open target. I'll meet you halfway. *Darlin*, out." The plane circled over them tipping its wings one more time before disappearing in the distance.

Brandon noted the plane's good luck signal. They were going to need it. Night was falling fast, and a hundred yards was a lot of cutting. Hopefully some of the area was open. "Let's get this show on the road. Mira, you've got the watch."

He waited until she turned around on the raft, then eased off into the water. Pain lanced through his leg, but the buoyancy of the water helped take pressure off it. "Hand me the machete and I'll give you a hand."

Rafà turned and his brow rose in question. "Are you sure?"

"I'm still in charge here. Now, hand it over."

Rafà complied and they began hacking and sawing in a flurry of activity and noise.

Chapter Forty-Four

"Brandon," she gasped when the raft tipped precariously. She turned to see him moving toward the trees, a machete in hand.

He turned and gave her a hard look. She used her hands to paddle the raft. "You can't walk on your leg and this water is teaming with deadly germs."

"If we don't cut those trees fast enough, germs won't matter. I'll live with the consequences."

She maneuvered the raft beside him. "I'm not happy with it, but I understand." She placed a hand on his chest and looked up into those intense green eyes. "How can I help?"

He took her hand and brushed a light kiss on her palm. "Keep watch, and don't lose faith."

As he moved away, she remembered his words from their morning in the roost. He was a professional and knew what he was doing. The loud buzz of the saw pulled her back to the present. *He's right*. She began to pray as she watched and listened. Perched on the raft, she pulled cut branches out of the way and used the pole to inch the raft forward. Unable to swim, she was limited in how she could help. Rafà and Brandon had to be exhausted from cutting vegetation. Each time a little vegetation was cleared, the raft moved closer to freedom.

She took her watch-duty seriously, and between

moving branches, she scanned the water behind them. With her eyes closed, she listened for sounds different from the normal swamp chirps and calls.

She opened her eyes and yelled over the buzzing saw. "Brandon, Rafà—Stop! I hear something."

Brandon eased to the edge of the raft as Rafà silenced the saw. "Chopper," both men exclaimed in unison.

"Dammit, someone saw the flare," Brandon cursed. "Rafà, get my mask." He turned to her. "We need to hide. The yellow trail on the water is leading them right to us. They'll cover this entire area with bullets."

Icy tendrils of fear jetted through her body, stiffening her muscles. "What are you trying to say? Just spit it out." She wasn't stupid—they couldn't run from a helicopter by climbing trees. Hadn't he muttered something to Rafà about a mask? Surely, he couldn't expect her to…"B-bran-don?" Terror cracked her voice as realization came in horrifying clarity.

Her fear of drowning had controlled her actions all her life. She'd tried learning the mechanics of swimming—but her efforts failed miserably. Finally, she'd avoided the water altogether. Now they were trapped. Submerging beneath the murky depths horrified her more than the helicopter.

"I can't." She edged back on the raft. "I'll drown. Can't you cover me up and hide me in the roots of one of the trees?" Her breath rasped in panic. Adrenaline iced her blood.

His corded arms pulled her to the edge of the raft, placing her legs in the water, straddling his chest. The raft shook precariously. Panicked, she grabbed his shoulders. He reached up and pulled her head down, taking her lips in a firm but tender kiss.

Leaning back, he looked at her. "I know you're scared." His thumbs rubbed calming circles on her upper arms. "Remember how I had to have complete faith in you when you did the surgery? I trusted you without reservations. I need the same trust from *you* now. This," he waved his hand to encompass their surroundings, "is my operating room. I swear to you, Mira, I won't let you drown."

She swallowed and took a deep breath. Her wary gaze scanned his face, noting the strength and utter confidence he had in his skills. His eyes looked back at her, filled with love and something else—compassion. He understood her fear and wasn't making light of it. Just like all the numerous times the last two weeks, he would keep her safe.

She smiled tremulously and wiped the tears from her cheeks. "I trust you."

"That's my girl."

The helicopter came closer. Rafà appeared from nowhere holding the mask and snorkel. Brandon took it and adjusted the strap as short as it would go. "This might be a little big and water could drip in around the seal. Just breathe through your mouth and not your nose. I'll keep you afloat just beneath the surface."

She tried not to shake as he placed the mask on her face and adjusted it. Obediently, she sucked in a breath through her mouth, surprised to feel the fresh air rush in through the tube. He pulled her off the raft and up against his chest. She wanted to cling to him like a baby animal clings to its mother—but allowed him to loosen her grip and turn her around. She drew comfort from the feel of his large body beneath hers. So strong and unyielding.

She floated in the water supported by Brandon as they moved backward, away from the raft. Rafà moved the supplies to an islet and disappeared in the tangled roots at the edge. Fear numbed her thoughts and body as the scene took on a surreal look. She concentrated, trying to control her fear.

You can do this—he's is depending on you. You are stronger than the fear—you are in control of your emotions. A fleeting memory of looking into the eyes of the snake strengthened her resolve.

As if sensing her turmoil, he tightened his grip and whispered, "You are my heart. Use my strength. I'll get us through this, love." He tightened his hold and kissed the back of her head.

The feel of his lips and the tightening of his arm sent warmth and a feeling of control through her. She was still scared, but felt stronger, more in control. She could do this—she had to do it.

Damn it, she would do it.

By the roar of its engine, the helicopter was nearly upon them.

"Mira, if something should happen, and I don't make it," he yelled over the din as the helicopter came closer, "Rafà and my sister will help you. Don't try to go it alone."

She ripped the snorkel from her mouth. "Don't even think of dying. I won't accept it as a possibility. We're a team. We all go—no one stays behind." Her voice strengthened as the sound of the chopper became deafening.

His words were an oath. "All right, we all go."

Gunshots erupted around them as Brandon

continued to back away from the open water. They were quite a distance from the raft, now, and suddenly, he stilled. Her heart quickened at the downdraft from the helicopter. Turbulence bent trees and rippled the water, pushing it outward and against her body. All around, the shrubs and vines writhed.

He touched her face—checked her mask and snorkel.

Then they sank.

She willed her limbs not to struggle against the strong arm holding her. She fought a life time of fear as the water covered her head. Little light penetrated the dark water. Pressure filled her ears as they sank lower. Swallowing hard, she held her breath. Her burning lungs begged for air. Breathe, Mira—in through the mouth—out through the mouth. She closed her eyes.

Think of happy things. You can do this—breathe. She pictured Brandon's beautiful eyes glinting at her— his mouth quirking up as he smiled. Those same eyes on the face of a small replica of the two of them. *Breathe—relax.*

The downdraft was directly above, her heart rate skyrocketed. *Phlat—phlat—phlat,* the blades chopped the air. Displaced water pushed them back into the plants. Tendril-like fingers trailed across her skin. It took every ounce of willpower she had not to bolt away from their touch.

Endlessly, the bullets pierced the surface of the water with sharp whines that whirred into dull plops as the water slowed them. The water churned and muddied by the wind made it impossible to see how near they came. *A blessing?*

The churning water stilled. *The helicopter was*

moving away. An explosion of sound and light rocked her senses. Brandon stood, bringing her head out of the water. She ripped the mask from her face and gaped at the hellish scene. The helicopter smoked profusely as it spun like an awkward insect swatted down. It continued to move away from them—then, the blades stopped turning, and it dropped. A fireball exploded upward, lighting the swamp with a satisfying orange glow.

Rafà stood near the islet holding a small hand-held rocket launcher. No need to ask what had happened to the helicopter. She was past being surprised at what these two kept pulling from the supply bag.

"You okay?" he asked as he navigated them toward the islet.

"We did it, Brandon. I didn't panic, and you didn't let me drown."

He dropped a kiss on her forehead. "I'm very proud of you."

The radio squawked in the pack. Rafà pulled the pack from the islet and spoke into the receiver. "Come in *Darlin*, this is Archangel."

"Holy crap, Rafà, it's great to hear your voice." Jackson's words came across the radio loud and clear. "You guys about ready to go home? The copter cleared out a lot of debris, so I should be there in about ten. Cajun out."

Rafà turned to Brandon, "How'd our SEAL do?"

"Let's move her up to squid. She was a champ." He wrapped both arms around her and squeezed. He turned his gaze to Rafà. "Why don't you go ahead and meet Jackson in case there were any survivors from the crash." He moved to the raft. "Mira and I will stay here with the supplies."

"Sure thing, Cap."

The raft was missing pieces where bullets had struck, but it floated. She clung to the side and gasped when Brandon hauled himself up onto the raft.

"You shouldn't have been pulling me around and sawing limbs. I was so involved with my fear I didn't think."

"It wouldn't have mattered. I did what had to be done. If I've added more damage to my leg, well, let's just say I know a really good doctor." He reached down to pull her aboard.

"I'm not letting you pull or lift me anymore. I can't believe how self-centered I've been." She glowered at him as she maneuvered her way to the other end of the raft.

"Just where do you think you're going?" he demanded as she let go of the raft and jumped toward the islet.

She caught the branch of a small shrub and pulled her body onto dry land. "I," she said in a huff, "am going to get my medical bag and examine your leg."

She reached her bag and pulled it toward her. She was angry because she had been lax in her duty. He could have permanently damaged his leg. She looked back at the raft, surprised to see a Cheshire grin on her husband's face.

"Why are you grinning?" she demanded as she surveyed her body expecting to find a hole in her shirt or anything which would bring a smirk to his face.

"I'm grinning because I'm crazy in love with the most beautiful woman in the—"

"Oh, Cap, say it isn't so." A young man appeared from behind the islet—waist deep in the shallow water.

"Tell me you haven't gone bonkers and fallen head over heels for some..." He caught sight of Mira and hushed. He gave her a mock bow. "Ma'am," he purred and flashed a grin at Brandon.

He looked like a Cajun prince. Tall and lanky with olive skin, the man dripped with swarthy good looks. He had an air of charm and sophistication with a killer smile.

Brandon cast a stern look in the man's direction. "Mira, this clown is Jackson Favre, our ride home. Jackson, my wife, *Doctor* Mira Falcon."

She stifled a laugh at the look on Jackson's face. His mouth gaped like a fish and his eyes popped open like oysters over a fire.

"Do you think you can stop ogling my wife long enough to get us out of here?" Brandon punctuated his words with a splash of water directly at Jackson's face.

"Sure thing. I've got the boat just a few yards back," Jackson answered without taking his eyes off Mira. "Hey, Cher, you need some help?" His accent became thick and dripped with New Orleans charm.

"Can it—goofball, the lady is taken. Pick up the equipment and let's get the hell out of here." Brandon's voice held a note of irritation and just enough command to cause Jackson to jump onto the islet and grab the supplies.

Rafà returned, sent a teasing look at Brandon, then swooped in swinging her up in his arms. "Doc—you sure you want to bring the grouch with us? We could fly away in Jackson's plane and just leave him here."

She laughed at Rafà's antics and blew Brandon a kiss. "Don't worry. I'll only go as far as the boat with him." She waited until they were out of sight before speaking. "Don't you dare let him walk. I think he damaged his leg again."

Rafà sobered. "I know, Doc. We're taking you first, so he doesn't do something stupid to keep you from worrying. Jackson and I have it all worked out. Here we are."

She looked at the inflatable boat with surprise. She hadn't expected anything quite so sturdy. After floating on the bamboo raft, this looked like a yacht. The supplies had already been placed in the center and he sat her down next to them.

Moments later, Jackson rounded the islet heading for the boat, pulling Brandon, in a small inflatable dinghy. Her heart nearly broke at the stoic look on Brandon's face. He sat up straight, shoulders back, looking like this was the way he traveled all the time.

He scrambled into the boat with as much dignity as possible and the other two men jumped aboard. Jackson started the engine and the boat sprang forward.

****

"Let's get the hell out of here. I'm supposed to be on my honeymoon." Brandon flung the order out and all three men broke into laughter.

Jackson joined in the playful conversation. "Your flight leaves in fifteen minutes, sir. I hope you're all packed."

As they approached the edge of the mangrove swamp and came to the open lagoon, the boat slowed. Each man picked up a gun and hunkered down. Mira followed their example, slumping down by the bags. They were serious now—all play forgotten. The open water presented a danger to them.

"How far from here?" he asked in a hushed

whisper.

"About fifty yards. It'll take a few extra minutes. I booby trapped the door. And, Cap…"

He looked back, unease tightening his gut. "What's wrong?"

"My hands are itching."

"Shit," Rafà and Brandon intoned in unison. Jackson had some kind of New Orleans mojo. When trouble was around, he itched.

"What's wrong?" she asked.

"Trouble," Brandon enlightened her before turning to Jackson. "Gun it."

The bow of the boat rose out of the water as it picked up speed. The reeds and small trees became a blur as they sped the short distance to the plane. About twenty feet away from the plane, the first shot rang out. Brandon and Rafà returned fire.

Jackson maneuvered the boat toward the yellow seaplane tethered in the reeds. He pulled the boat alongside. "Cover me—I've got to disarm the charges on the door." He jumped onto the small rungs by the door.

Rafà moved to cover him as Brandon shifted to lie near Mira. "Put Mira in first and get that big yellow duck running."

"Yeah, boss. Just keep them from messing up *Darlin's* new paint job. Come on, Cher, it's time to go." Jackson helped Mira up, shielding her body as he did so.

"What about Brandon?" she asked.

"Don't worry, he'll be in soon."

Brandon fired a volley of shots, allowing Jackson and Mira time to board. The plane made a whining noise and vibrated as the propellers engaged. The tiny raft slapped against the side of the metal craft.

Rafà tossed the equipment through the door and turned to him. "Your turn, Cap."

Bullets pelted the plane, ricocheting into the surrounding water.

He rolled inside as Jackson reached to grab Rafà who ignored the hand. "Find me a claymore and some rope. I want to send them a nice little present."

Jackson dug through the supplies and handed him the items. Rafà rigged the explosive and tied it to the boat's tiller.

Mira knelt at the edge of the plane. "You've got to stop him, he'll be killed."

"Strap in and get ready for takeoff. Now, Mira!" Brandon commanded when she hesitated.

Rafà dropped into the boat and gave it full throttle. He headed directly toward enemy fire.

Brandon pulled his rifle from the pack. "Jackson, be ready for my signal." He took aim on the boat, waiting.

Thirty yards from shore, Rafà jumped from the boat, leaving it running and heading for the rebels.

Still, Brandon waited. Tension rose in the plane as moments passed. He felt it but ignored it. The boat neared the shore and he fired. The explosion sent a giant fireball into the sky, flinging debris everywhere. The gunfire stopped.

Lying on his belly, Brandon reached down and grasped the hand reaching up from the water. Images of the previous mission flashed through his mind, images of Rafà falling from the copter, the guns firing and them taking off. A solid hand clasped his, and a feeling of triumph pulsed through him as he stared into the eyes of his friend. Rafà climbed in and pulled the door shut behind him. Now his mission was complete. He could relax and let down his guard.

"I'm tired of this place, Jackson, let's go home." He put his head down and lay still.

Jackson maneuvered the plane into the center of the lagoon, pushed the throttle and the plane rushed forward. He pulled back on the wheel and the plane lifted, gaining altitude.

They were on their way home.

Chapter Forty-Five

The plane rose, heading away from the nightmare, which had ensnared her for the last two weeks. The cabin walls rattled where bullets had penetrated, causing Mira to question their safety yet again. "Are you sure this thing will hold together long enough to get us home?" She shouted above the engine noise.

"She didn't mean anything, *Darlin.*" Jackson caressed the controls. He smiled and winked at her confused look. "She'll get us home just fine—though *someone* is going to owe me a new paint job."

"Yeah, yeah, just put it on my bill." Brandon rolled onto his back in obvious pain. "If I pay for it, do I get to pick the color? Canary yellow isn't what I'd call a *covert* color. How about something in camouflage? Maybe brown and green?"

Mira watched the interchange between the two men. Their bantering came only from longtime friendship. She had missed out on that kind of relationship in her life. She could almost envy the two of them—except the cost to keep their friendship was steep.

"Brandon, you need to get out of those clothes so I can check you out," she said.

"Woot!" Jackson hooted and Rafà whistled.

"I guess that did come out a little funny." She grinned as heat rose in her face. "Well, regardless of how funny it sounds—strip, sailor."

"Yes, doctor," he teased. "You should change, too. It's a long flight."

She looked around at the open space and then back at him. "Where? I'm not giving your friends a free show."

Whistles and cackles greeted her words.

"Can it, you two."

Jackson turned, serious once more. "Ma'am, if you open the little door at the back, I actually have a small bathroom. You could change in there if you'd like."

"You have a bathroom?" She couldn't believe the plane was big enough.

"Yes, ma'am. I've retrofitted *Darlin,* so I can live on her if need be."

An actual *bathroom.* What a treat. "After I—

"Go on." Brandon cut off her words. "I'm okay."

"Thanks, Jackson. I believe I'll freshen up." She pawed though the bags until she found her backpack and then made her way to the back of the plane.

Small was a generous term for the cramped cubicle she squeezed into. It did have all the amenities though, including running water. Sitting on the toilet, she removed her boots and then stood to strip out of her wet things, pausing as she caught sight of her face in the metallic mirror. Who was the woman staring back at her? The features were the same, but the eyes were much older—wiser.

She opened her backpack for some toiletries and felt the leather binding of the journals. So much had happened, they'd been shoved to the back of her mind. She smoothed the leather binding. Feelings of foreboding swept over her. The guerillas had ransacked her room at the clinic. Would she be safe when she got home? What if someone else wanted them? Her thoughts flew to Brandon's mention of the CIA. Would they be thrown back into danger because of these books?

Her instincts said yes.

She swept her gaze around the bathroom cubicle spying a small gap in the wall behind the toilet. Wrapping the journals in a shirt along with Rafà's vase, she pulled the wall covering back, and slipped them into the opening. She pushed the gap closed, stood, and brushed her hands. They would be safe on Jackson's *Darlin*. He wasn't about to let anyone come aboard and plunder his lady.

After freshening up, she quickly donned a clean shirt and pants—forgoing a bra. She picked up her wet things and headed out to share the protein bars she just found in her bag.

Brandon lay on his back, sound asleep.

Her heart turned over as she studied the relaxed lines of his face. Her soldier was finally resting. He had somehow managed to remove his shirt before succumbing to fatigue. Her eyes traveled over his chest and settled on his shoulder. The wound was one of many scars on his body. She vowed to kiss every one of them when they got home.

Medical kit in hand, she knelt beside him. She removed a syringe from the kit and injected him with a dose of morphine. The hell with what he might say about it. He didn't flinch or wake. He'd been strong long enough. It was time to let his body heal.

"Take over for a minute, Rafà." Jackson relinquished the controls to his friend and moved to kneel on the other side of Brandon. "How bad was he hurt, ma'am?"

"Please, call me Mira." She pointed to Brandon's feet and Jackson immediately removed his boots. Together they tugged off his pants revealing the horrendous damage to his leg. She looked up and saw the pain in Jackson's eyes. "You two are pretty close?"

He nodded and then swallowed. "He's like a brother and a father to me. I would do anything for him, ma'am."

"I understand, Jackson. I love him, too." She paused, collected her thoughts, and then said. "He nearly died. His shoulder will be okay, but his leg will probably never be the same."

His face tightened at her words. "I have a pull-down cot. It will be a lot more comfortable than the floor."

"It sounds perfect."

He moved to the other side of the plane and pulled a handle on the wall. A small bed folded down.

"I got him." Rafà spoke from the pilot's seat. "This lady is a beaut, but she likes your hands better than mine." He grinned and made the plane tilt just a little.

Jackson moved to take the controls. "Hey, treat her nice."

Rafà came and stood beside her. "You knock him out?"

"Yes, it's time he rested."

He bent down, lifted Brandon, and carried him to the cot. Taking out a blanket from below, he tucked it around him. Tugging tightly on the belt, he secured Brandon for the trip. With a mock salute, he left her alone.

She removed the wet bandage with a grimace. The wound looked surprisingly good for the conditions they'd been in. She thought back to the primitive care he'd undergone—cauterization in the rebel camp, riding in a filthy dump truck, lying under a maggot covered tarp, and wading through a mangrove swamp. He was one lucky man.

With tired hands, she used an alcohol swab to clean the ragged skin around the wound. The orchid had already begun to heal the tissue. Her heart lurched at the thought of what she could do if she had more of the plant. She could help so many. The plant truly was miraculous. She finished cleaning the healthy-looking pink tissue, placed a fresh bandage on the wound, then grabbed a blanket and a pillow from the cupboard below. Curled on the floor beneath the cot, she listened to his rhythmic breathing. The engine droned and the gentle vibrations of the floor soothed her tired body. Sleep soon claimed her.

****

Brandon woke. Alerted by the changing altitude of the plane, he lay still, acclimating to the dim light. Over the dry cotton of his mouth, he called out, "Mira? Rafà?"

An overhead light clicked on as something bumped against the bunk below him.

"Damn," Mira's muffled curse sounded beneath him.

He chuckled when she popped up beside him, a smile on her face, a hand rubbing her head. "Your vocabulary has expanded, sweetheart. I'm a bad influence on you." He waggled his brow at her.

Light pink crept up her neck and over her cheeks.

How could this uninhibited, passionate woman blush so beautifully? He cupped a hand against the pink. "You're so sexy when you blush."

She turned her head and planted a kiss on his palm. "How do you feel?" Her gaze scanned him professionally.

"Thirsty, grouchy as hell, and ready to sleep with you in a real bed."

"I can help with the first—only coffee will cure the second, and we'll work on the third." She opened a nearby cupboard and pulled out a bottle of water.

He drank deeply from the bottle as he looked at the love of his life. His face tightened as he pulled his serious mask into place. "Mira, when we land, I'll have to leave you for a while." At her protesting look, he explained. "I have debriefing which is classified. You won't be allowed to be with me. Afterward, I have something to sort out."

She gasped at his words. Her shoulders dropped like a heavy cloak weighed upon them. "Brandon, I'm your wife. I have a right to be with you."

He realized in an instant what she must think. He was such an ass sometimes. He pulled her into his arms. "No, it isn't what you're thinking. I love you and nothing has changed between us. But there's going to be an ugly battle between me and some of the brass. Something dirty is going on and I don't like it. I also don't trust any of them. I don't want them anywhere near you. Don't trust anyone but me, Jackson or Rafà."

She sucked in a breath, held it, and then breathed out slowly. "What do you want me to do?"

"That's my woman." He gently squeezed her hands. "If they question you, tell them as little as possible. Don't mention the journals, and if they do, tell them you lost them."

"You need surgery on your leg—it can't wait long."

"The Navy will see to it. I'll be fine." He did his best to sound convincing, but he too worried about his leg.

Could he be the strong man she needed him to be? She was the most wonderful thing ever to happen to him and he wanted her to have the best. Would a shattered old soldier make her happy? He was always self-confident in his work, but until now he'd had little or no personal life. Relationships were new to him. Would he measure up? He voiced none of this and kept his fears bottled inside.

"You can't do this alone," she said. "I want to be there for you. I need to be sure they give you the best treatment."

"Hey, Cap," Jackson spoke loudly from the front of the plane. "We'll be landing in about twenty minutes. I've gotten clearance to land at the base and they'll meet us with an ambulance. You're to be taken at once to the hospital and will be debriefed tomorrow. You want me to contact anyone else?" He looked back at the two of them with a questioning look.

"Have a message sent to my sister. Tell her I'm fine and back home." He looked at her "You'll like my sister. She'll be ecstatic I'm finally married."

"Time to buckle up." Jackson informed them. "Cher, if you like, you can sit in the copilot's seat."

Brandon laughed. "An honor has been bestowed upon you. He doesn't let just *anyone* sit there."

"He lets me," Rafà spoke up.

Jackson smirked at him. "That's 'cause you're so pretty."

Mira tucked the blanket tightly around Brandon, then strapped him in. "You're all mine, and don't you forget it."

Her trembling smile tugged at his heart. He pulled her face down and kissed her, only releasing her when they hit an air pocket and the plane bucked.

****

She gave him one long meaningful look, before squeezing his hand and going up front.

"Wow," she exclaimed as she sat in the copilot's seat. "It looks so different from up here. This is almost as exciting as riding the zip lines with Rafà."

Jackson smiled and made sure she was buckled in correctly, then spoke into his headset, answering someone below.

Minutes later the wheels touched down, jolting the tiny plane. The engine whined as Jackson hit the thrusters to slow the aircraft. He came to a near stop, then turned and taxied down a series of runways. They were finally home.

Her shoulders relaxed as the plane came to a stop. Flashing lights from several vehicles lit the area around the plane. She unbuckled and went to the cot, noting Brandon had already released the restraints. A blast of warm air, smelling of diesel, rushed in as Jackson opened the outer door. Two men eased through the door with medical bags and a litter. As they approached, Mira stepped closer to Brandon—an unconscious protective move. She knew it was okay to let these men take him, but she was reluctant to let him go.

"Step aside, ma'am," one man said.

Rafà and Jackson moved to stand beside her protectively, all three, blocking access to Brandon.

"Just one minute," she said, asserting herself. "State your name and rank, soldier." Her voice of authority was something the young man recognized, and he immediately paused and straightened.

"Ensign Jeffery Scot, ma'am. We're here to transport Lt. Commander Falcon."

"I'm Dr. Mira Falcon. Take utmost care with my husband. He took a bullet to his upper thigh which shattered the bone. It will require multiple surgeries and extensive rehabilitation. He has another bullet wound in his shoulder, has lost at least two pints of blood and suffered a major fever. His leg must be immobilized, and antibiotics administered stat."

"Yes, sir, ma'am," the young ensign stuttered, obviously surprised at her name.

Brandon reached out and took her arm. "Let them do their job, Mira."

She reluctantly stepped aside.

Chapter Forty-Six

"Tell me, Dr. Phelps, exactly why were you at the clinic? All Americans had been ordered to leave Honduras."

The man behind the desk looked like someone from a bad spy movie. Only the dark glasses were missing, and she attributed the fact to the indoor setting.

"Falcon. My name is Dr. Mira Falcon, and I don't have time for this. My husband is about to undergo surgery and I need to be there." How many times did she have to tell him the same thing? Was he dense or just trying to irritate her? She couldn't believe all that had happened in the last few hours.

Brandon had been rushed into the triage unit and she'd been left to sit and wait. She desperately wanted to be in the room with him, but a nurse had come out and taken her description of the care she had given him, and then she'd been left alone. Jackson and Rafà had gone off to debriefing. Then the man across the desk had shown up, informing her in clipped tones, they needed to talk.

"Exactly what are you trying to ascertain, Mr...?" She deliberately paused. "I'm sorry, what did you say your name was?" She felt a sense of triumph when his lips tightened.

"Simpson. What were you doing in hostile territory?"

"Enough, Mr. Simpson. I need to be with my husband. Am I under arrest? Do I need a lawyer?"

"No ma'am, but…"

She rose from the chair with all the urgency she felt. "Then goodbye, Mr. Simpson." She left the office and the man in a spin.

As she returned to the waiting area, she noticed a woman sitting on the couch. She was pretty, with dark hair and eyes. Those eyes had a faint look of familiarity about them.

"You must be, Mira, I'm Sandra, Brandon's sister. Jackson called me as soon as he touched ground. I was in DC for a conference and got here as quickly as I could."

"Yes, I'm Mira, Brandon's wife."

"Wife? He forgot that little surprise. How exciting." She held out her hand. "I'm so glad to meet you. Big brother has finally met his match."

"I don't know about being his match, but he's everything to me," she spoke the words softly and grasped the offered hand, holding on.

Sandra squeezed back and patted the seat next to her. "How'd you meet? He must have been on a mission, since he's been hurt."

"I *was* his mission, or at least part of it. He saved me from kidnappers." She hesitated to say much, since all of Brandon's missions were classified.

"That's my brother, all right. He's always saving the world." Sandra smiled. "I'm glad he slowed down this time and brought back some happiness with him. I hope we'll be great friends."

"Mrs. Falcon?" She jumped anxiously to her feet and hurried to the woman in scrubs.

"He's about to go under, you have about a minute if you'd like to see him." The nurse led her through a door to a curtained bed.

His skin looked dark against the crisp white sheets. "Hey, my love," he said in a slurred voice. Obviously, someone had gotten some needed sedation into her stubborn husband. Mira vowed to kiss the person on the mouth if she ever found him—or her. "Hey, you." She traced his face with shaking fingers. "Sandra and I will be right outside when you wake."

"S-s-sandy's here?"

She leaned down to brush her lips across his. "I love you, Brandon."

"You..." His voice hushed, and his eyes closed.

"We'll keep you informed, Mrs. Falcon," the nurse said and wheeled him away.

****

Two months after her kidnapping and rescue, Mira wished she'd been more insistent about staying with Brandon while he'd gone through his rehab. Instead, she did as he asked and returned to her old life.

Now, back at her old apartment in Chapel Hill, she resumed her research job at the university. If she had the journals, she could work on the code, but they were still on Jackson's plane. Safe, at least for now.

She could almost believe it had all been a nightmare followed by a beautiful dream—but— dreams didn't get pregnant.

Her face was gaunt. Weight loss from the trauma and constant morning sickness wreaked havoc on her skin. Coffee made her run for the bathroom, gagging. She smiled when Brandon's obsession with coffee flitted through her mind.

She hadn't told him yet.

He'd been so busy, struggling to walk and fighting with the military. How could she add anything else to his plate? His surgery had gone well, and the doctors were amazed at his miraculous healing ability. She hadn't told them about the orchid, expressing as much amazement as they at the unusual enzymes found in his blood.

As soon as he'd been able to get around, he'd insisted she get out of town while he raised a little hell with the brass. Weeks passed, and she only heard from him through quick phone calls. His last call had been longer and filled with so much news.

"Mira, I'm free."

The simple sentence came across the phone like a choir of angels singing hallelujah. Two months of hearings, investigations and worry had come to an end. "Everything worked out fine. I'm so glad you weren't here to see the ugly side of the military judicial system."

"Are you sure they're not going to come pull you out of my bed and court martial you?"

"No court martial, thank God. Some good people came to bat for me. The information I shared has proved very valuable. A spy has been caught and a traitor brought down. I can't explain the details, but believe it or not," he said with a chuckle, "your husband is now considered a hero."

"I've always known it and I didn't need an elite military task force to figure it out. When do I get to see you? I've missed you so much." Excitement made her antsy.

"It's going to be a little longer than I planned. I

hate to spring this on you, but the Navy offered me a deal I couldn't refuse. How do you feel about living in a jungle?"

Had she heard correctly? "A what?"

"We're moving to a small island near Belize. I'm going to train men in jungle survival."

Her voice wobbled, and she swallowed her tears. "Fantastic. It's your dream."

"Shush, baby. Don't cry. You know what it does to me. I promise I'm not going back. I'm finished fighting. I've got to go now. I'll see you in a few more weeks."

She cried for hours after he'd hung up. There were so many unanswered questions. She trusted his promise, but not the men who'd put him in danger. The call had been three weeks ago.

"Enough," she said aloud. Pulling her mind out of the past, she looked around at the apartment where she'd lived for years. It looked like she felt, devoid of color, and listless. She missed the vibrancy of the jungle, with all its sounds and smells—not to mention the colors. He had said they were going to live on an island with a jungle. It sounded fantastic, so what was taking so long?

A quick look down at her loose jeans and T-shirt, and she decided it was time for a few maternity things. She hadn't put on weight, but she did have a little bump in the middle. She ran a comb though her hair, which was much longer than it should be. Her curls had lost their bounce and over-all she looked like...*Damn, she looked horrible*. It was time to put her life back together, starting with her appearance. She grabbed her purse and started for the door.

The doorbell rang.

Her pulse raced as her steps quickened. Blood rushed in her ears nearly deafening her as her heart beat a staccato rhythm against her ribs. It was him—finally him. Her mouth widened into a smile, and she quickly swiped the tears from her cheeks. Reaching the door, she fumbled in her haste and had to turn the latch twice. Her heart in her throat, she snatched the door open.

Roguish in his military uniform, Jackson stood there, broad smile on his face.

Anticipation turned to dust and her body sagged. Emotion swamped her. She quickly blinked back tears and looked away.

"I'm sorry. You thought it was Brandon." He bent and pulled her into a big hug, then stepped back in surprise. "Damn, Cher. What have you done to yourself? You look like hell."

She flung her arms around him and burst into tears. He stiffened, patting her back with awkward taps. Her sobs grew louder. Her control was broken.

He steered her to the couch and sat with her as she continued to wail. "Now, now, Cher. I didn't mean it—really, you look just fine." He rocked her and spoke soothingly. "This isn't about what I said, is it?"

"N-no," she said between sobs. "I want Brandon. I feel as if he's deserted me." She sat up and tried to swipe the tears from her face. "Give me a minute, Jackson. Could you see if I have any soda in the fridge?"

She went into the powder room and splashed cold water on her face. Feeling better after her outburst, she headed for the kitchen. She grabbed the soda from his hand and gulped half of it down before saying, "I'm sorry. My hormones are a mess these days and I get so emotional."

He looked back at her, sympathetically, but with a blank stare.

"I'm pregnant, and I want my husband. I don't give a damn about military training or whatever—I want him here with me."

"You're pregnant?" Jackson grinned like he'd won the lottery. "Cap is going to be so excited about this."

"When do I get to see him?"

"Soon. After he cut that sweet deal with the Navy, he flew down to get the place ready for training."

"And just where do I fit into all of this?" Mira burst out, frustrated at the lack of information. "Does he still remember he has a wife?" She stopped at the look of hurt on Jackson's face.

"I'm sorry, Cher. Brandon should have handled this better but believe me he still loves you. He's preparing right now for your arrival."

"Why didn't he come himself? Why are you here, instead?"

Jackson took a moment as if collecting his thoughts. "He's making it safe."

"Why isn't it safe? Are there more rebels?"

He interrupted her tirade. "No—you have it wrong, Cher. Navy SEALs, active or retired, keep a low profile. We make a lot of enemies in our business. Those enemies don't disappear just because he's out of the military."

"I'm not waiting until he builds a fortress with an ivory tower to stick me in while he plays in the jungle. I'll pack a bag and let's go." She got up and headed for the bedroom.

Panic crossed Jackson's face "Wait a minute;

things aren't ready, yet." He struggled to regain his happy-go-lucky persona. "Brandon says the house should be ready soon and I'm supposed to fly you down next week." He smiled now back on track. "Hey, are you hungry, Cher? Let's go out and get something to eat and talk things over. The two of you are going to drive this old Cajun up a tree with all the drama."

"Drama?" She huffed and sat down on the couch. "Pardon me for saying so, but this is my life we're talking about."

He persisted. "Chinese?—or how about Mexican?"

All at once, she blew out a breath and relaxed. She knew how stubborn Brandon could be. He was trying to be all noble. Doing what macho men like him did— putting her safety before himself. "Italian, I can't hold down the others."

He grinned. "You want pizza or something more stylish?"

"I feel like being pampered, so let's do stylish. I'll go change."

"Sure thing, Cher." He pulled out his cell. "I'll call a cab."

Mira hurried into the bedroom and rummaged through her closet. Her choices weren't inspiring, but she had to choose something. Her hands rested on a green sheath—the exact same color as Brandon's eyes. She quickly stripped, put on the dress, then slipped into flat ballerina slippers.

As she looked into the mirror, she saw a sparkle in her eyes, which hadn't been there these last few weeks. She quickly pulled her hair back with a clip and brushed on some blusher and a little lip gloss. Satisfied she looked almost human, she picked up her purse and made her way to the living room.

Jackson hung up the phone when she entered. "Wow, you look great, Cher. I take back everything I said. You still need a little more color and fewer shadows in your face, but you look terrific."

"Are you always so observant and outspoken, Jackson?" She couldn't be annoyed at him even if she tried. He was just too darn nice.

He got to his feet and took her arm. "Is that a polite way of saying, I look too closely and say too much? My momma used to say something very similar—except her version was, 'stop being so nosy and hush.' " He played the Cajun boy to the hilt. She laughed at his mother's description. His eyes twinkled at her laughter.

She took his proffered arm. "Thank you. I haven't laughed in a long time."

She closed the door to the apartment, turned and stopped. The man standing beside the large black vehicle was big and handsome. He had dark hair and eyes and she felt something oddly familiar about him. When he smiled, she knew.

"Rafà," she yelled. With a running leap, she jumped into his arms. "I'm so happy to see you—and just look at you—you're gorgeous. I never would have suspected this under all that hair and scruff. You clean up pretty good soldier."

"Thanks, Doc. I'm happy to see you too. Don't ever let Cap hear you say such things about me. He's liable to cut off a few body parts to make me less appealing."

She stepped back and straightened her clothes. "Sorry, I wasn't very lady-like."

"I seem to remember you have a little wild side,

Doc. So, what's the plan?"

His words sounded achingly familiar.

Mira and Jackson spoke at the same time. "Food."

"Your taxi awaits."

As she reached the curb, Rafà clicked the automatic ignition and the large black car came alive with a purr. She looked at the car—a Humvee—yeah that was Rafà. He was all about big and bad. Jackson helped her up into the front as Rafà took the driver's seat. As soon as Jackson closed his door, the car took off with a squeal of wheels.

Dinner was a loud, fun-filled event, everyone catching up, but saying nothing important.

"When are you going to tell Brandon about the baby?" Jackson dropped the bombshell during dessert and Rafà choked. Jackson made quite a show of pounding his back.

Mira nearly strangled on the water she had in her mouth. Quickly she swallowed and burst into laughter. "Did you imagine you'd be an uncle this quickly, Rafà?" She reminded him of his toast to 'Uncle Rafà' after she had operated on Brandon.

"Nah, I was just being eloquent." Rafà flashed her favorite grin. The devilish one.

She was still laughing at Rafà's antics as they exited the Humvee at her apartment. It felt good, not being afraid. These last months without Brandon had been hard. Always looking over her shoulder expecting some rebel to jump out at her—demanding the journals. At times, she'd felt like someone was watching her.

She turned the key and stepped through the door. Chaos greeted her—just like when her room at the clinic had been trashed. Fear paralyzed her legs, but not her voice. She screamed.

Rafà pulled her behind him. Lightning fast, his weapon was in his hand as he scanned the room. Her hand trembled where she clasped his belt. Together, they moved further into the living room. Every part had been ransacked—lamps lay broken on the carpet as the curtains hung askew on their rods. Shredded cushions from the chairs filled the floor with bits of foam. Her bookcase lay on its side, books spilling from the shelves. Like before, her pictures lay in broken frames. She released her hold on Rafà, allowing him more freedom in his search. Pressing her balled fist to her lips, she watched him move away.

Jackson pulled his Glock from his ankle holster. "Stay here and let us check it out." He began a room by room search.

"They're gone," Rafà said as he came back into the room.

"Shouldn't we call the police?" she asked. "I don't have any valuables, but I can still check to see if anything is missing." She moved forward as if in a fog. How could this have happened? She had just been thinking about how safe she felt. Why would anyone want to rob her—she didn't have anything of value—and then it hit her—the journals.

"This isn't a normal robbery is it?" She fisted her hands to keep from touching her mementos strewn about the apartment. Her mind spun in a relentless circle. Her fears had been realized. Someone came after the journals. How did they know where to find her?

Jackson replaced his weapon and placed his hand in the small of her back. "This changes thing, Cher. We'll leave tonight." He pulled out his phone, spoke to someone, and hung up. "If there is anything here you value, get it. We won't be coming back. Be sure you have all your papers and passport. The plane will be ready by the time we get to the airport."

Mira watched the transformation as he spoke. Where was the carefree, funny Cajun? The man speaking now was one hundred percent soldier.

"I don't have much but I have some things—" She hushed when Jackson put a finger to his lips.

He leaned down and whispered into her ear. "The place might be bugged."

She nodded. "I don't want to stay here. I'll get some things together." She quickly packed a few items, loath to touch any of the articles handled by the intruders who had violated her home. She didn't look back at the apartment as they left. There was nothing for her here. She was going to her real home, Brandon.

Chapter Forty-Seven

Brandon looked around the room in the old plantation house and tried to see it through Mira's eyes. Would she like it? He'd had all the furniture shipped in from the states weeks ago and hoped to have it all finished before he sent for her. The antique canopy bed was king-sized and hopefully would appeal to her sense of romanticism. White mosquito netting added to the look, it was practical without the air conditioning. He'd agonized more over furnishing the house than building the barracks and setting up the program.

He had a long way to go to make this place what he wanted for her—but he couldn't wait any longer. Would she be happy here, sharing his dream? She had dreams of her own.

"Stop fretting," Sandy said from the door of the master bedroom. "Mira will ignore the room and all the rest and look only at you. I'm so happy for you. I wish you'd stop worrying. Everything will be perfect when she arrives."

"What if she doesn't like it?"

She laughed. "Mira's strong enough to stand up to you if something makes her unhappy. She'll tell you and you'll fix it."

His cell phone rang. He limped from the room leaning heavily on the wooden cane he despised. "What do you mean you'll be here in six hours? You're supposed to come next week. How is she—what's wrong?" Pulse racing, he fired questions at Rafà on the other end of the line.

"Just a minute, Cap."

Seconds later, his heart beat accelerated as he heard her soft voice. The sound had lived in his dreams for the past months. "Brandon, are you there?"

"Mira, oh God, Mira—it's so wonderful to hear your voice. How are you, darling?"

"If you hadn't been so damn stubborn and totally forgotten me, you would know."

Her voice held a note of ire, which had his groin tightening. *By God*, he loved it when she was mad. He wished he could see her face.

"I haven't forgotten you, believe me. I needed a little time to make things secure." There were so many things he wanted to say—needed to say, but not over the phone. He wanted to look into her eyes when he told her all those things, tightly bound in his heart.

"You have six hours—you'd better get your act together by then because once I land—you're never getting rid of me. And Brandon?" Her voice dropped to a low, husky murmur. "Do you think you could find us a bed this time?"

His heart swelled and nearly burst with love. "I—"

"Cap, I sure hope you're ready." Rafà interrupted. "This little whirlwind is on her way and we're bringing a little surprise." He dropped the words into the sentence with casual indifference.

"What kind of surprise? You know I don't like surprises." He heard only laughter on the other end.

"See you soon, Cap." The line clicked off.

Brandon stared at the phone for a moment, then

jumped into action.

****

Mira sat in the co-pilot's seat and stared out at the endless ocean and puffy white clouds. She fidgeted with excitement. They were flying to her new home. "What kind of house is it, Rafà?" She couldn't wait to start making this new place her home.

"I think it's pink," he remarked evasively.

"Yeah, it's pink." Jackson chimed in. "Brandon wants it to be a surprise, Cher."

"I'm to stop being so nosy and hush?" She laughed with Jackson, turned to stare out the window, and settled back into the seat. The doctor part of her was worried about Brandon, not the house. God, she hoped he wasn't doing too much. The wife part of her only wanted to be with the man she loved. The plane hit another air pocket and she grabbed her stomach.

"Can't you make this thing stop bumping?" She ran for the bathroom. A sip of water calmed her stomach this time—yea for progress.

A quick look at her hiding place, confirmed the journals were still safe. How much anguish had been caused by the damn things? She had thought the danger over when she left the jungle, but someone still wanted them. As soon as she settled in, she would make reading them a priority. Uncle Max might have risked his life to get them to her, and she intended to find out why they were so important.

"You okay in there?" Rafà's worried voice came from outside the bathroom door.

"I'll be out in a minute." She took the time to rinse her face and apply color to her cheeks and lips. She was ready.

The plane dropped altitude and islands with trees and mountains appeared as green dots in the blue ocean. Vivid green against azure blue. She drank it all in as she buckled into the seat. "How much longer?"

Jackson patted her hands in her lap "Ready, Cher? We'll be there in a few minutes."

"I'm more than ready. I'd speed this thing up if I could." She smiled and patted the plane. "No offense, *Darlin'*."

"Would you like to see an aerial view of your new home?"

She nodded, and her breathing quickened.

Jackson dipped low and flew around the island pointing out the old plantation and the out-buildings. Moving upward, he showed her the mountains with their waterfalls and jungle. He completed his circle of the island by flying over the sandy beach side and then back to the plantation.

"What do you think?"

She swallowed hard, overwhelmed at the enormity of her new situation. "I'm speechless—it's so beautiful. You said Brandon owns this? How can he own an island?"

Rafà commented from the back. "I'm sure Cap, will explain everything."

Moments later, Jackson landed on the water and taxied to a floating dock. She was unbuckled in seconds, anxiously waiting as they completed all the necessary landing procedures.

The door opened from the outside and light flooded in. A young Hispanic man greeted her. "Welcome, Señora Falcon."

She unbuckled and ran for the door.

Startled, the young man jumped aside. She pushed out of the plane before it was properly tied off.

Chapter Forty-Eight

Mira shaded her eyes against the bright sun, searching for her heart's desire.

Brandon stood, at the end of the dock against the backdrop of bright green trees and a blue sky. His white shirt, loose from his khaki pants, flapped in the gentle breeze. A Panama hat sat at a rakish angle on his dark curls. He leaned heavily on a wooden cane, unmoving, body tense.

Sunglasses hid his eyes, but she didn't need to see those burning green orbs to know what he was thinking. He stood there, allowing her to see him, waiting for her verdict. Her soldier was unsure of himself when it came to matters of the heart.

She beamed at him and took off running, just managing to keep from jumping on him, as she had done with Rafà. She enveloped him in her arms, pulling him tight against her body. God, he felt good.

Tilting her head back, she looked up at him. He removed his sunglasses and dropped them to the planking.

She saw it all, the gauntness of his face, the weight loss, and the scars of the battle he'd fought to heal. He was much more handsome than she remembered. Rather than detract, the changes wrought by his wounds enhanced his already handsome visage.

He lowered his head. Their lips met—tentatively at

first, a gentle taste, and then he ground his lips against hers. His tongue plunged between her lips drinking her sweetness, branding her as his.

She matched his ardor, kissing him back with all the love and desire restrained from months of waiting. She inhaled his male scent. A tinge of spice, ocean breeze—Brandon.

The floating dock swayed. He tightened his arms around her, pulled her head to his chest, fingers caressing her nape. His heart pounded loudly against her ear.

"I suppose you two want to get by?" he asked Jackson and Rafà, who waited by the plane—luggage spread at their feet.

"We've got all day, Cap. Take your time. We wouldn't want to rush anything. Besides, it's kind of nice watching the two of you. You're cute together." Rafà stood, arms folded in rakish nonchalance.

Brandon bent slowly and picked up his sunglasses. "You're lucky I'm in a good mood. Otherwise, your butt would be in the water by now." He turned and walked toward the jeep, never taking his arm from around her. "Hurry with the luggage. I don't want Mira to get sunburned out here." He grinned when the two muttered behind him.

A gentle breeze cooled her cheeks as the young man from the dock drove them toward home. They sat in the back of the jeep, fingers entwined—touching but saying nothing. Behind them, Rafà and Jackson drove a pickup truck carrying the luggage. They drove past old fields untended and now reclaimed by the jungle.

"Wait." She turned sideways, looking at the plants.

"*Alto*," he spoke to the driver and the car stopped.

"Is that coffee growing out there?"

He grinned, showing the dimple she found so endearing. "You bet it is. We are now the proud owners of a coffee plantation."

The day they'd picked coffee beans in the jungle flashed into her thoughts. Excited laughter bubbled from her lips. "We can have fresh ground coffee every day. We'll make our own blends. There's so much—"

He laughed, pulling her back and tucking her beneath his arm. "Give it time." He tapped the front seat and the car moved onward. "I have a great deal of work to get things up and running. The out-buildings are a little rough, but the plantation house isn't bad. We'll need to do some modernizing though." He looked down at her. "Are you sure you're up for this? It isn't going to be easy and it could get kind of lonely."

She turned and touched his face. "You still don't get it do you?"

"Get what?"

"I love you with all my heart, and I never want to be apart from you again. We could live in the jungle up a tree for all I care. As long as we are together, I'll be happy."

He swallowed, drawing her eyes to the bobble of his Adam's apple.

Still he held something back.

Manuel stopped the jeep before they reached the huge plantation house.

Mira took it all in. The house faded pink in color, balconies, porches, and wide shuttered windows gracing the sides. Spanish tiles, loose in places, covered the roof.

It was old and needed some love—but it seemed to

welcome her. She couldn't wait to explore it. "It's beautiful. I can't believe I'm going to live in a place so lovely. I've missed the color and vibrancy of the jungle."

Brandon tapped the front seat and Manuel moved forward. The car stopped outside a shaded courtyard. People poured from the house surrounding the jeep with laughter and greetings. She caught her breath at the welcome from these strangers. No. She looked closer. They weren't all strangers. There was Ana, and her little girl and Rosita. How wonderful to see them.

He helped her from the jeep. "Mira, these two little imps"—he pointed to a girl of about four and a boy about eight—"are my niece, Bonnie, and nephew Steve."

Sandra stood behind her two children. "It's so good to see you again, Mira."

"Can we cut the cake now?" Bonnie asked, pulling on Rosita's skirt.

"Shh. It's a surprise." Rosita led the little girl away.

He took her hand and led her into the house.

Her gaze moved around the large open entry room, admiring details, totally enthralled by the beauty of the old house.

"You look tired. Let me show you to our bedroom." He moved to the stairs, as the crowd from the courtyard melted away.

She laughed up at him. "We have a bedroom? With a real bed?"

"With Rosita in the house, I figured the dining table would be off limits. Though I did get one made from solid teak—very strong." He waggled his brows in devilment.

She gave him an accusing look. "You're incorrigible, but I love you anyway."

His rich laughter echoed in the giant hall. He closed the bedroom door, pulled her into his arms, and held her, gently rocking. "I'm never letting you out of my sight again." He growled low and guttural. "You better get used to it."

She leaned into him, wrapped herself around his lean body, unable to get close enough. After a few minutes the trip caught up to her and she swayed.

"Are you all right?" His voice became anxious as he lifted her onto the beautiful, canopied bed. "I didn't mean to rush you. We have all the time in the world."

She reached up, touched his cheek, loving the feel of his skin. Her fingers traced the contours of his face, relearning the hard angles. "I'm okay. Nothing a little food and seven months won't fix."

He stilled at her words, then jumped from the side of the bed. "We're going to have a baby?" His gaze fixed almost reverently on her belly. "Mira, you've made me the happiest man in the world."

"And you've made me the happiest woman. I was afraid to tell you before. You've had so much going on—the inquiries, separation from the service. I didn't want to add this to your burden."

"Burden? Our child could never be a—"

A tentative knock sounded at the door.

When he opened the door, Rosita stood outside with a tray of food.

"Thanks." He took the tray, closed the door, and moved to the bed. When she sat up, he placed the tray down and rushed to prop pillows behind her. He wiped her face with the damp cloth on the tray, insisting she eat as he quietly watched.

"You're not going to hover like this for the next seven months, are you?" she asked when he took the empty tray away.

"That depends. Are you going to be sick for the next seven months?"

She gave him an exasperated look as he continued to stare at her. "I'm fine. I was so excited I couldn't eat today, and the flight was bumpy. I'm okay now, really."

"Will you feel up to celebrating tonight?"

She patted the bed and beckoned him closer. "Come here."

He slid across the coverlet until he lay next to her.

"I don't want you to worry. I'm not sick and the baby's fine." At her words, he glanced down at her almost flat belly. She took his hand, placing it on the tiny bump that was their child. His face softened into a look of awe. He looked nothing like the hard-edged soldier she'd met in the jungle. He looked like a gentle lover and father.

Brandon pressed a soft kiss to her lips, then dipped his head to kiss her abdomen. "Rest for a while, sweetheart, and then I have a surprise for you—though not nearly as fantastic as yours." He pulled the cord on the ceiling fan and closed the blinds.

Before she could protest, he left the room.

Later, the door to the room opened, and Mira woke.

Ana entered, pausing at the foot of the bed." Are you rested now, doctor?"

"I'm fine, Ana. It's wonderful to see you looking so well."

"Señor Brandon, asks you to join him. We are to have a celebration."

"What does one wear to this celebration? I don't have many clothes."

"Señor Rafà, that scamp. He left you a package and suggests you wear the clothes inside."

What kind of clothes had he bought? She didn't remember him buying anything. Maybe he'd gone shopping with Sandra. She slipped off the bed and reached for the box on the wooden seat at the foot of the bed. Gently she pushed the tissue aside to reveal a simple white wedding gown. She gasped as her eyes smarted with tears. Her heart swelled with emotion as her fingers moved over the silky fabric of the gown. What was Brandon up to?

"I will help you dress, señora. Then we will go to the gazebo."

****

Brandon stood inside the restored gazebo. The structure sat amid a small grove of trees at the base of a tiny waterfall. It reminded him of the time Mira had bathed in the waterfall. The vision of her body beneath the falling water was etched in his memory. The old man he'd hired played a hauntingly beautiful melody on the mandolin. He looked past the be-ribboned seats and saw her.

His world stood still.

She was beautiful. Soft gold curls framed her face beneath the short veil. She held Rafà's arm as she walked down the rose strewn path and up the steps. His heart squeezed, nearly bursting with love as she walked toward him.

****

Rafà lifted her veil, kissed her cheek, then placed her hand in Brandon's. He reached over to a small table and handed her some flowers. Her heart raced as she looked at the bouquet. A single Blue Spider Orchid and a simple note were tucked between the green ferns.

To My Favorite Sister from your second-best man—Rafà.

Mira felt like she was in a dream. The kind every little girl has about white gowns and prince charming.

"Dearly beloved." An all too familiar voice came from in front of the small altar. "It is my pleasure to once more join this man and this woman in Holy Matrimony."

Joy bubbled up in her breast. Father Josè's presence made this so right.

****

Hours later, the celebration wound down and they returned to the house. Now it was just the two of them. Light glinted off her rings as Brandon pulled her hand to his lips. He'd had them commissioned. Platinum with small, yellow gold dots and a tiny cross. Similar to the ring rosary they had used in their first ceremony.

He pulled the ring rosary from his pocket, bringing it to his lips. "This rosary and my memories of you kept me going," he said as he kissed her gently on the lips.

Her eyes misted. What had she done to deserve a man like this? She couldn't wait to join him in the huge bed. She wanted to make more beautiful memories with this remarkable man—kiss away the hurts and worship his hard body.

"I love you, Mira, with all my heart and all my soul. I didn't know I still had a soul until you helped me release it from the place where I kept it buried. I want to spend the rest of my life showing you the strength of my love."

He deftly slid the zipper down her back. Sensation sizzled beneath his fingers with each inch of skin he exposed.

She wiggled out of the beautiful dress and stood before him in an almost-there bra and thong. The heat of his gaze burned across her skin. Sheer feminine pride tilted her chin up as a rosy flush bloomed in her cheeks. She gazed back at him, basking in his admiration.

His breath sucked in. "Dear lord in heaven," he uttered piously. "You're killing me."

She slid her hand slowly across the silky spread and fired an impish look over her shoulder. "We've never done this on a bed. Should we try it out?"

He quickly lifted her into his arms and placed her gently on the bed. He closed the netting and reached for her. "Yes, I think we should."

Thank you for purchasing
this publication of The Wild Rose Press, Inc.

For questions or more information
contact us at
info@thewildrosepress.com.

The Wild Rose Press, Inc.
www.thewildrosepress.com

To visit with authors of
The Wild Rose Press, Inc.
join our yahoo loop at
http://groups.yahoo.com/group/thewildrosepress/